**Rachel Lee** was hooked on writing by the age of twelve and practised her craft as she moved from place to place all over the United States. This *New York Times* bestselling author now resides in Florida and has the joy of writing full-time.

**Susan Carlisle**'s love affair with books began when she made a bad grade in math. Not allowed to watch TV until the grade had improved, she filled her time with books. Turning her love of reading into a love for writing romance, she pens hot medicals. She loves castles, travelling, afternoon tea, reads voraciously, and hearing from her readers. Join her newsletter at SusanCarlisle.com

*Publishers Weekly* bestselling and award-winning author **Elizabeth Heiter** likes her suspense to feature strong heroines, chilling villains, psychological twists, and a little romance. Her research has taken her into the minds of serial killers, through murder investigations, and onto the FBI Academy's shooting range. Her novels have been published in more than a dozen countries and translated into eight languages. Visit her at elizabethheiter.com

# Workplace Romance

# Workplace Romance:
# Life or Death

RACHEL LEE

SUSAN CARLISLE

ELIZABETH HEITER

MILLS & BOON

First Published in Great Britain 2024
by Mills & Boon, an imprint of HarperCollins*Publishers* Ltd,
1 London Bridge Street, London, SE1 9GF

www.harpercollins.co.uk

HarperCollins*Publishers*
Macken House, 39/40 Mayor Street Upper,
Dublin 1, D01 C9W8, Ireland

Workplace Romance: Life or Death © 2024 Harlequin Enterprises ULC.

*Murdered in Conard County* © 2019 Susan Civil Brown
*Firefighter's Unexpected Fling* © 2019 Susan Carlisle
*Secret Investigation* © 2020 Harlequin Enterprises ULC

Special thanks and acknowledgement are given to Elizabeth Heiter for her contribution to the *Tactical Crime Division* series.

ISBN: 978-0-263-32316-0

# MURDERED IN CONARD COUNTY

**RACHEL LEE**

# *Prologue*

*Three years earlier*

"Have either of you ever heard of Leopold and Loeb? They thought they could commit the perfect murder."

A large fire burned in the huge stone fireplace, casting dancing tongues of orange light and inky shadows around the cabin's sitting room. The wood sizzled and crackled, adding its dry music to the light and occasionally loud pops that sounded almost like gunshots.

The log walls, burnished by the years, added weight to the entire scene. Trophy heads of bighorn sheep, elk and deer hung everywhere, beneath each a plaque memorializing a past hunter.

Clearly this was a hunting lodge, one of generous size, able to house a fairly large party. But its heyday was in the past and now only three men occupied it.

It seemed like the last place on earth three men would plot murders.

Dressed in camouflage, their orange caps and vests tossed onto a nearby chest, they sat in a semicircle of comfortable lounge chairs in front of the fire, sipping brandy from snifters. Two of them enjoyed fat cigars with a surprisingly pleasant aroma.

"It was really cold out there," remarked one of them,

a man with dark hair and a luxuriant mustache who appeared to be about thirty, maybe a couple of years older. He'd been the one who had asked the question about Leopold and Loeb, but having received no response, he dropped it. For now.

"Good for the deer, Will," said the man nearest him. His name was Karl, and he looked like his Nordic ancestors, with pale hair and skin and frigid blue eyes. The deer he referred to had been field dressed and was hanging in a shed outside, protected from scavengers.

"Yeah," said Jeff, the third of them. He had the kind of good looks that could have gotten him cast on a TV drama, but he also had a kink in his spine from a military injury and he didn't quite sit or stand straight. He often endured pain but seldom showed it. "It's probably already frozen stiff."

"Like a board," Karl agreed. "Thank goodness we have a sling on our side-by-sides."

"And tomorrow maybe we'll get an elk," Jeff added. They'd won the drawing for a coveted license for an elk, and since they'd been hoping for one for years, this was no small deal.

Silence fell for a while, except for the crackling of the fire. Three men, looking very content, enjoying their hunting lodge after a successful day. Except one of them was not quite content.

Will spoke. "Do you two ever get tired of this hunting trip? Every year since we were boys, coming up here with our dads. Now just the three of us."

"Something wrong with the company?" Karl drawled.

"Of course not," Will answered. "It's just that I was thinking we've been doing this so many years, and we've never gone home empty-handed. Not much of a challenge, is it?"

Jeff nearly gaped. They'd spent the better part of three days tracking the buck that was now hanging in the shed. "We almost missed that mature eight-pointer. He was smart."

"We still got him," Will pointed out.

Karl spoke. "The elk will be even more of a challenge. What do you want, Will? To stop making these trips? I thought we were doing it more for the time away together. Three guys, brandy and cigars, traipsing around in the woods on the cusp of winter... A lot of guys would envy us."

"We aren't a lot of guys. In fact, I believe we're smarter than the average bear. All of us."

"So?"

"So, how about we hunt a different kind of prey? Not to kill but for the challenge."

"What are you talking about?" Jeff asked.

"You ever hear of Leopold and Loeb?" This time Will spoke more emphatically.

Both Karl and Jeff shook their heads. "Who were they?" Karl asked.

"Two guys who thought they were smart enough to commit the perfect murder. Back in the 1920s. But they got caught in twenty-four hours."

The other two men froze into silence.

"We're smarter," said Will presently. "Think of all the planning we'd have to do, a lot more than hunting deer or elk. And even without the murder it would be a helluva challenging game."

Silence, except for the fire, reigned for a while. Then Jeff said, "You *are* talking about a game, not a real murder, right?"

Will waved the hand holding his cigar. "The game would be the planning and stalking. Just like when we hunt deer. The kill hardly matters at that point. We only follow through because we want the meat and the rack. You can't hang a man's head on the wall."

That elicited a laugh from Karl. "True that." Even Jeff smiled after a moment.

"The most challenging game of all," Will continued. "How do we do it without leaving any evidence? How do we creep up on our prey?"

Karl snorted. "Men aren't as smart as deer, Will."

"But they're almost never alone."

After a bit, Jeff said, "Sorta like playing D&D when we were younger?"

"Like that," Will agreed. "Plotting and planning and stalking. That's all."

Presently all the men were sitting easily in their chairs and began to toss ideas around. If nothing else, it was an entertaining way to spend an icy evening.

# Chapter One

Blaire Afton slept with the window cracked because she liked the cool night breeze, and the sounds of animals in the woods. As park ranger for the state of Wyoming, she supervised a forested area with a dozen scattered campgrounds and quite a few hiking trails, most all the camps and trails farther up the mountain.

Her cabin was also the main office, the entry point to the park, and her bedroom was upstairs in a loft. The breeze, chilly as it got at night, even in July, kept her from feeling closed in. The fresh air seemed to make her sleep deeper and more relaxed, as well.

It also seemed to keep away the nightmares that still occasionally plagued her. Ten months in Afghanistan had left their mark.

But tonight she was edgy as all get-out, and sleep stubbornly evaded her. Maybe just as well, she thought irritably. Nights when she felt like this often produced bad dreams, which in turn elicited worse memories.

Sitting up at last, she flipped on the fluorescent lantern beside her bed and dressed in her park ranger's uniform and laced up her boots. If sleep caught up with her finally, she could crash on the sofa downstairs. Right now, however, early coffee was sounding delicious.

There was absolutely no way she could make her boots

silent on the open wooden staircase, but it didn't matter. All her staff were home for the night and she could bother only herself. Right now, bothering herself seemed like a fairly good idea.

The electric lines reached the cabin, having been run up the side of this mountain by the state, along with a phone landline that extended out to all the campgrounds in case of emergencies. Neither was perfectly reliable, but when they worked, they were a boon. Especially the electricity. Phone calls about vacant campsites didn't light up her life, nor did some of the stupid ones she received. Want a weather report? Then turn on the weather.

"Ha," she said aloud. The good news was that she had electric power this night. She walked over to her precious espresso machine and turned it on. A few shots over ice with milk and artificial sweetener...oh, yeah.

And since she was wide awake and had the power, maybe she should check her computer and see if she had internet, as well. Monthly reports were due soon, and if she had to be awake, she might as well deal with them. Reports weren't her favorite part of this job, and sometimes she wondered if some of them had been created by a higher-up who just wanted to be important.

When her coffee was ready and filling her insulated mug, she decided to step outside and enjoy some of the night's unique quiet. It wasn't silent, but it was so different from the busier daylight hours. Tilting her head back, she could see stars overhead, bright and distant this nearly moonless night. The silvery glow was just enough to see by, but not enough to wash out the stars.

Sipping her coffee, she allowed herself to enjoy being out in the dark without fear. It might come back at any moment, but as Afghanistan faded further into her past, it happened much less often. She was grateful for the incremental improvement.

Grateful, too, that the head forester at the national forest abutting her state land was also a veteran, someone she could talk to. Gus Maddox guarded a longer past in combat than she did, and there was still a lot he wouldn't, or couldn't, talk about. But he'd been in special operations, and much of what they did remained secret for years.

In her case, her service had been more ordinary. Guarding supply convoys sounded tame until you learned they were a desirable target. She and her team had more than once found themselves in intense firefights, or the object of roadside bombs.

She shook herself, refusing to let memory intrude on this night. It was lovely and deserved its due. An owl hooted from deep within the woods, a lonely yet beautiful sound. All kinds of small critters would be scurrying around, trying to evade notice by running from hiding place to hiding place while they searched for food. Nature had a balance and it wasn't always pretty, but unlike war it served a necessary purpose.

Dawn would be here soon, and she decided to wait in hope she might see a cloud of bats returning to their cave three miles north. They didn't often fly overhead here, but occasionally she enjoyed the treat.

Currently there was a great deal of worry among biologists about a fungus that was attacking the little brown bat. She hoped they managed to save the species.

A loud report unexpectedly shattered the night. The entire world seemed to freeze. Only the gentle sigh of the night breeze remained as wildlife paused in recognition of a threat.

Blaire froze, too. She knew the sound of a gunshot.

She also knew that no one was supposed to be hunting during the night or during this season.

What the hell? She couldn't even tell exactly where it came from. The sound had echoed off the rocks and slopes of the mountain. As quiet as the night was, it might have come from miles away.

Fifteen minutes later, the phone in her cabin started to ring.

Her heart sank.

TEN MILES SOUTH in his cabin in the national forest, August Maddox, Gus to everyone, was also enduring a restless night. Darkness had two sides to it, one favorable and one threatening, depending. In spec ops, he'd favored it when he was on a stealthy mission and didn't want to be detected. At other times, when he and his men were the prey, he hated it. The protection it sometimes afforded his troops could transform into deadliness in an instant.

As a result, he endured an ongoing battle with night. Time was improving it, but on nights like this when sleep eluded him, he sometimes forced himself to step outside, allowing the inkiness to swallow him, standing fast against urges to take cover. He hated this in himself, felt it as an ugly, inexcusable weakness, but hating it didn't make it go away.

The fingernail moon provided a little light, and he used it to go around the side of the building to visit the three horses in the corral there. His own gelding, Scrappy, immediately stirred from whatever sleep he'd been enjoying and came to the rail to accept a few pats and nuzzle Gus in return.

Sometimes Gus thought the horse was the only living being who understood him. *Probably because Scrappy couldn't talk*, he often added in attempted lightness.

But Scrappy did talk in his own way. He could communicate quite a bit with a toss of his head or a flick of his tail, not to mention the pawing of his feet. Tonight the horse seemed peaceful, though, and leaned into his hand as if trying to share the comfort.

He should have brought a carrot, Gus thought. Stroking the horse's neck, he asked, "Who gave you that silly name, Scrappy?"

Of course the horse couldn't answer, and Gus had never met anyone who could. The name had come attached to the animal, and no one had ever changed it. Which was okay, because Gus kind of liked it. Unusual. He was quite sure the word hadn't been attached to another horse anywhere. It also made him wonder about the horse's coltish days five or six years ago.

Scrappy was a gorgeous, large pinto whose lines suggested Arabian somewhere in the past. He was surefooted in these mountains, though, which was far more important than speed. And he was evidently an animal who attached himself firmly, because Gus had found that when Scrappy was out of the corral, he'd follow Gus around more like a puppy than anything.

Right then, though, as Scrappy nudged his arm repeatedly, he realized the horse wanted to take a walk. It was dark, but not too dark, and there was a good trail leading north toward the state park lands.

And Blaire Afton.

Gus half smiled at himself as he ran his fingers through Scrappy's mane. Blaire. She'd assumed her ranger position over there about two years ago, and they'd become friends. Well, as much as two wary vets could. Coffee, conversation, even some good laughs. Occasional confidences about so-called reentry problems. After two years, Scrappy probably knew the path by heart.

But it was odd for the horse to want to walk in the middle of the night. Horses *did* sleep. But maybe Gus's restlessness had reached him and made him restless, as well. Or maybe he sensed something in the night. Prickles of apprehension, never far away in the dark, ran up Gus's spine.

"Okay, a short ride," he told Scrappy. "Just enough to work out a kink or two."

An internal kink. Or a thousand. Gus had given up wondering just how many kinks he'd brought home with him after nearly twenty years in the Army, most of it in covert missions. The grenade that had messed him up with shrapnel hadn't left as many scars as memory. Or so he thought.

He was tempted to ride bareback, given that he didn't intend to go far, but he knew better. As steady as Scrappy was, if he startled or stumbled Gus could wind up on the ground. Better to have the security of a saddle than risk an injury.

Entering the corral, he saw happiness in Scrappy's sudden prance. The other two horses roused enough to glance over, then went back to snoozing. They never let the night rambles disturb them. The other two horses apparently considered them to be a matter between Scrappy and Gus.

Shortly he led the freshly saddled Scrappy out of the corral. Not that he needed leading. He followed him over to the door of his cabin where a whiteboard for messages was tacked and he scrawled that he'd gone for a ride on the Forked Rivers Trail. A safety precaution in case he wasn't back by the time his staff started wandering in from their various posts. Hard-and-fast rule: never go into the forest without letting the rangers know where you were headed and when you expected to return. It applied to him as well as their guests.

Then he swung up into the saddle, listening to Scrappy's happy nicker, enjoying his brief sideways prance of pleasure. And just like the song, the horse knew the way.

Funny thing to drift through his mind at that moment. A memory from childhood that seemed so far away now he wasn't sure it had really happened. Sitting in the car with his parents on the way to Grandmother's house. Seriously. Two kids in the back seat singing "Over the River" until his mother begged for mercy. His folks were gone now, taken by the flu of all things, and his sister who had followed him into the Army had been brought home in a box from Iraq.

Given his feelings about the darkness, it struck him as weird that the song and the attendant memories had popped up. But he ought to know by now how oddly the brain could work.

Scrappy's hooves were nearly silent on the pine needles that coated the trail. The duff under the trees was deep in these parts, and he'd suggested to HQ that they might need to clean up some of it. Fire hazard, and it hadn't rained in a while, although they were due for some soon to judge by the forecast. Good. They needed it.

The slow ride through the night woods was nearly magical. The creak of leather and the jingle of the rings on the bridle were quiet, but part of the feeling of the night. When he'd been in Germany he'd learned the story of the Christmas tree. The idea had begun with early and long winter nights, as travelers between villages had needed illumination to see their way. At some point people had started putting candles on tree branches.

Damn, he'd moved from Thanksgiving to Christmas in a matter of minutes and it was July. What the hell was going on inside his mind?

He shook his head a bit, then noticed that Scrappy was

starting to get edgy himself. He was tossing his head an awful lot. What had he sensed on the night breeze? Some odor that bothered him. That could be almost anything out of the ordinary.

But the horse's reaction put him on high alert, too. Something was wrong with the woods tonight. Scrappy felt it and he wasn't one to question an animal's instincts and senses.

Worry began to niggle at him. They were getting ever closer to Blaire Afton's cabin. Could she be sick or in trouble?

Maybe it was an annoying guy thing, but he often didn't like the idea that she was alone there at night. In the national forest there were people around whom he could radio if he needed to, who'd be there soon if he wanted them. Blaire had no such thing going for her. Her employees were all on daylight hours, gone in the evening, not returning until morning. Budget, he supposed. Money was tight for damn near everything now.

Blaire would probably laugh in his face if she ever guessed he sometimes worried about her being alone out here. She had some of the best training in the world. If asked he'd say that he felt sorry for anyone who tangled with her.

But she was still alone there in that cabin, and worse, she was alone with her nightmares. Like him. He knew all about that.

Scrappy tossed his head more emphatically and Gus loosened the reins. "Okay, man, do your thing."

Scrappy needed no other encouragement. His pace quickened dramatically.

Well, maybe Blaire would be restless tonight, too, and they could share morning coffee and conversation. It was gradually becoming his favorite way to start a day.

Then he heard the unmistakable sound of a gunshot, ringing through the forest. At a distance, but he still shouldn't be hearing it. Not at this time of year. Not in the dark.

"Scrappy, let's go." He touched the horse lightly with his heels, not wanting him to break into a gallop that could bring him to harm, but just to hurry a bit.

Scrappy needed no further urging.

"WE THINK SOMEONE'S been shot."

The words that had come across the telephone seemed to shriek in Blaire's ears as she hurried to grab a light jacket and her pistol belt as well as a shotgun out of the locked cabinet. On the way out the door she grabbed the first-aid kit. The sheriff would be sending a car or two, but she had the edge in time and distance. She would definitely arrive first.

The call had come from the most remote campground, and she'd be able to get only partway there in the truck. The last mile or so would have to be covered on the all-terrain side-by-side lashed to the bed of the truck.

If someone was injured, why had it had to happen at the most out-of-the-way campground? A campground limited to people who seriously wanted to rough it, who didn't mind carrying in supplies and tents. After the road ended up there, at the place she'd leave her truck, no vehicles of any kind were allowed. She was the only one permitted to head in there on any motorized vehicle. She had one equipped for emergency transport.

She was just loading the last items into her vehicle when Gus appeared, astride Scrappy, a welcome sight.

"I heard the shot. What happened?"

"Up at the Twin Rocks Campground. I just got a call. They think someone's been shot."

"Think?"

"That's the word. You want to follow me on horseback, or ride with me?" It never once entered her head that he wouldn't want to come along to help.

IT NEVER ENTERED his head, either. "I'm not armed," he warned her as he slipped off the saddle.

"We can share."

He loosely draped Scrappy's reins around the porch railing in front of the cabin, knowing they wouldn't hold him. He didn't want them to. It was a signal to Scrappy to hang around, not remain frozen in place. A few seconds later, he climbed into the pickup with Blaire and they started up the less-than-ideal road. He was glad his teeth weren't loose because Blaire wasted no time avoiding the ruts.

He spoke, raising his voice a bit to be heard over the roaring engine. "Have you thought yet about what you're doing for Christmas and Thanksgiving?"

She didn't answer for a moment as she shifted into a lower gear for the steepening road. "It's July. What brought that on?"

"Danged if I know," he admitted. "I was riding Scrappy in your direction because I'm restless tonight and it all started with a line from 'Over the River' popping into my head. Then as I was coming down the path I remembered how in the Middle Ages people put candles on tree branches on long winter nights so the pathways would be lit for travelers. Which led to…"

"Christmas," she said. "Got it. Still weird."

He laughed. "That's what I thought, too. My head apparently plays by its own rules."

It was her turn to laugh, a short mirthless sound. "No kidding. I don't have to tell you about mine."

No, she didn't, and he was damned sorry that she carried those burdens, too. "So, holidays," he repeated. No point in thinking about what lay ahead of them. If someone had been shot, they both knew it wasn't going to be pretty. And both of them had seen it before.

"I'll probably stay right here," she answered. "I love it when the forest is buried in snow, and someone has to be around if the snowshoe hikers and the cross-country skiers get into trouble."

"Always," he agreed. "And doesn't someone always get into trouble?"

"From what I understand, it hasn't failed yet."

He drummed his fingers on his thigh, then asked, "You called the sheriff?"

"Yeah, but discharge of a weapon is in my bailiwick. They have a couple of cars heading this way. If I find out someone *has* been shot, I'll warn them. Otherwise I'll tell them to stand down."

Made sense. This wasn't a war zone after all. Most likely someone had brought a gun along for protection and had fired it into the night for no good reason. Scared? A big shadow hovering in the trees?

And in the dead of night, wakened from a sound sleep by a gunshot, a camper could be forgiven for calling to say that someone *had* been shot even without seeing it. The more isolated a person felt, the more he or she was apt to expect the worst. Those guys up there at Twin Rocks were about as isolated as anyone could get without hiking off alone.

He hoped that was all it was. An accident that had been misinterpreted. His stomach, though, gave one huge twist, preparing him for the worst.

"You hanging around for the holidays?" she asked. Her voice bobbled as the road became rougher.

"Last year my assistant did," he reminded her. "This year it's me. What did you do last year?"

"Went to visit my mother in the nursing home. I told you she has Alzheimer's."

"Yeah. That's sad."

"Pointless to visit. She doesn't even recognize my voice on the phone anymore. Regardless, I don't think she feels lonely."

"Why's that?"

"She spends a lot of time talking to friends and relatives who died back when. Her own little party."

"I hope it comforts her."

"Me, too." Swinging a hard left, she turned onto a narrower leg of road that led directly to a dirt and gravel parking lot of sorts. It was where the campers left their vehicles before hiking in.

"You ever been to this campground?" she asked as she set the brake and switched off the ignition.

"Not on purpose," he admitted. "I may have. Scrappy and I sometimes wander a bit when we're out for a day-off ride."

"Everything has to be lugged in," she replied, as if that would explain all he needed to know.

It actually did. *Rustic* was the popular word for it. "They have a phone, though?"

"Yeah, a direct line to me. The state splurged. I would guess lawyers had something to do with that."

He gave a short laugh. "Wouldn't surprise me."

Even though Blaire was clearly experienced at getting the side-by-side off the back of her truck, he helped. It was heavy, it needed to roll down a ramp, and it might decide to just keep going.

Once it was safely parked, he helped reload the ramp and close the tailgate. Then there was loading the first-aid supplies and guns. She knew where everything went, so he took directions.

With a pause as he saw the roll of crime scene tape and box of latex gloves. And shoe covers. God. A couple of flashlights that would turn night into day. He hoped they didn't need any of it. Not any of it.

At least the state hadn't stinted on the side-by-side. It had a roof for rainy weather, and a roll bar he could easily grab for stability. There were four-point harnesses as well, no guarantee against every danger but far better than being flung from the vehicle.

These side-by-side UTVs weren't as stable as three-wheelers, either. It might be necessary for her job, but if he were out for joyriding, he'd vastly prefer a standard ATV.

She drove but tempered urgency with decent caution. The headlights were good enough, but this classified more as a migratory path than a road. Even knowing a ranger might have to get out here in an emergency, no one had wanted to make this campground easily accessible by vehicle. There were lots of places like that in his part of the forest. Places where he needed to drag teams on foot when someone got injured.

Soon, however, he saw the occasional glint of light through the trees. A lot of very-awake campers, he imagined. Frightened by the gunshot. He hoped they weren't frightened by more.

The forest thinned out almost abruptly as they reached the campground. He could make out scattered tents, well separated in the trees. Impossible in the dark to tell how many there might be.

But a group of people, all of whom looked as if they'd dragged on jeans, shirts and boots in a hurry, huddled together, a couple of the women hugging themselves.

Blaire brought the ATV to a halt, parked it and jumped

off. He followed more slowly, not wanting to reduce her authority in any way. She was the boss here. He was just a visitor. And he wasn't so stupid that he hadn't noticed how people tended to turn to the man who was present first.

He waited by the vehicle as Blaire covered the twenty or so feet to the huddle. Soon excited voices reached him, all of them talking at the same time about the single gunshot that had torn the silence of the night. From the gestures, he guessed they were pointing to where they thought the shot came from, and, of course, there were at least as many directions as people.

They'd been in tents, though, and that would muffle the sound. Plus there were enough rocks around her to cause confusing echoes.

But then one man silenced them all.

"Mark Jasper didn't come out of his tent. His kid was crying just a few minutes ago, but then he quieted."

He saw Blaire grow absolutely still. "His kid?"

"He brought his four-year-old with him. I guess the shot may have scared him. But… Why didn't Mark come out?"

Good question, thought Gus. Excellent question.

"Maybe he didn't want to take a chance and expose his boy. They might have gone back to sleep," said one of the women. Her voice trembled. She didn't believe that, Gus realized.

Blaire turned slowly toward the tent that the man had pointed out. She didn't want to look. He didn't, either. But as she took her first step toward the shelter, he stepped over and joined her. To hell with jurisdiction. His gorge was rising. A kid had been in that tent? No dad joining the others? By now this Jasper guy could have heard enough of the voices to know it was safe.

He glanced at Blaire and saw that her face had set into lines of stone. She knew, too. When they reached the door of the tent, she stopped and pointed. Leaning over, he saw it, too. The tent was unzipped by about six or seven inches.

"Gloves," he said immediately.

"Yes."

Protect the evidence. The opening might have been left by this Jasper guy, or it might have been created by someone else. Either way...

He brought her a pair of latex gloves, then snapped his own set on. Their eyes met, and hers reflected the trepidation he was feeling.

Then he heard a sound from behind him and swung around. The guy who had announced that Jasper hadn't come out had followed them. "Back up, sir." His tone was one of command, honed by years of military practice.

"Now," Blaire added, the same steely note in her voice. "You might be trampling evidence."

The guy's eyes widened and he started to back up.

Now Blaire turned her head. "Carefully," she said sharply. "Don't scuff. You might bury something."

The view of the guy raising his legs carefully with each step might have been amusing under other circumstances. There was no amusement now.

"Ready?" Blaire asked.

"Yup."

She leaned toward the tent and called, "Mr. Jasper? I'm the ranger. We're coming in. We need to check on you." No sound answered her.

"Like anyone can be ready for this," she muttered under her breath as she reached up for the zipper tab. The metal teeth seemed loud as the world held its breath.

When she had the zipper halfway down, she parted the canvas and shone her flashlight inside.

"Oh, my God," she breathed.

# Chapter Two

Blaire had seen a lot of truly horrible things during her time in Afghanistan. There had even been times when she'd been nearly frozen by a desire not to do what she needed to do. She'd survived, she'd acted and on a couple of occasions, she'd even saved lives.

This was different. In the glare of the flashlight she saw a man in a sleeping bag, his head near the front opening. Or rather what was left of his head. Worse, she saw a small child clinging desperately to the man's waist, eyes wide with shock and terror. That kid couldn't possibly understand this horror but had still entered the icy pit of not being able to move, of hanging on to his daddy for comfort and finding no response.

She squeezed her eyes shut for just a moment, then said quietly to Gus, "The father's been shot in the head. Dead. The kid is clinging to him and terrified out of his mind. I need the boy's name."

Gus slipped away, and soon she heard him murmuring to the gathered campers.

Not knowing if she would ever get the boy's name, she said quietly, "Wanna come outside? I'm sort of like police, you know. You probably saw me working when you were on your way up here."

No response.

Then Gus's voice in her ear. "Jimmy. He's Jimmy."

"Okay." She lowered the zipper more. When Gus squatted, she let him continue pulling it down so she didn't have to take eyes off the frightened and confused little boy. "Jimmy? Would you like to go home to Mommy? We can get Mommy to come for you."

His eyes flickered a bit. He'd heard her.

"My friend Gus here has a horse, too. You want to ride a horse? His name is Scrappy and he's neat. All different colors."

She had his attention now and stepped carefully through the flap, totally avoiding the father. She wondered how much evidence she was destroying but didn't much care. The priority was getting that child out of there.

The floor of the tent was small and not easy to cross. A small sleeping bag lay bunched up, a trap for the unwary foot. Toys were scattered about, too, plastic horses, some metal and plastic cars and a huge metal tractor. She bet Jimmy had had fun making roads in the pine needles and duff outside.

As soon as she got near, she squatted. His gaze was focusing on her more and more, coming out of the shock and into the moment. "I think we need to go find your mommy, don't you?"

"Daddy?"

"We'll take care of Daddy for you, okay? Mommy is going to need you, Jimmy. She probably misses you so bad right now. Let's go and I'll put you on my ATV. You like ATVs?"

"Zoom." The smallest of smiles cracked his frozen face.

"Well, this is a big one, and it definitely zooms. It's also a little like riding a roller coaster. Come on, let's go check it out."

At last Jimmy uncoiled and stood. But there was no way Blaire was going to let him see any more of his father. She scooped him up in her arms and turned so that he'd have to look through her.

"Gus?"

"Yo."

"Could you hold the flap open, please?"

Who knew a skinny four-year-old could feel at once so heavy and light? The flashlight she carried wasn't helping, either. She wished she had a third arm.

"Are you cold, Jimmy?" she asked as she moved toward the opening and bent a little to ease them through.

"A little bit," he admitted.

"Well, I've got a nice warm blanket on my ATV. You can curl up with it while I call your mommy, okay?" Lying. How was she going to call this kid's mother? Not immediately, for sure. She couldn't touch the corpse or look for ID until after the crime techs were done.

"Gus? The sheriff?"

"I radioed. There's a lot more than two cars on the way. Crime scene people, too."

"We've got to get this cordoned off."

"I'll ask Mr. Curious to help me. He'll love it. The kid?"

"Jimmy is going to get my favorite blanket and a place to curl up in the back of the ATV, right, Jimmy?"

Jimmy gave a small nod. His fingers dug into her, crumpling cloth and maybe even bruising a bit. She didn't care.

Walking carefully and slowly with the boy, almost unconsciously she began to hum a tune from her early childhood, "All Through the Night."

To her surprise, Jimmy knew the words and began to sing them with her. His voice was thin, frail from the shock, but he was clinging desperately to something familiar. After a moment, she began to sing softly with him. Before she reached the ATV, Jimmy's head was resting against her shoulder.

When the song ended, he said, "Mommy sings that." Then he started to sing it again.

And Blaire blinked hard, fighting back the first tears she'd felt in years.

GUS WATCHED BLAIRE carry the small child to the ATV. He'd already recovered the crime scene tape and there were plenty of trees to wind it around, but he hesitated for a moment, watching woman and child. He could imagine how hard this was for her, dealing with a freshly fatherless child. War did that too often. Now here, in a peaceful forest. Or one that should have been peaceful.

His radio crackled, and he answered it. "Maddox."

"We're about a mile out from the parking area," came the familiar voice of the sheriff, Gage Dalton. "Anything else we need to know?"

"I'm about to rope the scene right now. The vic has a small child. We're going to need some help with that and with finding a way to get in touch with family as soon as possible."

"We'll do what we can as fast as we can. The witnesses?"

"Some are trying to pack up. I'm going to stop that."

He was as good as his word, too. When he clicked off the radio, he turned toward the people who had dispersed from the remaining knot and started to fold up tents.

"You all can stop right there. The sheriff will be here soon and you might be material witnesses. None of you can leave the scene until he tells you."

Some grumbles answered him, but poles and other

items clattered to the ground. One woman, with her arms wrapped around herself, said, "I feel like a sitting duck."

"If you were," Gus said, "you'd already know it." That at least took some of the tension out of the small crowd. Then he signaled to the guy who'd tried to follow them to the tent and said, "You get to help me rope off the area."

The guy nodded. "I can do that. Sorry I got too close. Instinct."

"Instinct?"

"Yeah. Iraq. Know all the parameters of the situation."

Gus was familiar with that. He decided the guy wasn't a ghoul after all. He also proved to be very useful. In less than ten minutes, they had a large area around the victim's tent cordoned off. Part of him was disturbed that a gunshot had been heard but no one had approached the tent of the one person who hadn't joined them, not even the veteran. The tent in which a child had apparently been crying.

But it was the middle of the night, people had probably been wakened from a sound sleep and were experiencing some difficulty in putting the pieces together in any useful way. Camping was supposed to be a peaceful experience unless you ran into a bear. And, of course, the sound of the child crying might have persuaded them everything was okay in that tent. After all, it looked untouched from the outside.

Scared as some of these people were that there might be additional gunfire, they all might reasonably have assumed that Jasper and his son were staying cautiously out of sight.

Once he and Wes, the veteran, had roped off the area, there wasn't another thing they could do before the cops arrived. Preserve the scene, then stand back. And keep witnesses from leaving before they were dismissed by proper authority. He could understand, though, why some of them just wanted to get the hell out of here.

The fact remained, any one of that group of twelve to fourteen people could be the shooter. He wondered if any one of them had even considered that possibility.

Blaire settled Jimmy in the back of the ATV after moving a few items to the side. She had a thick wool blanket she carried in case she got stranded outside overnight without warning, and she did her best to turn it into a nest.

Then she pulled out a shiny survival blanket and Jimmy's world seemed to settle once again. "Space blanket!" The excitement was clear in his voice.

"You bet," she said, summoning a smile. "Now just stay here while we try to get your mommy. If you do that for me, you can keep the space blanket."

That seemed to make him utterly happy. He snuggled into the gray wool blanket and hugged the silvery Mylar to his chin. "I'll sleep," he announced.

"Great idea," she said. She couldn't resist brushing his hair gently back from his forehead. "Pleasant dreams, Jimmy."

He was already falling asleep, though. Exhausted from his fear and his crying, the tyke was nodding off. "Mommy says that, too," he murmured. And then his thumb found its way into his mouth and his eyes stayed closed.

Blaire waited for a minute, hoping the child could sleep for a while but imagining the sheriff's arrival with all the people and the work they needed to do would probably wake him. She could hope not.

HE HADN'T KNOWN the kid was there. God in heaven, he hadn't known. Jeff scrambled as quietly as he could over rough ground, putting as much distance between him and the vic as he could.

He'd been shocked by the sight of the kid. He almost couldn't bring himself to do it. If he hadn't, though, he'd be the next one The Hunt Club would take out. They'd warned him.

His damn fault for getting too curious. Now he was on the hook with them for a murder he didn't want to commit, and he was never going to forget that little boy. Those eyes, those cries, would haunt him forever.

Cussing viciously under his breath, he grabbed rocks and slipped on scree. He couldn't even turn on his flashlight yet, he was still too close. But the moon had nosedived behind the mountain and he didn't even have its thin, watery light to help him in his escape.

His heart was hammering and not just because of his efforts at climbing. He'd just killed a man and probably traumatized a kid for life. That kid wasn't supposed to be there. He'd been watching the guy for the last two weeks and he'd been camping solo. What had he done? Brought his son up for the weekend? Must have.

Giving Jeff the shock of his life. He should have backed off, should have told the others he couldn't do it because the target wasn't alone. Off-season. No tag. Whatever. Surely he could have come up with an excuse so they'd have given him another chance.

Maybe. Now that he knew what the others had been up to, he couldn't even rely on their friendship anymore. Look what they'd put him up to, even when he'd sworn he'd never rat them out.

And he wouldn't have. Man alive, he was in it up to his neck even if he hadn't known they were acting out some of the plans they'd made. An accomplice. He'd aided them. The noose would have tightened around his throat, too.

God, why hadn't he been able to make them see that? He wasn't an innocent who could just walk into a police station and say, "You know what my friends have been doing the last few years?"

Yeah. Right.

He swore again as a sharp rock bit right through his jeans and made him want to cry out from the unexpected pain. He shouldn't be struggling up the side of a mountain in the dark. He shouldn't be doing this at all.

He had believed it was all a game. A fun thing to talk about when they gathered at the lodge in the fall for their usual hunting trip. Planning early summer get-togethers to eyeball various campgrounds, looking for the places a shooter could escape without being seen.

The victim didn't much matter. Whoever was convenient and easy. The important thing was not to leave anything behind. To know the habits of the prey the same way they would know the habits of a deer.

Did the vic go hiking? If so, along what trails and how often and for how long? Was he or she alone very often or at all? Then Will had gotten the idea that they should get them in their tents. When there were other people in the campground, making it so much more challenging. Yeah.

He had believed it was just talk. He'd accompanied the others on the scouting expeditions, enjoying being in the woods while there were still patches of snow under the trees. He liked scoping out the campgrounds as the first hardy outdoorsy types began to arrive. And that, he had believed, was where it ended.

Planning. Scouting. A game.

But he'd been so wrong he could hardly believe his own delusion. He'd known these guys all his life. How was it possible he'd never noticed the psychopathy in either of them? Because that's what he now believed it was.

They didn't give a damn about anyone or anything except their own pleasure.

He paused to catch his breath and looked back over his shoulder. Far away, glimpsed through the thick forest, he caught sight of flashing red, blue and white lights. The police were there.

He'd known it wouldn't be long. That was part of the plan. Once he fired his gun, he had to clear out before the other campers emerged, and not long after them the cops.

Well, he'd accomplished that part of his task. He was well away by the time the campers dared to start coming out. But the little kid's wails had followed him into the night.

Damn it!

So he'd managed to back out of the place without scuffing up the ground in a way that would mark his trail. No one would be able to follow him. But now he was mostly on rocky terrain and that gave him added invisibility.

The damn duff down there had been hard to clear without leaving a visible trail. It had helped that so many campers had been messing it around this summer, but still, if he'd dragged his foot or... Well, it didn't matter. He hadn't.

But then there had been the farther distances. Like where he had kept watch. His movements. Too far out for anyone to notice, of course. He'd made sure of that.

So he'd done everything right. They'd never catch him and the guys would leave him alone. That's all he wanted.

But he hated himself, too, and wished he'd been made of sterner stuff, the kind that would have gone to the cops rather than knuckle under to threats and the fear that he would be counted an accomplice to acts he hadn't committed.

Now there was no hope of escape for him or his soul.

He'd done it. He'd killed a man. He was one of them, owned by them completely. Sold to the devil because of a threat to his life.

He feared, too, that if they were identified they would succeed in convincing the police that he was the killer in the other cases, that they were just his friends and he was pointing the finger at them to save his own hide.

Yeah, he had no trouble imagining them doing that, and doing it successfully. They'd plotted and planned so well that there was nothing to link *them* to the murders except him.

At last he made it over the ridge that would hide him from anyone below, not that the campground wasn't now concealed from view by thick woods.

But even if they decided to look around, they'd never find him now. All he had to do was crawl into the small cave below and await daylight. Then he would have a clear run to his car to get out of the forest.

All carefully planned. He'd be gone before any searcher could get up here.

Damn, he wanted a cigarette. But that had been part of their planning, too. No smoking. The tobacco smell would be distinctive, so they avoided it unless campfires were burning.

Who had come up with that idea?

He couldn't remember. He was past caring. He slid into the dark embrace of the cave at last, with only a short time before dawn.

Past caring. That was a good place to be. He envied the others. Instead he kept company with the remembered cries of a young boy.

BLAIRE WISHED SHE could do more. She was the kind of person who always wanted to take action, to be useful, but right now the police were in charge, using skills she didn't have to look for evidence, so she kept an eye on the little boy in the bed of her ATV and on the scene where some officers were busy questioning other campers and the rest were busy photographing the scene and hunting for evidence. Pacing back and forth between the two locations, she imagined she was creating a rut.

At least Jimmy slept. She hoped he slept right through when they removed his father in a body bag. She hated the thought that such a scene might be stamped in his mind forever.

She knew all about indelible images. She wished sometimes for a version of brain bleach. Just rinse your head in it and the dark, ugly stuff would be washed away.

Nice wish. She was old enough, however, to realize how unrealistic such a wish was. Life was the accumulation of experiences, and you could only hope that you'd learn from all of them, good or bad.

Gus stayed close to the line, attentive as the officers questioned the witnesses. Dropping by from time to time, she heard the same story repeated by everyone. They'd been asleep. Awakened suddenly by the loud, sharp clap. At first they hadn't even been sure they'd heard it.

Some had sat up, waiting to see if it came again. Others considered rolling over and going back to sleep.

Then came the sound of Jimmy's crying. Yes, he sounded scared but that might be a reaction to the sudden, loud noise. He was with his father, so he'd be okay.

Only slowly had some come to the realization that perhaps they'd better look outside to see what had happened. By then there was nothing to see, and the night had been silent except for the little boy's sobbing.

Which again they ignored because he was with his father. Except for Wes.

"I was in Iraq. I'll never mistake a gunshot for anything else. When the boy kept crying, I knew. I just knew someone had been shot. Maybe suicide, I thought. I was the first one out of my tent. The others took another couple of minutes. Regardless, I'm the one who ran to the emergency phone and called the ranger. No, I didn't touch a thing."

Wes paused, looking down, saying quietly, "It was hell listening to that kid and not acting. But his dad might have been okay. My appearance might have just scared the boy more." His mouth twisted. "They don't make rules of engagement for this."

"I hear you," Gus said. Several deputies who were also vets murmured agreement.

The sheriff spoke. "You did the best thing."

Except, thought Blaire, she'd moved in, opened the tent, stepped inside and took the boy out. She'd interfered with the scene. Next would be her turn to be grilled.

By the time they came to her, however, they were allowing the others to pack up as long as they were willing to leave contact information with the deputies. The early morning sun cast enough light on the world that details had emerged from the night, giving everything more depth. Making the trees look aged and old and maybe even weary. But that might be her own state of mind. Usually the forest gave her a sense of peace, and the trees offered her a stately temple.

The sheriff, Gage Dalton, and one of his deputies, Cadell Marcus, she thought, joined her just outside the roped area.

"Yes," she said before they even asked, "I touched the front of the tent. I was wearing gloves. I pulled the zipper down partway, poked my flashlight in and saw the scene. I had to get the little boy out of there."

Dalton nodded. "Of course you did. So what did you first see as you approached?"

"The zipper was pulled down from the top. I don't know how familiar you are with camping gear, but these days you can get tents with zippers that open both ways. A top opening allows in air while keeping protection down low from small critters. Anyway, it was open six or seven inches. Then I opened it more."

She paused, closing her eyes, remembering. "I didn't think about it at the time, but the inner screen wasn't closed. Doesn't necessarily mean anything because we don't have much of a flying insect problem up here."

Gage nodded. "Okay."

Cadell was making notes.

"Anyway, almost as soon as I poked the flashlight in, I saw the victim and I saw his son clinging to him. My only thought at that point was to get the child out of there as fast as I could. I asked Gus to pull the zipper down the rest of the way. I entered, trying not to disturb anything, and picked the boy up. I carried him to my ATV, where he's sleeping now."

"Did you notice anything else?"

She shook her head and opened her eyes. "Frankly, once I saw that man's head, I was aware of nothing else but the little boy. I seem to recall some toys being scattered around, the boy was out of his sleeping bag which, if I remember correctly, was pretty balled up, and that's it. I was completely focused on removing the child while trying not to step on anything." She paused. "Oh. I turned so Jimmy wouldn't be able to see his father."

Gage surprised her by reaching out to pat her upper arm. "You did the right things. We just needed to know where any contamination might have come from."

"What about Jimmy?" she asked. Concern for the

child, kept on simmer for the last couple of hours, now bubbled up like a pot boiling over.

"Sarah Ironheart has called child services. They're contacting the mother." He paused. "Do you think Jimmy trusts you?"

"Insofar as he can. He let me put him in my ATV to sleep." She smiled without humor. "I think the space blanket did it."

"Probably. I'm wondering, if I put you and him in the back of my car, we can take him to town to the social worker. His mom should be on the way."

She hesitated, hating to walk away from what was clearly her job. This campground was her responsibility, and once the cops left…

"Go ahead," said Gus. "I'll meet your staff when they arrive in the next hour and explain. I'm sure they can fill in for you."

The sheriff spoke. "And after the techs are done I'm leaving a couple of deputies up here so the scene won't be disturbed. You're covered."

He gave her a half smile as he said it.

"Yeah, CYA," she responded. "Okay." She couldn't bear the thought of waking Jimmy only to turn him over to a stranger without explanation. The car ride to town would give her plenty of opportunity to reassure him, and maybe by the time they reached Conard City his mom will have arrived.

She looked at Gus. "I promised him a horse ride."

"We might be able to work in a couple of minutes when we get to your HQ. If that's okay with Gage."

"Fine by me. That little boy needs everything good he can get right now."

# *Chapter Three*

Jimmy woke quickly. At first he looked frightened but he recognized Blaire and when she told him they were going to take a ride in a police car, he seemed delighted. Not once, not yet, did he ask the dreaded question, "Where's my daddy?"

They sat in the back of Gage's official SUV and Gage obliged him by turning on the rack of lights but explained people in the woods were still sleeping so he couldn't turn on the siren.

Jimmy appeared satisfied with that. Then Blaire began the onerous task of explaining to him that they were taking him to his mom and finally he asked, "Where's my daddy?"

Her heart sank like a stone. How the hell did you explain this to a four-year-old? It wasn't her place. He'd need his mom and a social worker for this.

She cleared her throat. "He can't come with us right now."

After a moment, Jimmy nodded. "He's helping the police, right?"

She couldn't bring herself to answer and was grateful when he didn't press the issue, apparently satisfied with his own answer.

Which gave her plenty of time to contemplate the kind

of monster who would shoot a man while his young son was nearby. Only in battle when her comrades were in danger had she ever felt a need to kill, but she felt it right then and memories surged in her, the past burst into the present and she wanted to vomit.

But Jimmy fell asleep and they sailed right past her headquarters building without offering him the promised horse ride. Gus, who had been following them down, pulled over and gave a hands-up signal as they drove past. Letting her know he'd figured it out.

It was good of him to offer to stay and inform her staff what was going on. She could hardly stop to call and radio, and she couldn't wait for them herself, not with this trusting, precious little boy cuddled up against her.

Just as well. She wasn't sure what world she was inhabiting. Afghanistan? Conard County? The state park? Images, like mixed-up slides, kept flashing in her mind and she had to make a huge effort to focus on the back of Gage's head, on the fact she was in his vehicle. On the boy curled against her so trustingly.

That trust was killing her. Nobody should trust her like that. Not him most especially. He was just a kid and when he found out and finally understood what had happened, he might never trust another soul in his life.

Almost without realizing it, as the town grew closer and the day grew brighter, she was making a silent promise to herself. Somehow she was going to find the SOB who'd done this. If the cops didn't get him first, she wasn't going to give up the hunt.

Because someone deserved to pay for this. Someone deserved to die.

MILES AWAY, THE killer was hotfooting it down a mountainside to his vehicle. The cries of the child rang loud in his head and he thought bitterly that he should have just kidnapped the kid and carried him along.

He'd been angry at his friends. He'd been scared of them, maybe even terrified. But now he loathed them. He wished he could find a way to get even that wouldn't involve putting himself in prison for life.

Thoughts of revenge fueled him as he raced toward safety.

GUS HAD LOADED the ATV onto Blaire's truck and brought everything down to her HQ, where he waited patiently. As staff members reported for their day's work, he explained what had happened and told them to avoid the upper campground, so they wouldn't get in the way of the police.

While he was telling them, an ambulance brought the body down. Silence fell among the six men and women who were about to fan out to their various jobs. They stood, watching it pass, and for several long minutes, no one spoke.

Then Gus's radio crackled. It was one of his own staff.

"You coming back today, Gus, or you want me to stand in?"

"I'm not sure." He was thinking of Blaire. She might need more than a cup of coffee after this. "You take over, Josh. I'll let you know what's up."

"Terrible thing," Josh said. "You can bet we're going to be on high alert today."

"Good. We don't know which direction the perp took off when he left. Or whether he'll shoot again."

That made the local crew shift nervously and eye him. *Oh, hell,* he thought. He'd just messed up everything. What could he say? He couldn't very well send them out to patrol the other campgrounds. Not after this. They were seasonal workers, not trained for this kind of thing. And he was still more used to talking to other soldiers than civilians. He needed to guard his tongue.

"You got stuff you can do nearby?" he asked, scanning them.

One spoke. "Blaire's been talking about replacing the fire rings at the Cottonwood Campground."

"Nearby?"

"Yeah."

"Then do that."

"We'll need the truck to cart the concrete and the rings."

Gus nodded. "Okay. Good idea. Stick together. I'm almost positive the threat is gone, though."

"I'll feel better tomorrow," one said sarcastically.

He helped them unload the ATV, then fill the truck bed with bags of concrete and steel fire rings. Finally, he turned over the keys and watched them drive away. East. Away from the campground where the shooting had occurred. Not that he could blame them.

Then he went inside and made a fresh pot of coffee. He eyed the espresso machine because he loved Blaire's espresso, but he didn't know how to use it. Maybe he'd remedy that when she got back, ask for instructions.

While he waited for the coffee he went outside and whistled for Scrappy. Five minutes later, the gelding emerged from the woods to the north, looking quite perky. He must have picked up some sleep during all the uproar.

When the horse reached him, he patted his neck, then was astonished—he was always astonished when it happened—when Scrappy wrapped his neck around him, giving him a hug.

The horse was a mind reader? No, a mood reader. He

patted and stroked Scrappy until the horse needed to move and pranced away.

"You getting hungry?"

Scrappy bobbed his head emphatically. If that horse could talk...

He had some feed in one of the saddlebags and put it on the edge of the porch, making sure Scrappy's reins wouldn't get in his way. Water. He needed water, too.

He went back inside and looked around until he found a big bucket in a supply closet. That would do.

A little while later, cup of coffee in his hand, he perched on the step of the small porch and shared breakfast with Scrappy. Maybe his best friend, he thought.

But his mind was wandering elsewhere, to Blaire, to the murder, to the little guy who'd lost his father.

It had been a while, thank God, since he'd felt murderous, but today was shaking him back into that old unwanted feeling.

A sleeping man. His child nearby. What kind of person would take that shot without a threat driving him? And how offensive could a sleeping man be? Kid aside, the killer had to be the worst kind of coward.

Afraid of where his thoughts might take him, because he'd spent a lot of time getting himself past the war, he forced himself to notice other things. The play of the light on the trees as the sun rose ever higher. The bird calls. Even more entertaining were the squirrels darting around, jumping from branch to branch and walking out on slender twigs, looking like high-wire daredevils. Even at times hanging upside down while they gnawed a branch. Weird, they usually did that only in the spring and fall.

BLAIRE RETURNED IN the late morning, looking absolutely wrung out. A police vehicle dropped her off, then turned around and headed back down the mountain. Gus rose as she approached, but she lowered herself to the porch step, eyeing Scrappy, who'd found a clump of grass to investigate.

"You must want to get back," she said.

"I most likely want to get you a cup of coffee. Regular because I don't know how your espresso machine works." He lowered himself beside her and asked, "Awful?"

"Awful," she agreed. "That poor little boy. At least his mother was already there when we arrived. But then he asked the question he didn't ask before."

"What's that?"

*"Where's Daddy?"*

"Oh. My. God." Gus didn't even want to imagine it, but his mind threw it up in full view, inescapable.

"Yeah." She sighed, leaned against the porch stanchion and closed her eyes.

"Your crew is out working on fire rings at Cottonwood. They didn't seem too eager to split up."

Her eyes opened to half-mast. "I don't imagine they would. I'm not too eager myself. God, what a monster, and it's too soon to hope he's made his way to the far ends of the Earth. He could be hanging around out there."

He couldn't deny it. "Look, we've both been up most of the night. If you want to sleep, I'll stand guard here until your people are done for the day. If not, let me get you some coffee."

"Coffee sounds good," she admitted. "I may be over-tired, but I'm too wound up to sleep. What I really want is to wrap my hands around someone's throat. A specific someone."

He could identify with that. He'd just finished brewing a second pot of coffee so he was able to bring her a piping mug that smelled rich and fresh. He brought one for himself and sat beside her once again.

"I'm still trying to wrap my mind around the kind of person who would do something like that," she said. "It had to be in cold blood. Nothing had happened as far as anyone knows."

"His wife?"

"She's already been gently questioned. Nobody who'd want to kill him, nobody who'd had a fight with him recently, Gage told me."

"Well, great. The trail is awfully lean."

"If it's there at all." She sighed and sipped her coffee. "You must need to get back."

"My assistant is filling in. Unless you want to get rid of me, I'm here for now."

She turned her head, looking straight at him for the first time, and he noted how hollow her eyes looked. "Thanks. I'm not keen on being alone right now."

"Then there's no need." He paused. "We've shared a whole lot over cups of joe."

"That we have." She tilted her head back and drew several deep breaths as if drinking in the fresh woodland scents. "I'll share something with you right now. If the police don't have much success quickly, I'm going to start a search of my own. I know these woods like the back of my hand. He can't have come in and out without leaving some trace."

He turned his mug in his hands, thinking about it. "You're right. If it comes to that, I'll help you. But we can't wait too long. One rain and everything will be lost."

"Yeah." Again she raised her coffee to her lips, and this time she nearly drained the mug. Rising, she put her foot on the step. "I need more caffeine. If you want, I'll make espresso."

"Only if I can watch and learn. Then you'll never get rid of me."

That at least drew a weak laugh from her. Once inside, he leaned against the narrow counter with his arms folded and watched her make the beverage. From time to time she told him things that wouldn't be immediately obvious, like turning the handled filter to one side to create the pressure.

"Espresso has to be brewed under pressure."

But her mind was obviously elsewhere, and to be frank, so was his.

"People get murdered," she remarked as she finished and handed him a tall cup holding three shots. "Doctor as you like. Ice in the freezer, thank God, milk in the fridge, sweetener in these little packets."

"Ice will water it down," he remarked.

"Yeah, but I like mine cold unless it's winter. Your choice."

He went for the ice, saying, "People get murdered... But what? You didn't finish that thought."

"No, I didn't." Her own cup in hand, she scooped ice into it and topped it with milk. "People get murdered, but not often by strangers while sleeping in a tent with their little son."

"Agreed."

"Outside?" she asked.

"I hate being stuck indoors." Another leftover from years in the military. He never felt all that safe when four walls held him and cut off his view.

They returned to the front steps. Scrappy looked almost as if he were sleeping standing up. Usually, he curled up on the ground, but not today. The tension the two of them were feeling must be reaching him, as well.

"I like your horse," she remarked. "Wish I could have one."

"Then get one."

"It's not in my nonexistent budget. And I don't get paid enough to afford one. Besides, I'm so shackled by things I need to do he might not get enough exercise."

"You're even more understaffed than I am."

"No kidding."

It was easier to talk about budgets and staffing than what had happened during the wee hours this morning. He sipped his espresso, loving the caffeine kick because he was tired, too, from lack of sleep, and waited. There'd be more. They were both vets. Memories had been stirred up, especially for her because she'd had to see it all.

Yeah, there'd be more. Because she'd had to help the kid.

But as noon began to approach, she said nothing more, and he had nothing to say. He was cramming the memories back into the dark pit where they belonged and he decided she must be doing the same.

Unfortunately, burying them wasn't a permanent solution. Like zombies, they kept rising anew and they were never welcome. And sometimes, like zombies, they'd devour you whole and all you could do was hang on. Or give in because there was no fighting it.

He glanced down into his cup and realized he'd finished his espresso. He'd have liked some more but decided not to ask.

At long last she turned to look at him, for the first time that day her blue eyes looking almost as brilliant as the sunny western sky. "That kid is going to have problems. He may not have seen the mess, he may not understand what happened, but he would remember that he left his dad behind in a tent on a mountainside. His mom will tell him about it later, but he's going to remember leaving his dad."

Gus nodded. "Yeah, he will." Of that he was certain. "The question will be whether he believes he abandoned his father."

She nodded and looked down at the mug she held. "More espresso?"

"I'd like that."

Those blue eyes lifted again. "You sure you don't have to get back?"

"Not today. I have a good staff. But even so, I'm in no rush to face the inevitable questions about what happened over here."

"Me neither." Her eyes shuttered briefly. "So my crew are out replacing fire rings?"

He'd told her that but under the circumstances didn't feel she'd slipped a memory cog. Overload. She must be experiencing it. "Yeah, it was the first thing they thought to do when I explained what had happened. Besides, I exceeded my authority."

Her head snapped around to look at him again. "Meaning?"

"I suggested today would be a good day to stick together."

After a few beats, she nodded. "You're right. I didn't even think of that. The creep could still be out there."

"I don't think there's any question that he's still out there. The only question is, did he leave the forest or is he hanging out somewhere?"

Her charming, crooked smile peeked out. "Correcting my precision now?"

He flashed a smile back at her. "You know why."

Of course she knew why. With a sigh, she rose. "Let's go make some more coffee. If I tried to sleep I wouldn't rest anyway, so I might as well be wired."

Inside the cabin was dim. Because of the harsh, cold winters, the builders hadn't been generous with windows except at the very front where visitors would enter. Consequently, the rear room that housed the small kitchen and dining area was dim and needed the lights turned on. Blaire flipped the switch, then turned on the espresso maker.

"How many shots?" she asked Gus.

"It's funny, but I'm not used to thinking of coffee in terms of shots."

That drew a faint laugh from her. She picked up and wagged a double shot glass at him. "How many of these?"

He laughed outright. "Okay, two."

She nodded and turned back to the machine.

"You gonna be okay?" he asked as the pump began pushing water through the coffee grounds. Noisy thing.

"Sure," she said, leaning against the counter and watching the espresso pour into the double shot glass. "I'm always okay. It's not necessarily pleasant, but I'm okay."

Yeah, *okay* was a long way from being happy, content or otherwise good. He shook his head a little and pulled out one of the two chairs at the small table, sitting while he watched her. "This day is endless."

"What brought you this way this morning?"

"I was restless and couldn't sleep. Scrappy was agitating for a ride so I decided to saddle up. I think he was feeling my mood."

"That wouldn't surprise me. Animals are very sensitive to energy, at least in my experience." She placed his mug in front of him again. "You know where the fixins are."

Making himself at home in her kitchen felt right. At

least at the moment. He dressed up his espresso and waited for her to make her own. "Plans for today, since you can't sleep?"

"I'm probably going to run this morning like a broken record in my head." She finished pouring milk into her mug, added a few ice cubes, then turned. "Outside, if you don't mind. The walls are closing in."

He knew the feeling well. He held open the front door for her and resumed his perch on the step. She paced for a bit on the bare ground that probably served as a parking lot when people checked in and were directed to their campgrounds.

"I keep thinking," she said, "that the crime scene guys aren't going to find much that's useful. The ground was a mess, did you notice? People had obviously scuffed it up pretty good last night even if they didn't this morning."

"I saw," he said in agreement. "What are you thinking?"

"That this guy knew what he was doing. That he didn't just walk into a random campsite and shoot someone through an opening in their tent."

He sat up a little straighter. He must have been more tired than he realized not to have thought of this himself. "You're saying stalking."

"I'm suggesting it, yes. No bumbling around in the dark as far as anyone knows. Certainly some of the people in the other tents must be light enough sleepers that they'd have heard activity."

"Maybe so." He was chewing the idea in his head.

"So, if he planned in advance he had to watch in advance. He'd have done that from a distance, right?"

He nodded. He'd done enough recon to know the drill. "Say he did."

"Then the cops might not find anything useful at the scene."

He nodded, sucking some air between his front teeth as his mouth tightened. "What are your plans for tomorrow? Got any time for reconnaissance?"

"I can make it."

"Can you ride?"

"Sure."

"So shall I borrow an extra mount or do you want to walk a perimeter first?"

She thought about it. "Walk," she decided. "We don't want to miss something."

"This assumes the cops don't find something today."

"Of course."

Their eyes met and the agreement was sealed. They'd do a little searching of their own.

That made him feel a bit better. He hoped it did for her, too.

THAT EVENING, JEFF pulled his car into the lodge's small parking area and went to face the music. He'd made a mistake and wished he could figure out a way of not telling Will and Karl. Desperately wished. Because things were going to get worse now.

But Jeff was acutely aware that he was a lousy liar. He could see them when they arrived tomorrow and pretend that everything had gone off without a hitch, but it wouldn't take them long to realize he was being untruthful.

The bane of his existence.

He let himself in and began to build a fire on the big stone hearth. That task was expected of the first to arrive, and given that the nights were chilly at this altitude, even in the summer when it had been known to snow occasionally, a small fire burning all the time was welcome.

The heavy log construction of the lodge acted like an insulator, too. Once it had caught the chill, it hung on to it until it was driven out.

The others weren't expected until late tomorrow, though. Fine by him. There was plenty to eat and drink and maybe he could find a way to omit mentioning his oversight. His major oversight.

Besides, it might amount to nothing. One shell casing? How much could that tell anyone? That he'd used a hollow-point bullet in a .45? Lots of folks bought hollow points and even more owned .45s. Hollow points were less likely to pass through the target and cause collateral damage, while still inflicting far more damage on the target than a full metal jacket.

He couldn't have been sure what he'd be facing when he opened that tent a few inches, but he knew he wanted to kill his target without killing anything else.

They'd find the remains of the bullet at autopsy anyway. A popular brand that could be purchased in an awful lot of places. No, that wouldn't lead to him.

But the shell casing automatically ejected by his pistol? He should have scooped that up, but in his panic to get away, he'd clean forgotten it was lying on the ground. What if it had retained his fingerprints?

Not likely, he assured himself. The way he'd handled those bullets, any fingerprints should be just smears. The heat of the powder burning before it ejected the round from the shell should have wiped out any DNA evidence.

So yeah, he'd made a mistake. It wasn't a god-awful mistake, though. Hell, they couldn't necessarily even link it to the shooting, regardless of bullet fragments they might find at autopsy. No, because *anyone* could have been shooting out there at any time. That brass casing might be months old.

So no, it wasn't a catastrophe.

He spent a great deal of time that evening sipping beer and bucking himself up, dreading the moment tomorrow when his friends would come through the door.

Friends? He wasn't very sure of that any longer. Friends would have taken his word for it that he wouldn't squeal on them. Friends should have trusted him rather than threatening him.

Thinking about those threats put him in the blackest of moods. He wasn't a killer. He *wasn't*. He'd killed, though. In self-defense, he reminded himself. Because failing to take that guy out would have been signing his own death sentence. Yeah, self-defense, not murder.

That proved to be a small sop to his conscience, but he needed one. While the cries of the child had begun to fade to the background, the memory of them still made him supremely uncomfortable.

He'd caused that. Did self-defense justify that? He hoped the kid was too young to understand what had happened.

Because he hated to think of the nightmares he'd caused if the kid wasn't.

## Chapter Four

The morning was still dewy when Blaire awoke from troubled, uneasy dreams. At least she'd finally been able to crash after a day that had seemed like a nightmare that would never end, a day during which she'd become so exhausted she had often felt as if she were only slightly attached to her own body.

She'd had the feeling before, in combat and the aftermath, but not since then. Not until yesterday.

It hadn't just been lack of sleep that had gotten to her. Jimmy had gotten to her. He had caused her an emotional turmoil unlike any she had felt since one of her comrades had been hit in a firefight. Or blasted by a roadside bomb.

All she could remember was how he'd been crying and clinging to his dead father. Yeah, he'd perked up well enough after she'd carried him away, singing to him, and he loved the silvery blanket, but how much trauma had he endured? How much had he understood and how much of that would stay with him forever?

She had no idea how good a four-year-old's long-term memory might be, but she suspected those memories were stronger if they carried a huge emotional impact. Heck, that was true for most people. Some events just got etched into your brain as if by acid.

Her staff showed up, trickling in around 8:00 a.m. The

first thing they wanted to know was news about the shooting. She had none. Then they asked if they could keep working on the fire rings as they had yesterday.

Of course they could. It wasn't like the job hadn't been done, and from what she'd seen yesterday afternoon, she figured there was hardly a camper left in the park. When she climbed into her truck to check out all the sites, she found she was right: only one hardy camper remained, a guy who always spent nearly the entire summer here. He was friendly enough, but clearly didn't want to strike up any lengthy conversations. Most days he sat beside a small fire drinking coffee. Beans seemed to be his preferred meal. Sometimes he went fishing in the tumbling stream a couple of hundred yards behind his campsite, and she'd occasionally seen a couple of freshly cleaned fish on a frying pan over his small fire.

"Nothing better than fresh fish," she inevitably said.

"Nothing," he always agreed before they went their separate ways.

Finally, because she couldn't ignore it any longer, she drove up to the site of yesterday's horror. She left her truck in the small parking lot next to a sheriff's vehicle but eschewed her ATV. She needed the walk back to the site, needed to stretch her legs and try to clear the air. When she got there, she felt a whole lot better.

The deputies Gage had promised stood guard. Seeing them, she wished she'd thought to bring a thermos of soup or something with her. Their only seat was a fallen log outside the taped-off area, and neither of them looked as if they were having a good time.

"Boring duty, huh?" she asked as she approached. Her uniform identified her as theirs identified them. She couldn't remember having met either of them before. They looked almost brand spanking new. Together they formed a sea of khaki, hers interrupted with dark pants and a dark green quilted vest over her shirt. Both of the deputies looked as if they wished they'd brought a vest or jacket with them.

"I suppose you can't light a fire?" she said. "The firepit is outside the crime scene area and you guys look cold."

"We ran out of coffee," one admitted frankly. His chest plate said his name was Carson. "We'll be relieved soon, though, Ranger. Only four hours at a stretch. If they need us up here tomorrow, we'll both be better prepared."

"You're not from around here, huh?" That seemed apparent. Anyone who lived in these parts knew how chilly it could get up here even at the height of summer.

"That's obvious, I guess," said the other guy. His last name was Bolling and his face was so fresh looking he could have passed for eighteen. Which she guessed was possible, however unlikely. "I'm from a small town in Nevada and I got sick of being hot."

Blaire had to laugh, and the two men joined her. She looked at Carson. "You, too?"

"Different town, more Midwestern. I wanted mountains. Visions of hiking and skiing. That kind of thing."

"I'll bet you never thought you'd be standing guard like this in the middle of nowhere."

"Not high on my list," Bolling said. "So is the skiing good?"

"We still don't have a downhill slope right around here. Something goes wrong with every attempt. But if you want to off-trail cross-country, that's great. So is snowshoeing. Just check in with me or with the national forest before you go. I need to know you're out here and you need to know if we have avalanche conditions. Mind if I walk around a bit?"

Carson chuckled. "I think you're in charge of this place except for the roped-off area."

"Yeah, that's yours."

She circled the campground, eyeing the signs of the hurried departures yesterday. And they had been hurried. Sure, it was unlikely the shooter was around or they'd have known it for certain, but she couldn't blame them for wanting to get the hell away from here.

Death had visited a few tents over. And it was not a natural death. Uneasiness would cause almost anyone to want to get as far away as possible.

She knew she and Gus had planned to check out the area together, but he also had responsibilities at the national forest. Her load was a lot lighter, for the most part. She could afford to set her staff to replacing fire rings, especially now that they were empty of campers.

She had no idea what she expected to find that the scene techs hadn't. They'd probably applied their version of a fine-tooth comb to most of the area, even beyond the circle of yellow tape.

But she kept walking slowly anyway. A campground was an unlikely place to pick up a trail, though. People were in constant motion at their sites and places in between. All of them had to traipse to one of the two outdoor chemical toilets, which meant they either walked around tents or passed between them. Kids, especially, scuffed the ground and kicked up needles and duff.

She paused at one spot where she had to smile. It seemed some kids had been laying out roads, probably to use to play with miniature cars. There were even a couple of twigs broken off trees and firmly planted to make the road look tree-lined. Clever.

How many kids had she seen last night? Not many, but

that didn't mean they weren't there. Their parents might have insisted they stay inside tents.

Then she spied something red that was half-buried in earth and squatted. A small metal car, she realized as she brushed the debris away. She hoped it wasn't someone's favorite.

Just in case she got a letter in a week or so from some youngster, she slipped it into her vest pocket. It wouldn't be the first time she'd heard from a kid who'd left something behind and who couldn't come back to retrieve it. Usually it was an inexpensive, small item that the parents didn't consider worth the time and effort to return for. She could understand both sides of that issue, but she didn't mind sending a toy back if it made a boy or girl happy. In fact, just doing it always made her smile.

Since Afghanistan, her smiles had become rarer and far more precious to her when she could summon a genuine one. Gone were the days when laughter came easily. She hoped both would return eventually. She had to believe they would. A battlefield was a helluva place to lose all your illusions, and while humor had carried most of them through, it had become an increasingly dark humor. Something that no one on the outside would ever understand.

Swallowing her memories yet again, she forced herself to move slowly and sweep the ground with her eyes. The guy had to have come from somewhere. He wasn't a ghost.

There was a basic rule to investigation: whoever took something from a scene also left something behind. She'd first learned that in Afghanistan when they'd been tracking the people who had attacked them or one of their other convoys. Nobody could move over even the rockiest ground without leaving traces, however minor.

But this damn forest floor was a challenge unto itself.

So much loose debris, easily scuffed and stirred. Even the wind could move it around. Moreover, under the trees it was soft, softer than a carpet, and footprints would disappear quickly unless boots scraped. Weight alone didn't make a lasting impression, not unless it rained, and rain here at this time of year was rare enough. They certainly hadn't had any in the several days leading up to the murder.

Eventually she called it a day. A wider perimeter would need the help that Gus promised and it might be a wild-goose chase anyway.

The killer was obviously skilled, had clearly taken great care not to leave a trail behind him.

Which left the question: Why Jasper? And why when his kid was there? Was Jimmy an unexpected complication for him? Too late to back out?

She seemed to remember one of the campers saying Jasper had brought his son up here just for the weekend. Yeah, if someone had been stalking him, Jimmy was probably a complete surprise.

She found herself once again hoping Jimmy could forget that night. If he retained any memory of it at all, she hoped it was of a space blanket and a ride in a police car. Not what had happened inside that tent.

Heading back, she passed the two cold deputies again. They no longer sat, but were moving from foot to foot. Too bad she hadn't picked up another survival blanket to offer them. "Much longer?" she asked.

Bolling looked at his watch. "A little less than an hour."

She nodded. "Keep warm." As if they could do much about it without lighting a small fire, which they didn't seem inclined to do. Maybe they didn't know how.

Shaking her head, knowing their relief was already on

the way, she headed back to her truck, walking among the tall trees and the occasional brush that looked parched.

The peace she usually found in these woods had been shattered, she realized. The niggling uneasiness she'd been trying to ignore hit her full force during her walk back to her truck. A killer had stalked these woods. He might still be out there. He might be watching even now. And he could always return to repeat his crime.

She told herself not to be fanciful, but she'd spent time in a place where such threats were as real as the air she breathed and the ground she walked on.

The guy could be out there right now, savoring his kill, enjoying his apparent success, wanting to see everything that happened. Hadn't she read somewhere that criminals often came back to the scene, especially to watch the cops?

Or it could be another kind of killer. The kind who got a kick out of reliving his actions. Who enjoyed the sense of power the killing gave him. Or the secret power of being so close to the very cops who were supposed to find him. Cat and mouse, maybe.

His motivation scarcely mattered at this point, though it might become useful eventually. No, all that mattered right now was that these woods were haunted by the ghost of a dead man and the evil of a murderer. That a little boy's cries might have soaked into the very trees and earth, leaving a psychic stain.

God, was she losing it?

But her step quickened anyway. Back to HQ. Back to check on her team. To call the sheriff and ask if they'd learned anything at all.

Despite every effort to ignore the feeling, she paused

and looked back twice. The sense of being watched persisted, even though she could detect nothing.

An icy trickle ran down her spine.

A THOUSAND YARDS away in a small hide left by some hunter in a past season, Will and Karl peered through high-powered binoculars. They'd happened on this point during reconnaissance during their spring planning and were delighted with it.

Here, below the tree line, there were few spots where one could see any great distance through the grid work of tree trunks and the laciness of tree branches. Not much brush under these trees, but not much open space for any appreciable distance.

This was a natural forest, not one neatly replanted by a lumber company, which would have given them corridors to peer along. No, here nature did her best to scatter the trees everywhere, giving each a better chance at a long life.

Some saplings added to the screening effect, huddled around the base of mother trees that, science had learned, actually provided nutrients to their offspring. On occasion, an older tree would sacrifice its life to ensure the growth of the new ones. Roots underground were carriers of messages and food.

Will had read about it. It tickled him to think of how much a forest was invisibly intertwined. When he was in a fanciful mood, he'd sometimes close his eyes and imagine a brightly lit neural-type network running beneath his feet, messages passing among the sheltering trees.

Then there was that massive fungus scientists had discovered under the ground that turned out to be a single organism covering square miles. As he started thinking about that, however, Karl spoke, shattering the moment.

"Jeff did it."

Yes, he'd done it. The solitary tent surrounded by crime scene tape and the two deputies wandering around as if they wished they were anywhere else… It was all the diagram he needed. But he remained anyway, peering through the binoculars, both enjoying the success and wanting to annoy Karl, who felt no appreciation of the miracle under them, buried in the ground.

Once he'd tried to tell Karl about it. Once was enough. It didn't even matter to him that it was actual science. Not Karl. He prided himself on being hardheaded. Will could tell him about it, and Karl would absorb the information factually and move on, finding nothing entrancing about it.

That was the only thing he didn't like about Karl. Had never liked, even though they were good friends in every other way. Karl had a distinct lack of imagination. A trait that proved helpful in this endeavor, were Will to be honest about it.

While he himself might see a network of patterns and possibilities and race down various avenues of attack, Karl remained firmly grounded in their scouting expeditions and what they knew and didn't know. He wasn't one to make even a small assumption.

Although sending Jeff on this expedition had left them both wondering if he'd just walk into the nearest police station.

They had that covered. Two against one, if Jeff tried to nail them, the two of them would nail him. They were each the other's alibi.

Not that they'd need one. This was their fifth kill in the last two summers, and neither he nor Karl had ever left a shred of evidence. Hell, the murders hadn't even been linked to one another.

They'd vastly overshadowed careless Leopold and Loeb. Funny, though, Will thought while watching the campground, seeing the ranger stray around out farther looking for something. He and Karl hadn't been content to prove the point and stop at one.

No. He and Karl had discovered a real taste for this kind of hunting. Deer could be slipperier, of course, but hunting a human? They weren't nearly as evasive, but they were so much more dangerous to take down.

It was always possible to leave traces, and cops would be looking, unlike when you took a deer during season with a license. They'd be paying attention to anything out of line. And if you weren't cautious enough, your victim might get wind that he was being stalked.

It wasn't the top thing on most people's minds, which had aided them, but one of their vics had had an almost preternatural sense that he was being followed. When they realized he seemed to be taking evasive action, they'd nearly salivated over the prospect of taking him out. A *real* challenge.

He studied the campground below once again, satisfying himself that no one seemed to be acting as if there was something significant to find.

Karl spoke, lowering his own binoculars. "Jeff's a wimp. I still can't believe he managed this."

"We kind of put him on the spot," Will reminded him.

Karl turned his head a bit to look at him. He shifted as if he were getting tired of lying on his stomach on the hard rock. "Would you have killed him?"

"I said I would."

"But he's one of us."

Will put down his own binoculars, lifting a brow. "He's one of us until he screws us. How far do you trust him?"

"More than I did a few days ago."

"Exactly. He's in it all the way now. But if he'd backed off, neither of us would have had a choice."

Karl nodded. "I know. I wish to hell he hadn't found out. Been jumpy since I learned he knew what we're doing. He's always been a bit of a coward. I like the guy, always have. We grew up together, went to college together. Joined the same fraternity, screwed the same girls…"

"Hey, that's almost as much of a crime these days as shooting someone."

Karl afforded one of his cold smiles. "Guess so, but I seem to remember those sorority gals fighting to get an invitation to our parties. And it wasn't a secret we were looking to get laid."

"Usually that was true. I remember a few who didn't seem to be clued in, though."

Karl nodded and lifted his binoculars again.

There *were* a few, Will recalled. Girls who were taken by surprise and had to be silenced before they got someone in trouble. Silencing them had been pathetically easy, though. All they'd had to do was tell them the stories they'd make up about the girls. How they'd come off looking like two-bit hookers. The strength of the fraternity, its numbers.

In a smaller way, he and Karl had that strength now, more so with Jeff actively involved.

God, how had that man pieced it all together from a few snips of conversation he'd overheard between Will and Karl? Why had he even believed it? What had been the clue that had made Jeff realize it was no longer a game?

Someday he was going to make Jeff spill the beans. But not yet. Jeff was entirely too nervous. He didn't want to do anything that might make Jeff take flight.

"I don't like that ranger," Karl remarked.

Will picked up his binoculars, focused them again and found the woman. "Why not?"

"She just picked up something from the ground and put it in her pocket. She's actively searching outside the crime scene area."

"She won't find anything useful," Will said, although sudden uncertainty made his stomach sink.

"She shouldn't if Jeff did what we said. But she just found something and picked it up. I couldn't tell what it was."

"Hell."

He zeroed in on the woman more closely, but she scanned the ground for a little while longer before waving to the deputies and heading for the parking lot. She didn't seem to be in a hurry, which could well be the best news for them.

At least until she started down the rutty walking path to the parking lot. Her step quickened, then quickened again and he saw her looking over her shoulder.

"What the hell?" he muttered.

She paused again and looked back.

"She senses we're watching," Karl said abruptly. "Look at something else."

"But…" Will started.

"No *buts*. If she'd found something she'd have showed it to the deputies. Instead she just stuck it in her pocket. Let it go."

Will, who'd been letting a lot go without much trouble for the last few years, suddenly found himself unable to do that. What had she picked up? It had been important enough to tuck in her pocket. Why hadn't she given it to the deputies?

Karl was probably right, he assured himself. But the way she'd looked back, twice… His stomach flipped again.

"Let it go," Karl said again. "People can often tell when they're being watched. It's some kind of instinct. But since she couldn't see anyone, she's probably convinced she imagined it."

"It would be easy enough," Will remarked. His literal-minded Karl might not get it, but Will himself had no desire to be any closer to that campsite. Something might be lurking down there, although he didn't want to put a name to it. He often told himself he didn't believe in ghosts or all that crap.

But the truth was, he feared they might exist.

That was one thing he hadn't considered when he'd embarked on this venture with his friends: that he might be collecting ghosts that could haunt him. Where was it written that they had to stay where they were killed?

He swore under his breath and rolled onto his back, looking up at the graying sky. "It's going to rain. Maybe we should go."

"It rarely rains up here."

"Don't you smell it?" He had to get out of here. Now. Because he honestly felt as if *something* were watching him.

"Well, we're supposed to meet Jeff at the lodge this evening," Karl said grudgingly. He pulled out a cigar from an inner pocket on his jacket. "Just a few puffs, first."

They were far enough away that the tobacco smell should waft away to the west, away from the campground and the deputies if it could even reach that far.

Giving in, Will pulled out a cigar of his own and clipped the end with his pocket tool before lighting it from a butane lighter. Then he held the flame to Karl, who did the same. The cellophane wrappers got shoved deep into their pockets.

It *was* relaxing, Will admitted to himself. Staring up

at the graying sky that didn't look all that threatening yet. Lying still, refusing to think about all the worrisome problems that had been stalking *him* since they embarked on this venture.

Would he undo it? No way. He'd gotten thrills for a lifetime the last couple of years.

"What's eating you?" Karl asked after a few minutes. "You're edgy."

Well, there was no way Will would tell him that he didn't like being within range of the scenes where any of the victims had died. He stayed away once the deed was done. It was always Karl, whether it had been his kill or not, who wanted to go back and look the site over. Some quirk or odd fascination.

"Coming back could be dangerous," he said finally, although he didn't say how. No need for that.

"They would never look up here. You know that. We can look down on them, but when we checked it out two months ago, we realized this position was well shielded from below. Different sight lines. You know that. Besides, those deputies look bored out of their minds."

"Yeah." He puffed on his cigar, liking the way it tasted and gave him a mild buzz. "That ranger was acting weird."

"She probably just wants the campground back. Funny, though," Karl added.

"Yeah?"

"Every campground in the park emptied out. Talk about having an impact."

"Kind of a broad-brush response," Will agreed. That hadn't happened before. He pondered that reaction for the next ten minutes while drawing occasionally on his cigar. Maybe it was because this park was so small. While they'd chosen the most rustic of the campsites, farthest from the ranger's cabin and the entrance, the distance wasn't huge.

If people thought a killer was hanging out in these woods, yeah, they'd get the hell out.

Abruptly, he returned to the moment as a huge drop of rain hit the tip of his nose. While he wandered in his thoughts, the sky had darkened considerably, and for the first time, he heard the rumble of thunder.

He spared a thought for those deputies standing guard below, not that he cared about them. The rain would mess up the scene even more, covering any inadvertent tracks Jeff might have left. Not that he thought any had been left. They'd picked a time when the campground would be full and well scuffed up by the campers. Probably covered with bits of their trash, as well.

He looked at his cigar, hating to put it out. He bought only expensive ones and felt guiltier about wasting them than he felt about wasting food.

He sat up and Karl did, too, after some raindrops splattered his face.

"We've seen enough for now," he told Karl.

"Yeah. Jeff did the job. If he followed all his instructions, we're clear."

Will looked at him. "Of course we're clear. Why wouldn't we be? He's been doing the stalking part with us since the beginning. He practiced the approaches. He's as good as either of us."

"Maybe."

Will sometimes thoroughly disliked Karl. Not for long, but there were moments. This was one of them. "No *maybe* about it," he said firmly.

The sky opened up, settling the question of what to do with the cigar as sheets of rain fell. He cussed, ground out his cigar and tossed the stogie to the ground, kicking leaves and pine needles over it. The rain would take care of it. Karl followed suit.

Together they rose, gave one last look back down the mountain, then started heading over the crest and back to their vehicle. Another successful hunt.

Irritated as he'd begun to feel, Will smiled as the rain hid them in its gray veils. Jeff had graduated. Maybe they ought to throw him a small party.

# Chapter Five

Gus spent a lot of time thinking about Blaire the next two days. He'd hated leaving her at night, knowing she was going to be all alone in the park. But he didn't want to hover and make her feel that he was doubtful of her ability to care for herself.

Dang, those campers from the other campgrounds had bailed even before the cops had released the folks at the crime scene. Word had traveled on the wind, apparently, and nobody wanted to be camping out here when there'd been a murder.

An unusual murder. It wasn't as if Jasper had been killed by his wife after an argument, or as if he'd gotten into a fight with someone else at the campground.

No, to all appearances this shooter had been a stranger. That might change once the cops dug into Jasper's background more deeply, but the people at the surrounding campgrounds weren't going to take a chance that it wasn't a grudge killing.

Even a few of the national forest campgrounds had cleared out. The farther they were from the state park, the less likely people had been to leave, but there was still a marked quiet.

Weird, especially since people booked sites months in advance to make sure they'd have a place to pitch a tent or park an RV. Weirder still when you considered how hard it was to find a place to camp anymore. Gone were the days he remembered from childhood where you could drop in almost any place and find a site.

Anyway, once he got things sorted out with his staff, leaving Holly Booker in charge of the front office and the rest of his people out doing their regular jobs with guns on their hips and in their saddle holsters, he headed for Blaire's place again. The need to check on her had been growing more powerful all day.

Once upon a time being a ranger had been a relatively safe job. Well, except for problems with wildlife, of course. But that had changed over the last decade or so. Rangers were getting shot. Not many, but enough that anyone who worked in the forest needed to be alert to strange activity.

Now they'd had this killing, and he wasn't convinced the shooter had left the woods. What better place to hide out than in the huge forests on the side of the mountain? And what if he hadn't settled whatever problem had caused him to do this in the first place?

Lack of knowledge about the victim frustrated him, but since he wasn't a member of the sheriff's department he thought it very unlikely they'd give him any useful information. Investigations were always kept close to the vest, and for good reasons.

Reasons that didn't keep him from feeling frustrated nor ease his concern about what might be going on over in the state park. Most of his staff were certified as law officers for the US Forest Service and carried weapons. Things were different on the other side of the line. Blaire was the only park ranger over there who was an authorized law officer. The rest were civilian seasonal hires. Given this was Wyoming, he figured any of them could come armed to work, but he had no idea what training they might have.

He was confident of Blaire's training, especially with her Army background, but come sunset she'd be all alone in that deserted park. The last two nights hadn't worried him so much with cops crawling all over the crime scene, but tonight?

He was worried.

He'd gone on a few solo missions when he'd been in spec ops, but he always had backup at the other end of his radio: a helicopter that could swoop in quickly if he got in trouble. Only once had that failed him, and he'd had to travel for three days as surreptitiously as he possibly could before he got a radio connection and found a reasonably safe place for the chopper to come in. But there was only that once.

Blaire was over there with no one nearby. He was the closest thing to a backup she had, and training combined with the recent murder made him feel he could back her up a whole lot better over there.

Holly was happy to take over for him. She seemed to like the office work almost as much as she enjoyed taking small groups on tours of the wildflowers and wildlife. She said she just liked meeting the people, and she had a natural way of making everyone feel like a friend.

He kind of lacked that ability. Too much had closed up inside him over the years. Trust didn't come easily, and chitchat was largely beyond him. Holly had a gift, and he didn't mind taking advantage of it when she enjoyed it.

For himself, he preferred to be out in the woods riding Scrappy, occasionally stopping by campgrounds for a few words with people, and if he chatted much it was with hikers. Loners like himself.

Scrappy seemed in no particular hurry this evening. He

ambled along and Gus swayed in his saddle, enjoying the soothing sound of creaking leather. During a number of missions in Afghanistan, he'd ridden horseback on saddles provided by the Army, but this was somehow different. Hell, he'd never be able to put his finger on the triggers that could send him into rage or cause him to get so lost in memory he didn't know where he was.

Edginess was a constant companion. He lived with it as he lived with bouts of anxiety. Mostly he controlled it. Sometimes he thought that Scrappy was his personal comfort animal.

They reached the end of the trail and Scrappy turned toward the ranger's cabin and Blaire without any direction from him. He guessed he was getting predictable.

Blaire was sitting on her porch step as the twilight began to deepen. She waved when she saw him and stood.

"Coffee?" she called.

"When have I ever said no?"

He swung down from the saddle as Blaire went inside, presumably to bring him some coffee. He'd just reached her step when she reemerged carrying two insulated mugs. Even in midsummer, when the sun disappeared behind the mountains, the thin air began to take on a noticeable chill. She was wearing a blue sweater and jeans, and he pulled a flannel shirt out of his saddlebag to wear.

Scrappy eyed him from the side with one warm brown eye, then began to explore his surroundings. He'd tossed the reins loosely over his neck so they didn't get caught on something. Probably wouldn't be long before he shook them off anyway.

Blaire sat, and he sat beside her, resting his elbows on his knees, taking care to keep space between them. He didn't ever want her to feel as if he were encroaching.

"You hear anything?" she asked.

"Not a peep. You?"

"Nada. I did wander around up there at the outer edge of the campground. I found where some kids had been making roads in the duff and picked up a miniature red car in case someone calls me or writes about it."

"Really? For a miniature car?"

She looked at him, a crooked smile tipping her mouth. "You had a deprived childhood, Gus. Small things can be the most important stuff in the world to a kid. This is a little tow truck. Even has a hook on the boom."

He felt a smile grow on his own face. "Really cool, then."

"Clearly." She laughed quietly. "You know, this place is this deserted only at the height of winter. An awful lot of people have canceled reservations and most haven't even asked for their deposits back."

"Really? I know we're quiet, too, at least on your side of the forest, but I didn't check cancellations."

"Ah," she said. "Holly is taking over."

Something in the way she said that made him uncomfortable. He decided to take the possible bull by the potential horns. "*Not* because she's a woman. She happens to like it."

"Did I say anything?"

"Your voice was hinting."

She laughed, a delightful sound. Like him, she seemed to have trouble laughing at times, but when she relaxed enough he enjoyed hearing the sound emerge from her. He was glad the laughter hadn't been totally wiped out of her. Sometimes he wondered if *he* had much left.

He glanced up the road that led to the higher campgrounds, especially the one where the murder had happened. "It seems so out of the blue," he remarked.

"I know. Especially with the kid there. I keep wondering who would do a thing like that. Had the boy's presence been unexpected? Did the shooter even see Jimmy before he pulled the trigger?"

"Questions without answers right now," he remarked unhelpfully, then hated the way that sounded. "Sorry, I didn't mean anything by that." He took a long swallow of hot coffee.

"I didn't think you did. It's true, though. I have all these questions rolling around in my head, and the answers are beyond my knowing. I wonder if the sheriff will even share anything with us. Probably not."

"Not unless he thinks it would be useful, is my guess." Gus shifted, watching Scrappy knock the end of a branch with his nose, as if he found it entertaining to watch it bounce. It was probably easier to understand that horse's mind than the killer's mind.

After a few minutes, she spoke again. "One of my seasonals gave me chills earlier. Dave Carr. You've met him, I think?"

"Yeah, doesn't he lead backcountry ski expeditions in the winter?"

"That's him."

"So how'd he give you chills?" Turning until he leaned back against the porch stanchion, Gus sipped more coffee and waited to hear.

"Apparently there was a buzz going around town yesterday and early this morning. Some people are claiming there's a serial killer running around the mountains all the way up to Yellowstone and over to Idaho."

Gus stiffened. "Why in the hell?"

"Five murders in two years. Of course, that doesn't mean much. They were all in different places, and you can't even say all of them were killed in tents. They were all asleep when they got shot, but one guy was in the bed of his pickup, pulled over at a turnout on an access road up near Yellowstone. Sleeping, yeah, but out in plain sight." She shook her head a little. "From what Dave said, there's really nothing to link the killings."

"Other than that they all happened in the mountains and the victims were all sleeping."

"*Presumed* to be sleeping. That's talk. I'd have to ask Gage if he can check on the murders, and right now he's probably too busy to be worrying about what happened hundreds of miles away."

"True." He settled again but turned the idea around in his head. Linking murders was a chancy thing at best, especially if widely spread apart. The killer would have to leave some kind of "calling card." And if he had, wouldn't someone have picked up on it by now?

Blaire put her mug down on the porch, linked her hands as she leaned forward to rest her arms on her thighs and stared into the deepening night. "I was up at the scene. Oh, I already told you that. Sheesh, I'm losing my wits."

"I doubt it. Little car, roads in the duff."

She flashed a smile his way. "Yeah, and they were making little trees out of the ends of branches. I bet those kids were having a blast."

"I would have," he admitted. "I was really into making roads and hills to drive my cars and trucks over. My dad told me once I ought to get into model railroading, build my own scenery."

"Why didn't you?"

"I didn't have a place to do it, or the money, even though I was working at a sandwich shop, and then the Army."

Her crooked smile returned. "The Army would do it."

"Didn't leave me a whole lot of time for anything else.

So, you were up at the scene? Why do I feel you have more to say about that?"

"Probably because you're perceptive and I do. Yeah, I was up there yesterday, about midday. Two miserable deputies standing watch, neither of them prepared for how chilly it can get in the thin air up there. I felt sorry for them. Anyway, I felt as if I was being watched."

That definitely snagged his attention. He'd learned the hard way never to dismiss that feeling. "But you didn't see anyone?"

"Not a soul, other than the deputies. It felt as if the woods were still trying to get back to normal after all that happened. Not quite the same, if you know what I mean."

"Disturbed. Yeah. I've felt it."

"So anyway, maybe it was my own reaction to events and the feeling that some animals have moved away for a while. I couldn't blame them."

"Me neither." He drained his mug and was about to set it down when Blaire asked, "You want some more? I have to admit I'm feeling reluctant to go to sleep tonight."

He eyed her closely. "Did you sleep last night?"

"Mostly. I guess it hadn't sunk in yet. Tonight it's sinking in." Rising, she took his mug and her own. "If you want to come inside?"

"I'm kind of enjoying the night. Unless you'd rather be indoors."

"Not especially."

He stared out into the woods, noting that Scrappy had wandered closer to the cabin again. The horse seemed calm and content, which was a good sign. Nothing going on out there to put him on edge.

Now he, himself, was a different story. Almost always on edge. He wished he could contain it some way so that he could help Blaire relax because despite her outward demeanor, he sensed she was wound up tight inside.

She returned with more coffee and the surprising addition of a small package of cinnamon rolls. "Sugar's good for whatever ails you."

He summoned a smile. "Until you're diabetic."

"I'm not. My kingdom for a chocolate bar. I'm a chocoholic."

"A common affliction." He opened the package of rolls, which sat on a silvery tray, and helped himself to one, waiting for the next development. Because there would be one. They'd spent enough time chatting over the last two years for him to have learned the rhythms of their revelations. She had more to say. She was troubled.

"There's something wrong with this situation," she said eventually.

"No kidding."

She shook her head a little. "I don't just mean the murder. But think about it. The shooter knew to walk up to a tent. I'm betting a specific tent. You?"

He thought about it. "There were plenty to choose from. Okay, let's assume he had a specific target in mind."

"But if it wasn't some guy he knew…" She paused. "Jimmy's presence is bothering me. A lot. If the shooter knew Jasper, he'd know about Jasper's kid. If he knew Jasper well, he'd probably know the guy liked to bring his kid camping with him. So… This is an awful place to take out a man you're mad at if you know he might have a child with him. It'd make more sense to get him near work or home."

"Maybe so." He was listening to her spin a theory and wouldn't interject anything unless he saw a glaring flaw. So far, he didn't. People who were mad at someone didn't usually follow them to an out-of-the-way campground to off them. Unnecessary effort, no special benefit. Bigger chance of getting caught, actually.

As if she were reading his thoughts, she said virtually the same thing. "You want to get rid of someone you hate, do it in a heavily populated area without witnesses. Not out here where you might stand out like a sore thumb. Someone's got to know the shooter was in this area, and I seriously doubt he's a local."

He made a sound of agreement.

"I'm not used to thinking this way," she said slowly. "If I go off the rails, let me know."

"Like I'm used to thinking this way?"

That drew a fleeting smile from her, but it didn't reach her eyes. Damn, he wanted to see her blue eyes smile again.

"Anyway," Gus continued, "what I'm getting at is that the victim may have been selected at random. And that our killer must have done some scouting beforehand. How else would he know how to get in and get out so quickly and easily? He couldn't have just been wandering in the woods in the middle of the night."

He was slipping into tactical ways of thinking, and wasn't at all certain that was the right direction to take with this. It wasn't a military operation. No reason to think the killer had been thinking of...

The thought halted midstream. His mind swerved onto a slightly different track without much of a hitch. "Planned operation," he said. He felt her gaze settle on him, almost as warm as a touch. Damn, he needed to ignore the attraction he felt for her. It wouldn't be good for either of them. Besides, right now it seemed to be important to her to puzzle out this murder. Like they had any real information.

"Planned operation?" she repeated.

"Yeah. It crossed my mind for some reason." The only

reason possibly being that occasionally he was distractible. He never used to be that way, but since coming home for good, he had his moments of wandering. To escape unpleasant thoughts mostly, he imagined. "I'm starting to think tactically."

She turned toward him, attentive. "Yeah," she said quietly. Same wavelength.

"So, say this was planned. How long was Jasper at the campground?"

"Two and a half weeks. I checked."

"Long enough to figure out his habits, to get a sense of the area and people around him. Long enough to plan an approach and egress."

She nodded and turned more, pulling up one leg until it was folded sideways on the porch in front of her, half a cross-legged posture. Nodding again, she sipped her coffee, evidently thinking about what he'd said.

Which, frankly, sounded like a load of crap to him now that he'd said it out loud. Was he proposing some kind of mastermind killer? To what end? Even a soldier like him wouldn't be thinking of such things if he wanted to get rid of somebody. Hell no. Get 'em in a dark alley late at night, shiv 'em in the middle of a crowd... Escape routes were easier to come by than on a nearly unpopulated mountain. Any one of those campers might have responded immediately to the gunshot. No killer had any way to know no one would.

"Doesn't make sense," he said before she could raise a list of objections that would probably mirror his own. "No reason for anyone to treat the murder tactically. Habitual thinking on my part."

"But not necessarily wrong." She looked down into her mug, remaining quiet again.

He turned his head to find Scrappy meandering around

the gravel parking lot at the edge of the woods. He loved that gelding. Probably the only living thing he allowed himself to love anymore.

"Love," he said, for no particular reason, "is a helluva scary proposition. Friendship, too, for that matter."

"Where'd that come from?"

He turned his head, meeting her eyes. "The horse, believe it or not. He's got a long life expectancy. Iraq and Afghanistan taught me to be stingy with my feelings."

"Yeah, it sure did." She closed her eyes briefly. "Maybe too stingy. I don't know. That little boy really upset me, his terror and knowing he is going to grow up without his father. But I've seen it before. Half the world seems to live in that condition."

He nodded. Nothing to say to that. It wasn't only lost comrades who haunted his nightmares, though. Plenty of civilians did, too.

"Well," she said, "if you think there's any possibility that this guy was stalking the victim, then we owe it to ourselves and everyone else to take a look-see."

"For a distant sight line."

She nodded. "A place someone could watch from and not be noticed."

He looked up the mountain. "We'll have to cover a lot of territory." No denying it. Hundreds if not thousands of acres.

"Let's start with some parameters. How far out would the guy have to hide? Would he choose upslope or down? Whatever we decide, we can expand the area later if we need to."

"We could be wasting our time."

"It's better than doing nothing at all."

With that he felt complete agreement.

THEY'D THROWN A party for him. Even a bottle of champagne, decent champagne. Jeff felt pretty good and kept his lone slipup from Karl and Will. He figured that one shell casing couldn't give him away. Like he'd already thought, the heat of the exploding powder it had contained probably would have burned away any oils his fingers might have left behind. No reason to mention it.

At best they might find a partial, and fat lot of good it would do the cops even though he'd been fingerprinted when he joined the Army. A partial wouldn't create a match strong enough to stand up on its own. He knew because he'd looked it up.

But once they parted ways, he began to gnaw worriedly on the idea of that shell casing anyway. Useless, he kept telling himself, but part of him couldn't believe it.

So, without telling the others, he decided to go back and scout around a bit. If they hadn't found the casing, he'd remove it. Simple. Make sure there was nothing there. And he'd drive up just like any other tourist so there'd be no risk.

But that shell casing was haunting him, causing him so much anxiety that he was having trouble sleeping.

Worse, it was probably too soon to go back. He had to be sure the local authorities felt the site had nothing left to offer them, that they were totally ready to release it and forget about it.

And he'd need a cover story in case anyone wondered about him being up there. Time. He had to make himself wait a little longer.

He had a couple of weeks before he started teaching again. If he wanted to. He'd considered applying for a sabbatical for the fall term, and his department chair was agreeable, asking only that he give the department a couple of weeks warning so they could arrange for a stand-in.

But the idea of the sabbatical no longer enticed him. Sitting in his comfy little house on the edge of Laramie was proving to tax him psychologically.

Because of what they'd made him do. Because of what he'd done. Because the cries of a young child still echoed in the corridors of his mind.

Hell, if he were to be honest, the shell casing was the least of his worries. The biggest worry was how he would live with himself now. And an equally big worry was that they would insist he do this again. That they wouldn't buy that he now was so deeply involved he couldn't talk.

Damn, this was supposed to have been a *game*. Not real killings, merely the planning of them. How had Will and Karl moved past that? He'd never guessed they were so warped.

How could he have known them for so long and failed to realize they were probably both psychopaths? No real feeling for anyone else.

And how could they have known him for so long and not believe him when he said he'd never tell. Loyalty would have stopped him. But they didn't believe him, they didn't trust him, and that told him even more about them.

Friends? He'd have been better off with enemies.

Finally, anxiety pushed him to look up the state park's website. He needed to make a plan for going back there, maybe with a metal detector. After all, people still sometimes panned for gold in the streams in these mountains. It wouldn't be weird for someone to want to wander around with a metal detector hoping to find a nugget.

So he could get a metal detector and look around until he found the shell casing and then get the hell out. Easy plan. No reason to tell the others because he still didn't want them to know he'd left that casing behind.

*Slow down,* he told himself. *Take it easy.* Don't make a mistake that could get him into serious trouble.

He hadn't really looked at the park's website before. They'd taken a brief drive up the road to do recon and that didn't require a website. All he had needed to find was that rustic campground that vehicles couldn't. It had been easier than anticipated, too. GPS was a wonderful thing, as was a satellite receiver to track where he was. No need for a nearby cell repeater.

Thus he really didn't know anything about Twin Rocks Campground. The web page had the usual scenery pictures, one of an RV campsite, another of a rustic site and some general information for day hikes. Clearly nobody had spent a whole lot of time or money on this page.

He was about to move on to something else when he saw a name at the bottom of the page:

*Blaire Afton, Chief Ranger.*

Everything inside him felt as if it congealed. He had seen her from a distance on their one recon, but had thought he was mistaken.

Blaire Afton. That couldn't be the Blaire Afton he'd met in the Army and asked to go out with him. She'd declined, then he'd been injured in that training accident and mustered out. Turning to her brief bio page, he looked at her photo. It was the same Blaire Afton.

He hadn't really known her.

But what if she remembered him? What if his name came up somehow and she recalled him, either from the Army or from him passing her on his way up the road?

Suddenly a partial fingerprint on a shell casing seemed like a bigger deal. If the cops mentioned that it seemed to belong to a Jeffery Walston, would she remember the name after all this time? What if she saw him at the park and remembered his face?

He closed his laptop swiftly as if it could hide him from danger. Bad. Bad indeed. He knew the ranger, however slightly. She might be able to identify him if they somehow came up with his name. But Jeffery Walston wasn't an unusual name. It could be lots of guys.

Unless she saw him at the campground running around with a metal detector. Unless she connected him to the location of the murder.

God, he'd better stay away from her. Far away. But that shell casing was practically burning a hole in his mind.

If he'd had the guts, he might have killed himself right then. Instead he sat in a cold sweat and faced the fact that he'd probably have to fess up about the shell casing...and God knew what else.

He'd smoked, hadn't he? Thank heaven it had rained. He couldn't have left any DNA behind, could he? Surely that casing wouldn't still hold enough skin oil to identify him, either by partial print or DNA.

Surely.

But he stared blankly as his heart skipped beats, and he didn't believe it one bit. He'd broken the rule. He'd left enough behind to identify him.

God help him when the others found out.

Whatever the risk, he had to go back and make sure he found that casing and picked up any cigarette butts, rain or no rain.

And try to avoid Blaire Afton.

But he knew what the guys would tell him. He knew it with leaden certainty. Jeffery Walston might be a common name, but if Blaire Afton could link it to a face, well...

They'd tell him to kill her. To get rid of her so she couldn't identify him. Or they'd get rid of him. Squeezing his eyes closed, he faced what would happen if he ran into the ranger. He had to avoid her at all costs while cleaning up the evidence. If she saw him...

He quivered, thinking about having to kill another person, this time one he knew, however slightly.

God, he still couldn't believe the mess he'd gotten into, so innocently. Just playing a game with friends.

Until he learned the game was no game.

Terror grew in him like a tangled vine, reaching every cell in his body and mind. He had to go back and remove any evidence. No, he hadn't been able to go back for the casing while the cops were poring over the site, but they had to be gone by now. So he had to hunt for the casing and remove it if it was still there. Then he needed to go to the observation point and remove anything that remained of his presence there. Then he'd be safe. Even if Karl and Will got mad at him, he'd be safe, and so would they.

It didn't help that the kid had screamed and cried until he couldn't erase the sound from his own head. It chased him, the way fear was chasing him. He was well and truly stuck and he could see only one way out that didn't involve his dying.

He needed to calm down, think clearly, make sure he knew exactly what to do so he didn't make things worse. Reaching for a pill bottle in his pocket, he pulled out a small white pill. For anxiety. To find calm.

He had a lot of thinking to do.

# Chapter Six

"I'm off the next two days," Gus said to Blaire two nights later. "I've got time to do some poking around if you can manage it."

She nodded. As the night thickened around them, the hoot of an owl filled the air. A lonely sound, although that wasn't why the owl hooted.

She murmured, "The owl calls my name."

"Don't say that," Gus said sharply. "I don't take those things lightly and you shouldn't, either. We've both seen how easily and senselessly death can come."

Little light reached them. The moon had shrunk until it was barely a sliver, and clouds kept scudding over it. Still, he thought he saw a hint of wryness in her expression.

"Superstitious much?" she asked with a lightness that surprised him, mainly because it meant her mood was improving. "I was thinking of the book."

"Oh." He'd reacted too quickly. "Some indigenous peoples consider the owl's hoot to be a bad omen. I was thinking of that."

"That's okay. And really, any of us who've gone where we've been probably pick up some superstitions. Heck, my mother even handed me a few when I was a kid. The *knock-on-wood* kind. And she hated it if anyone spilled salt."

He gave a brief laugh. "Yeah, I learned a few of those, too. You got any Irish in the family? My mom was Irish and I think she picked up a tote bag full of stuff like, *never leave an umbrella open upside down in the house.* More than once I saw her leap up, telling me not to do that."

"I never heard that one."

"It's a belief if the umbrella is open upside down it'll catch troubles for the house and family. There were others, but I left most of them behind." He paused. "Except this." Reaching inside his shirt, he pulled out a chain necklace. "My Saint Christopher medal. Apparently, he's not really a saint after all, but plenty of us still carry him around."

"Belief is what matters." She stood, stretching. "Are you heading back or do you want to use the couch? I think it's comfortable enough."

He rose, too. "That'd be great. Let me see to Scrappy and give Holly a call. And what about you? Can you get some time off tomorrow?"

"I can take two days whenever I want. Given that we're deserted right now, nobody really needs to be here. But Dave's my assistant. He'll stand in for me. I was thinking of going to town, too. I need some staples and a few fresh bits for my fridge."

INSIDE, BLAIRE SCANNED her small refrigerator in the back kitchen to see what else she might need to add to the list she'd been building since she last went grocery shopping. She didn't consume much herself, but she kept extra on hand for Dave, in case he worked late and for when he filled in for her on her days off.

Come winter she'd have to keep the fridge full to the brim because getting out of the park could sometimes be uncertain. Right now, however, when she was able to take a day or two every week, it wasn't as big a concern.

She called Dave on the radio, and he said he'd be glad to fill in for her tomorrow. *Good guy, Dave.*

Much as she tried to distract herself, however, her thoughts kept coming back to the murder. And to Gus. She'd learned to trust him over the two years since they'd met. They had a lot in common, of course, but it was more than that. At some point they'd crossed a bridge and for her part she knew she had shared memories with him that she would have found nearly impossible to share with anyone else.

Now, like her, he wanted to do some investigating up at the campground. Being in the Army had given them a very different mind-set in some ways, and when you looked at the murder as if it were a campaign, a mission, things popped to mind that might not if you thought of it as merely a random crime.

She was having trouble with the whole idea of random. Especially since Dave had told her that people were starting to talk about other murders, as well, and that they might be linked somehow.

Tomorrow she was going to make time to talk to the sheriff. She didn't know how much he'd tell her, but it was sure worth a try. She needed something, some kind of information to settle her about this ugly incident. She'd never be comfortable with the idea that that man had been murdered, never feel quite easy when she recalled little Jimmy's fear and sobbing, but she had a need to…

Well, pigeonhole, she guessed. Although that wasn't right, either. But even in war you had ways of dealing with matters so you could shove them in a mental rucksack out of the way.

This murder wasn't amenable to that because there were too damn many questions. War was itself an answer to a lot of things she'd had to deal with. Yeah, it was random, it was hideous, it was unthinkable. Life in a land of nightmares. But it had a name and a way to look at it.

Jasper's murder had nothing to define it except "murder."

So she needed a reason of almost any kind. An old enemy. Someone who bore a grudge. His wife's lover. Damn near anything would do because just *murder* wasn't enough for her.

She was pondering this newly discovered quirk in herself when the door opened and Gus entered, carrying his saddle with tack thrown over his shoulder. "Where can I set this?"

"Anywhere you want to."

For the first time she thought about his horse. "Is Scrappy going to be all right? I mean, I don't have a covered area for the corral here."

"I used some buckets from your lean-to. He's got food and water. And he's used to this." Gus lowered the saddle to the floor near the sidewall where there was some space. "I often go camping when I can get away, and he's happy to hang around and amuse himself, or just sleep."

"Oh." She felt oddly foolish. "I didn't know."

"Why should you? And, of course, being the nice person you are, you want to know he's okay."

She shook her head a little. "I think I care more about animals than people these days. Sorry, I was lost in thought. I just realized I have a driving need to make pigeonholes."

"Pigeonholes?"

"Yeah." She turned to go to the back and the kitchen. "Beer?"

"Thanks."

She retrieved two longnecks from the fridge and brought them out front. He accepted one bottle, then sat on the edge of the couch that filled one side of the public office space. Her living room, such as it was.

"I always liked this sofa," he remarked. "You lucked out. All I have are some institutional-type chairs."

"The last ranger left it. It doesn't suffer from overuse." She smiled. "In fact, you're the only person who uses it regularly."

"Yeah, I come visit a lot. Do you mind?"

"Of course not. If I did, I'd have told you a long time ago."

He twisted the top off his beer, flipped it into the wastebasket that sat in front of the long business desk that separated the public area from her office and raised it in salute. "Back to pigeonholes."

She didn't answer immediately, but went instead to get the office chair from behind the long bar and bring it around. She sat on it facing him, as she had so many past evenings. "Maybe not pigeonholes," she said finally, then took a sip of her beer. Icy cold, her throat welcomed it. The air was so dry up here.

"Then what?"

"Maybe what I'm trying to say is that I need some context. This murder is so random."

"That it is." He leaned back, crossing his legs loosely at the ankles. "So what do you need to know?"

At that she had to laugh. "Motive. Identity. All that stuff nobody probably knows yet. Nice as that would be, I realize I won't be told until the case is closed. But I still need something. Who was the victim? What did he do? Why was he here with his son and not the rest of his family?"

"Did he have any enemies?" he added.

She nodded, feeling rueful. "Context. I guess I don't

want to believe he was chosen randomly by someone with an itch to kill. That makes me crazy."

"It'd make anyone crazy. Anyone who cares, that is." He sighed and tipped his head back as he swallowed some more beer. "I guess we have to wait for our answers."

She leaned forward on her chair, cradling her frigid beer in both hands. "I need to deal with this. It's unreasonable to be uneasy simply because I don't have all the answers. I had few enough of them in Afghanistan."

"It wasn't answers we had over there. It was one big reason. If any of us had stopped to ask *why*, we might have had a bigger problem. But the reason was baked in from the moment we arrived. It was a war. This isn't a war. I don't blame you for being uneasy. Hell, the whole reason I rode over here tonight was because I couldn't stop feeling uneasy about you being alone over here. I'd have been over here last night but I know how damn independent you are."

"Gus…"

He held up a hand and she fell silent. "Let me finish. This is no criticism of you, or an expression of doubt in your abilities to look after yourself. No, I was uneasy because we've got a big question mark with a gun running around out there and that's a lot more difficult to protect yourself against than some known."

"Known? How so?"

"How many sandbag walls did you sit behind in Kandahar? How much armor did you wear every time you poked your nose out? Can we turn this cabin into a fortress? Not likely. It's a whole different situation, and being alone out here isn't the safest place to be, not until we can be sure the killer has moved on."

She nodded slowly, accepting his arguments. And though she could be fiercely independent and resented any implication that she was somehow less capable than a man, fact was, she was touched by his concern for her.

She stared down at her hands, cradling the beer she had hardly tasted, and remembered her early days here. She'd been on maybe her third or fourth night, feeling a mixture of pride at her recent promotion and a bit of discomfort about whether she was ready for the responsibility. Being alone out here, though, had always felt soothing. Comfortable. A long way away from ugly thoughts, pain and anguish.

Then Gus had come riding out of the spring mist that clung close to the ground that day. Wisps of it parted before him and Scrappy. Except for his green jacket, the brass badge and the Forest Service hat, she'd have wondered who the hell was riding in when the park hadn't officially opened for the season.

Iconic, she'd thought then. Even for a girl raised in the West, he looked iconic.

He'd raised a hand to wave, calling, "I'm Gus Maddox, the head ranger at the national forest next door." He and his horse had come closer. "You must be Blaire Afton?"

Thus had begun a relationship that had started as two strangers with similar jobs, then had been welded by sharing that they were both vets and sometimes had some difficulties dealing with the past. The revelations had come slowly, carefully. Trust was hard won in some areas. But now she trusted him completely.

In all that time, they had remained friends who treated each other as colleagues and occasionally as comrades. When they met up, either at one of their cabins or in town for coffee, they had the kinds of conversations she'd had with the guys in her unit in the Army.

As if there was a line that couldn't be crossed. Had they still been in the service, that line would definitely be there. But that was in the past, and now was now, and she felt ever increasing urges to know him in other ways.

A striking man, he'd have made almost any woman drool. She was a little astonished to realize she was getting to the drooling stage with him.

For some reason, the thought cheered her up, drawing her out of the uneasy darkness that had been haunting her since the murder. It was like a permission slip to get out of the serious stuff for a little while.

She looked at the bottle in her hand and noticed she'd hardly made a dent in that beer. Good. This was no alcohol-fueled mood.

Rising from her chair, she went to sit on the couch, not too close, but not exactly tucked into the far end, either. Even from more than a foot away, she could detect his aromas, wonderful aromas, the faint scent of man mixed with the outdoors, a bit of horse and a bit of beer. Very masculine.

Very sexy.

Oh, God, was she about to do something stupid? His gray eyes, eyes the color of a late afternoon storm rolling in over the mountains, had fixed on her and settled. It was a frank stare.

She was crossing the invisible line. He sensed it. All of a sudden she was nervous and afraid to move. She didn't want to make him uncomfortable. She didn't want to risk the precious friendship they'd built, and in her experience taking a relationship beyond that eventually led to a parting of ways.

And what if they *did* have sex? Would they become uncomfortable with one another afterward? It might prove to be a major sacrifice.

But his eyes held hers, drew her as if they were magnetic. "Blaire?"

Frank words emerged. There was little she hadn't told him about the bad things in the past, and dissembling with Gus seemed impossible now. "I'm telling myself not to go where I'm thinking about going."

That made him smile. Man, she loved the way the corners of his eyes crinkled when the smile reached them. "You are, huh? Afraid of repercussions?"

"Aren't there always repercussions?"

"Depends." Leaning to one side, he put his beer bottle on the battered end table. Then he took hers from her hands and put it beside his.

"You," he said, "are the most attractive woman I've known in a long time. Like you, I've been trying not to risk our friendship. But a lot of good things can begin between friends."

She nodded as her mouth went dry. A tremor passed through her.

"I get your reluctance. I share it. But I want you."

Oh, boy. Magic words. They lit her up like a thousand sparklers, tingling in every cell. She felt almost as if she couldn't catch her breath.

He reached out and took her hands. His touch was warm, his fingers and palms a bit calloused from hard work. He looked down at her smaller hands, then squeezed her fingers and drew her over until she sat beside him.

"I don't want to mess things up, either," he said. "But a hug ought to be safe, shouldn't it?"

He was quite a perceptive man, she thought as she nodded and let him gently pull her closer. He'd sensed what she was thinking and had turned out to be thinking along the same lines. As his arm wrapped around her, cuddling her to his side, she felt as if a spring-tight tension in her released. She relaxed, more completely than she had in a long time. She softened.

In the hollow of his shoulder, she found a firm pillow, and she could hear the beating of his heart, strong and steady. The arm he had wrapped around her gave her a gentle squeeze, then his hand began to stroke her arm.

Apparently trying to make sure matters didn't progress further until and unless they were both ready, he began to talk about tomorrow. "Do you have good topographic maps for the area we're going to explore?"

"Yeah. Down to a meter or so. Some geology students did it as a class project a while back. There may be some differences, though. The mountain moves."

"That it does. Rocks fall, landslides happen... But whatever you have, let's mark out a plan of action tomorrow."

"Sounds good."

"But first you want to go to town, right?"

"I need a few things, but that could wait. What I really want is to talk to the sheriff."

"I've had cause to talk to Dalton quite a few times when we've had problems. He's a good man."

She nodded, loving the way the soft flannel of his shirt felt beneath her cheek. "He used to head up the crime scene unit before he was elected sheriff."

"And before that, undercover DEA." He gave a muted laugh. "That guy has a lot of experience under his belt. Even if he can't share details with us, maybe he can offer a few opinions or speculations."

"A sense of what might have been going on," she agreed. "He doesn't strike me as a man who likes the idea of a random killing, either."

"Stranger killings are the hardest to solve." A slight sigh escaped him. "More beer?"

"I misjudged my mood."

She felt, rather than saw, his nod, then his movements

as he reached for his own bottle and took a few swallows. Tentatively she let her hand come to rest on one of his denim-clad thighs. She felt the muscles jump a bit at the touch, then relax. God, he was as hard as steel. Must be all that riding.

But he didn't reject her touch, nor did he do anything to encourage it. Her hand began to absorb his warmth, and she felt an even deeper relaxation filling her. Like a cat finding sunlight, she thought with some amusement at herself.

"I'm making too much of this," she remarked. "Too much. These things happen."

"Sure, they happen all the time in the desolate woods at a campground. If I thought you were making too much of this, I wouldn't have ridden over tonight. I'm concerned, too. You're right about needing a reason. Without it, we have no idea what this killer might be planning. Not a good time to be hanging out alone."

"But Jasper wasn't alone. He was in a campground with at least eight other camping groups. A really strange place to pull this."

"Which may be the biggest clue we have. Only problem is what to do with it."

Absently her fingers had begun to stroke the taut denim on his thigh. She'd always loved the feel of worn denim, but it never occurred to her that she was self-comforting. Well, possibly in the depths of her mind, but she wasn't ready to face that.

Her self-image was one of toughness. She'd survived Afghanistan and all that went with that. She'd helped lead convoys through hell, and for all she was supposed to be a noncombatant, being female, she'd seen plenty of combat. She could handle a lot, and getting in a tizzy over a random murder struck her as an extreme overreaction.

Until she remembered Jimmy.

"It's the kid," she said presently, her voice evincing the slightest tremor. She hated the sound of weakness. "I should be able to just let this go, Gus. Let the sheriff handle it. But I can't and it's because of that little boy. Sure, maybe the guy had a ton of enemies. Maybe he was a drug dealer or a mob type, or whatever. But what kind of sick twist would have him shot when he was in a tent with his little boy?"

"That's troubling, isn't it?" Surprising her, he put his beer down then laid his hand over hers, clasping it lightly. "It bothers me, too. When it happened, I could see it might tear you apart."

"It was awful, Gus! That poor little kid! He didn't understand what had happened, thank God. And I'm fairly sure he didn't see how badly his father was wounded. I tried to keep my back to all that. But my God! What kind of sicko would do that?"

Gus didn't answer immediately. "Maybe he didn't know the child was there. But a sicko any way you look at it, kid or no kid. The man was sound asleep in a tent. No chance to defend himself."

"And no chance to protect Jimmy. That shooter could have hit the boy, too. Accidentally or not. Everything about it makes me furious."

"I feel pretty angry myself," he agreed.

But as her thoughts roamed even further backward in time, Blaire remembered her days in the Army. "Too many kids get traumatized," she said after a minute. "Too many. I just hope Jimmy has no clear memories of that night."

"Me, too." He squeezed her hand. "You did what you could to protect him, Blaire. You took good care of him, from what I could see."

"Little enough." She lowered her head, closing her eyes. "It's killing me," she admitted. "I want to get that guy. And I'm sure the impulse has mostly to do with Jimmy."

"Hardly surprising." He turned a little, drawing her into a closer embrace. "We can only do what we can," he reminded her. "Tomorrow we'll check with the sheriff to make sure we won't get in the way. Then we'll build our strategy."

"I don't recall any ops planning that happened like this." Meaning the way he held her. She felt the laugh begin in his belly and roll upward until it emerged, a warm, amused sound.

"Nope," he agreed. "I remember always standing, or if we could sit, it was on miserable folding chairs around a table that was always gritty with dust. Hell, *we* were almost always gritty. We rigged a shower at our forward operating base and you'd barely switch into a clean set of camos before you'd be dusty again."

"It seemed like it. This is way more comfortable."

"By far."

She realized she was smiling into his shoulder. She wanted to wrap an arm around his waist but stopped herself. Lines that shouldn't be crossed. She never wanted to lose Gus's friendship.

She spoke. "I appreciate you not coming over last night to watch over me."

"I don't think I'm watching over you now. I've got a higher respect for your abilities, and it's not my place, anyway. I just kept getting this sense that it might be easier for you not to be alone at night."

"Given what happened, you're right." In Afghanistan she'd almost never been alone. That was the whole idea of a unit. But she didn't have a unit here to watch her back and there might still be a deranged killer out there running around in the woods. With everyone fleeing the campground, that didn't leave many targets for him.

"This brings me back to the random thing," she remarked. "If he's still hanging around out there, looking for someone else to shoot, the target population just shrank to next to nothing."

"I thought about that," he agreed. "My end of the forest isn't quite as deserted as yours, but I'm not sure that should make me feel complacent."

"Then there's what Dave said this morning. People have started talking about scattered killings in the woods over the last few years. Some are calling for all of them to be investigated as one case."

"I'm sure Gage would do it if he had some proof."

"Exactly. When my computer is being reliable, I've spent hours today looking up news articles." She fell silent, wishing she could let go of all of it and just enjoy this rare opportunity to be so close to Gus.

"And?" he prompted her.

"I think I found the murders that concern some people." She sensed him grow more alert, a bit stiff.

"And?" he asked again.

"And people might be right. There are similarities but also differences."

"The gang-working-together idea?"

"Makes you wonder." Her heart grew heavy at the thought. "Gang. It sounds so much worse in a way."

"Also maybe easier to solve. More people, more chances for a slipup."

She tilted her head and he obligingly tilted his so they could look at one another from a distance of about three inches.

"You're a glass-half-full kinda guy."

"I try. Wish I could say I always succeed."

She smiled, lifted her hand a bit and lightly touched his cheek. "You're a good influence."

"When I'm not in a dark pit." But he didn't seem to want to discuss that. "So, would it feel more like operational planning if I brought over a folding camp table and sprinkled a little dirt on it?"

The laugh escaped her. She hadn't even realized she was trembling on the cusp of one, but there it came. He had such a good effect on her, Gus did. He could steer a course through the difficult things and eventually bring back a happier mood. At least in her.

She was well aware he carried his own troubled memories, and he'd shared them with her. At least some of them. But like a cork, he always managed to bob back up. She could use a touch of that.

"Sure. I could even cut up the map."

He laughed again, his gray eyes dancing. "Absolutely. After all, every battle occurs at the juncture between four map sections..."

"In the dark and in the rain," she completed for him. An old saying, truer than she would have believed until she faced it.

"We do so much on computers now," she remarked, remembering scrolling through maps that were downloaded from a satellite.

"When the connection worked. I didn't like the limited view on the computer, though. Call me old-fashioned, but I always wanted a big paper map."

"Well, that's what I've got. Better yet, they're rolled, not folded, so no tears, and no corners at a point where we want to be."

He chuckled again. "There we go. I couldn't ask for

better. Do you have any idea how the terrain may have changed since the mapping?"

"Some, but I've never done a complete survey. Basically, I'm here to make sure campers are safe and that no one commits vandalism or annoys anyone else. I know the ground I routinely cover pretty well. Then comes winter and it all changes anyway."

"Yeah. And we're out there with an eye on possible avalanche risks after a heavy snow." She knew he had pretty much the same winter tasks.

"I'm not exactly looking for boulders that might have moved a few feet." Closing a park didn't mean no one would use it. A surprising number of people showed up to cross-country ski on fresh unpacked snow, or to hike around on snowshoes. Hardy types, but they weren't always aware of winter dangers.

Yes, there was a sign out front, and in several other locations, warning people they entered at their own risk. But that didn't mean Blaire didn't keep an eye out. She lived here year-round, including the deep winter months, so if someone needed something and could get to her, they'd find help.

The hard part was keeping out the snowmobilers. The amount of damage they could do, even in the dead of winter, was appalling. It was a constant battle, even though there weren't that many places where the woods opened up to give them a path.

She closed her eyes, though, and thought about what it was like up here in the winter. Beautiful. Quiet. Serene. Almost magical. She found peace here. It filled her and mostly drove away the ghosts that followed her so restlessly.

"I wish it were winter," she heard herself murmur.

"Yeah. Me, too."

She realized he'd helped ease her tension to the point that she was getting sleepy. Much as she hated to do it, she eased away from him. "Let me get you some blankets."

"Tired?"

"I guess I've been more wound up since the murder than I realized."

He smiled and stood, offering his hand to help her up. "Sleep is always good. I think we both learned that the hard way. Where are the blankets? I can get them."

She pointed up to the loft. "My bedroom."

"Then just toss them down to me."

"Okay. You know where the half bath is?" Of course he did. This wasn't his first visit to this cabin. She must be even more worn out than she had thought.

After she tossed pillows and blankets down to him and said good-night, she pulled her boots off and flopped back on the bed. God, how had she grown so tired?

Then she faced it. She hadn't been sleeping well since the murder. She'd been on edge, wound up, and tossing and turning.

But right now, calm seemed to have descended. Gus was downstairs. She could let go of everything and let relaxation seep through her every cell.

Problems could wait for morning.

And almost before she finished the thought, she fell soundly asleep, still dressed, her legs hanging over the edge of the bed.

DOWNSTAIRS, GUS MADE his bed on the sofa, glad he'd decided to stay tonight. He got the feeling that Blaire seriously needed company. He could understand that.

Being locked inside your own head with your own worries and thoughts could be crazy-making. He'd been there and now tried to avoid it as much as possible.

Sometimes it was okay. Like her mentioning the winter woods. Like her, he loved that peaceful beauty. Or when he was out taking a lazy ride with Scrappy. But maybe being with Scrappy wasn't really being alone, he thought wryly.

He stepped outside to make sure his horse was okay and found that Scrappy had settled onto the ground, having evidently found himself a soft enough spot to curl up in. Scrappy plainly thought the world was safe tonight.

Back inside he reacquainted himself with the fact that a six-foot couch wasn't quite long enough for his six-foot-two length, but it wasn't impossible. Prop his head up a bit on the pillow and he just about made it.

Judging by the quiet from above, he guessed Blaire had fallen out quickly. Good. He suspected she might not have been sleeping well. Well, why should she? This murder had been bound to reawaken old wounds, even if only to a small degree. He felt some mental twinges himself. But like her, he wondered who could have committed an act like that.

A very sick man.

Which didn't comfort him even a little. It only made the perp more unpredictable.

Then, with nothing else he could do, he scooched onto his side and sought sleep. As with most soldiers, it wasn't hard to find.

# Chapter Seven

Morning brought the dread visit to Jeff. The champagne they'd toasted him with the first night had worn off. Now they wanted to discuss their next move.

He wanted no part of it, and as they began to talk in the most general terms over coffee and sweet rolls, his mind ran around frantically trying to find a way to step out of this. To get away. To have no further part in their sick game.

Because he finally had to admit it wasn't just shocking, it was sick. He hardly recognized his friends anymore. They weren't the men he'd believed them to be.

Sociopaths. Psychopaths. Whatever. It didn't matter. They were strangers to him now, as if they'd been possessed by demons.

How could he get away from this? He couldn't commit another murder. He didn't want to know anything about what they intended to do next. No way.

But fear held him silent. Maybe too silent because Karl finally said to him, "What the hell is wrong with you, Jeff? You're as silent as a tomb."

That made Will laugh. Maybe in the past a phrase like that would have amused Jeff. Now it only made him feel ill.

Karl dropped his joking manner. "What's going on,

Jeff?" This time it sounded like an inquisition, barely veiling a threat.

Jeff's mind, already skittering around like a cornered rat trying to find an escape, was now joined by a wildly hammering heart. He had to say something, preferably something that would get him out of this mess. He'd done his killing. They knew he couldn't squeal. He'd implicate himself as a murderer, not as an accomplice.

But what could he say that wouldn't make things worse?

He had to clear his throat to make sound emerge. "You didn't tell me there was a kid there."

"Kid?"

"Little one. In the tent with his father."

"Did he see you?" Will's immediate concern, Jeff thought bitterly. For his own safety.

"No. Too dark. Hell, I could barely see him. But I had to listen to his screams all the way up the mountain."

The two of them exchanged looks. Jeff was rapidly reaching the point where he didn't care. If they killed him, at least he'd be out of this.

"We didn't know there was a kid," Karl said.

"Great planning," Jeff answered bitterly. "What if I'd hit him, too? You wanna talk about a manhunt?"

The other two were silent for a minute or so. Then Karl remarked, "They wouldn't be able to find us anyway. You didn't leave a trail."

Didn't leave a trail. Well, that was the big problem, wasn't it? A missing shell casing. And he was rapidly getting to the point where he didn't care if they knew.

"I left one thing," he blurted out.

Two heads swiveled to look at him, and neither looked very friendly. "What?" Karl demanded.

"A shell casing."

Will swore. "We warned you."

"Warn all you want. I forgot it. Do you know how many people were in that campground?" He was winding up now and didn't care where it took him. "Lots, and as soon as I fired my pistol, the kid started shrieking and the whole place woke up. I didn't have time to pull out my penlight and look for a casing. I had to get the hell out."

Although the truth of it was, he hadn't even remembered the casing. He might well have been able to find it and remove it. The chance the police hadn't found it was slim, but he was going to have to go back and look for it anyway, because he couldn't take the chance that he'd left evidence that could identify him and that it was still lying out there waiting to be found.

Bad enough he'd had to commit the murder. He sure as hell didn't want to *pay* for it.

"It's probably no big deal," Karl said a few minutes later. "The heat of the exploding powder probably would have burned it clean."

"And if it didn't?" Will demanded.

Karl shrugged. "Say it's got a fingerprint or two. Partials at best. And Jeff's never been fingerprinted, have you?"

Jeff couldn't force the lie past his throat. It was as if a vise clamped it and wouldn't let him speak.

"Jeff?" Will's voice had tightened and lowered until it almost sounded like a growled threat. "Fingerprints?"

Jeff wished he were already dead. He'd like to be out of body, watching this all from the ceiling. He wasn't going to get out of this, though. His silence was already an answer.

"When I enlisted in the Army. They took everyone's prints."

Karl swore and jumped up from his chair.

Will looked at him. "You said there'd be nothing left," Jeff said.

"There shouldn't be. That doesn't mean there won't be."

Jeff cringed instinctively as Will raised his hand. He expected to be struck, and having experienced that once before years ago, he knew it would be painful. The man was religious about staying in shape, and part of that was bodybuilding.

But Will didn't strike him. He lowered his hand and said, "We ought to bury you out back right now."

Jeff felt a flare of anger, a welcome relief from the terror he'd been living with. These men were supposed to be his friends? What alternate universe had he been living in?

He leaped up and glared at both of them. "I never wanted to do this, and you know it. I only killed that guy because you threatened to kill me if I didn't. I'm not happy about it. And if I made a freaking mistake, I'm the only one who'll go down for it, and you know it!"

"How are we supposed to know that?" Will asked.

"Simple, you jackass. No matter what I might tell the cops, you could tell them I'm nuts. There's nothing to implicate *you*. Why would I even bother? I told you months ago I'm not a rat."

"And we warned you about leaving behind any evidence," Karl growled. "Damn it, Jeff, are you missing some screws?"

"No." Jeff was getting fed up beyond containment. "You're clear. What do you care if I get picked up?"

"You need to go back and find it," Karl said. "Because the crime scene people might not have. You need to look for the shell casing, Jeff."

"How could they have missed it?"

"They're not big-city cops. A bunch of rubes. They'd miss their own noses if they didn't have mirrors."

"I can't go back there," Jeff said finally, and sagged into his chair.

"Why not?"

"Because the time we went on recon, I saw the ranger."

Will waved a hand. "Wait a minute. Why were you walking up the road? We told you to avoid that!"

"Remember, you took me on the recon. And the night of the killing. I came in from the back just like you said."

"Then why..." Karl trailed off as if he couldn't find words.

"It's simple," Jeff admitted. "I knew the ranger when we were in the Army. Just briefly. If she saw me when we drove up there, she never recognized me. As far as she was concerned, I was a total stranger."

Karl and Will exchanged long looks, then Karl said, "You're a jerk, Jeff. A total jerk. What if she remembered you afterward? What if she wonders what the hell you were doing there? You should have told us. We'd have found another place."

"I'm telling you..."

"You don't get to tell me anything. There's only one solution for this. You go back and kill her."

GUS AND BLAIRE decided to make a small social occasion out of the morning. Gus took Scrappy back to his corral just as the first morning light was dusting the eastern sky with pink. A half hour later, as the rim of the sun just started to lift above the mountains, he picked up Blaire in his green Forest Service truck. Some of the large tools rattled in the back but that was par.

She climbed in beside him, a smile on her face. For now they were out to banish the ugly things and reach for the good ones. One of the best was breakfast at Maude's diner. For a little while she could allow her concern about what had happened to that man, Jasper, and by extension his little boy, move into the background.

She used to be better at putting things aside. She'd quickly learned when she was overseas that you just couldn't let things weigh on you constantly or you'd wear yourself out, or worse, become useless. Compartmentalizing, she thought it was called. Well, for the duration of breakfast she was going to compartmentalize the murder.

Maybe in a way what made it so hard for her was the protectiveness she felt for all the people camping in the park. As if she were their caretaker or something, which was ridiculous. Still, she handed out bandages, topical antiseptics, advice on a whole bunch of things, like starting a fire in a firepit, and even, at times, how to assemble a tent.

Mothering adults. Did she have an overinflated sense of her own importance? Or did inexperienced people just decide to go camping?

Only some of Maude's morning regulars had arrived at the café, so they had no trouble finding a seat. Blaire had loved Maude's—or the City Diner as it was properly named—since the first time she had visited it. It was vintage in every respect, right down to the matching tape covering cracks in the upholstery of chairs and booths. The tabletops, some kind of plastic laminate, had been wiped so many times that they showed white spots. And the aromas…ah, the aromas. At this hour, they were mostly of coffee and frying bacon or ham, and enough to create an appetite even on a full stomach.

Her stomach was far from full.

They both ordered omelets filled with cheese and ham. Blaire chose rye toast on the side, but Gus asked for a double helping of home fries with his meal. And, of course, coffee, but this time Blaire ordered one of the lattes Maude had started making a few years ago, from what she understood. One concession to modernity.

It would have been nice to get through the meal without a reminder, but an older man rose from a nearby table and came over to speak to them with little preamble.

"So what's with that murder? You got any leads yet?"

Blaire weighed a response. This would be a bad time to shoot from the hip. Gus was looking at her, probably deciding that since the murder had happened in *her* park, she should answer. "The police are looking into it. Right now, you probably know as much as I do."

The man nodded, rubbing his chin. Calloused skin rasped on beard stubble. "Folks are talking about some other murders, too. Been five of them in the mountains."

"I wouldn't know about them."

He shook his head. "I think people are inclined to make up stories because it's more interesting, if you know what I mean. Well, I thought maybe you could give me some ammo to stop some of that talk."

"Sorry, I know as much as you do."

He glanced at her name tag. "Thanks, Ranger Afton." Then he returned to his table.

"So much for forgetting for half an hour," she mumbled as she lifted the latte to her lips.

"I guess once you poked your nose out, someone was going to ask about it."

"He could have been a bigger nuisance," she admitted and pulled a smile from somewhere. "So much for our little social hour."

"We can try it again around a campfire tonight."

Her smile broadened. "I like the sound of that." And she did. It had been a while since she'd done that, and never with Gus. Sometimes she held campfires with storytelling for guests at the camp, especially when there were quite a few children of appropriate age.

She enjoyed those times, times when all the bad stuff at the back of her mind went into dark corners and stayed there.

After breakfast, they walked over to the sheriff's office. Blaire didn't spend a whole lot of time with the police, but she knew a few of the officers and greeted them. Gus seemed to know everyone there who was getting ready to go out on patrol or settling into a desk. He was, after all, law enforcement himself.

She still found it hard to get to know people. Brief conversations with campers, or informative campfires, were different somehow. Odd, but she hadn't always been that way. Something had happened to her in her time in the Army. It was almost as if she were afraid to commit any real emotion, as if she feared the person would just leave. As so many of her friends had during that year in the 'Stan.

She gave herself an internal shake, telling herself not to go there. It was over except inside her own head. Ghosts. Just ghosts.

Velma, the eternal dispatcher, waved them back to Gage's office with a cigarette in her hand. Over her head on the wall a huge no-smoking sign hung.

Blaire stifled a giggle.

"Skip the coffee," Gus whispered as they entered the back hallway. "Some of the deputies say it tastes like embalming fluid."

Another reason to laugh. Was she ready for that? She guessed she was. But everything changed the instant they stepped into Gage Dalton's office.

The sheriff, one side of his face scarred by an old burn, motioned them to sit in the chairs facing his desk. If she sat just right, Blaire could see around the tippy stacks of paper and the old-fashioned cathode-ray tube monitor on the computer. That thing needed to be put out to pasture, she thought.

"Need a bigger desk?" she heard herself ask.

Gage chuckled. "I need not to have to keep every report on paper as well as on the computer. Don't ask me why. I keep thinking I should make an executive decision to put a halt to the duplication, but then a clerk over at the courthouse reminds me we'll always need a paper trail. What if the computers go down or get hacked? I still need an answer for that one. So, what's up?"

Gus looked at Blaire, so she spoke first. "We want to do a perimeter check, but we don't want to get in your way. And if there's anything you've discovered about the murder that you can share, it'd be really helpful."

Gage looked at both of them. "Don't you have your own park to watch?" he asked Gus.

"Right now I want to help catch this guy so Blaire isn't out there all alone at night wondering if he's still in the woods."

Gage nodded. "I hadn't thought of that. We've been presuming he's long gone. No reason to hang around. And as near as we can tell so far, he picked Jasper at random. He worked as an accountant for an oil company. No reason to have any enemies. God-fearing, churchgoing and nobody so far has a harsh word to say. Although that could change."

She couldn't help herself. "How is Jimmy? The little boy?"

"His mom says he doesn't seem to be aware of what happened, but she's taking him to therapy anyway. He's going to need help, at the very least, with dealing with his dad being gone for good."

"I should say so." She shook her head, remembering that sobbing little boy in her arms on a cold, cold night.

"His mom says she can't separate him from the rescue blanket, so you made a hit with that one."

"Space blanket," she said. "That's what I told him. Maybe he'll dream of being an astronaut." She sighed. "But back to the big questions. I'm hearing from one of my team members that people are talking about this murder being related to others."

"I'm hearing that, too. I have some investigators looking into it and consulting with other police departments. We'll see if we can find any links. God knows we need something more than a spent shell casing."

Gus leaned forward. "He left a shell casing behind? That's amateurish."

"Yeah, it is," Gage agreed. "Very. So the likelihood that he's responsible for other murders that left no evidence behind is pretty slim."

"Blaire had an idea," Gus said. He looked at her.

"It's probably silly," she said, ready to dismiss it.

"Nothing's silly," Gus replied, "and certainly not from you with where you've been. Spit it out."

She shrugged one shoulder. "It seems random. But when you add in the other murders people have mentioned, maybe... Maybe it's not one guy acting alone. Especially since I'm hearing that they're all different, but you say they left no evidence behind."

Gage nodded thoughtfully. "I'm not ready to agree, but it's an interesting notion. Let me see what I get back from other agencies. Then there's the question of what you mean by a perimeter search."

Gus spoke. "We were talking about how this guy had to have somewhere to watch the campground. To make sure when it was safe to go in, to choose his target, whatever. A staging location. We thought we might find something."

"Point is," Blaire admitted almost ruefully, "I'm not good at sitting on my hands. This might turn up evidence."

"You're thinking in bigger terms," Gage remarked. "Tactical terms."

Blaire nodded. "It's our training."

"It's good training. It's also a great idea. The likelihood that he just hung around until everyone went to sleep bugs me. But with kids running around the place, he'd probably be seen."

"Probably," they agreed as one.

"Go for it. At this point the likelihood we'll get anything useful off that shell casing is slim. I'll be able to match it to a weapon if we ever find it, but right now…" Gage shook his head. "Find me a pistol while you're at it."

A few minutes later, they were heading out with Gage's promise to share any information he received on the other murders. Not this investigation, of course. He couldn't breach that confidentiality. But the others? Most were probably cold cases by now. Few secrets he couldn't share.

Before they got out the door, however, Connie Parish and Beau Beauregard, both deputies, suggested coffee at Maude's. Blaire exchanged looks with Gus and got the impression that he felt that might be significant. He nodded to her and she smiled.

"Sure," she said.

Maude's had quieted some after the breakfast hour, and they had no trouble finding a relatively private booth. Coffee arrived automatically, and it seemed Maude had decided Blaire was a latte drinker, because that's what she received in a tall cup. Not that she was about to complain.

"Primarily," Connie said, speaking first, "I'm worried about you being out at the campground all alone, Blaire, especially at night. So is Beau. This was such a random killing, and the guy could still be out there. Wouldn't be the first weirdo we've had playing hermit in those mountains."

"Nor the last," Beau remarked. "The *he always kept to himself* kind don't always limit that to the apartment next door."

Despite herself, Blaire was amused. "What do you think we're dealing with here?"

"Damned if I know. The vic was an accountant. For an oil company," Connie said. "Now, how likely is that to get you shot on a camping trip? Oh, I suppose there could be reasons, but I can't imagine any. If he'd angered someone at the company, why follow him out here? This feels so random."

"At least it appears to be," Gus agreed. "But if you really think about it, a lot of life is random. Even so, maybe he had some debts he couldn't meet. Gambling, drugs."

"That's so cliché," Blaire murmured, unexpectedly drawing a laugh from the other three. "Well, it is," she protested. "Easy fallback position. Blame it on the vic."

He shrugged. "You're right. But we have so little to go on, at least as far as I know."

Turning her latte in her hands, Blaire studied it as if it might have answers. Afghanistan had been nothing like this, she thought. Nothing. It struck her as odd that one murder was bothering her so much after all that she'd lived through. Yet somehow this one murder seemed scarier. Maybe because it was so far inexplicable.

Beau spoke. "We were thinking we'd feel better if you had a dog, Blaire."

Her head snapped up. "A dog?"

"A trained police dog," Beau clarified. "I spoke to Cadell Marcus yesterday. I don't know if you've met him, but he trains our K-9s. He's got a Malinois almost ready to go, and he said he'd be willing to pass her to you, or just let you keep her for a while, whichever you prefer."

This was so unexpected, Blaire had to think about it. She liked dogs. Hell, they'd had a few bomb sniffers with them in Afghanistan. She felt great respect for a dog's abilities. But she'd never thought of wanting or needing her own K-9.

"That isn't extreme?" she said finally.

"Hardly," Gus said drily. "I slept on your sofa last night because I didn't like the idea of you being alone out there. I know you can take care of yourself, but that didn't keep me from worrying one bit. Some things seem to be engraved on my DNA."

She might have laughed except right now she felt far from laughter. A man was dead, they didn't know why and some creep might be haunting the woods.

Before she could make up her mind, Gus spoke. "I was also thinking about getting her a horse. At least for now. We want to ride around up there looking for evidence of a staging area or an isolated camp. Gideon Ironheart's the man for that, right?"

Connie nodded. "My uncle-in-law," she explained to Blaire. "In case you don't know."

"I thought everyone in the county knew how all the Parishes are related," Gus said. "It's one of the first things I heard about."

Connie flashed a grin. "For a while we just kept expanding. Anyway, if you want, I'll call Gideon. I'm sure he'll be glad to bring a mount to the park for Blaire. How well do you ride?"

"I'm pretty much a novice," Blaire warned her, but she had to admit she liked the idea of being able to ride around the mountain instead of hiking for a few days while they hunted for any kind of evidence. "I did some riding while I was in Afghanistan but I haven't done much since."

"Gideon will have a gentle, patient horse. He'll take care of everything."

"And the dog?" Beau prompted.

Blaire had to hesitate. Much as she liked dogs, she wasn't sure she wanted one living with her. She'd become attached, for one thing. For another, animals weren't allowed in the park. "You know we don't allow pets in the park. Mainly because people don't keep them leashed. They chase deer and other animals. Then, most people don't scoop up after them. So how can I have a dog and tell campers they can't?"

"Get him a K-9 vest," Beau said. "That should do all your explaining for you."

He had a point, but she still hesitated. "Let me think about it," she said finally. "Right now the place is completely empty, but give it a few days. Fears will subside and there'll be plenty of people around. Then none of you will have to worry about me being alone."

She was touched by their concern. Inwardly she was aware of her own uneasiness because of the incomprehensibility of this murder, but she didn't want to display it. She'd been to war. If she could survive that, even with some emotional damage, she could certainly survive this. And she had a reasonable, tested belief in her ability to look out for herself. Not that she was a superhero or anything, but she could handle quite a bit.

Everything except someone creeping up on her in her sleep. But she had locks and a sturdy building. She wasn't sleeping in a tent like Jasper.

But something else was going on with the idea of getting a dog. "We had bomb-sniffing dogs in Afghanistan."

"Yup," Gus agreed, then waited.

"We lost a few." She closed her eyes. "Getting attached... I'm not ready to do that again, okay?"

"Okay," said Connie. "Let me call Gideon. We'll get you a horse on loan so you can roam around with Gus and check out the area faster. I bet he can get one up there by late this afternoon. Will you be around?"

Gus spoke. "It's my understanding that Blaire wants to lay in some supplies. Then?"

The question was directed at her. "Just some supplies. Gage said he'll let us know what he learns. Beyond that, I have no business." She turned her head toward Gus. "You?"

"The same." He looked at Connie and Beau. "Figure we'll be back in place at the park by two or a little after."

Connie nodded. "I'll call Gideon now."

THE TRIP TO the grocery felt almost like emerging from night into day. It was so damn normal, she thought as she and Gus wended their way through the aisles, sharing a cart. She even decided to splurge a little on a box of frozen clam strips and a bag of frozen North Atlantic cod. Her freezer wasn't large, so she had to resist a whole lot more than that and stick to staples like boneless, skinless chicken breasts that provided a good protein base for almost anything, some frozen veggies and canned goods that would keep for a while.

When she was done, she realized she'd bought more than she usually did, and looked at the sacks she piled into the back of Gus's truck.

"I overdid it," she remarked.

He laughed. "You, too?"

She shook her head a little. "I share with my staff once in a while, but you can't eat everything out of a box or a can. It gets boring."

"Jars," he said. "I depend on jars. Tomato sauce, Alfredo sauce, things like that."

She nodded. "I'm stocked with enough soup cans to feed an army, I believe."

"I love soup."

They were both pretty cheerful as they pulled out of town and began rolling toward the mountains and the park.

Gus brought up the problem of storage. It seemed a safe enough topic, she supposed, because with each passing mile the shadow of the murder seemed to be looming larger.

"Can't you get the state to give you a bigger refrigerator and freezer? It seems awfully small if you can't get out of the park for some reason."

"Mostly I only have to worry about myself," she answered. "I always have some backup in the cupboards during the summer, and come winter I've got the world's biggest freezer."

He laughed. "True that."

The road into the park began to rise before them, and way up above the mountain peak storm clouds seemed to be brewing. But something else was brewing inside Blaire, and finally she decided to address it directly.

"I must be crazy."

"Why?" He turned the wheel a bit trying to avoid a pothole. The truck bumped only a little.

"Because it's ridiculous to think the murderer might still be up there hiding out in the woods. And that even if he is, that he might kill someone else."

"I don't think that's crazy." Surprising her, he freed one hand from the wheel to reach over and squeeze hers. Just a quick squeeze because as the road grew rougher, he needed both hands to control the truck. "It would be easier to dismiss the idea if we knew why Jasper was killed. A reason for it. But as it stands, the whole damn thing is an ugly mystery, and now the possibility that five other murders might be linked makes it even worse."

"Serial killer," she said. The truck engine strained a little as the climb became steeper. A short distance with a steep grade that the park system kept talking about leveling out.

"Well, we don't know that, either. But as long as it's a possibility, there's no reason to feel crazy for worrying."

"I guess not. I didn't used to be so easy to creep out."

He snorted. "You're not used to this situation. Overseas we knew we were always at risk and the threat could come from anywhere. Here, we don't expect those things. It's so out of place in the park that it's downright jarring."

"So is this road," she remarked, trying to change the subject. She didn't want to give in to the morbid maundering of her imagination, especially since her experience in Afghanistan had given her enough vivid images and memories to fill in the imaginings. The important thing was to keep control of her mind.

Yeah. She'd been working on that for years. It ought to be a perfected skill by now, but occasionally the wrong stuff still popped up and disturbed her.

"We've been talking about resurfacing this road," she remarked as the truck jolted yet again. "I don't think we're high on the state's priority list, though. We're a small campground, comparatively speaking."

"With the national forest right next door, what do you expect?" he asked lightly. "We get the roads. If people want to drive a huge RV in, they come to us. On the other hand, your campgrounds offer a lot more privacy."

"Yeah. We get a lot of tent campers. Pop-up trailer

types. Not so many big RVs, but quite a few smaller ones at lower altitudes where we have hookups."

Covering familiar ground, talking about stuff he already knew, probably because she was trying to cover up her crawling sense of unease. Like when she'd been on missions. Knowing the enemy was out there, never knowing when he might strike.

"You looking forward to having a horse for a few days?" he asked, bringing them around a hairpin bend where the road went from pavement to gravel.

"Yeah, except it occurred to me, too late, I know next to nothing about caring for one. Heck, those saddles we used in Afghanistan were nothing like the one you have."

"Well, I'll share a secret with you."

"What's that?"

He flashed a smile her way. "I'll help you take care of the horse. In fact, I'll bring Scrappy over and the two can share your corral for a few days. Make a party of it."

Her discomfort subsided a bit. "A party? Seriously? When we're looking for evidence to lead us to a killer?"

He laughed. "Thought you'd like that one."

At last they pulled through the official entrance to the campground and into the small parking lot in front of her cabin. Dave was sitting on the front porch on a battered lawn chair with his feet on the railing. He waved as they pulled up. A man of about forty, mostly bald, with a friendly face and a personal uniform of plaid shirts and jeans, he made people feel welcome. Blaire sometimes wondered if *she* did.

"Didn't expect you back so soon," Dave remarked. "I thought when you said you wanted a couple of days you planned to be scarce around here."

Blaire smiled. "I do. Someone's lending me a horse and Gus and I are going to take some rides in the mountains."

Why did she feel as if she couldn't share the truth with Dave? He wasn't one for gossip, and what did it matter anyway? It wasn't as if she were embarking on a top secret mission where a little talk could cost lives.

She was slipping back into the military mind-set. Whether that was good or bad, it was too soon to say. She guessed she'd find out.

"So you want me to hang around?" Dave asked. "Or come back tomorrow? I don't see two horses and it's getting kind of late in the day to take much of a ride anyway."

Blaire chewed her lip momentarily. "Would filling in for me tomorrow be a problem?"

"I'd planned to anyway. And an extra day if you want. My wife and kids went to Buffalo to visit her family, so it's not like anyone's going to miss me."

Gus spoke. "I need to go over to my place to get my horse and some supplies. If you could hang out here, I'll take Blaire with me and she can drive my truck back over while I bring Scrappy." He eyed Blaire. "If that's okay with you?"

"That's fine," she agreed. She liked the idea that Gus was evidently planning to stay another night, and that he'd help her learn how to take care of the horse that Gideon should be bringing.

"Just one thing," Gus said. "Gideon Ironheart is bringing a horse for Blaire to ride for a few days, so if it arrives while we're gone?"

Dave nodded. "That I can handle. The corral out back is still good, mainly because I fixed it up last spring. You never know when the state might decide it would help to get us mounts. On the other hand, the way the road paving argument is going, I figure I'll be walking or using the ATVs for years to come."

"They work," Blaire pointed out with humor.

"Sure, but they don't go everywhere a horse could."

She half smiled. "And they tear up the terrain."

"Exactly." Dave pretended to be struck by the thought. "I never thought of that. Sheesh, Blaire, you ought to pass that along to the powers that be. Hey, guys, the ATVs damage the environment."

"Probably no more than the campers," she retorted. "Okay, that's how we'll do it, then." She looked at Gus. "How long should we be?"

"An hour at most. By truck my cabin isn't that far away if you take the wood trail."

She knew what he meant. There was a road between the two cabins, basically two ruts that ran between the trees, but it shaved off a lot of travel time. Gus's truck had high suspension for dealing with the rugged terrain around the forest. It could probably handle it better than most ATVs.

Thanking Dave yet again, she climbed back into the truck with Gus, and they headed along the wood trail toward his headquarters.

# Chapter Eight

Gus loaded the back of his truck with all kinds of horse needs, like bags of feed, currycombs and so on. He believed in taking care of any animal in his care, and some that simply needed help. When it came to Scrappy, however, it felt as if he were taking care of family.

Instead of taking the trail back to Blaire's place, he took the wood road. He led the way on Scrappy with her following behind in his truck. The day was beginning to wane. The sun had disappeared behind the mountain he was traveling over, and the light had become flat. It was still daytime, the sky above a brilliant blue, but the shadows beneath the trees seemed to have deepened anyway.

The forest didn't feel right, he thought. He supposed that was something left over from the war, but it was a feeling he couldn't dismiss anyway. As if a threat could lurk behind any tree.

Maybe it could. Some lunatic had killed a man inoffensively sleeping in his tent. Killed him with his young son beside him. What kind of person did that? The question had been bugging him since the outset.

The kind of person who would do that was exactly the reason he couldn't bring himself to leave Blaire alone again. He'd fought his instincts the first nights after the murder, but finally he couldn't continue an internal war that clearly wasn't going to sign a cease-fire.

He was worried for Blaire. She was out there alone at night, and if the campground had been full to the rafters, he'd have felt he was extraneous. But everyone had fled after the murder, and there was still no sign of a return.

People had become spooked. Unless they caught the bad guy, Blaire's campground might remain mostly empty for the rest of the season. That meant she'd be all alone out there in the woods at night after her seasonal staff went home for the day. Ordinarily that wasn't something she, or he, would worry about.

Now he was worrying. The woods didn't feel right, and instinct was crawling up and down his spine telling him this wasn't over. How he could be sure of that, he didn't know, but he remained on high alert for anything that didn't seem normal. Anything that might indicate an important change of some kind.

For certain, he was in agreement with Blaire that something about the murder seemed more like a planned operation. An assassination. Which made him truly eager to learn anything he could about the victim, but no one was going to feed that information to him. Police stuff. Civilians not wanted.

Yeah, he was a law enforcement officer, but only in the national forest. If the murder had happened over there, he'd be part of the investigation. This was different. He didn't have a clear idea of Blaire's role vis-à-vis this kind of thing. But wasn't she, too, law enforcement in the park? But maybe not for major crimes. Maybe she was expected to rely on local authorities. It wasn't as if she had the manpower to do much else.

But still... Maybe she could press Gage a little more. Maybe, given her position, he might be willing to share more with her than information about the other murders that were now worrying people.

And man, hadn't that seemed to come out of nowhere? All of a sudden people worrying about other murders that had happened in the woods over the last couple of years. Linked? How likely was that? He had no idea.

He just knew that his gut was screaming this wasn't over, and he couldn't stop worrying about Blaire.

Tomorrow they'd pack up some supplies and do a survey of the surrounding area. The killing had been planned. Of that he was certain. And that meant someone had spent at least a little time surveying the campground and the victim. Which also meant a greater likelihood the guy had left some kind of evidence behind.

He just hoped his need to protect Blaire wasn't offending her. She had experience in combat, in military operations, and while she hadn't been in special ops the way he had, it remained she was no greenhorn. He'd often felt kinship with the way her mind worked.

So maybe he should ask her if she resented his hovering. He couldn't blame her if she did. Yeah, he should ask. He should do her that courtesy.

He also needed to be wary of his attraction to her. He'd felt it when they first met, and it hadn't lessened any with time, but he honestly still didn't feel emotionally fit to engage in a meaningful relationship deeper than friendship. And from things she'd said occasionally, he believed she felt much the same way: wary.

A misstep could kill their friendship, and he treasured that too much to risk it. Still, sometimes his body ached with yearning when he thought of her or was around her.

*Careful, dude. Just be careful.*

The radio on his hip crackled and he lifted it to his ear. A satellite transceiver, it usually worked, but occasionally dense woods could interfere a bit. No real interference right now, though.

"Maddox," he said into the receiver.

"Hey, boss," came the voice of Tony Eschevarria.

"What's up?" Gus asked.

"You said you'd be out of pocket the next two days?"

"At least. Over at the state campground."

"Weird, that killing," Tony remarked, his voice crackling a bit. "Listen, a deputy is here. He's looking for you and I can send him over that way if you want."

"Sure thing. I should be there in about twenty minutes."

"I hope he's got good news, Gus."

"Me, too," Gus answered. "Me, too."

He clipped the brick back in its belt holder, then leaned forward to pat Scrappy's neck. The saddle creaked a bit, a sound he'd always loved, and nearly vanished in the shivering of deciduous tree leaves in the gentle breeze. The storm that had appeared to be building over the mountains hadn't materialized, but he swore he could smell it. Tonight, maybe.

The wood road, as they called it, little more than a cart track, had once been used by lumberers gathering wood to build the old mining town on Thunder Mountain, abandoned more than a century ago. Still, the cart tracks had been convenient enough that they'd been kept clear by usage over those years.

At last the track emerged onto a portion of paved roadway just above Blaire's cabin. A truck and horse trailer now filled part of the gravel lot, and Dave was standing out front talking to Gideon Ironheart. Gus smiled. He'd always liked Gideon.

The man had once been an ironworker who'd walked the high beams, but when he came here to visit his estranged brother, Micah Parish, he'd fallen in love with one of Micah's colleagues in the sheriff's office. At least that was the story. Anyway, these days Gideon raised horses, trained them for their owners and rescued mustangs. His two teenage children often led trail rides for tourists, sometimes at the national forest.

While Blaire parked the truck, he dismounted Scrappy and called a greeting to Gideon, who walked over with an extended hand. "I hear you're planning to do a little exploring with Blaire Afton."

"That's the plan. Thanks for the help."

Gideon grinned. "It's good for the horses to have a little adventure every now and then. I might have some big paddocks but they offer little new to explore. Lita will enjoy herself a whole bunch."

"Lita's the horse?" He heard Blaire's footfalls behind him as she approached.

"Most well-behaved mare a body could ask for." Gideon turned, smiling and offering his hand. "You must be Blaire Afton."

"I am," she answered, shaking his hand. "And you're Gideon Ironheart, right?"

"So I've heard."

Gus was glad to hear her laugh. "Your reputation precedes you," she said. "I heard someone call you a horse whisperer. So, you whisper to them?"

Gideon shook his head. "Most of so-called whispering is knowing horses. They communicate quite well if you pay attention and, if you listen, they decide to please you. Sort of like cats."

Another laugh emerged from Blaire. Gus felt like a grinning fool, just to hear her so happy.

"Let me introduce you," Gideon said. "Then I'm going to ride her up the road a ways to work out the kinks from being in the trailer. After that, she's yours as long as you need her."

"Somebody say that to me." Dave pretended to groan. "We need horses up here so badly I even took a wild hair and repaired the corral for them. Sell that to the state."

"I would if I could," Gideon answered. "I've got some fine mounts that would love working up here."

Gus and Dave helped him open the trailer and lower the ramp, then Gideon stepped inside and led an absolutely gorgeous chestnut out of the trailer.

"Oh, wow," Blaire breathed.

Gideon walked her slowly in a circle, leading her by a rein, then brought her toward Blaire. "Get to know her. Pat her neck first, don't approach her from the front until she gets to know you. Remember, she's got a big blind spot in front of her nose. And talk to her so she'll recognize your voice."

Blaire apparently didn't feel any reluctance to make friends with the horse. She wasn't quite as big as Scrappy, but still large. But then, Blaire had ridden in Afghanistan so this wasn't exactly utterly new to her.

It wasn't long before it became evident that Lita liked Blaire. Five minutes later, the horse wound her neck around and over Blaire's neck and shoulder, a horse hug.

"There you go," said Gideon. "She's yours now. Need anything in the way of supplies?"

Gus recited the list of items he'd brought with him, from bags of feed to grooming supplies.

"You'll do," Gideon agreed. "Call me if you need anything at all."

"You could send another horse," Dave laughed. "As long as you're lending them."

NOT TEN MINUTES after Gideon drove off, Dave helped carry the groceries inside, then left to spend the evening at home. He once again promised to take over for Blaire the next day if needed.

Blaire swiftly put away the groceries with an obliging Gus's help. Then the Conard County deputy arrived.

A big man, appearing to be in his sixties, he unfolded from the SUV. He had long inky hair streaked with gray, and his Native American ancestry was obvious in his face. He looked at them from dark eyes and smiled.

"Micah Parish," he said, shaking their hands. "I saw my brother headed on out." He pointed with his chin toward Lita. "New acquisition?"

"A loaner," Blaire answered. "You're storied in these parts, and I don't even spend that much time in town so I don't get all the gossip."

Micah chuckled, a deep rumbling sound. "I'm storied because I broke some barriers around here."

Gus doubted that was the only reason.

"You talked to my daughter-in-law, Connie," he said. "And, of course, she talked to me. Then Gage talked to me. Seems like folks are worried this murder might be linked to others in the mountains. So, I'm here to share information. Thing is, Gus, I was sent first to you. Somebody's nervous about the national forest."

"The killer, you mean?" Gus frowned. "Has there been a threat?"

"No." Micah looked at Blaire. "You got maps of the whole area?"

"How much do you want?"

"Most of the mountain range on up to Yellowstone."

"On my wall. Come in. Do you want some coffee?"

"My wife, Faith, tells me the day I turn down coffee I'll be at the Pearly Gates."

She pointed him to the large map hanging on the wall and went to start a pot of coffee. For a minute or so, there was silence from the front room, then Micah and Gus began to talk.

"The thing here is this," Micah said. "Can't imagine why no one noticed it before. Hey, Blaire?"

"Yes?" She punched the button to start the pot, then came round into the front room.

"Okay to use the pushpins to mark the map?"

"Go ahead." She didn't usually do that, but the map wasn't inviolate. There was a corkboard beside it, and other than an announcement of a campfire group every Friday evening, it was simply covered with colored pushpins.

Micah pulled a pad out of his jacket pocket and flipped it open. Then he read from it and began sticking red pushpins into the map along the mountain range. "Nobody's perfect," he remarked as he stuck the last pin in place. "I can only approximate the GPS readings on this map."

He stepped back a bit. "These are in order, marking those five murders that everyone is worried about." He pointed to the highest pin. "Number one."

Then as his finger trailed down along the pins to the one in the state campground, he called the order. There was no mistaking it. The murders had moved southward through the mountains.

"As you can see, it's not anywhere near a perfect line, but it's too close to ignore. All of the victims were isolated, but *not* alone. Like the one in your campground, Blaire. It's as if the killer wanted the body to be found immediately."

She nodded, feeling her skin crawl.

"Anyway," Micah continued, "Gage sent me to warn you, Gus, because the forest might be next in line. Although what you can do about it, I don't know. That's a whole lot of territory. But judging by the previous timing, the threat won't be too soon. You'll have time to figure out what you can do."

"What I can do?" Gus repeated. "Right now I must have thirty hikers out in the woods, plus about sixty families camping mostly at the southern side. I can't just empty the park indefinitely. Not even for this. Damn, I can hear HQ hit the roof."

Micah smiled faintly. "So can I. All you can do is have your people remain alert. These instances might not even be linked. There sure hasn't been anything like the Jasper murder with a kid in the tent."

Blaire had been studying the map closely and eventually spoke. "It looks as if someone is trying to make these events appear random."

The men looked again, and both nodded.

"Not doing very well," Gus remarked.

"Actually, take a closer look. Every one of these killings occurred in a different jurisdiction, including two that happened across the state line. That would make linking them very difficult because the different jurisdictions operate independently. That's clever."

"If it's one killer," agreed Micah.

"It looks," said Gus, "like a carefully planned operation."

Silence fell among the three of them. Blaire's skin tightened the way it often had before going on a transport mission, knowing that danger lay ahead, but having no idea what kind, or from where.

Micah muttered, "Well, hell," as he stared at the map. "That would explain a lot." He faced them. "Gage was going to send you some of the reports, the ones he can get. I'm not sure who'll bring them up or when. Most of these cases are cold and getting colder. And from what he said, none of them have any evidence except bodies. Very useful."

"But there are two murders every summer, right?" Blaire asked. "That's what I heard."

"So it appears, not that you can be sure of much with a sample set of five. All right, I'll head back on down and pass this information to Gage. Good thinking, Blaire. You may have hit on something important."

"Important but probably useless," she responded. "Somebody with brains is behind this but finding that brain isn't going to get any easier."

"Maybe that'll change," Gus offered. "We might find something useful in our survey over the next few days. Or just thinking about all the murders from the perspective you provided might generate some ideas."

"Criminal masterminds," Micah rumbled, and half snorted. "Word is they don't exist."

Blaire couldn't suppress a smile. "That's what they say. They also say that every perp brings something to the scene and leaves something behind. Nobody's apparently found anything left behind except bodies and the bullets in them. Oh, and one shell casing."

"Yeah. The reports will verify it when Gage gets them, but from what he mentioned this morning to me, all the weapons were different, too. God help us."

Micah stayed just long enough to finish a mug of coffee, then headed back down the mountain toward town. Gus helped Blaire with grooming Lita and feeding her, along with taking care of Scrappy, and she had to admit a certain excitement at the prospect of riding around the mountains with him in the morning.

It had been a long time since she'd been in the saddle, and she'd realized during those days in Afghanistan that she really loved to ride, that she enjoyed the companionship of a horse, and that a horse could be as much of an early warning system as a trained dog. They reacted to strangers by getting nervous, for one thing.

When the horses were taken care of, they headed back inside. "I need a shower," Blaire remarked. "I smell like horse. And since you were here last night, you probably are starting to feel truly grungy."

"I'm used to grungy," he reminded her. "But I'll never turn down a hot shower. You go first."

"It's a luxury, isn't it?"

She'd never realized just how much of one it was until those long missions in the 'Stan. Sometimes she'd felt as if dust and dirt had filled her pores and could never be scrubbed out. She ran upstairs to get clean clothes.

She would have liked to luxuriate in the shower, but she needed to save hot water for Gus. Making it quick, she toweled off swiftly and climbed into fresh jeans and a long-sleeved polo with the state park logo on the shoulder. From the tiny linen cupboard, she pulled out fresh towels for him and placed them on a low stool she kept in the corner for holding her clothes.

In the front room, she found Gus unpacking fresh clothes from a saddlebag.

"Always ready?" she asked lightly.

"That's the Coast Guard, but yeah. A change of clothes is always a handy thing to have around. I'll hurry."

"I'm done. If you want to use up all the hot water, be my guest."

He laughed, disappearing down the short, narrow hallway from the kitchen into her bathroom. A short while later she heard the shower running.

Now to think of dinner. Fortunately that had been at the back of her mind while she'd been shopping, and it was easy enough to choose a frozen lasagna and preheat the oven. She'd gotten lazy. She could have cooked for two, but in the summers she avoided cooking even for herself, except when her freezer gave her fits. She had plastic containers full of things like pea soup and stew on her refrigerator shelf, but none of them held enough for two. The lasagna did.

Gus apparently believed in conserving water, because he emerged from the bathroom, his hair still wet and scented like her bar soap, before the oven beeped that it was preheated.

He looked over her shoulder, giving her the full force of his delightful aromas. "Oh, yum," he said. "I assume you're making dinner?"

"I wouldn't make this much just for me."

He laughed. "So you were thinking about me when we were at the store."

She was thinking about him a lot, she admitted to herself. Maybe too much. But she could deal with that later once things settled down around here.

She put the lasagna in the oven, still covered by its plastic sheeting per directions, then filled their mugs with more coffee. "Front room?" she asked.

"Let me go hang up this towel." He pulled it from around his neck. "Be right there."

She carried the coffee out to the front room, placing his cup on the rustic end table and hers on the counter that separated the room from the workspace. Everything here was rustic, which she liked, but it also felt empty without the usual comings and goings of campers.

She settled behind the counter on her swiveling stool, feeling it might be a safer move than sitting beside him on the sofa. She didn't know why she needed to feel safe as he posed no threat to anything except possibly her peace of mind.

Afraid of damaging their friendship, she didn't want him to even guess how sexually attractive she found him. The pull hadn't worn off with familiarity, either. It seemed to be growing, and in the last couple of days it had grown by leaps and bounds.

He joined her just a few minutes later and dropped onto the couch. "Okay," he said. "There's one thing I want to know, and I want complete truth."

Her heart skipped a beat and discomfort made her stomach flutter. "That sounds ominous."

"It's not." He waved a hand before picking up his coffee mug and toasting her with it in a silent *thank-you*. "I just want to know if I'm driving you nuts by hovering. You're a very capable woman. You don't need a man for much."

She nearly gaped at him, then laughed. "Sexist much?"

"I don't want you to think I'm *being* sexist," he answered. "That's all."

"Ah." She bit her lower lip, but she felt like smiling. "I don't. I just thought you were being a concerned friend."

"Okay, then. It's just that you've taken care of yourself in some pretty sketchy places and situations. I *know* that, and I don't underrate it."

She nodded, liking him even more, if that was possible. "Thank you, but I'm glad you've decided to help. How much ground can I cover alone? And to be quite honest, I feel uneasy. *Really* uneasy. This whole situation stinks, and I don't care how many pins have marked that map, how do we know the killer has moved on? He might hang out in the woods. And if I were to go start poking around by myself, I might make him nervous enough to act, but he might hesitate if I'm not alone. Heck, despite what Micah Parish pointed out with those pins, how can I know I don't make an attractive target out here if I'm by myself?"

"That's my fear," he admitted. "My main fear. This guy obviously likes killing. You might look like a pear ready to pluck."

"I hear most serial killers escalate, too. Speed up." She leaned forward, her elbows on the polished pine counter, and wrapped her hands around her mug. "I've always hated being blind and I was on too many missions where we were just that—blind and waiting for something to happen. That's what this feels like."

"I hear you." Leaning back on the sofa, he crossed his legs, one ankle on the other knee. "I don't like this whole thing. One bit. I could be completely off track, though. Comparing this to anything we went through overseas on missions might really be stretching it. Those instincts could be completely wrong."

"But what are they telling you?"

"Probably the same thing yours are. There's something more than a single murder going on, and I don't mean five of them." He drummed his fingers on his thigh. "That was a really interesting point you made about the murders all being in different jurisdictions. It's not like there's a free flow of crime information between them. Not unless someone has reason to believe the crimes are linked, or they know the perp has crossed jurisdictional lines."

She nodded. "That was my understanding."

"Cops are like anyone else, they're protective of their turf."

"They don't even like the FBI, from what I hear."

"And if this really does cross state lines, the Bureau could get involved. Another reason not to open their eyes."

"Gage has."

"Gage was a Fed once himself," Gus replied. "I suspect he's less turf conscious than many."

Shaking her head, she tried to ease the tension that was

growing in her neck. "There are moments when I feel as if I'm overreacting. I have no more evidence that this killer might act around here again than we have evidence period. And it's driving me nuts not to know a damn thing about why or how this happened."

He put his coffee aside and rose. "Neck tight?"

"Like a spring."

He came around behind her and began to massage her shoulders and neck. "Tell me if I press too hard or it hurts."

At that all she could do was groan with the pleasure of it. "Don't stop."

"I won't. You're tight as a drum."

She could well believe it. Part of her couldn't let this go, couldn't just brush it off. The police were dealing with it. The other part of her wouldn't just leave it alone. They needed more than a spent shell casing. A whole lot more, and if some guy had watched the campsite long enough to know how to approach and when, then he must have left something behind. *Something.* She knew optics, knew how far it was possible to see with a good scope or binoculars. He could have been more than a hundred yards away. All he needed was a sight line.

Her neck was finally letting go. Her head dropped forward and she felt the release. "Thank you."

"Okay now?"

"Yup. For now."

Dinner was ready. The oven timer beeped, letting her know. "Hungry?" she asked.

"Famished. And I suggest an early night. We should start at first light."

From the woods farther up the road, in the trees, Jeff watched in frustration. Wasn't that ranger ever going to go back to his own park? He was all over Blaire like white on rice.

He'd been told he needed to take Blaire out, but he wasn't at all sure she'd even remember their brief encounter or connect him to any of this. Why should she?

But he knew why he was here. This was his punishment for having lost that shell casing. This was his punishment because he'd known Blaire long ago. He shouldn't have told the guys that he'd passed her on his first recon out here. Hell, she hadn't recognized him then. He was probably just another face among hundreds she saw every summer, and he hadn't really noticed her. Why would she remember him any better than he'd remembered her?

But he had his marching orders. Kill or be killed. Damn, damn, damn, how had he walked into this mess? How had he honestly believed his friends were just playing a game? He should have known Will better. Should have recognized the cold streak in him.

Should have? Psychopaths were notorious for being able to hide their missing empathy, for seeming like people you really wanted to know. So many were successful con men because they appeared so warm and likable. Hard for a mere friend to begin to suspect such a thing.

But that was Jeff's conclusion now, too late. And Karl was probably no better, or else how could they have turned this "game" so deadly? He'd been wrestling with that since he had first realized what was going on, but almost immediately they'd snared him right into this mess. His life or someone else's.

He wished he had more guts. Evidently, for him anyway, it took less guts to shoot someone else.

So now here he was, under orders to kill Blaire Afton, which he *really* didn't want to do, and she might as well have a bodyguard. What was he supposed to do? Take them both out?

He ground his teeth together and leaned his head back against a tree trunk, wishing himself anywhere else on the planet. He couldn't shoot both of them. There was enough of an uproar over the first murder.

And he still had the cries of that child hammering inside his head. He didn't lack feeling the way the other two guys did. He wished he could have shot anyone except a guy with a little kid. Why those two had picked that man...

He'd assumed it was because he was camping alone. And at first he had been, or so it had seemed. Somewhere between the time the details had become fixed and when he'd crept into that campground to shoot the man, a child had arrived. How could he have missed that?

But he knew. In his reluctance to carry out the killing, he hadn't been as attentive as he should have been. No, he'd sat up there higher in the forest, just like this, with his eyes closed, wishing he was in Tahiti, or even the depths of Antarctica.

Reluctantly, he looked again and saw the national forest truck was still parked alongside the state truck. He wondered about the chestnut horse that had been delivered that day and was now out in the corral with the forest ranger's horse.

Maybe the two were lovebirds. Maybe they planned a nice ride in the forest and up the mountainside. Why else would there be another horse in the corral? And if that was the case, how would he ever get Blaire alone so he could shoot her? He sure as hell didn't want another body to add to his conscience.

He ached somewhere deep inside over all this and was beginning to feel that he'd be hurting over this murder until the day he died. Crap, the Jasper guy had been bad. His kid had made it worse. And now he was supposed to kill someone he had actually known however long ago and however briefly?

This time he carried a rifle so he could shoot from a distance, but he also had his pistol. He pulled it out of his holster and stared at it. All he had to do was take himself out and all of this would be over.

He turned it slowly in his hand and thought about how easy it would be. The victim had died instantly. He never moved a muscle, and while Jeff wasn't terribly educated in such things, he had expected at least some twitching or even moaning, shot to the head notwithstanding.

But the kill had apparently been instantaneous. No muscle twitching, no moan, then the kid had started screaming and Jeff had hurried away as fast as he could without pounding the ground with his feet.

As his more experienced "friends" had told him, no one would dare come out to check what had happened for a minute or two, giving him time to slip away. They'd been right. Except for the kid's squalling, the campground had remained silent and still. Confusion and self-protection had reared long enough for Jeff to vanish into the shadows of the night. All without so much as scuffing his feet on the pine needles, dirt and leaves.

No trail. No sound, certainly not with the boy screaming. No evidence other than losing a shell casing.

And now all because of that casing, and the possibility that Blaire might remember his face or name after all these years, he was back here facing another nightmare.

The night was deepening. Lights came on in her cabin. Smoke began to rise from a chimney. It was getting cold out here, so maybe it was cooling down inside.

Maybe, he thought, he ought to try popping her through

the window. Sure, and that ranger would come barreling after him instantly.

Nope.

A sound of disgust escaped him, and he brought his weary body to its feet. He had to find a protected spot for the night. He hadn't bothered to locate one while there was still daylight, and through his distress he felt some annoyance with himself.

He grabbed his backpack with one hand and turned to head deeper into the woods, away from any chance encounter with someone coming up that road. He'd spend another day watching. What choice did he have?

Well, said a little voice in his head, he *could* go back to Will and Karl and confess that he was a complete failure and leave it to them to shoot him.

Except he had a very bad feeling about that. Their little game of not getting caught meant that however they chose to remove him they'd have to make it look like an accident. Which meant he could die in all sorts of ways, from a fire, to a car accident, to a rockfall. Ways that might make him suffer for quite a while.

He wouldn't go out as easily as his own victim had. No way. They'd come up with something diabolical that would keep them in the clear.

It finally was dawning on him that he had plenty of good reason to hate the two men he had always thought were his closest friends. Plenty of reason.

Clouds raced over the moon, occasionally dimming the already darkened woods even more. Each time he had to pause and wait for the light to return. All so he could find a sheltered place where the wind wouldn't beat on him all night and he could bundle up in a sleeping bag.

Maybe his mind would work better in the morning.

Maybe he'd find a solution one way or another. A good solution. Hell, maybe he'd find a way out of this altogether.

Vain hope, he supposed. It was hard to hide completely anymore. Very hard. And he had no idea how to stay off the grid.

Damn it all to hell! There had to be a way. And if that way was killing Blaire Afton, what was she to him? Nothing. Not as important as his own life.

Because that's what it really came down to. Who mattered more.

He was almost positive that despite what he'd done, he mattered more. Blaire had gone to war. She probably had a body count that far exceeded anything he could do.

Hell, maybe she even *deserved* to die.

He turned that one around in his head as he finally spread out his sleeping bag against the windbreak of a couple of large boulders.

Yeah. She deserved it.

Now he just had to figure out the best way to do it.

Feeling far better than he had in a couple of days, he curled up in his sleeping bag with some moss for a pillow, and finally, for the first time since he'd killed that guy, he slept well.

## Chapter Nine

Dawn was just barely breaking, the first rosy light appearing to the east, as Blaire and Gus made a breakfast of eggs, bacon and toast. They ate quickly, cleaned up quickly, then with a couple of insulated bottles full of coffee, they went out back to the corral and found two horses that looked ready for some action.

Gus helped Blaire saddle Lita, carefully instructing her on the important points of the western saddle. They weren't so very different from the saddle she had used a few times in Afghanistan.

He saddled Scrappy with practiced ease, and soon they were trotting up the road toward the rustic campsite where a man had been killed. They hadn't talked much, but Gus wasn't naturally chatty in the morning, and Blaire didn't seem to be, either.

The horses seemed to be enjoying the climb, prancing a bit, tossing their heads and whinnying once in a while as if talking to one another.

"I hope you slept well," Blaire said, breaking the prolonged silence. "That couch is barely long enough for you. Oh, heck, it's not long enough at all."

"It was fine. And yeah, I slept well. You?"

"Nightmares." She shook her head as if she could shake loose of them.

"About anything in particular?"

"I wish I knew. No, just woke up with the sensation of having spent a frightening night. I probably ought to be glad I can't remember. For too long, I could."

He knew exactly what she meant. Long after coming home, long after returning to civilian life, he'd relived some of his worst experiences in his dreams. "This situation hasn't been good for the mental health."

"No," she admitted. "I'm beginning to feel as if I'm teetering on a seesaw between the past and present." She paused. "Hey, that's exactly the thing I've been describing as being uneasy. I just realized it. Yeah, there was a murder, it was heinous, but that alone can't explain why tension is gripping me nearly every single minute."

"Maybe it could." But he didn't believe it.

Another silence fell, and he would have bet that she was considering her post-traumatic stress and how this event might have heightened it.

Everyone had it to some degree. Some were luckier, having it in smaller bits they could more easily ignore. Some couldn't get past it at all. He figured he was somewhere in the middle, and after all this time he had a better handle on it. Hell, he and Blaire had spent hours over coffee discussing it, as if talking about it would make those memories and feelings less powerful.

Maybe it had. The last few months he'd thought the two of them were moving to a better place. Now this. Not a better place at all.

When they reached the turn to the rustic campground, they paused. "Want to look over the scene again?" he asked her.

"I'm thinking. How much could the crime scene techs have missed? They certainly found the shell casing."

"True. So let's start circling farther out."

But she chose to circle the evident edge of the camping area, with all the sites in clear view. She drew rein at one point and looked down.

Gus followed her gaze and saw the small metal cars in the dirt, roadways still evident. Kids playing. Kids whose parents had been stricken enough by events that they'd left without getting these toys. Maybe the youngsters had been upset enough not to care about them, or had even forgotten them in the ugliness of what had occurred.

"Sad," Blaire remarked.

"Yeah."

They continued on their way, and through the trees he could see the tent where the man had been killed, and the crime scene tape that still surrounded the area. He wondered if anyone would clean that up or if it would be left to Blaire and her staff.

He asked, "Are they done with the scene?"

"I don't know. I need to ask. Then I guess we get to do the cleanup."

That answered his question. "I'll help."

She tossed him a quizzical look. "I thought you had your own responsibilities."

"I do, but Holly's in her element. She always enjoys standing in for me. One of these days, I bet she replaces me."

That drew a smile from Blaire and he was relieved to see it. She'd been awfully somber this morning.

After the first circuit, during which they'd noted nothing of interest, they moved out another fifty yards. The woods grew thicker but when he looked uphill, he saw more than one potential sight line. Not far enough, maybe, before they were blocked by the growth, but they were still there. He felt, however, that a watcher would have stationed himself a much longer way out if he could. Away from chance discovery.

"Kids like to run in the woods," Blaire remarked. "Several times a year we have to go looking for them. You?"

"No different for us."

"They're usually farther out than this. Far enough that they completely lose sight of the camp. Too much of a chance that someone would stumble over our killer here."

"The same thought crossed my mind."

Another smile from her. "Well, we're on the same wavelength quite a bit."

"So it seems." Mental echoes of one another at times. When he wasn't appreciating it, he could become amused by it. Right now he knew exactly what she was doing when she moved her reins to the left and headed them uphill.

"Hundred yards next?" he asked.

"Yes, if you agree."

"Why wouldn't I?" He was enjoying her taking charge and doing this her way. He'd never minded women being in charge, even though he hadn't come across it often in spec ops, and he had no trouble seeing Blaire as a complete equal. They'd walked the same roads, to some extent, and shared a lot of experience. Now they even had similar civilian jobs.

The only thing that troubled him was the attraction that kept goading him. Boy, that could blow things up fast. Then there was the protectiveness he was feeling. Even though she had said she didn't mind him hanging around, he had to hope she wasn't beginning to feel like he didn't trust her to take care of herself.

That would be demeaning. Not at all what he wanted her to feel.

They reached a point on the second circle where she

drew rein sharply. He paused, just behind her, and strained his senses when she said nothing. Waiting, wondering if she had heard or seen something.

Then he noticed it, too. At first the jingle and creak of harness and saddle had made him inattentive to sound, but now that it was gone, he could hear it. Or not hear it as the case was.

She turned Lita carefully until she could look at him sideways. "The birds."

He nodded. They had fallen silent.

"Could be a hiker," she said quietly. "I don't have any registered at the moment, but simple things like letting someone know where you're going up here don't always seem important to people."

"I know," he answered just as quietly. "Not until we have to send out huge search parties to hunt for someone with a sprained ankle who can barely tell us which quadrant he's in. Don't you just love it?" Then he fell silent, too, listening.

A breeze ruffled the treetops, but that was nothing new. The air was seldom still at that height, although here at ground level it could often become nearly motionless because of the tree trunks and brush.

None of that explained the silence of the birds, however. No, that indicated major disturbance, and he doubted he and Blaire were causing it, or they'd have noticed it earlier.

Problem was, he couldn't imagine what could be causing the unusual silence. The birds were used to ordinary animals and threats in the woods, and if the two of them on horseback hadn't silenced them, what had?

Another glance at Blaire told him the silence was concerning her. The birds had to feel threatened.

Then, almost in answer to the thought, a boom of thunder rolled down the mountainside.

"Great time for Thunder Mountain to live up to its reputation," Blaire said.

They both looked up and realized the sky just to the west had grown threateningly inky. It was going to be bad.

"Better head back," he said.

She nodded reluctantly.

He understood. This search of theirs had only just begun, and now they were having to cut it short. Who could guess how much evidence might be wiped away by a downpour. Probably anything that there might be.

She started to turn Lita, then paused.

He eased Scrappy up beside her, trying to ignore the electric tingle as their legs brushed briefly. "What?" he asked.

"I just felt...something. The back of my neck prickled. Probably the coming storm." She shrugged and started her mount back toward the road.

Gus followed. Her neck had prickled? He knew that feeling and he seriously doubted it was the storm.

Growing even more alert, he scanned the woods around them. He didn't see a damn thing.

HELL'S BELLS, JEFF THOUGHT. He saw the growing storm, although he doubted it would hit that quickly. What annoyed the dickens out of him was that the two were headed away, probably back to the cabin. He couldn't keep up with those horses unless he tried to run, and he figured he'd either make too much noise and be heard, or he'd break an ankle and die out here.

Regardless, any chance he might have found to take out Blaire was lost for now. Instead he had to figure out how to weather this storm without freezing to death. Nobody needed to draw him a map about how dangerous it was to get wet up here. He'd done enough hunting to know.

Having to hunker under a survival blanket while trying to keep his gear dry and hoping he hadn't chosen a place where he'd quickly be sitting in runoff didn't please him one bit.

Thunder boomed again, hollow but louder. Time to take cover, and quickly. He found himself a huge boulder that looked as if it sank into the ground enough to prevent a river from running under it and began to set up his basic camp. Only as he was spreading his survival blanket, however, did he realize it had a metallic coating.

Damn! Would it be enough to attract lightning? Or would he be safe because of the high trees and the boulder? Except he knew you shouldn't shelter under trees during a storm. So where the hell was he supposed to go?

The first big raindrop that hit his head told him he was out of time. He'd just have to set up here, and if he was worried about the survival blanket maybe he shouldn't use it. Just sit here and get drenched and hope the rain didn't penetrate his backpack. Out of it, he pulled a waterproof jacket that was too warm for the day, but it might be all he had to prevent hypothermia in a downpour.

*Or use the damn blanket,* he argued with himself. Getting struck by lightning would at least get him out of this mess. It would probably be a much better end than going back to his so-called friends without having completed this task.

Task. Murder. *Might as well face it head-on, Jeff,* he said to himself, then spoke aloud. "You're a killer now. You killed a man you didn't even know for no good reason at all except to save your own damn neck."

The woods had lost their ability to echo anything back at him. Maybe it was the growing thickness of the air, or the rain that had begun to fall more steadily. The only good thing he could say about it was that any evidence he'd left behind would be washed away.

He pulled the survival blanket out of his backpack and unfolded it, tucking it around himself and his gun and gear. A bolt of lightning would be a good thing right now.

And he didn't give a damn that this blanket must stick out like a sore thumb. Somebody finding him and taking him in for any reason at all would be almost as good as a lightning strike.

Miserable, hating himself, hating the weather, he hunkered inside the blanket.

BLAIRE HELPED GUS as much as she could with the horses. The saddles went under the lean-to to be covered with a tarp that was folded in there. The horses... Well, horses had withstood far worse for millennia, but Gus left the wool saddle blanket on their backs and gently guided them under the lean-to.

Blaire patted Lita on the neck and murmured to her. Her flanks quivered a bit as the thunder boomed, but she remained still.

"If they were free, they'd run," Gus said. "Unfortunately, I can't let them do that. They could get hurt on this ground."

She nodded, stroking Lita's side. "They'll be okay?"

"Sure. I'm positive Lita has been through storms at Gideon's ranch, and I know for a fact Scrappy's been through a bunch of them. I just want them to feel comfortable under the lean-to."

She nodded. "And if they get wet..."

"The wool saddle blankets will help keep them warm. They'll be fine, Blaire. Scrappy's never been pampered and I'm sure Gideon doesn't have enough barn space to bring his animals inside. Nope, they'll withstand it. Unlike us. Can we make some coffee?"

She laughed and led the way inside, but she honestly wasn't feeling very good. This storm threatened to kill any possibility of finding some evidence to help locate the killer. Maybe they'd been asking for too much. "Gus? Espresso or regular?"

"I could use espresso for the caffeine, but on the other hand regular might give me an excuse to drink more hot liquid, and I feel like I'm getting a little chilled."

"You, too? I think the temperature must have dropped twenty degrees while we were riding back. Maybe we'll need a fire." Then she put her hands on her hips and tipped her head quizzically. "So, coffee? Espresso or regular?"

He grinned. "That was an evasion. I can't make up my mind. Whichever you want."

"Some help."

He followed her around to the kitchen. "Want me to bring in some wood? And do you want the fire in the fireplace or in the woodstove?"

The cabin had both. Blaire didn't know the history, but there was a nice stone fireplace next to a Franklin stove that could really put out the heat. She preferred the stove in the winter, but right now it wasn't that cold.

"Let's start with the fireplace, if that's okay."

"More romantic."

She froze as that comment dropped, but he was already on his way out to get wood. What had he meant by that? Anything? Nothing?

Dang. Her heart started beating a little faster as she wondered if he'd been joking. Since first meeting him, she'd been quashing the attraction she felt toward him, but it was very much alive and well. Those simple words had nearly set off a firestorm in her.

More romantic?

Oh, she wished.

With effort, she focused her attention on making a pot of fresh regular coffee. If he still wanted more caffeine later, it wasn't hard to make espresso.

GUS GAVE HIMSELF quite a few mental kicks in the butt as he gathered logs and kindling into a large tote clearly made for the task. Hadn't he seen a wood box inside? In a corner on the front side of the room? Serving as an extra seat beneath a tattered cushion? Maybe he should have checked that out first.

But after what had slipped out of his mouth, he was glad to be out here under the small lean-to alongside the cabin. The corral was out back with another lean-to, but this was the woodshed, capable of holding enough fuel for an entire winter. Right now he looked at nearly six cords of dry wood. Good enough.

He took more time than necessary because if he'd walked out on a mess of his own making with his casual comment, he needed a way to deal with it. Problem was, that would all depend on how she had reacted to it. Maybe she'd taken it as a joke. He half hoped so, even though truth had escaped his lips.

A fire in the fireplace *would* be more romantic. The question was whether this was the time or place. Or even the right relationship. She might be no more eager than he to risk their friendship.

And romance could tear it asunder if it didn't work out. Funny thing about that, how a relationship that could be so close could also be a god-awful mess if it went awry.

He ought to know. He hadn't spent his entire life living like a monk. He'd had girlfriends. He'd considered asking one of them to marry him, too. He thought he'd found true love at last. Just like a soap opera.

And just like a soap opera it had turned out that when he was away on assignment, she liked to fool around. Being alone wasn't her cup of tea at all.

That one had hurt like hell. Mostly the betrayal, he'd decided later. He couldn't even be sure afterward that he'd really loved her. Maybe he'd been more in love with the idea of having a wife, and maybe a kid or two, and coming home after a mission to a family.

It was possible. He might well have deluded himself.

Or possibly he'd been every bit as scorched as he'd felt.

Inside he found Blaire heating up canned clam chowder as if nothing had happened.

"If you're allergic to shellfish, tell me now," she said. "I can make you something else."

"Not allergic, thank God. Life without shellfish would suck."

She laughed lightly as he went out to the fireplace and built a nice fire on the hearth. When he finished, he had a nice blaze going and she'd placed bowls of soup, a plate of crackers and some beer on the kitchenette table, where he was able to join her.

"If the bowls weren't so hot, I'd suggest eating in front of the fire," she said. "You did a nice job."

"You do a nice job of heating up canned soup," he retorted, drawing another laugh out of her. Man, he loved that sound.

"Yeah. I'm not much of a cook. Mom tried to teach me, but I felt no urge to put on an apron."

Which might be what led her to the military. No standard role for this woman. He liked it.

After dinner he insisted on taking care of washing up. When he'd dried his hands and came out to the front room, he found her staring at the map Micah Parish had stuck with pins.

"It's a definite plan," she murmured.

"I agree," he said, coming up beside her.

"But the killings are so far apart in time as well as location, there's no reason to expect him to act again anytime soon."

"You wouldn't think."

"So he's atypical for a serial murderer. Not escalating."

"Not yet anyway."

She turned her head to look at him. "This is so stupid, feeling uneasy that he might be hanging around. He's probably gone home to think about his next move."

"Maybe."

She arched a brow. "Maybe?"

He shook his head a little. "This guy appears to be smart, unless this is all chance," he said, pointing at the map.

"But if he *is* smart?"

"Then what better way to throw us off than by breaking the pattern?"

She caught her breath. "So I'm not crazy."

"Did I say you were?"

She shook her head and faced him. "You feel it, too."

"Call it combat sense. I don't know. I've got this itch at the base of my skull that won't leave me alone. I tried to act like the murder was over, the guy had gone away. That's why it took me two days to start hovering around you. Because I can't escape the feeling that this isn't over. Don't ask me why. It's just there, an itch. A sting like a pinprick in my brain. Anyway, there's no one else here for him to go after, so I started worrying about you."

She dropped her head, looking down at the wooden floor. "Yeah. From the outset I haven't been able to shake it. Something about that murder… My God, Gus, I can't get over it. What kind of monster shoots a sleeping man when his small son is right beside him? He's got no limit, evidently. So what next? My seasonal staff?"

"Or you," he said quietly.

She whipped around and faced the fire, placing her hands on her hips. It was a defiant pose, he thought.

"Let him try," she said. "Besides, this is all speculation."

But neither of them believed it. Not completely. Finely honed senses were pinging and couldn't be ignored.

WILL WAS FED UP with Jeff. He didn't bother to discuss it with Karl. He didn't want any kind of debate, even though he and Karl were very much on the same wavelength.

Jeff must be dealt with. Not necessarily killed but hamstrung enough that he'd never murmur a word about any of this. And while Karl might think that being responsible for one murder would be enough to shut him up, Will didn't.

Damn, he hated overdeveloped consciences.

He, Jeff and Karl had been friends since early childhood. Their fathers had been hunting buddies and when the boys were old enough, they'd joined the hunts with them. Always spending a few weeks here at this lodge, sharing plenty of laughter, talk and beer. It had never occurred to him that friendship with Jeff could become an Achilles' heel.

Of course, when he'd started this damn game, he'd never intended to start killing, so it had never struck him it might be best not to mention it to Jeff.

So he'd sat here in this very chair shooting off his mouth about a game. All because he'd recently come across the story of Leopold and Loeb and had wondered if the three of them could prove they were smarter. Actually, it wasn't really a question, because Leopold and Loeb had been nowhere near as smart as they had believed.

Still, it had been intended to be a game, just as he had said that night. For a while, the stalking and planning had been enough, but then one night Karl had said, "The thrill is going away."

Fateful words. The first few times, they'd simply shot to miss, to cause a bad scare. And they'd been careful not to let Jeff know what was up, because they'd learned long ago that Jeff's conscience was probably bigger than Jeff himself. Besides, they knew him for a weakling. He hated confrontation, and when they were kids he'd been inclined to run away rather than stand up for himself.

Wimp.

So now here they were. They'd managed to pressure Jeff into killing one man just to make it impossible for him to run to the cops. But had they *really* made it impossible?

He had sensed Jeff's fear. Not that Jeff's being afraid was anything new, but the guy was afraid that he and Karl would kill *him*. They would if it became necessary. Regardless, he and Karl were certain they'd left no traces behind so even if Jeff went running to the cops, they could claim they knew nothing at all and Jeff must have gone nuts.

After all, they were, every one of them, respectable people without police records. He and Karl were pillars of their community. Jeff was…well, an underachiever. Not a man to like taking risks even to get ahead.

Now this. Jeff had been in the Army with that ranger woman. She'd glimpsed him on their first survey trip when they'd gone to pick the campground for the hit. He said he was sure she hadn't recognized him.

But Jeff had recognized *her* and that stuck in Will's craw like a fish bone. Not good.

Karl didn't like it, either. There was a link now, and Jeff was that link. They either had to get rid of Jeff or get rid of the ranger. Neither of them especially wanted to kill Jeff. He'd been part of their entire lives, and his father had been like a beloved uncle to them.

But one or the other had to go. If that woman ranger remembered Jeff being there, and found just one thing, anything, that made her draw a connection, there was going to be hell to pay.

Jeff had called just an hour ago on the sat phone, telling Will that a thunderstorm had him pinned down and he couldn't act tonight, especially with another ranger there. Will figured he just needed some goading.

For Pete's sake, pinned down by a freaking thunderstorm? Jeff needed to grow some cojones. If there were two rangers there, so what? Take them both out, then get the hell out of there. At the least, it would make this case stand out from the others in case the growing talk made the authorities think about the murders being linked.

Frustration with Jeff was nothing new these days. Will growled to himself, then pulled his tablet out of its case and looked at the map on which he'd been following Jeff's every move. Jeff had no idea that Will and Karl could track him, not that it probably mattered to him.

But it mattered to Will and Karl. If the man took a hike anywhere near a cop, they wanted to be able to step in. So far Jeff hadn't entertained any such thoughts, at least none that he'd evinced.

But that didn't ease Will's frustration any. He and Karl had agreed that after this murder they needed to take some time off. Maybe a couple of years. Find another way to amuse themselves. If they did that, any links someone might perceive would go up in smoke.

He settled back in his chair, puffing on his cigar, staring at the red blinking dot on his map. It came and went, but he was fairly certain that was because the wimp was huddling under a survival blanket, hiding from the rain. Each time the dot returned, it assured him that Jeff hadn't moved.

*But damn it, Jeff,* he thought. The rain would make a perfect cover to just get the job done. No one would hear a thing. It was likely any evidence would just wash away if the downpour was as heavy as Jeff had said.

He was also fairly certain that Jeff wouldn't leave another shell casing behind. So, use the high power rifle and take out the rangers and get out of the rain.

Sometimes Jeff didn't think too well.

Hell, maybe most of the time.

Will set the tablet aside and sat smoking his cigar with one hand and drumming his fingers with the other. He needed a way to motivate Jeff. Soon. This couldn't continue as long as there was a whisper of a chance that that ranger might remember him somehow, especially if his name came up. If the cops had found some kind of evidence.

Will sat forward suddenly, unpleasant feelings running down his spine. If Jeff had left behind a shell casing, maybe he'd left even more behind. He clearly hadn't been cautious enough.

Well, of course not. The wimp had been afraid. He'd scurried away leaving that casing behind and who knew what else. One of his cigarette butts? God knew how the police might be able to use something like that.

He picked up the sat phone and called Jeff. "Still raining?" he asked. He hoped so.

God, maybe he should just go out there, kill Jeff himself, then take out the ranger to be extra careful. Yeah, somehow make Jeff nearly impossible to identify because he *could* be linked to Karl and Will.

*Hell!* He was beginning to think more like a movie or television show. What was he going to do? Murder Jeff, cut off his fingers and face, then murder a ranger so she wouldn't suddenly remember Jeff's name?

No, Jeff was supposed to kill the ranger, tie up the last important loose end, and it was the least he could do considering he'd left that damn shell casing behind. First rule in this game: leave nothing behind. Nothing.

Jeff answered, his voice shaking.

"Why are you shaking?" Will demanded.

"Cold," came the abbreviated answer.

"Man up," Will said shortly. "Take advantage of the rain and just take the woman out. Then you can get inside again and warm your delicate toesies."

"Shut up," Jeff said. It sounded as if he'd gritted the words out between his teeth.

"I will not shut up. I might, however, come out there and kill you myself to close this out."

Complete silence answered him. Then, suddenly, he clearly heard the sound of rain beating on the survival blanket for just a few seconds before the line went empty. He glanced at the tablet and saw that Jeff had disappeared again. The son of a gun had cut him off. Probably deliberately.

But no, a few seconds later he heard Jeff's voice again and saw the dot reappear on the map.

"I'll get her tomorrow," he said. "And you know what, Will?"

God it was almost impossible to understand Jeff with his voice shaking like that. "What?"

"She saw me, all right. I don't think she recognized my face but she might have. Anyway, she knows we went up there five days before I killed that guy, and at some point she's going to put that together."

Will felt stunned. Ice water trickled down his spine. "You lie."

"No, I lied the first time. I don't trust you, and I didn't want to kill *her*, and now that's exactly where I am because you and Karl are goddamn psychopaths who don't give a flying fig about anyone else on this planet. I have half a mind to come to the lodge and kill the two of you for getting me into this."

"You don't have the stones."

"Are you sure of that? But to cover my own butt I have to make sure that woman can't put me together with this mess. That's all on you, jerk. All of it. When this is done, I want nothing to do with the two of you ever again. Buy out my share of the lodge, then stay out of my life."

Yeah, like they'd pay him a dime. But now was not the time to get into that, or even think about it.

"Has it occurred to you," Jeff asked, his voice quavering, "that she may have recognized me, but she also saw the two of you?"

"All the more reason to erase her," Will said sharply.

"No, you're not getting it, you ass. If I turn up dead, she may remember you two and give your descriptions."

That silenced Will. For once he hadn't thought of something.

"And if you think killing me will save you, think again. I turn up dead, everyone knows we're friends... Nah, you'll be under the microscope."

Dang, thought Will, maybe the guy had some stones after all.

Several seconds passed before he spoke again. "Then you'd better take her out and tie off the loose end. We told you that you could be our next target, and we're not stupid. We can make it look like an accident." Will felt his own bravado covering his sudden uncertainty.

"Yeah. Sure."

"Just do it, Jeff."

"I will, damn it. But just leave me alone. I'm not sitting out here in this miserable rain and cold because I enjoy it."

Then he disconnected, leaving Will to listen to the static of a disturbed signal.

After a minute or two, Will put down the phone and picked up his tablet. Jeff was still there. Will looked across the room to the gun rack, which held seven rifles, some good for hunting, but a couple for much longer-range shooting. Damn near sniper rifles. His dad and Karl's had often liked to practice target shooting over a thousand yards.

Jeff had one of those rifles with him right now. He didn't even have to get close to the woman.

But Will thought about going out there and using one of them on Jeff. He studied the map on his tablet, bringing up the terrain. No roads nearby. He'd have to hike through the night, a dangerous thing to do even without a storm.

Hell! He almost hurled the tablet in frustration. If Jeff didn't take that damn woman out by tomorrow night, he and Karl were going to have to do something about Jeff.

No escaping it. Especially since Jeff had pointed out that she'd seen all three of them. They'd have to get rid of him in a way that wouldn't jog her memory so they could stay clear of her.

Or they'd have to kill them both along with that nosy federal ranger.

Either way, if Jeff failed, they'd have to mop up. They should have gotten rid of him as soon as they learned he'd figured out what they were doing. Honoring an old friendship this way had proved to be the biggest head-ache they'd had so far.

He was coming to hate Jeff.

THE WIND HAD picked up considerably and was blowing rain so hard against the window glass that it sounded like small pebbles.

"Will the horses be okay?" Blaire asked.

"Yeah," Gus said. "They know how to hunker together and they've got pretty thick hides. If they didn't there wouldn't be any horses."

"I guess you're right. I know I wouldn't want to be out there in this."

"Not if I can avoid it," he agreed.

She rubbed her arms as they sat on the couch sepa-rated by a couple of feet. "This place doesn't usually feel drafty." She paused. "Let me take that back. It can in the winter because of the temperature differential between the glass and the log walls. That's when I put up the shut-ters. No shutters tonight."

She had already pulled on a cardigan, but now she rose and went to sit on the rug in front of the fire. Closer to the heat and warmth.

"Is that a wood box over there?" Gus asked.

She twisted and followed his pointing finger. "Yes, it is. I think it's full. I should have mentioned it rather than you going outside to get wood."

"I think by the time I got to the door you were in the kitchen starting soup. It's okay." Rising, he went to the box, lifted the long seat pillow off it and looked inside. "I certainly won't have to go out for more wood tonight."

She pulled her knees up under her chin and wrapped her arms around them. "This fire feels so good. But there went all hope of finding any evidence out there. This rain is heavy enough to wash it all away. And the wind will probably knock down the tent and the crime scene tape. Of course, that'll make the area fresh and clean again."

"There are advantages." He joined her on the floor, sitting cross-legged. "There had to be some place he was hanging out to observe from. I doubt the rain will wash that away. And if we find it, we might find something useful."

She glanced at him. "So you still want to go on the hunt tomorrow?"

"If this weather improves. But absolutely. If you're like me, you want to feel like you're actually accomplishing something, not sitting on your hands. I mean, I'd settle back if the police had the guy."

"So would I. But until then…" She turned her attention back to the fire. "I can't stop hearing that little boy cry. It makes me so mad. Furious. Someone needs to pay."

"Yeah. I'm with you."

Watching the flames leap, she thought about what she'd just revealed to him and herself. It *was* about the boy, she admitted. As much as anything, she wanted that boy to grow up with the satisfaction of knowing his father's killer had been caught and sent to prison. Yeah, she was worried he might still be hanging around, and she couldn't blame Gus for being concerned about her safety. Every night, with the campers all gone, she was out here all alone. It wasn't as if she never needed to emerge from this cabin during the hours when her staff weren't here.

Nope. And if this guy was in it just for the thrill, she'd make a great target. Maybe he even thought she might have found some evidence. After all, she'd been the first person to approach the tent.

"Oh, heck," she said in a burst of frustration. She reclined on the rug, staring up at the dancing shadows on the ceiling. "I hate feeling like everything is messed up and I can't do anything to sort it out. Things were a lot clearer in the Army."

"*Some* things were," he agreed. "But that kind of thinking is what makes it so hard to adjust to the return to civilian life."

"I'm sure. I've been guilty of it more than once." She rolled on her side and propped her chin in her hand. "I don't remember my life before the Army being so messy, but maybe that's not true. No way to tell now. And I'm probably misremembering a lot of things from my military days. Nothing is all that clear-cut."

"Except lines of authority, and even those can get muddy."

He unfolded his legs and stretched out beside her, also propping his chin in his hand. "What I'm trying to think about now is how I'm in a warm cabin with a full belly and a good friend instead of stuck in a frigid cave hoping the paraffin flame will actually make the instant coffee hot."

"Good thoughts," she said after a moment. Then a heavy sigh escaped her. "This is a form of PTSD, isn't it?"

"What is?"

She closed her eyes a moment. "I need to face it. A gun report. A man shot in the head, in vivid Technicolor for me, a crying kid and now I've been paranoid since it happened. The paranoia isn't based in any evidence, merely in my past experience."

She opened her eyes and found him staring at her, appearing concerned, his eyes as gray as the storm outside. He spoke. "Then we're both having PTSD. I feel the paranoia. You might be right. It might be a leftover reaction. But what if it isn't? I'm not prepared to stake everything on dismissing this. It's not like I was walking down a street and heard a backfire. This is a whole different level."

He had a point, but she hated not being able to trust her own judgment. "It's awful," she said frankly. "Not being able to trust myself. It's a new thing."

"You didn't feel this way in Afghanistan?"

"Not often. That's what I meant about everything being so clear. There were bad guys, there were good guys, and if there was any doubt, it didn't last long. But this is different. I'm worrying about the stupidest possible thing. That a killer, who has most likely already moved on so he won't be found, might be stalking *me*. I have absolutely no evidence for that. It's just a feeling. A phantasm."

He reached out to grip her shoulder firmly but gently. "Given how many times a *feeling* has saved my life, I'm not going to dismiss this one, and neither should you. When the guy is locked up, then we can kick our own butts for our reactions. But on the off chance…" He didn't complete the sentence. He just gave her shoulder a squeeze, then let go.

"We're hot messes, Gus," she remarked after a few minutes.

"Sometimes. Not always. We're luckier than a lot of people. Holding steady jobs. Having friends."

"One *real* friend," she said honestly.

He shook his head a little but let it pass. She figured he didn't see any point arguing with the plain truth. She knew a lot of people, but as for counting friends of the kind she could truly share her mind and heart with, Gus was it. He'd been there. He understood. Considering she wasn't a hop away from a support group, Gus was priceless in that regard.

But it was more than his understanding. Gus had been there any time she needed someone. Like now. Running around with this paranoid fear clawing at her, he'd been right beside her, his mere presence making her feel safer.

"Thanks for being you," she said quietly. "Your friendship means the world."

His expression softened from concern. "I could say the same to you. Two slightly bent vets who've spent the last two years sharing things we couldn't share with most people. Then we're pretty much on our own in separate parks, tied up too much to go seeking the company of other vets. There's a support group in town, but how often could we get there? Honestly."

"Not frequently," she admitted. Her days off were generally jam-packed with things she needed to do, and come winter there was often no getting out of here at all. But Gus always managed to find his way over here on Scrappy.

She shifted her position so she could look at the fire again. Staring at him was awakening feelings in her that had absolutely nothing to do with paranoia. She was afraid she might simply leap into his arms.

*No time for this,* she warned herself. Not now. No way did she want to do something that would make him feel it was necessary to get out of here. He'd never evinced any sexual interest in her that she could be sure of, and she'd been careful to avoid the same.

Sometimes it seemed as if their shared experience was a wall between them. Maybe it was. Who knew what might happen if they knocked down that wall and moved past friendship.

"You ever dated much?" he suddenly asked, surprising her.

She turned to see him. "Yeah. A bit."

"Never found the right one?"

Forgetting her concerns for a moment, she smiled. "Apparently not. You?"

"I got really serious once. It turned out to be a big mistake. When I left town, she found someone else to fill in until I returned."

"Ouch!" She winced. "I don't know that I ever had that going on. Of course, I never got serious. Nobody inspired that in me."

"A tough nut, huh?" But his eyes danced a little.

"Maybe. Or maybe I'm just too damn picky."

"Picky is a good thing to be."

Taking her by surprise, he rolled onto his back, then drew her toward him until her head rested on his shoulder and his arm wrapped her back.

"Gus?" Her heart leaped with delight.

"A little comfort for us both," he answered. "Not that it's going to last long because the soles of my boots are starting to get too warm. You?"

"Yeah." She gave a quiet little laugh. "At least I'm not cold now."

"Always a good thing. Except those summers when we wished we were on an iceberg."

"Yeah. Huge extremes." Unable to resist, she snuggled a little closer and inhaled his scent. Wonderful. And the way her boots were getting warmer, she figured they'd both be safe. Another couple of minutes and they'd have to back away from the fire or completely change position.

But right now she wanted to revel in the rare experience of physical closeness with another human being. With a man. Since coming home she'd avoided it, feeling that she was too messed up to get involved without hurting someone.

Yeah, she was adapting pretty well, but if her paranoia

of the past few days didn't make it clear that she wasn't completely recovered, nothing would.

And if she couldn't trust her own mind and feelings, she wasn't fit to be anyone's companion.

Then she felt her feet. "Aw, damn," she said, pulling away from his delicious embrace and sitting up. If the heat from the fire had penetrated the thick soles of her work boots, it would steadily get hotter for a while, and those soles wouldn't cool down quickly. *Been there, done that,* she thought as she tugged at laces. *Bad timing, though.*

Gus half laughed and sat up, reaching for his own boots. "You're right. I just wasn't ready to let you go."

The words warmed her heart the way the fire had warmed her boots. She tossed him a sideways smile, as she pulled her boots off and set them to one side. Stockinged feet were always comfortable in here unless the floor got really cold. That seldom happened so her feet were generally warm enough.

She realized she was growing thirsty. Beer with dinner had been great, but the soup had been salty as had the crackers. "Something to drink?" she asked.

"Sure." He rose with her and they walked around to the kitchen. "This is sort of like a shotgun house," he remarked.

"I think it was built piecemeal by adding at the back, but I'm not sure. At least I have the loft for a bedroom."

"I bet it's toasty on winter nights."

"Oh, yeah." She opened the refrigerator, revealing a couple of bottles of juice, a few more beers and soft drinks. "Or do you want coffee or tea?"

"I told you I never refuse coffee, but if it's too late for you..."

It wasn't. In fact, it wasn't that late at all, she thought

as she glanced at the digital clock on the wall. She turned on the espresso machine, then said, "Latte?"

"Perfect."

Outside, the wind howled and rain beat on the windows, but inside all was warm and dry. Blaire was really glad not to be out there tonight.

# Chapter Ten

Jeff had just about had it. After his reaming out over the satellite phone from Will, the person he most wanted to shoot was Will. Followed, probably, by himself.

But neither of those things was going to happen. Nope. Instead he sat there shivering under a survival blanket that, while it was keeping him dry, was too open to keep him warm. The storm had dropped the temperature fast, and at this higher altitude it never got exactly hot to begin with. His fingers, even inside gloves, felt so cold he wondered if he'd get frostbite. Being reduced to eating energy bars didn't help much, either.

But he had to keep the blanket spread to protect his backpack full of essential items, like food and survival equipment, and even though it *shouldn't* make any difference, he didn't want to expose either his rifle or his pistol to the rain. They should still fire, but... What about the scope he might need? It wouldn't help to have it full of water or steamed up when he found his opportunity.

If he ever found his opportunity.

*Don't leave a trail or evidence behind.* The first rule, one they had repeated until his brain felt like it was being cudgeled. So maybe Blaire had recognized him. It didn't mean she'd connect him to the murder.

But since he'd admitted to knowing her, other thoughts

had danced unprompted through his head. Maybe she had recognized him. Maybe she would wonder why he never registered for a campsite or signed in as a hiker. What if, by chance, she put him together mentally with the murder, or simply mentioned it to the law because it started to nag at her.

The way he'd begun to be nagged by the moment of recognition.

Or what if they found a fingerprint on that damn shell casing. She'd recognize his name if they mentioned it to her. Oh, she'd probably be able to tell them more than the Army could after all these years. It hadn't been for long, but they'd trained side by side for a few weeks. How much had he shared with her?

He couldn't recall now. Too long ago, and he hadn't placed any undue emphasis on avoiding chitchat about personal things like families and high schools and other friends. Hell, for all he knew he'd mentioned Will and Karl to her. What if she remembered *that*?

Oh man, maybe he should just risk his neck and slide down this sodden mountain through slippery dirt and duff, banging into rocks. And once he got there, he could burst into that damn cabin and take out two people before they could react. They wouldn't be expecting him at all.

And he had been a pretty good marksman even before the Army and he'd kept it up with all the hunting trips and target practice.

He *liked* shooting. A target range was one of his favorite places to spend time.

Or it had been before he'd killed a man.

His alternatives had become so narrow since Will and Karl had told him to kill a man or be killed himself. He could go to the police, turn himself in.

Yeah. And if he pointed a finger at those two, which he

increasingly wanted to do, they'd have each other for alibis. Friends? Friends? Really? He couldn't think of them that way anymore. He'd told them he'd keep his mouth shut, but they'd threatened him anyway.

Psychopaths.

After the way Will had talked to him tonight, he was beginning to wonder if they wouldn't kill him anyway even if he got rid of Blaire Afton.

He swore loudly. There was no one to hear, so why not? He needed to vent the horrible stew of overwhelming anger, hatred, fear and self-loathing he was now living in. Thanks to Will and Karl.

His friends. Lifelong friends. Why had he never before noticed they were missing something essential? That thing that made most people humane: compassion.

How could he have missed that they were basically ice inside and only pretended to be like everyone else?

Well, he'd missed it until just recently, and now he was paying for his blindness. Kinda astonishing that he could know someone for so long and not see the rot at their core.

Now there was rot at his, as well. When this was over, he swore to himself, he would never again speak to either of them. Never. He would banish them from his life and try to find some way to make up for the ugliness that had planted inside him.

But first he had to get through this, and if he was going to get through this, he needed to act soon or there'd never be any atonement.

He shook his head sharply, trying to get rid of the thought. Atonement? Later. Because right now he wasn't sure there could ever be any, even if he spent the rest of his life trying.

He was a wimp. Will had called him that and he was

right. If he weren't such a wimp, he'd have put the gun to his own head.

But then, unbidden, came thoughts of his wife and soon-to-be-born child. He'd managed not to think of them once through this whole mess, managed to keep them separate and clean, and prevent their memories from making him feel any uglier than he already did.

Now they surged to the forefront, and one question froze even his shivering from the cold. How in the hell could he ever touch Dinah again with these soiled hands?

IN THE CABIN, the lattes were almost drained from their tall cups. Gus had drawn Blaire close to his side and kept an arm around her while they sipped and watched the fire dance.

"We'll go out again tomorrow," he told her. "If there's anything left to be found, we'll find it."

She wanted to believe him, but she knew she had to look, unlikely though it was. She wouldn't rest unless she tried. That was how she was built.

"Promise you won't hate me?" he said a few minutes later.

"I don't think I could do that," she said honestly. He'd been there every time she'd needed him for an emotional crisis in the last couple of years. Every time she'd needed him for anything.

"Oh," he answered, "it's always possible."

She shook her head a little. "Why are you afraid I'd hate you?"

"Because I want to cross a line."

She caught her breath as her heart slammed into a faster rhythm. "Gus?" she nearly whispered.

"I want to kiss you," he said quietly but bluntly. "I'm

going out of my mind wanting you. I realize you probably don't feel the same but…"

"Hush," she said, hardly able to keep her breath.

He hushed instantly and started to draw his arm away. That was not at all what she wanted. She twisted around until she was pressed into him and able to look straight at his face.

"Kiss me. Just do it. And don't stop there."

She watched his expression change radically. It went from a little intense to soft warmth. "Blaire, I wasn't…"

"No, but I am. I know I've been trying to hide my attraction to you because I didn't want to damage our friendship, but—" She stopped, all of a sudden afraid that she'd gone way too far, that he might want to get out of here without even that kiss he'd asked for.

Then he spoke, hardly more than a murmur. "I was worried about the same thing. What we have is already irreplaceable."

She nodded, her mouth going dry, her throat threatening to close off and her heart hammering hard enough to leap out of her breast. She'd blown it, and she hadn't been this frightened since her first exposure to hostile fire. "We can keep it," she said hoarsely and hopefully. "We're grown-ups."

"I want a lot more than a kiss from you," he said. "A lot. But if you change your mind…"

"I know how to say no. I'm not saying it."

He started to smile, but before the expression completed, he clamped his mouth over hers in the most commanding, demanding kiss she'd ever felt. Her heart soared as his tongue slipped past her lips and began to plunder her mouth in a timeless rhythm.

Electric sparkles joined the mayhem he'd already set

loose in her, filling her with heat and desire and a longing so strong it almost made her ache.

She'd waited forever, and now the wait was over. He was claiming her in the only way she'd ever wanted to be claimed.

She raised a hand, clutching at his shirt, hanging on to him for dear life. This felt so right, so good. So perfect. *Never let it end.* Then she felt his hand begin to caress her, first down her side, then slipping around front until he cradled her breast.

His touch was gentle, almost respectful, as he began to knead sensitive flesh through layers of sweater, shirt and bra. Those layers might as well have not been there. The thrill from his touch raced through her body all the way to her center until she had to clamp her thighs together. She felt her nipple harden, and when he drew back slightly from the kiss she had to gasp for air.

"You're so beautiful," he whispered, releasing her breast just long enough to brush her hair back from her cheek. "Beautiful. I've had to fight to keep my hands off you."

Music to her soul. When he released her she almost cried out, but he stood and drew her up with him. Then she looked down as he pushed the cardigan off her shoulders and reached for the buttons of her work shirt. She wished she were wearing lace and satin, fancy lingerie, instead of simple cotton, but the wish vanished swiftly as he pushed the shirt off her shoulders and let it fall to the floor.

His gaze drank her in, noting her in a way that made her feel as if he truly never wanted to forget a single line of her. Then with a twist, he released the back clasp of her bra and it, too, drifted to the floor as she spilled free of her confinement.

"Perfect," he muttered, bending his head to suck one of her nipples.

She gasped again as the electric charge ran through her and set off an ache at her center that could be answered only one way. Helplessly she grabbed his head, holding him close, never wanting the sensation to end.

She felt his fingers working the button of her jeans, then his hands pushing them down along with her undies. Then, taking his mouth from her breast, causing her to groan a protest, he urged her back onto the couch.

Her eyes, which had closed at some point she couldn't remember, opened a bit to see him tug her pants off and toss them away. Then without a moment's hesitation he began to strip himself, baring to her hungry gaze the hard lines of a male body at its peak of perfection.

"You're gorgeous," she croaked as he unwrapped himself.

"Not as gorgeous as you," he said huskily.

Man, he was ready for her, and her insides quivered and clenched in recognition. All of him was big, and right now all of him was hard, too.

He reached for her hands and pulled her up until she was pressed against him, front to front, and his powerful arms wrapped around her. As he bent his head to drop kisses on her neck, she shivered with delight and with being naked against his heated nakedness.

There was no feeling in the world, she thought, like skin on skin, like having his hard, satiny member pressed against the flat of her belly, an incitement and a promise.

"Want to go up to the loft or make a pallet down here?" he asked her between kisses.

She sighed, hanging on to her mind with difficulty while he busily tried to strip her to basic instincts. "Climbing that ladder isn't sexy."

"Unless you're the one climbing behind."

Her sleepy eyes popped all the way open as she felt as if she were drowning in the gray pools of his. They wrapped around her like his arms, the color of the stormy sky outside, but bringing a storm of a very different kind. And with them came a sleepy smile.

Teasing her. At a time like this. She loved it as warmth continued to spread into her and turn into heat like lava. Her legs began to quiver, and all she wanted was to feel his weight atop her and his member hard inside her.

He must have felt her starting to slip, because suddenly his hands cupped her rump, such an exquisite and intimate experience, and lifted her. Then he put her carefully on the couch.

"Before one of us falls down," he said thickly, "I'll make that pallet."

Damn, she hated that he'd let her go, but there was nothing she could do except press her legs together in anticipation, waiting for the moment he would satisfy the burgeoning ache inside her.

He grabbed the folded blankets she had given him the night before and spread them on the rug before the hearth, folding them in half for extra padding. The pillow soon joined it. Then before she could stir much at all, he once again lifted her and laid her down on the bed he'd made for the two of them.

Softness below, hardness above, heat from one side and a chill from the other. Sensations overwhelmed her, each seeming to join and augment the hunger he had awakened in her. "Gus…" she whispered, at once feeling weak and yet so strong. Her hands found his powerful shoulders, clinging. Her legs parted, inviting his possession.

Nobody in her life had ever made her feel this hot so swiftly. No one. It was as if he possessed a magic connection to all the nerve endings in her body, so that his least touch made every single one of them tingle with awareness and need.

He kissed her mouth again, deeply but more gently. His hands wandered her shoulders, her neck, and then her breasts. After a few minutes of driving her nearly crazy with longing, his mouth latched onto her nipple, sucking strongly until she arched with each pull of his mouth, feeling devoured but hungrier still. Her hips bucked in response, finding her rhythm, and then, depriving her of breath, he entered her.

Filled, stretched and finding the answer she had so needed, she stilled for just a moment, needing to savor him, needing the moment to last forever.

He must have felt nearly the same, because he, too, stilled, then caught her face between his hands. Her eyelids fluttered and she looked into his eyes, feeling as if she could see all the way to his soul.

Never had any moment felt so exquisite.

HUNGER WASHED THROUGH Gus in powerful waves. He'd had good sex before, but this was beyond any previous experience. Something about Blaire had lit rockets in him, driving him in ways that stole his self-control.

Part of his mind wanted to make this flawless, to give her every possible sensation he could before completion. Most of him refused to listen. There'd be another time for slow exploration, gentle touches and caresses. Time to learn all that delighted her.

Right now he could not ignore the one goal his body drove toward. After those moments of stillness that had seemed to come from somewhere out among the stars, his body took over again, leaving his brain far behind.

A rocket to the moon. A journey beyond the solar

system. A careening sense of falling into the center of the universe.

Everything that mattered was here and now. All of it. Blaire and he became the sole occupants in a special world beyond which nothing else existed.

He pumped into her, hearing her gasps, moans and cries, goaded by them and by the way her hips rose to meet his. Her nails dug into his shoulders, the pain so much a part of the pleasure that they were indistinguishable.

He felt culmination overtake her, felt it in the stiffening of her body and the keening cry that escaped her. He held on to the last shred of his self-control until he heard her reach the peak once more.

Then he jetted into her, into the cosmos. Into a place out of time and mind, feeling as if his entire soul spilled into her.

EVENTUALLY HE CAME BACK to their place in time, aware that he had collapsed on her, that his weight might be uncomfortable. But she was still clinging to his shoulders, and when he tried to roll off she made a small sound of protest, trying to hang on, then let him go.

"My God," he whispered.

"Yeah," she murmured in reply.

Perspiration dried quickly in the heat from the fire. He rolled over and draped an arm around her waist. "You okay?"

"Okay? I don't think I've ever been better."

He saw her smile dawn on her puffy lips. He'd kissed her too hard, but at least she wasn't wincing. That kiss had come from deep within him, expressing a desire he'd been trying to bury since he'd first met her.

But since she wasn't complaining, he wasn't going to apologize. She wiggled around a bit until she faced him and placed her hand on his chest. "We can do this again, right?"

If he hadn't spent every ounce of energy he had on her, he'd have laughed and proved it. Instead he returned her smile and said, "Believe it."

She closed her eyes, still smiling, and ran her palm over his smooth skin. "All this time and I never dreamed how perfect you are without clothing."

"Perfect? You're missing the scars."

"Battle scars," she retorted. "I have a few, too. You didn't point them out and I'm blind to yours. Just take the heartfelt compliment. I knew you were in great shape, I just never imagined such a striking package."

"I can say the same. I've been pining for you since day one."

A quiet little laugh escaped her. "We were behaving."

"We wanted to take care of our friendship."

Her eyes opened wider. "I know. Have we blown it?"

He shook his head slowly. "I don't think so."

"Me, either. This feels incredibly right."

He thought so, too. Holding her close was no longer ruled by the passion between them. He felt a different kind of warmth growing in him, the sense that an emptiness had been filled, that places perennially cold in his heart were thawing. He gave himself up to the gift that felt perilously close to a peace he had forgotten existed.

He was not the kind of man who wished for the impossible, but at that moment he wished he could stay in this place forever, with Blaire in his arms, with the warmth in his heart and soul. To cling to feelings he'd lost so long ago, that had become the detritus of war.

He spent a lot of time *not* thinking about the war. Sometimes it was like trying to avoid the elephant in the room, but he tried to focus on the present day and the needs of the forest he protected and the people he served. Just taking care of Mother Nature and offering a bandage to a kid who'd cut his finger on a sharp piece of wood, those things made him feel good about himself.

So he tried not to remember. Still, the demons roared up out of the depths from time to time. They did for Blaire, too, and when it happened they got together whether in town for a trip to the diner or at one of their headquarters. Sometimes they hardly had to speak at all. A simple word or two would convey everything that was necessary.

They'd been balm for each other for a long time. He actually depended on her and she seemed to depend on him. But this was so very different. This wasn't dependence of any kind. This was a meeting of two souls with a hunger for something greater.

She ran her hand over his back, not paying any special attention to the burn scar that wrinkled his back on one side. "Your skin feels so good," she murmured.

He stroked her side in return. "So does yours. Plus your curves. Enough to drive a guy crazy. Did that give you any trouble on duty?" He'd seen more than enough men crossing the line with women in their units.

"Some. Funny thing, though. After infantry training I wasn't an easy target anymore. Most of them wisely didn't press the issue."

He liked the thought of her scaring the bejesus out of some young fool who thought he was entitled to take what he wanted, to expect some woman to be grateful for his attentions.

"I was also luckier than some because my superiors weren't into sexual harassment at all."

"Fortunate. I saw some of that stuff. I'm glad it overlooked you."

And there they were, returning to the safe—safe?—

ground of their military experience. He could have sighed, and it was all his fault.

Then he found the escape hatch before he totally destroyed the mood. His stomach growled. A giggle escaped Blaire.

"Yeah," he said. "I guess the soup didn't stick. Want me to wander into the kitchen and find something for both of us?"

IN THE END, they slipped into jeans and shirts and went barefoot into the kitchen together. She did have a few things handy, things she didn't usually buy in any kind of quantity because they were too tempting. But tucked into her freezer, lying flat beneath a load of other food, was a frozen pizza.

"I can doctor it with canned mushrooms and some fresh bell peppers," she offered. She'd splurged on a couple of peppers at the store. In fact, as she looked inside her fridge, she saw a whole bunch of splurges she'd hardly been aware of making. Her mood? Or because she had hoped that Gus would stay the night again? The latter, she suspected. Regardless, her usually bare refrigerator was stuffed to the gills tonight.

"Mind if I look around?"

She waved him toward the fridge. "Help yourself. And if you like to cook, so much the better."

But cooking never became involved. He found her brick of white Vermont cheddar cheese, an unopened package of pepperoni slices that she'd almost forgotten she had and a box of wheat crackers in the cupboard. He wielded her chef's knife like a pro and soon had a large plate full of sliced, crumbly cheese with crackers and pepperoni. It looked like a professional job.

"I suppose I should have saved the pepperoni for the

pizza," he said as he carried the plate into the living room and pulled the end table around to hold it. She followed with two cans of cola.

"That pizza is a desperation measure," she answered. "I can always get more pepperoni."

They curled up on the couch together. She tucked her legs beneath herself.

These moments were heavenly, she thought as she nibbled on crackers and cheese. Everything felt so right. She only wished it could last. And it might, for the rest of the night.

But her PTSD was still gnawing at the edges of her mind, trying to warn her of the threat outside, a threat held at bay only by the violent storm.

Except she couldn't be certain there was any threat at all. Just leftover tatters of her mind from some seriously bad experience.

She tried to shake it off and let her head lean against Gus's shoulder. He didn't seem to mind at all. Every so often he passed her a cracker holding a bit of cheese or pepperoni. Taking care of her.

A sudden loud crack of thunder, sounding as if it were right in the room, caused her to start. The bolt of lightning flashed even through the curtains that were closed against the night.

"Wow," she murmured. It awoke memories she didn't want, causing her to leave the comfort of being close to Gus. She rose and began to pace rapidly, wishing the room were a lot bigger.

"Blaire?"

She glanced at him, taking in his frown, but she suspected he knew exactly what was going on. That crack of thunder had sounded like weapons fire. Too loud, too close. Her hands suddenly itched to be holding her rifle, her body to be ducking down behind something until she could locate the threat.

At least she didn't try to hide. She hadn't lost her sense of where she *really* was, but the sound had awakened deeply ingrained impulses. At least there'd been only one crack of thunder. The grumbling continued, but that's all it was, grumbling.

"It was just thunder," Gus said.

But she could tell he was reminding himself as much as her. Some things, she thought, would never be normal again. She hated the fireworks displays the town put on, so she stayed out here rather than joining the celebration. At least fireworks were forbidden in the state park and in the national forest.

Which, of course, didn't mean she never had to put a stop to them and threaten people with arrest if they didn't listen. But walking up to a campsite where people were setting off bottle rockets, reminiscent of the sound of mortars, and firecrackers that sounded like gunshots... That was an effort of will on her part.

"Yeah," she answered Gus.

"I'd pace along with you but I think we'd collide."

"I'm sorry."

"Don't be. It jolted me, too. I'd been out about six months when a kid lit a string of fireworks right behind me. Firecrackers, probably. I swung around instantly into a crouch and I really didn't see him. Didn't see the fireworks. I hate to think what might have happened if my buddy hadn't been there to call me back."

She nodded, understanding completely. Gradually the tension the bolt had set off in her was easing, and after a couple of more minutes she was able to return to the couch. She sat near him, but not right beside him. She didn't think she was ready to be touched yet.

He still held the plate of crackers and cheese that they'd made only a moderate dent on. "Have some more," he said, holding it toward her. "Eating something usually brings me back to the present. Especially something I never had overseas."

The fire had begun to burn down and she considered whether to put another log on it. Mundane thoughts. Safe thoughts. Her taste buds were indeed bringing her back from the cliff edge. Tart cheese, crunchy, slightly bitter wheat crackers. An anchor to the present moment.

At last she was able to look at Gus and smile. The magic of the evening was beginning to return.

JEFF GAVE UP. He didn't care if someone spotted him. He popped open a can of paraffin used to heat foods on the trail and lit the flame with his lighter. Then he set it in front of him, holding his freezing hands over it. Within minutes the survival blanket caught some of the flame's heat and began to reflect it back toward his face.

Thank God. He'd begun to think his nose would fall off from frostbite, although he was sure it wasn't *that* cold. Having to sit out here like this was pure misery, and he wondered that he hadn't started shivering. Although his insulated rain jacket was probably capturing his body heat as effectively as it kept the rain out.

As soon as his fingers felt a little better, he reached inside his jacket and pulled out a pack of cigarettes from his breast pocket. They were a little crushed, but still smokable, and damn he needed a smoke.

The misery of the night was beginning to drive him past moral considerations. He hated his friends even more now, but step by step he made up his mind to get Blaire Afton out of the way so he never needed to do this again.

One shot. He was pretty good at several hundred yards.

Maybe more. That other ranger wouldn't be able to find him fast enough if he picked his spot and knew all the places for concealment or quick escape. First thing in the morning, he promised himself. Then he was going to shoot Blaire in the same way he would shoot a game animal.

After that, having bought a few days, he was going to move to Timbuktu or some other faraway place so that Will and Karl would leave him alone. Forever. He just wanted to be left alone forever. Dinah and his baby would be better off without him. Yeah, he could run as far as he wanted.

And he didn't care if it was called running because, damn it, he needed to run for his life. He no longer trusted those guys not to kill him anyway. They weren't going to let him go simply because he'd done what he'd been told to do.

Then another thought crept into his brain. Why shoot Blaire if it wasn't going to save his own life?

Double damn, he thought. Why had he needed to think of that? Because, he reminded himself, killing her would give him time to make plans and extricate himself. He couldn't just march out of here tomorrow and be on a plane by midnight. Nothing was that easy, even without thinking of his family.

He started making a mental list as he continued to warm his hands. Passport. Cash. Arranging for his bank and credit cards to accept charges from overseas. Clothes. He needed to take at least some clothing with him. He wasn't rich like the other two and couldn't be needlessly wasteful.

But he *did* have enough to get away to some cheaper place, and enough to sustain him until he could find some kind of work. He didn't mind getting his hands dirty, he was strong and healthy, and educated. He ought to be able to find something somewhere.

Regardless, he figured if he left the country, Will and Karl would lose all interest in him. He wouldn't be around to make them nervous, or to annoy them. Out of sight, out of mind would most likely apply because he didn't think either one of them would want to waste time tracking him down in some other country.

Yeah. Kill the woman and hightail it. The plan would work. He just needed to take care the other ranger couldn't find him first. Hell, he ought to shoot the man, as well. Will had suggested it. It would certainly buy him time to leave this park behind, to get out of the mountains.

Another thing to hash over in his mind as he sat there in misery. He hardly even noticed that the storm rolled out after midnight. All *that* did was make the night colder.

Damn, his life sucked.

# Chapter Eleven

Blaire and Gus made their way up to her loft bedroom instead of feeding the fire on the stone hearth. Heat rose and it had filled the loft, which captured it. Blaire's predecessor had used the room farthest back in this cabin for a bedroom, but it hadn't taken long for Blaire to figure out the loft stayed warmer on frigid winter nights. She burned less fuel and didn't need to use space heaters. She now used the back room for storage.

Her successor would probably change everything around, a thought that occasionally amused her. As it was, she had a tidy space, big enough for a queen bed, a small chest of drawers, a night table, a chair and a lamp. Inconvenient as far as needing a bathroom, but it was a small price to pay.

She had to warn Gus to watch out for his head, though. The loft ceiling nearly scraped her head.

"This is cozy," he remarked. The light had several settings and she had turned it on low so he was cast in a golden glow.

"*Cozy* is a pleasant word for *tiny*," she answered. "But I like it."

"I can see why. Nice and warm, too."

Three or four minutes later they were both tucked under her comforter, naked and locked in tight embrace.

This time Gus used his mouth and tongue to explore her, at one point disappearing beneath the covers to kiss and lick her sweet center until she thought she was going to lose her mind. When she was sure she couldn't stand it anymore, she turned the tables, rising over him to discover his defined muscles, the hollows between them and finally the silky skin of his erection. It jumped at her first touch, and she felt an incredible sense of power and pleasure, unlike anything she'd ever felt.

But he was doing a lot of that to her, giving her new sensations and a new appreciation of sex. This was in no way the mundane experience she'd had in the past. This was waking her to an entirely new view of being a woman.

She enjoyed his every moan and shudder as her tongue tried to give him the same pleasures he had shared with her earlier. Finally his hands caught her shoulders and pulled her up. Straddling his hips, she took him inside her, then rested on him, feeling as if they truly became one.

Their hips, welded together, moved together, and the rising tide of passion swept her up until it carried her away almost violently. They reached the peak together, both of them crying out simultaneously.

Then, feeling as if she floated on the softest cloud, Blaire closed her eyes and drifted away.

LYING LIKE SPOONS beneath the covers, Gus cradled her from behind, holding her intimately. She felt his warm breath against the back of her ear, and even as sleep tried to tug at her, she spoke.

"That was heaven."

"If that was heaven, sign me up." Then he gave a whispery laugh. "I'm sure it was better."

She smiled into the dark in response. "I don't think I've ever felt this good."

"Me, either." He pressed a kiss to her cheek, then settled back again. Their heads shared the same pillow and she could feel his every move. "I hate to be the practical one, but the storm has passed and if you want to ride out in the morning…"

She sighed. "We need to sleep. I know. I've been fighting it off because I don't want to miss a minute of this."

"This won't be the last minute," he answered. "Unless you tell me to take a hike, I plan on being right here with you tomorrow night."

She hesitated. "What about Holly?"

"She always wanted to replace me."

Blaire gasped. "Seriously?"

He chuckled. "Not really. But she enjoys ruling the roost sometimes. Which is the only reason I can ever take a vacation or get to town. Holly is the best, but she's told me more than once that she likes being able to point at me when someone's unhappy."

"Ooh, not so nice." She was teasing and she could tell he knew it when he laughed.

"She has her moments, all right." She felt him pull her a little closer. "Sleep," he said. "It's going to be a long day in the saddle."

IN THE EARLY MORNING, before the sun had risen when the light was still gray, Gus went to the corral out back to check on the horses. They regarded him almost sleepily and stood close together because the chill had deepened overnight. Remembering summers elsewhere, he sometimes wondered how folks could ever really think of this climate as having a summer. A few hot days, but up here in the forest on the mountain little of that heat reached them. Eighty degrees was a heat wave.

The lean-to over one part of the corral, against the

cabin, seemed to have done its job. The wind must have been blowing from a different direction because the feed was dry and if the horses had gotten wet at all, he couldn't tell. Even their blankets seemed mostly dry.

They nickered at him, apparently glad to see a human face. He could well imagine. The night's rain had left a lot of mud behind, and that wasn't good for them to stand in. He needed to move them out of here soon.

He loved the morning scents of the woods after a storm, though. The loamy scent of the forest floor, the pines seeming to exhale their aroma with delight...all of it. Fresh, clean and unsullied by anything else.

Well, except horse poop, he corrected himself with amusement. Grabbing a shovel that leaned against the cabin wall, he scooped up as much as he could find and dumped it into the compost pile on the other side of the fence. He wondered if the compost ever got put to use. He knew some folks came up to grab a load or two of his in the spring for their backyard gardens. Maybe they came here, too. He turned some of it and felt the heat rise. Good. It was aging.

Smelly, though, he thought with amusement. So much for that fresh morning aroma.

The sky had lightened a little more as he returned inside, wondering if he should start breakfast or let Blaire sleep. He was used to running on only a couple of hours of sleep in the field. Today wouldn't be a problem for him. He didn't know about her.

As he stepped inside, he smelled bacon. Well, that answered the question. He passed the kitchen area to the bathroom, where he washed his hands, then returned to Blaire.

"Morning," he said. "I hope I didn't wake you when I got up."

"Not really. I was starting to stir. How are the horses?"

"Champs. They're fine, but they really need a ride today. At the moment they're standing in mud."

She turned from the stove to look at him and he thought he saw a slight pinkening of her cheeks. "Bad for them?"

"Bad for their hooves if they stand too long. A few hours won't cause a problem, I'm sure, but I know they'd feel better if they could dry off their feet."

"Who wouldn't?" She turned back to the stove and flipped some strips of bacon.

"Can I help?"

"Make some toast if you want it. We've got power this morning, amazingly enough. I was sure that storm would have left us blacked out. Anyway, the toaster's over there. We don't have to use the flame on the stove."

He found a loaf of wheat bread next to the toaster and a butter dish with a full stick. He dug out a knife and began by popping two slices of bread into the toaster. "Did you ever see those four-sided metal tents you could use to make toast over a gas flame?"

She thought a moment. "Those things with the little wooden handles so you could pull down the piece that held the bread in place against the grill? My great-grandmother had one, but I never saw her use it."

"I've sometimes thought I'd like to find one somewhere. Power goes out over at my place, too, and I like my toast."

"Then we ought to look for one. Now that you mention it, that would probably help me out a lot in the winter."

He watched her fork bacon onto a plate with a paper

towel on it. She immediately placed more strips in the pan. "I stuck my nose outside," she said. "It's cold, isn't it?"

"Relatively. We'll need jackets and gloves for certain."

"Then we should eat hearty. Stoke the internal heater."

He absolutely didn't have any problem with that.

THEY RODE OUT after the sun crested the mountains far to the east. It hung red and hazy for a while, then brightened to orange. Soon it became too brilliant to look at.

The cold clung beneath the trees, however. At Gus's suggestion they started circling the murder scene about two hundred yards out.

"He had to watch for a while before moving in," Gus said needlessly as they had already discussed this. "So he'd have some kind of hide. Maybe use one left by another hunter."

She was riding beside him as their path through the trees allowed it. A slight shudder escaped her. "I don't like the way you phrased that. *Another* hunter. Like this guy was after deer or elk."

She had a point. "I hope you know I didn't mean it that way."

"I do," she acknowledged.

"You okay?"

"Hell, no," she answered frankly. "Ants of bad memories are crawling up and down my spine, and occasionally all over me. If you mowed this forest to the ground, maybe then I'd be able to believe there isn't an ambush out here waiting for us."

"I read you." Yeah, he did. It might all be PTSD from their time in war, but whether it was didn't matter. They couldn't afford to ignore it until they were *sure* the shooter wasn't out here.

A little farther along, she spoke again. "We started this whole idea to find evidence."

"True."

"How much could be left after that storm last night? Seriously."

He shook his head but refused to give in to the despair that sometimes accompanied the memories. His brain had a kink in it since Afghanistan and all he could do was make the best use of it he might. Ignoring it never won the day.

They used both GPS and a regular compass to navigate their way around a wide arc. The GPS didn't always catch a weak satellite signal through the trees, but as soon as another satellite was in place it would strengthen. In the interim, when the signal failed, they used the old-fashioned method.

About an hour later, Blaire made a sound of disgust. "I haven't yet been able to see the Jasper tent through the trees. If someone was going to observe, he'd need the sight line or he'd have to be a lot closer. What's the smart money?"

Gus reined in Scrappy and waited until Blaire came fully beside him, their legs almost touching.

"Here." He reached into his saddlebag and pulled out a huge pair of binoculars that would have served a sniper's crew well. "Look upslope and see what catches your attention."

"Why up?"

"Because if there's a high spot up there, or even along this arc, those trees aren't necessarily going to matter. We don't have to see *through* them."

She gave him a crooked smile. "Which is why you were special ops and I wasn't." She looked upslope again. "You're right, I'm probably looking in the wrong direction."

"We should look both ways. In case he might have found an open sight line here, too."

"I hope we're not on a fool's errand," she remarked as they moved forward.

"We've got to look. Neither of us is the type to sit on our hands." Nor did he want to tell her that he could swear he felt eyes boring into the back of his neck. Those sensations had never let him down in the 'Stan, but they hadn't always been right, either.

Even so... "You know, Blaire, we're both concerned he's still hanging around, but I can't understand why he would."

"I can't understand why he killed that poor man in the first place. Besides, I've heard criminals like to come back to the scene. To relive their big moment. To see what the cops are doing. We're looking. Maybe he's interested in that. Maybe it makes him feel important."

"Possibly." He tilted his head a little, looking at his display and seeing the GPS was down again. He pulled the compass out of his breast pocket to make sure they were still following their planned route. So far so good. He looked downslope again but saw only trees. A lot of trees. He could have sighed. "That was good reasoning, you know."

She had been looking upslope with the binoculars. "What was?"

He smiled. "Your rationale for why he still might be here. Maybe our senses are completely off-kilter."

She lowered her head for a moment, then said something that made his heart hurt. "I hope not. I'm still learning to trust my perceptions again."

THEY WERE GETTING too close, Jeff thought. He'd made his way back to the hide atop a big boulder from which he'd watched the campground. It would give some hunter a panorama for tracking game. For him it gave a view of the killing field.

He caught himself. That was too dramatic. That called to mind the most god-awful massacre, and he didn't want to associate with that, even in a private moment of thought.

But putting his binoculars to his eyes, he watched the two of them. If he took Blaire out now, the guy might dismount to take care of her. Would he have time to get away before the man came looking for him?

He looked up the slope and recalled the night of the shooting. He'd had to go into the campground that night, right to the tent. This time he could keep a much safer distance and just hightail it. It wasn't as far, and he knew the way. He ought to since he'd covered the path so many times.

Shooting Blaire might spook the horses, too. The guy—Gus, he thought—might get thrown. That would be helpful. Of course, a man could probably run faster over this terrain than a horse could. But would he leave Blaire if she was bleeding?

Yeah, if she was already dead.

Crap.

He rolled over again and watched the two of them. If they came up any higher, he was going to have to retreat from this spot. He had little doubt they'd find it. It worked as a deer blind, not a human blind. The guy who'd built this nest hadn't wanted it to be impossible to find in subsequent years. Too much work had gone into it, such as moving heavy rocks for a base.

Damn, he wanted a cigarette. The thought made him look down and he realized he'd left a heap of butts already. Damn! He scooped them up and began to stuff them into a pocket. Not enough to leave a shell casing behind. No, now he'd leave DNA for sure. Maybe Will was right to scorn him.

No, Will wasn't right. Will wasn't right about a damn thing except he needed to make sure Blaire didn't have a sudden memory of him and make a connection.

Then Jeff was going to clear his butt out of this country.

His thoughts stuttered a bit and he wondered if his thinking was getting screwed up. Energy bars barely staved off the cold and he was almost out of them. Maybe his brain was skipping important things.

But he knew one thing for sure. If he went back without killing that woman, Will and Karl were going to kill *him*. So he had to do it. Just to buy time.

He needed those two to split up a little more. More space between them, more distance. He didn't want to add *two* people to a body count that shouldn't even exist.

He closed his eyes briefly, wishing himself on another planet. Or even dead and buried. Anything but lying here watching a woman he had nothing against, waiting for an opportunity to shoot her as if she were a game animal.

It was self-defense, he told himself. Indirectly, perhaps, but he needed to defend himself and this was the only way. Self-defense. He kept repeating it like a mantra.

GUS DREW REIN and Scrappy slowed, then stopped. Realizing it, Blaire slowed Lita down and looked over at him. "Something wrong?"

"Scrappy just started to limp. Maybe he's got a loose shoe or something. I need to check. Give me a minute?"

"Of course." She watched him dismount, then turned her attention to the woods around them. She just didn't see any place yet that would have given the shooter a clear view of the campground. They needed to get higher, unless Scrappy was truly lame, in which case they'd have to head back.

Because she was busy telling herself this was a fool's errand, they'd never find anything useful and it was simply born of their military training that required them to act against a threat... Well, she wouldn't necessarily mind if they had to call this off. She loved being out here on horseback, and Lita was a great mount, but the sense of danger lurking around every tree was ruining it and probably ridiculous besides.

Since she'd left the combat zone for the last time, she'd been forced to realize how powerful post-traumatic stress could be. She hadn't been inflicted with it as badly as some of her former comrades, but she had it. Enough to make her uneasy for no damn good reason, like the last few days.

A random murder had occurred. It might not even be random at all. They wouldn't know that until the police collected more evidence. But right now, riding through the woods, hoping to find the place from which the shooter could have observed the campground, had its footing more in her memories than in the present.

Yeah, it was creepy, but *this* creepy? She needed to talk herself down. Needed to accept that the killer was long gone and every bit of the uneasiness she couldn't shake was being internally generated by a heap of bad memories that couldn't quite be buried.

Then maybe she could get back to doing her job, and Gus could get back to doing his. Holly and Dave might not mind standing in for them for a while, but it wasn't fair. They both had jobs to do and they were letting them slide because neither of them could quite believe in the safety of the woods.

That thought caused her to sit back in the saddle.

Couldn't believe in the safety of the woods? Seriously? This retreat she had come to in order to escape the bustle of the busy, populated world because it somehow grated on her and kept her on alert too much? It no longer felt safe?

God, this was bad. Maybe she needed to get some counseling. Never had the detritus of her military experience gotten this far out of hand. Nightmares, yeah. Disliking crowds, yeah. But the woods? The safe haven she'd found here?

"It seems he got a stone in his hoof," Gus said, dropping Scrappy's right foreleg to the ground.

"Do we need to go back?"

"Nah. I've got a tool in my saddlebag. I'll get it out in a minute and then we can move on."

She watched him come around Scrappy's left side and unbuckle the saddlebag. "Is he bruised?"

"I don't know yet. He didn't limp for long, so I hope not."

"Well...if he needs a rest..." She trailed off as it hit her how far away they were now from everything. Miles from her cabin. Probably miles from the dirt road. Could they shortcut it through the woods? Maybe. It all depended on how many ravines were lurking between here and there. So far they'd been lucky. At any moment the mountain could throw up a huge stop sign.

"It'll be fine," Gus said as he pulled out the tool. "We can always walk them, but I don't think it'll be necessary."

Blaire felt the punch before she heard the report. She started to fall sideways and grabbed the saddle horn only to feel it slip from her fingers. She felt another blow, this one to her head as she wondered with confusion why she was on the ground. Then everything went black.

JEFF HAD A clear escape route. He could run up to the cave like a mountain goat, nothing in his way from here. When the guy dismounted his horse and started to check its hoof, it seemed like a fateful opportunity. He had a clear shot at Blaire, and from over two hundred yards he had no doubt he could make it.

If he was one thing, he was a superb marksman with this rifle. One shot was all he'd need.

He looked downslope and liked what he saw. Damn fool ranger wouldn't be able to reach this spot fast. Too many rocks, a ravine that looked deep enough to swallow him and his horse. It made great protection for Jeff.

Okay, then.

Lifting his rifle to his shoulder, he pulled the bolt to put a shell in the chamber. Then, with his elbows resting on a rock, he looked through the scope. Suddenly Blaire was big, a huge target.

Holding his breath, steadying his hands until the view from the scope grew perfectly still, he fired. He waited just long enough to see Blaire fall from her horse.

Then he grabbed his pack and gun and started to run uphill. He didn't wait to see the result. He didn't need to. He was a damn fine shot.

What he hadn't seen was that the man was looking right in his direction when he fired.

GUS REMOVED THE STONE from Scrappy's foot and tossed it away. Bending, he looked closely and saw nothing worrisome. He straightened and looked up at Blaire, who was still straddling Lita. "He might be a bit tender later, but he's fine to continue."

"Good," she said.

Then the entire world shifted to slow motion. He saw

a flash from up in the woods some distance away. His mind registered it as a muzzle flash. Only then did he hear the familiar *crack*.

Before he could act, he saw red spread across Blaire's sleeve and begin to drip on her hand. He had to get her down. *Now.*

She reached for the saddle horn, but before he could get there, she tipped sideways and fell off Lita. He heard the thud as her head hit the ground.

Everything inside him froze. The clearheaded state of battle washed over him, curling its ice around everything within him, focusing him as nothing else could.

He left Scrappy standing and dealt with Lita, who was disturbed enough by the sound and Blaire's tumble to be dancing nervously. He feared she might inadvertently trample Blaire as she lay on the ground, so he grabbed her by the bridle, then grabbed Scrappy with his other hand.

He knew horses well enough to know that Scrappy might react to Lita's nervousness and begin to behave the same way. While it wasn't usually necessary, he used the reins to tie Scrappy to a tree trunk along with Lita.

They nickered and huffed, an equine announcement of *let's get out of here*, but he was sure they weren't going anywhere.

Only then, what seemed like years later but couldn't have been more than a half minute, he knelt next to Blaire. She had the rag doll limpness he recognized as unconsciousness, and he feared how badly she might have hit her head.

But there was a sequence, and the first thing he needed to do was stanch the blood from her wound. Time slowed down until it dragged its heels. Only experience had taught him that was adrenaline speeding up his mind, that time still moved at its regular pace.

With adrenaline-powered strength, he ripped the sleeve of her jacket open and kept tearing until he could see where the blood was heaviest. Then he tore her shirt and revealed her shoulder, turning her partly over to see her back as well as her front.

A through-and-through wound, bleeding from both sides, but not through the artery, thank God. Bad enough, but no spurts. Grabbing the sleeve he had just torn, he ripped it in half and pushed it against the two holes, front and back, as hard as he could.

He could use her jacket sleeve for a tourniquet, he thought, but his mind was only partly on first aid. "Blaire. Blaire?"

Her unconsciousness worried him as much as anything. How hard had she hit her head? Head wounds could be the absolute worst, even though he was sure he could stop the bleeding from her shoulder.

He kept calling her name as he wound the jacket sleeve around her shoulder, making it tight. Stop the bleeding. Find a way to wake her up.

Only then could he search out the shooter, and he damn well knew where he was going to start.

BLAIRE CAME TO with a throbbing head and a shoulder that was throbbing even harder. She cussed and suddenly saw Gus's face above hers.

"Thank God," he said. "You hit your head."

"How long was I out and who shot me?"

"You were out for about two minutes and I don't know yet who shot you. But I saw the muzzle flash."

"Then go get him, Gus."

"No. I REALLY WANT to but I'm worried about you. I need to get you help."

She tried to sit up, wincing a bit, so he helped her, propping her against a tree.

"I don't think you lost a lot of blood," he said, "but if you start to get light-headed, you know what to do."

"Not my first rodeo," she said between her teeth. "The blow to my head wasn't that bad. I'm not seeing double or anything. The headache is already lessening. The shoulder... Well, it hurts like hell but I can't feel any serious damage." She moved her arm.

"The shooter messed up," she said after a few moments. "Just a flesh wound. He must have used a full metal jacket." Meaning that the bullet hadn't entered her shattering and spinning, causing a lot of internal damage.

"Blaire..."

She managed a faint smile. "I always wanted to say that."

He flashed a grin in response. "Your head is okay."

"My shoulder's not too bad, either."

He rested his hand on her uninjured shoulder, aware that time was ticking, both for her and for the escaping shooter. "I'm going to radio for help for you. Then, if you think you're okay by yourself for a bit, I'm going after that bastard."

With her good arm, she pushed herself up. "I'm coming with you."

"Stop. Don't be difficult, Blaire. You've been shot."

She caught his gaze with hers. "I've also been in combat. So have you. Trust me, I can judge my own fitness. There's a ravine up there and I know the way around it. What's more, he obviously has a long-range weapon. Do you? Do you really want to go after him alone? He could be perched anywhere."

He frowned at her, a frown that seemed to sink all the way to his soul. "You might start bleeding again."

"If I do, I'll tell you. This feels like you've got me bandaged pretty well. Quit frowning at me. I won't be stupid."

"Riding up there is stupid," he said flatly. But looking at her, he realized he was fighting a losing battle. If she could find a way to get herself back on Lita, she'd follow him. Never had he seen such a stubborn set to a woman's jaw. He wanted to throw up his hands in frustration. "I'm trained for this," he reminded her. "Solo missions."

"I'm trained, too," she retorted. With a shove, she reached her feet and remained steady. "See, I'm not even weak from blood loss. I'm *fine*."

Well, there were different definitions of that word, but he gave up arguing even though he had an urge to tie her to that tree. But, he understood, if that shooter realized she was still alive, he might be circling around right now. He could get in another shot without being seen.

"Hell and damnation," he growled. But he gave in. Better to keep her close.

He had to help her mount Lita since she had only one workable arm, but once she was astride the horse, feet in the stirrups, she looked fine. No paleness to her face, no sagging. Maybe the wound wasn't that awful.

It was her left shoulder that was injured and she was right-handed. Like many of the rangers out here who needed to go into the woods, she carried a shotgun as well as a pistol. The shotgun was settled into a holster in front of her right thigh, and before he would allow her to move, he asked her to prove she could pull it out and use it with one arm. She obliged while giving him an annoyed look.

"It's a shotgun," she said. "I hardly have to be accurate."

If he weren't getting hopping mad, he might have

smiled. "I just need to be sure you can use it. And I'm radioing this in, like it or not. We aren't going to play solitary superheroes out here."

Damn! He'd gone from violent fear that she was dead into relief that she was reasonably okay and now he was so mad he was ready to kill.

Someone had shot her. Why? Hell, he didn't care why. Whoever it was, needed to be grabbed by the short and curlies, tied up in handcuffs and marched to jail.

As they moved farther upslope, his radio found an area with clear satellite transmission, and he gave the sheriff's office a rundown as they rode, including that Blaire had been wounded but was riding at his side. He asked they be tracked, and dispatch promised they would.

Insofar as possible, he thought as he hooked the radio onto his belt again. He kept glancing at Blaire to be sure she was still all right and wondered if she had any idea how distracting she was. This wasn't helping the search much. His concern for her wasn't making him a better hunter.

He would have liked to be able to shield her with his body, but since there was no way to know if the guy might circle around and take another shot, there was no safe place for her to ride. He suggested she lead the way because she knew how to get around the ravine, and all he had to do was point out where he had seen the muzzle flash. Plus, he could see if she started to weaken.

She was a born navigator with a lot of experience. She guided with surety, part of the trip taking them away from the area from which he'd seen the flash, much more of it angling toward it and up as they left the ravine behind.

He glanced down into that ravine as they crossed a narrow ledge of rock and realized there'd have been no way to cross it directly. None. The shooter was probably counting on it to slow them down.

But their horses moved swiftly when the terrain allowed. Soon they found a trampled muddy place that he'd probably been using. From there his trail was clear for about twenty feet or so, giving them direction, then it disappeared in the sopping duff and loam beneath the trees.

She drew rein and waited for him to catch up to her. "He probably followed as straight a path uphill as he could. For speed?"

He nodded. "I agree."

"And there's a road on the other side of that ridge," she said, pointing. "Not much of one, little more than a cart track used by hunters, but he could have left a vehicle there."

"I bet." He paused. "Let's speed up. This is a rough climb. He had to get winded. To slow down."

But the horses wouldn't, he thought. They'd just keep climbing steadily and as quickly as they could, as if they sensed the urgency. They probably did. Horses were sensitive animals.

He kept one eye on Blaire while he scanned the area around them. The guy might have angled away from a straight path. It all depended on how scared he was and how much time he thought he'd have. If the shooter thought Blaire was down, he might think he had a lot of time.

He hoped so. The fury in him had grown cold, a feeling he remembered from other conflicts. He was riding its wave, heedless of danger to himself, focused on the mission, focused on Blaire's safety. Nothing else mattered.

She, too, was scanning around them, but he had little hope they'd see much. The shooter probably had the sense to wear woodland camouflage, although the higher they climbed the thinner the trees grew. They were nowhere near the tree line, but for some reason the growth here was thinner. He tried to remember if there'd been a fire here at some point. The ground was plenty brushy, but the trees didn't seem as big or as stout as they had farther below.

Then he saw it. A flash of movement above them.

"Blaire."

She halted and looked back at him.

"I think I saw him. We're sitting ducks right now. We'd better split up." He hated to suggest it, given that she was wounded, probably suffering a great deal of pain and maybe even weakening. But together they made a great target.

"Where?" she asked quietly.

"Eleven o'clock. About three hundred yards upslope."

"Got it."

Then with a brief nod she turned Lita a bit, angling away from where he'd seen the movement. Misleading as if she were going to look elsewhere.

He did the same heading the other direction, but not too much, teeth clenched until his jaw screamed, hoping that their split wouldn't tell the guy they'd seen him.

Then Blaire called, "I think I saw something over here."

Did she want him to come her way? Or was she sending their intended misdirection up to the shooter?

"I'll be there in a minute," he called back. "Need room to turn around."

"Yo," she answered, her voice sounding a little fainter.

The brief conversation gave him the chance to look up again to the spot where he'd seen movement. There was more movement now. Rapid. Then something happened and he heard rocks falling. A man's shape, suddenly visible, lost its upward momentum and instead he seemed to be scrambling frantically.

*Gotcha,* he thought with burning satisfaction. "Now, Scrappy." He touched the horse with his heels, speeding him up. If ever he had needed this horse to be sure-footed, he needed it now. Scrappy didn't disappoint.

With amazing speed, the horse covered the ground toward the man, who was still struggling as more rocks tumbled on him from above. The guy had evidently made a serious misstep and gotten into a patch of very loose scree.

Taking it as a warning, Gus halted Scrappy about two hundred feet back, then dismounted, carrying his shotgun with him. He approached cautiously, aware that the guy was armed and desperate.

Then he swore as he saw Blaire emerge from the trees on the other side. He was hoping to have dealt with this before she entered the danger zone. He was, however, glad to see she'd unholstered her shotgun and angled Lita so she could use it.

"Keep a bead on him," Gus called to her as he hurried carefully toward the man.

The guy turned over, his rifle in his hands, looking as if he were ready to shoot. Gus instantly squatted and prepared to take aim, but the man evidently realized he was outnumbered. If he shot in any direction, one of two shotguns would fire at him.

"Put the rifle away," Gus demanded, rising and making it clear that he was ready to shoot. "Now."

He could see the guy's face clearly, reflecting panic. He looked around wildly, his feet pushing at the scree beneath him but gaining no purchase.

"Give up," Blaire called. "You wouldn't be the first man I've shot."

Well, that was blunt, Gus thought, easing closer to their quarry. Vets didn't like to say things like that. He hoped to hell that wasn't the blow to her head talking.

"I've got him," Gus called when he was ten feet away. Resignation had replaced panic on the guy's face. He took one hand from his rifle, and with the other tossed the weapon to the side.

Then he said the strangest thing: "I'm so glad I didn't kill her."

## Chapter Twelve

A half hour later, with Jeff Walston securely bound in zip ties, Gus heard the sound of helicopter rotors from overhead. Medevac was on the way, and as he'd been told over the radio, a couple of cops were riding along.

Good. He needed to be away from the source of his anger. He had enough experience to know he wouldn't take it out on his prisoner, but he had never liked the uncomfortable, conflicting emotions the situation brought out in him. The guy could have killed Blaire. Maybe had wanted to. It would have been easy for Gus to treat him like a soccer ball.

But he didn't. Instead he sat beside Blaire, whom he'd helped to dismount and sit against a tree. For all she had claimed it was just a flesh wound, it was taking a toll on her. He was amazed at the strength and determination that had brought her this far.

"I wouldn't have minded having you on my team over there," he told her.

"That's quite a compliment," she murmured. "Thanks, Gus."

"You're remarkable."

"I'm a soldier." That seemed to be all she needed to say. From his perspective, it was quite enough.

Because of the chaotic winds aloft so near the peak of

the mountain, the helicopter couldn't come very close or low. Through the trees he caught glimpses of three people sliding down ropes to the ground, and after them came a Stokes basket.

Then another wait.

"I wish I could go to the hospital with you," Gus said. "But the horses…"

"I know. Take care of the horses. They were good comrades today, weren't they?" She smiled wanly. "Gus?"

"Yeah?"

"I think I was running on adrenaline."

That didn't surprise him at all, but before he could respond, three men burst out of the trees in tan overalls. He instantly recognized Seth Hardin, a retired Navy SEAL who'd helped build the local rescue operations into a finely honed operation.

They shook hands briefly as the other two put Blaire on the basket and strapped her in. Gus repeated her injuries to the two EMTs, then watched them race back through the woods to get Blaire onto the helicopter.

Seth remained with him. "I'll keep watch over the prisoner if you want to head back."

Gus nodded. "I need to take care of two horses. But FYI, I didn't touch the guy's weapon or much of anything except to put the zip ties on him."

Seth arched a brow. "That must have required some restraint."

"Exactly." They shared a look of understanding, then Gus rose. "You armed?"

Seth patted his side, pointing out the rather obvious pistol attached to his belt. "Of course."

"You want one of our shotguns? He said he's alone but…"

"Hey, you know what we're capable of. I'll be fine. I'm

just going to make sure this creep can't move an inch, then I'll stand back and pay attention. It won't be for long. The second chopper is supposed to be following with some more cops. You just get out of here. You don't need to wear a neon sign to tell me how worried you are about Blaire."

JEFF WALSTON WANTED to spill his guts. He started talking in the helicopter and by the time Gus was able to reach town, they had a pretty clear picture of the so-called Hunt Club.

It was an ugly one. Micah Parish filled him in as Gus drove to the hospital. Gus listened with only one ear. He could get the nitty-gritty later, but right now he was badly worried about Blaire. Blood on the outside of the body didn't necessarily mean there wasn't internal bleeding. She'd held on, probably longer than she would have without a flood of adrenaline coursing through her, but now the question was how much damage had she worsened with her stubbornness.

At the hospital they wouldn't tell him much except that she was now in recovery. He could see her when she woke up.

The wait was endless. His pacing could have worn a path in the waiting room floor. Still, pieces began to fall together in his mind. He began to see exactly where he wanted to go.

It kind of shocked him, but as it settled in, he knew it was right.

BEFORE BLAIRE EVEN opened her eyes she knew where she was. She'd been in the hospital before, and the odors plus the steady beeping of equipment placed her firmly in her present location.

As she surfaced slowly from the drugs, memory returned. Being shot, the insane ride through the woods that she would have been smarter not to do, helping Gus capture the bad guy. The ride in the Stokes basket up to the helicopter. Then nothing.

She moved a little and felt that her wound had changed. Probably surgery, she thought groggily. Yeah, her throat felt raw, so there'd been a breathing tube.

It was over. She'd be fine. She didn't need a doctor to tell her that. She'd been in worse condition once before from a roadside incendiary device. That time she'd been saved by luck as much as anything, being on the far side of the vehicle.

"Blaire."

A quiet voice. Gus. He was here. Warmth suffused her, and a contradictory sense of happiness. Lying post-op in a hospital bed seemed like an odd place to feel that warmth.

At last the anesthesia wore off enough that she could open her eyes. They lighted instantly on Gus, who was sitting beside her bed.

"Blaire," he said again, and smiled. A wide, genuine smile that communicated more than words. She was okay and he was happy and relieved about it. Then she sensed him gently taking her hand.

"Welcome back," he said. "You're fine."

"What was that all about?" she asked, her voice thick. "The guy. What was he doing?"

He told her about The Hunt Club, about how the man they had captured had been forced into committing two murders by threats against his life.

"Sport?" That almost made her mind whirl. "They were doing this for sport?"

"Two of them, evidently. They've been rounded up. The full truth will come out with time, but right now the man we caught seems eager to talk."

"Good." Then she slipped away again, still under the influence of surgical medications.

She had no sense of how much time had passed, but when she came to again, her shoulder throbbed like mad. "Damn," she said.

"Blaire?" Gus's voice again. "What's wrong?"

"My shoulder hurts worse than when I was shot."

"I'm not surprised. No adrenaline now, plus I guess they had to do some work inside you. One of the docs said you were lucky your lung didn't collapse."

Those words woke her up completely. "What?"

"You were bleeding internally. Next time you want to ride a horse when you've been shot, please reconsider." Then he pressed a tube into her hand. "Top button. Call the nurse for some painkiller."

She certainly needed some. She pressed the button and a voice came over the speaker over her head. "Nurse's station."

"Something for pain, please."

"Be there shortly."

Then she dropped the tube and her fingers reached for Gus. He replied by clasping her hand.

"Listen," he said. "You were tough. You *are* tough, as tough as anyone I've known."

Something important was coming. She could sense it. All of a sudden she didn't want that nurse to hurry. She wanted to listen to him.

"I know we've avoided this," Gus continued. "But I refuse to avoid it any longer. Nearly losing you... Well, it kind of yanked me out of stasis."

"You, too?"

He nodded. "We don't have long. I'm sure you're about to get knocked out again. But tuck this away for when you're feeling better because I don't want to take advantage of you."

"How could you?" She thought she heard the nurse's rubbery steps in the hall. Her heart began to accelerate. "Gus?"

"I love you," he said simply. "And if you don't mind, I'd like to marry you. But don't answer now. Just put it away until you're back on your feet. I promise not to pressure you. I just needed you to know."

Just as the nurse wearing blue scrubs appeared in the doorway, she felt her heart take flight. "Pressure away," she said. Then the needle went into the IV port. "I love you, too," she said before she vanished into the haze again.

A MONTH LATER, they stood before Judge Wyatt Carter and took their vows. They'd agreed to keep their jobs, to feel out their path into the future.

And they'd promised each other they were going to attend the trials of The Hunt Club. A game? Just a game had cost five lives? It was an appalling idea. It appalled Blaire even more to recognize Jeff Walston and remember they'd served briefly together. A man known to her!

But that faded as they stepped out of the courthouse into a sunny August morning. The bride wore a street-length white dress and the groom wore his best Forest Service uniform.

A surprising number of people awaited them outside and began to clap. Turning to each other, they kissed, drawing more applause.

They had friends and had found love and a new way of life.

"Upward," he murmured. "Always. I love you."

\* \* \* \* \*

# FIREFIGHTER'S UNEXPECTED FLING

**SUSAN CARLISLE**

To Brandon Ray.

Some family you love even though they married in!

# CHAPTER ONE

SALLY DAVIS PULLED her bag and a portable bottle of oxygen out of the back of the ambulance. The heat from the burning abandoned warehouse was almost unbearable. Her work coveralls were sticking to her sweating body.

This structural fire was the worst she'd seen as a paramedic working with the Austin, Texas, Fire Department over the last year. Her heart had leaped as the adrenaline had started pumping when the call had woken her and the dispatcher had announced what was involved. These were the fires she feared the most. With a warehouse like this, there was no telling who or what was inside. There were just too many opportunities for injury, or worse.

She watched as the flames grew. The popping and cracking of the building burning was an ironic contrast to the peace of the sun rising on the horizon. She didn't have time to appreciate it though. She had a job to do.

Moments later a voice yelled, "There's someone in there!"

Sally's mouth dropped open in shock as she saw Captain Ross Lawson run into the flames. Even in full turnout gear with the faceplate of his helmet pulled down and oxygen tank on his back, she recognized his tall form and broad shoulders. Sally's breath caught in her chest. What was wrong with him? Her heartbeat drummed in her ears as she searched the doorway, hoping…

Sally had seen firefighters enter a burning building before but never one as completely enveloped as this one. She gripped the handle of her supply box. Would Ross make it out? Would there be someone with him?

The firefighters manning the hoses focused the water on the door, pushing back the blaze.

Every muscle in her body tightened as the tension and anticipation grew. Ross was more of an acquaintance, as she'd only shared a few shifts with him since moving to Austin. However, he and her brother were good friends. More than once she'd heard Kody praise Ross. From what little she knew about him he deserved Kody's admiration.

Right now, in this moment, as she waited with fear starting to strangle her, she questioned Ross's decision-making. Since she had joined the volunteer fire department back in North Carolina, Sally had been taught that judgment calls were *always* based on the safety of the firefighter. She doubted Ross had even given his welfare any thought before rushing into the fire.

The loss of one life would be terrible enough but the loss of a second trying to save the first wasn't acceptable. In her opinion, Ross was taking too great a risk, the danger too high. He hadn't struck her as a daredevil or adrenaline junkie but, then again, she didn't know him that well. Was this particular characteristic of Captain Lawson's one of the reasons Kody thought so highly of him?

James, the emergency medical tech working with her, stepped next to her. "That takes guts."

A form appeared in the doorway, then burst out carrying a man across his shoulders. The sixty pounds of fire equipment he wore in addition to the man's weight meant Ross was carrying more than his own body weight. Sally had to respect his physical stamina, if not his reckless determination.

Two firefighters rushed to help him, but he fell to the ground before they could catch him. The man he carried rolled off his back to lie unmoving beside him, smoke smoldering from his clothes.

"You take Captain Lawson. I'll see to the man," Sally said to James as she ran to them.

Ross jerked off his helmet and came up on his hands and knees, coughing.

Placing the portable oxygen tank on the ground, she went to her knees beside the rescued man, clearly homeless and using the warehouse to sleep in, and leaned over, putting her cheek close to his mouth. As the senior paramedic at the scene, she needed to check the more seriously injured person. Ross had been using oxygen while the homeless man had not.

Her patient was breathing, barely. She quickly positioned the face mask over his mouth and nose, then turned the valve on the tank so that two liters of oxygen flowed. By rote she found and checked his pulse. Next, she searched for any injuries, especially burns. She located a couple on his hands and face. Using the radio, she called all the information in to the hospital.

"We need to get this man transported STAT," Sally called to her partner.

Another ambulance had arrived and took over the care of Ross, leaving James free to pull a gurney her way. With the efficiency of years of practice, they loaded the man and started toward the ambulance. She called to the EMT now taking care of Ross. "How's he doing?"

The EMT didn't take his eyes off Ross as he said, "He's taken in a lot of smoke but otherwise he's good."

"Get him in a box. I still want him seen," she ordered.

Ross shook his head. "I'm fine." He coughed several times.

"I'm the medic in charge. You're going to the hospital to be checked out, Captain."

He went into another coughing fit as she hurried away. She left the EMT to see that the stubborn captain was transported back to the hospital.

Minutes later she was in the back of the ambulance—the box, as it was affectionately known—with the homeless man. While they moved at a rapid speed, she kept busy checking his vitals and relaying to the hospital emergency room the latest stats. The staff would be prepared for the patient's arrival.

The ambulance pulled to a stop and moments later the back doors were opened. They had arrived at the hospital. A couple of the staff had been waiting outside for them. Sally and one of the techs removed the gurney with the man on it.

As other medical personnel began hooking him up to monitors, she reported quickly to the young staff nurse, "This is a John Doe for now. He was in a burning warehouse. Acute smoke inhalation is the place to start."

Just as she was finishing up her report, the gurney with Ross went by. She followed it into the examination room next to the John Doe. Ross's coat had been removed and his T-shirt pulled up. He still wore his yellow firefighter pants that were blackened in places. Square stickers with monitoring wires had been placed on his chest connecting him to machines nearby. Aware of how inappropriate it was for her to admire the contours of his well-defined chest and abdomen, she couldn't stop herself. The man kept himself in top physical shape. It was necessary with his field of work but his physique suggested he strove to surpass the norm. No wonder he'd been able to carry the man out of the burning building.

His gaze met hers. Heated embarrassment washed over her and she averted her eyes. Ogling a man, especially one that she worked with, wasn't what she should be doing.

Ross went into another round of heavy coughing that sent her attention to the amount of oxygen he was receiving. The bubble in the meter indicated one liter, which was good. Still, at this rate it would take him days to clear the smoke from his lungs.

Sally stepped closer to his side and spoke to no one in particular. "How's he doing?"

One of the nurses responded. "He seems to be recovering well. We're going to continue to give him oxygen and get a chest X-ray just to be sure that he didn't inhale any more smoke than we anticipated."

"I'm right here, you know." Ross's voice was a rusty muffled sound beneath the mask. He glared at her. This time her look remained on him.

"You need to save your voice."

He grimaced as a doctor entered. What was that look about? Surely, he wasn't afraid of doctors.

Slipping out of the room as the woman started her examination, Sally stepped to the department desk and signed papers releasing Ross and the John Doe as her patients into the hospital's care. Done, she joined the EMTs at her ambulance.

She gave James a wry smile. "Good work out there this morning."

"You too," he replied as he pulled out of the drive.

In the passenger seat, she buckled up, glad to be out of the back of the box. She wasn't a big fan of riding there.

She shivered now at the memory of when she'd been locked in a trunk and forgotten while playing a childhood game. To this day she didn't like tight spaces or the dark. Being in the square box of the ambulance reminded her too much of that experience. It was one of those things she just dealt with because she loved her job.

Sally leaned her head back and closed her eyes. Ross's light blue gaze over the oxygen mask came to mind. She'd met Ross Lawson soon after she had moved to Austin and gone to work for the Austin Medical Emergency Service, the medical service arm that worked in conjunction with the fire department that shared the same stations and sometimes the same personnel when a fireman was also qualified to work the medical side. As an advanced paramedic, she was assigned Station Twelve, one of the busiest houses of Austin's forty-eight stations. It just happened that it was the same station where her brother and Ross worked. She hadn't missed that twinge of attraction when she and Ross had first met any more than she had this morning. But she had never acted on it and never would.

A relationship, of any kind, was no longer a priority for her. She'd had that. Her brief marriage had been both sad and disappointing. Now she was no longer married, all she wanted to do was focus on getting into medical school. It had been her dream before she'd married, and it was still her dream. At this point in her life a relationship would just be a distraction, even if she wanted one. She was done making concessions for a man. Going after what she wanted was what mattered.

The ambulance reversed with a beep, beep, beep. It alerted her to the fact that they had arrived at the firehouse. When they stopped, she hopped out onto the spotless floor.

She loved the look of the fire station. It was a modern version of the old traditional fire halls with its redbrick exterior and high arched glass doors. A ceramic dalmatian dog even sat next to the main entrance. The firefighters worked on one side of the building and the emergency crew on the other. They shared a kitchen, workout room and TV room on the firefighter side. They were a station family.

James had backed into the bay closest to the medical side of the building. The other two bays were for the engine, quint truck and rescue truck. They hadn't returned yet. The company would still be at the warehouse fire mopping up. When they did return, they would also pull in backward, ready for the next run.

Before she could even think about cleaning up and heading home, she would have to restock the ambulance and write a report. The ambulance must always be ready to roll out. More than once in the last year she'd returned from a call only to turn around and make another one.

"Hey, Sweet Pea."

She groaned and turned to see Kody loping toward her. "I told you not to call me that," she whispered. "Especially not here."

He gave her a contrite look. "Sorry, I forgot."

"What're you doing here anyway?"

"I left something in my locker and had to stop by and get it. My shift isn't until tomorrow."

Sally smiled. She couldn't help but be glad to see her older brother. Even if it was for a few minutes. He was a good one and she had no doubt he loved her. Sometimes too much. He tended toward being overprotective. But when she'd needed to reinvent her life, Kody had been there to help. She would always be grateful.

"I heard that Ross was the hero of the day this morning." He sounded excited.

"Yeah, you could say that." He'd scared the fool out of her.

"You don't think so?"

Sally started toward the supply room. "He could have been killed."

Kody's voice softened. "He knows what he's doing. I don't know of a better firefighter."

"He ran into a fully enveloped burning warehouse!" Sally was surprised how her voice rose and held so much emotion.

"I'm sure you've seen worse. Why're you so upset?"

"I'm not upset. It just seemed overly dangerous to me. Instead of one person being hurt there, for a moment I thought it was going to be two. He has a bad case of smoke inhalation as it is." She pulled a couple of oxygen masks off a shelf.

"How's he doing?" Kody had real concern in his voice.

She looked for another piece of plastic line. "He's at the hospital but he should be released soon. They were running a few more tests when I left."

"He's bucking for a promotion, so I guess this'll look good on his résumé. See you later."

"Bye." She headed back to the ambulance with her arms full. She had no interest in Ross's ambitions and yet, for some reason, his heroics had been particularly difficult for her to watch.

Ross returned to the station a week after the warehouse fire. He had missed two shifts. The doctor had insisted, despite his arguments. He liked having time to work on his ranch but the interviews for one of the eight Battalion Chief positions were coming up soon and he should be at the station in case there were important visitors. Now that he was back, he needed to concentrate on what was ahead, what he'd planned to do since he was a boy.

Thankfully the man he'd gone in after was doing okay. He would have a stay in the burn unit but would recover.

Just as Ross and his grandfather had. Ross rolled his shoulder, remembering the years' old pain.

He'd hated to miss all that time at the station, but it had taken more time to clear his lungs than he had expected. Still, he had saved that man's life. He didn't advocate running into fully engulfed houses, but memories of that horrible night when he was young had compelled him into action before he'd known what he was doing.

Memories of that night washed over him. He'd been visiting his grandpa, who'd lived in a small clapboard house outside of town. He'd adored the old man, thought he could do no wrong. His grandfather had taught Ross how to work with his hands. Shown him how to mend a fence, handle a horse. Most of what he knew he'd learned at his grandfather's side. His parents had been too busy with their lives to care. So most weekends and holidays between the ages of ten and fourteen Ross could be found at his grandfather's small ranch.

The night of the fire, Ross had been shaken awake by his grandpa. Ross could still hear his gruff smoke-filled voice. "Boy, the place is on fire. Get down and crawl to the front door. I'll be behind you."

The smoke had burned Ross's throat and eyes, but he'd done as he was told. He'd remembered what the firefighter who had come to his school had said: "Stop, drop and roll." Ross had scrambled to the door but not before a piece of burning wood had fallen on his shoulder. But the pain hadn't overridden his horror. He'd wanted out of the house. Had been glad for the fresh air. He'd run across the lawn. It had been too hot close to the house. Ross had coughed and coughed, just as he had the other morning, seeming never to draw in a full deep breath. He'd looked back for his grandpa but hadn't seen him. The fear had threatened to swallow him. His eyes had watered more from tears than smoke.

Someone must've seen the flames because the volunteer fire department had been coming up the long drive. Ross had managed between coughs and gasps of air to point and say, "My grandpa's in there."

The man hadn't hesitated before he'd run toward the house. Ross had watched in shock as he'd entered the front door. Moments later he'd come out, pulling his grandpa onto the porch and down the steps and straight toward the waiting medics. It wasn't until then that Ross had noticed the full agony of his back.

Both he and his grandpa had spent some time in the hospital. They'd had burns and lung issues. His grandfather had been told by the arson investigator that he believed the fire had started from a spark from the woodstove. Ross only knew for sure he was glad his grandpa and he had survived. Regardless of what had started the fire, Ross still carried large puckered scars on his back and shoulder as a reminder of that fateful night.

Last week, the moment he'd learned there was someone in the house he'd reacted before thinking. His Battalion Chief hadn't been pleased. Only because the outcome had been positive had Ross managed to come out without it damaging his career. He had been told in no uncertain terms that it wasn't to happen again. The message had been loud and clear: don't have any marks against you or you won't make Battalion Chief.

It was midafternoon when he was out with the rest of the company doing their daily checkup and review of the equipment that he saw Sal walking to the ambulance. Her black hair was pulled up away from her face and she wore her usual jumpsuit. She glanced at him and nodded. Memories of the look of concern in her eyes and a flicker of something else, like maybe interest, as she'd watched him in the hospital drifted through his mind.

Ross had known she was Kody's sister before she'd joined the house. Over the past year they had shared shifts a few times. With him working twenty-four hours on and forty-eight off and her not being able to work the same days as her brother, they hadn't often been on the same schedule. Still, he'd heard talk. More than one firefighter had sung her praises. A few had even expressed interest in her. They had all reported back that they had been shot down. She wasn't interested. There was some speculation as to why, but Ross knew, through Kody, that she was a divorcée. Maybe she was still getting over her broken marriage.

Swinging up on the truck, Ross winced. He had hit something, a door facing or a piece of furniture, on his way out of the burning house. At the hospital they had been concerned with the smoke inhalation and he'd not said anything about his ribs hurting because he hadn't wanted to be admitted. The pain was better than it had been.

He checked a few gauges and climbed out again. This time he tried not to flinch.

Sal came up beside him and said in a low voice, "I saw your face a minute ago. Are you all right? Are you still having trouble breathing?"

"No, I'm fine. I'm good."

She gave him a skeptical look as her eyebrows drew together. "Are you sure?"

"Yeah." If he wasn't careful, she'd make him see a doctor. Did she have that God complex firefighters joked about? The one that went: What's the difference between a paramedic and God? God doesn't think he's a paramedic.

She scrutinized him for a moment. It reminded him of when his mother gave him that look when she knew he wasn't being truthful. "You were in pain a second ago."

He'd been caught. She wasn't going to let it go. Had she been watching him that closely? He'd have to give that more thought later. "I have a couple of ribs that were bruised when I came out of the house."

"Did you tell them at the hospital?"

Now he felt like he had when his mother had caught him. Ross gave her a sheepish look. "No."

"That figures." She shook her head. "You firefighters. All of you think you're superheroes."

He grinned. "Who dares to say we're not?"

She just glared at him. "Feeling like one of those a minute ago?"

He relaxed his shoulders. "I've been wrapping it. I just have trouble getting it tight enough without help."

"You shouldn't be doing that. You need to stop that and just take it easy. Ribs take a while to heal."

"It's hard to do that when you have chores to do at home."

"Don't you have a wife or girlfriend who could help with those?"

"I don't have either." He'd never had a wife. Had come close once but it hadn't worked out.

"Come in here—" Sal indicated the medical area "—and let me have a look. Get rid of that bandage." She didn't wait for him, instead she walked toward the door as if she fully expected him to follow her orders.

Ross hesitated a moment, then trailed after her. He looked back over his shoulder. He didn't need any surprise visits from the bosses just when he was being looked over for more injuries. He hated showing any signs of weakness.

He rarely came to this side of the building. Sal was in the spacious room with a couple of tables and chairs, and a wall of supply cabinets.

She pushed a stool on wheels toward him. "Take your shirt off, then have a seat."

He couldn't do that! She would see his scars. He didn't completely take his shirt off around people for any reason. How to get around doing so had become a perfected art for him. The other morning at the hospital it had been a fight, but he'd convinced first the EMT and then the hospital staff it wasn't necessary to take his shirt off.

She left him to go to a cabinet across the room. Ross took a moment to appreciate the swing of her hips before he pushed his T-shirt up under his arms.

When she returned, she had a pair of scissors in her hand.

"Hey, I don't think you'll need those."

She smirked. "They're to cut the bandage if I need to." She then gave him an odd look but said nothing about his shirt still being on.

He explained, "It hurts too much to lift my arms."

She nodded, seeming to accept his explanation. "Your bandage is around your waist, not your ribs. It wasn't doing you any good anyway."

He gave her a contrite look. "I told you I'd done a poor job of it."

"You're right about that. It doesn't matter. I'm taking it off. And you're leaving it off."

"Is that an example of the tender care I've heard so much about?" Ross watched her closely.

Her gaze met his. "I save that for people who shouldn't know better."

One of his palms went to the center of his chest. "That was a shot to my ego."

She huffed. "That might be so but I'm stating truth. Can you raise your arms out to your sides?"

He winced but he managed to do as she requested. Sal

stepped closer. She smelled of something floral. Was it her shampoo or lotion? Whatever it was, he wanted to lean in and take a deeper breath. Her hands worked on the bandage, removing it; her fingers journeyed across his oversensitive stomach. He looked down. Her dark hair veiled her face. It looked so silky. Would it feel that way if he touched it?

No! What was going on? He'd never acted this way around any of the other women he worked with. He hardly knew Sal. She was the sister of one of his best friends. Was he overreacting because he'd not had a date in so long? Whatever it was, it had to stop. His sister wanted to set him up on a blind date. Maybe he should agree.

Sal gathered the bandage in her hand, stepped away from him and dropped the wad into a garbage can.

Ross couldn't help but be relieved, but he was disappointed at the same time. He lowered his arms.

"Okay, arms up again. Show me where you hurt."

With his index finger, he pointed to the middle of his left side. Sal bent closer. Seconds later, her fingers ran over his skin. "Does it hurt here?"

"Yeah."

"I can see some yellowing of the skin. You should've said something at the hospital." She straightened.

Why did she sound so put out? "You've already said that. Besides, the chest X-ray was clear."

She stepped closer. "I'm going to check you out all the way around."

In another place and time, that would have sounded suggestive. And from another person. He and Sal had never had that kind of interaction.

She ducked under his arm and stepped around to his back and then returned to his front before moving away.

Ross missed her heat immediately. He didn't even know her, and he was having this reaction. Why her? Why now?

"If that isn't better in a few days, you need to have another X-ray. You also need to take some over-the-counter pain reliever for the next few days."

Even in a jumpsuit more suited for a male, Sal looked all female. He must have messed up his mind as well as his side in that fire. These thoughts had to stop here.

Her quipping "You can pull your shirt down now" brought him back to reality.

Ross walked toward the door, tucking his shirt in as he went. "Thanks, Sal."

"By the way, I think what you did at that house was both brave and stupid."

# CHAPTER TWO

Ross didn't often get involved in the social side of the fire department but he was making an exception this time for two reasons. One, the annual picnic was a good place to take Olivia and Jared, his niece and nephew, while they were visiting. Two, it would be nice if he was seen by the bosses interacting positively with his fellow firefighters and the first responders at his station. He needed any edge he could get to gain the promotion.

The event was being held at one of the large parks in town. Not being a family man, Ross had only been to a few of them. There would be the usual fare of barbecue, baked beans, boiled corn and Texas-sized slices of bread. Desserts of every kind and drinks would also be provided. Along with the food were child-friendly games and crafts. Jared and Olivia were excited about the games. He was more interested in the menu; it was some of his favorite food groups.

Ross looked around the area for a parking space. The weather was clear. It would be a perfect day for the event. He scanned the vehicles to see if any belonged to the members of his station. Kody had said he would be there. Would Sal be with him? Why would he care about that? She'd been on his mind too much lately.

Ross enjoyed having the kids around. They came for

a weekend now and then, but this time they were staying for a little more than a week while his sister and her husband were out of town. Normally, they would have stayed with his parents but they were off on a cruise. He had sort of volunteered and then been asked to take them for ten days. On the days he worked, a friend's wife had agreed to watch them.

He pulled his truck into a spot in the already half-full parking lot teeming with people. Seconds later, Jared and Olivia were climbing out, their eyes bright with excitement.

"Yay, there's face painting. I want to go over there." Olivia pointed to a tent not far away.

"I want to go ride the pony," Jared said over his sister.

Ross raised his voice above it all. "Circle up here. We need to have a couple of ground rules. Number one, we stay together, and number two, we stay together. If I lose you kids, your mother and father will be mad at me." He grinned at them. "Got it?"

"Got it!" they chimed in.

"Okay. Why don't we go have lunch first, then we can make the rounds and do anything you like afterward?"

He raised a hand for a high five. Jared and Olivia enthusiastically slapped his palm.

They made their way to the buffet-style line that had formed under a large shelter and joined it.

The kids each held their plates as he served pulled pork onto their sandwich buns. While he was filling his plate with ribs, he looked across the table to see Sal taking some as well. How long had she been there? "Hey, I didn't see you over there."

This was the first time he'd ever seen her in anything but a jumpsuit. Today she was wearing a simple sky blue T-shirt that was tucked into tight, well-worn jeans. A thin belt drew his attention to her hips. She looked fit but not skinny. Her hair flowed down around her shoulders. This version of Sal was very appealing.

Her eyelids flickered and she said shyly, "Hi, Ross. I think you're a little busy to notice much."

"You're right about that." He looked for the kids and found there was a gap between him and them. He saw Sal's grin and forgot what he was doing. He hurriedly returned to picking out his ribs and moved forward. The kids each added a small bag of chips to their plates. When they were all finished, they picked out canned drinks from large containers filled with ice.

When Ross turned around after getting his, he noticed Sal pulling her drink out of a bucket next to his. It didn't appear anyone was with her. Their eyes met and she gave him a soft unsure smile. She looked away over the sea of picnic tables and walked away. Would she have joined them if he'd asked? Did he want her to?

"Come on, kids, let's see about finding a place to sit." He nodded forward. "Jared, head out through the picnic tables that way."

The boy did as Ross said and he and Olivia followed. As they moved along, a number of people he knew spoke to him. He called "hi" and kept moving. Finally, he saw Jared doing a fast walk toward an empty table. Relieved they had found one, Ross settled in for his meal.

He spied Sal weaving through the tables, obviously searching for a place to sit.

She came close enough that he raised his hand and called, "Hey, Sal, come join us. We have room."

Her face brightened at her name, but when she turned his way she looked hesitant, as if trying to figure out a way to refuse, but she came their way.

As she set her lunch down next to Olivia's and across from him, she said, "Thanks. Kody and Lucy are coming but they're running late." She looked around her. "There sure are a lot of people here. I had no idea that it'd be like this." She slipped her legs under the table.

"Austin's isn't a tiny fire department. The families really turn out for the picnic." What was happening to him? He didn't invite single women he worked with to join him for a meal. It was against departmental policy for firefighters and medical personnel at the same station to see each other. But this wasn't a date. He was just being nice.

He wasn't dating right now anyway. In college, he'd dated as much as any of his friends. During the early years of joining the department he'd done the bar scene with some of the other bachelors for a few years but that had got old fast. It was hard to see about the ranch and work his odd hours and keep that lifestyle.

Once he'd been serious about someone, but it hadn't worked out. She'd hated his schedule and had been afraid he might be hurt or killed. After a messy breakup, he'd decided to concentrate on his career and not worry about the aggravation of maintaining a relationship for a while. For now, he'd like to keep things casual, uncomplicated. Maybe after making Battalion Chief he would give serious thought to settling down. But that wouldn't or couldn't include seeing someone he worked with.

"I see." She glanced at Jared and Olivia. "I didn't know you had children."

Olivia giggled.

"This is my niece and nephew. They're spending a couple of weeks with me while my sister and her husband are out of town. Sal, this is Jared and Olivia."

Olivia gave her a curious look. "Your name is Sal? That's a boy's name."

"That's what your uncle calls me at work. My name is really Sally."

His niece wrinkled her nose. "I like Sally better."

Ross did too. It suited her. To think he had never really wondered what her full name was.

Sally looked down at Olivia and smiled. "You know, I do too."

That was interesting. Why didn't she ever correct anybody at the station?

Sally turned her attention to her food and the rest of them did as well. She handed over a napkin to Jared. Ross looked at him. He had barbecue sauce running down his chin.

The boy took it from her.

"Good sandwich?" Sally asked, smiling.

"Yes." Jared grinned.

"I can tell. Mine's good too."

"Uncle Ross's must be good too because it's all over his face." Olivia pointed to him.

They all laughed.

"He looks like a clown," Olivia blurted out.

They all broke into laughter again.

"What?" He wiped his mouth and looked at the napkin. There was a lot of sauce on it.

"It's still on there," Jared stated.

Ross tried again to clean his face.

"It's *still* on there," Olivia said with a giggle.

"You guys are starting to hurt my feelings." Ross liked the sound of Sally's laughter—sweet and full-bodied.

"Here, let me see if I can help you." Sally held up her napkin. "Lean toward me."

Ross did as she suggested as she shifted toward him. Their eyes met and held for a moment. There was a flicker of something there. Awareness, curiosity, interest?

Sally blinked and her focus moved on. A moment later she rubbed a spot on his cheek and sat back.

"She got it," Olivia announced.

However, she had left a warmth behind for him to think about.

"Jared," Sally said a little too brightly, as if she had been affected as well. "How old are you?"

"Nine."

"What do you like? Football? Baseball…?" Her attention remained on him as if she was truly interested.

"Soccer."

"Soccer. I've watched a few games but I don't know much about the rules."

Ross grinned as Jared lapsed into a full monologue about soccer playing. It hadn't taken long for Sal, uh, Sally to find the kid's sweet spot.

When he ran out of steam Sally was quick to ask, "Olivia, do you have something special you like to do?"

"I like to draw."

"Do you draw people, or animals or landscapes?" Sally took a bite of her sandwich while waiting for an answer.

Olivia wrinkled her forehead. "Landscapes? What's that?"

"Pictures of trees and grass," Jared offered.

"That's right." Sally gave him a smile of praise.

"No, I like to draw horses. I drew a picture of Uncle Ross's horses."

Sally's attention turned to him. She seemed surprised. "You have horses?"

"I do. I own a few acres out west of town."

"You need to come see Uncle Ross's horses sometime. They're beautiful." Olivia let the last word trail out. "Their names are Romeo and Juliet."

Sally smiled at her. "Are they, now?" She looked at him with a teasing grin on her lips. "Interesting names for horses."

"Hey, they were already named when I bought them."

She grinned. "So you say."

They returned to eating their meals.

As they finished, Olivia asked, "Uncle Ross, can I go have my face painted now?"

Jared turned to him. "And I want to ride the pony."

"We can't do both at the same time. Who's going first?"

Both their hands went up.

Sally covered her smile with a hand.

Ross looked at her and shook his head sadly. "I can handle a company of men at a fire with no problem but give me two kids."

Her look met his. "I think you're doing great."

She did? For some reason he rather liked that idea.

Sally pushed her plate to the center of the table. "Maybe I can help. I can take Olivia to have her face painted while you take Jared to ride the pony. We can meet somewhere afterward."

Ross looked at the children. "That sounds like a plan, doesn't it, kids?"

They both nodded.

He looked around. "Okay, we'll meet over there by the flagpole."

Sally stood. "Then we'll see you in a little while. Olivia, bring your trash and we'll put it in the garbage on the way."

To his surprise Olivia made no argument about cleaning up. Instead she did as Sally asked. As they headed toward the face-painting booth, Olivia slipped her hand into Sally's. She swung it between them.

Sally strolled with Olivia across the grassy area toward the activities. Ross's niece and nephew were nice kids. They seemed to adore him and he them. Her ex-husband, Wade, had never really cared for children. He'd always said he wanted his own but he'd never liked others', thought they were always dirty. More than once he'd worried they would get his clothes nasty when they were around. Thinking back, she didn't understand what she'd seen in him. How she'd even thought herself in love.

Wade had been the local wonder boy. Everyone had loved him, thought he was great. She had too, which was why she'd given up almost everything she loved to make him happy. They hadn't been married long when she'd learned he was having an affair. She'd tried to work it out but Wade wasn't going to change his ways. How had she been so oblivious? What she had thought was real and special had all been a lie. Finally, she'd filed for divorce.

Her judgment where men were concerned was off. All her trust was gone. Never would she be taken in like that again. She mentally shook her head. She wasn't going to ruin a nice day thinking about her ex-husband.

Half an hour later, she and Olivia were on their way to the flagpole. Olivia had a large fuchsia star on one cheek and smaller ones trailing away from it up across her forehead, along with a smile on her lips. Sally couldn't help but smile as well at how proud the girl was.

As they approached the pole, Ross and Jared walked up. The grin on Ross's face when he saw Olivia made Sally's grow. He had such a nice smile. Wide, carefree and inviting. She'd really been missing out on something special by never having seen it before. Most of their interactions had been working ones where there had been no time for smiles.

Ross went down on one knee in front of Olivia. "I love your stars."

Sally watched the similar-colored heads so close together. Ross would make a good father someday. "How was your pony ride, Jared?"

"It was fun, but not as much fun as riding Uncle Ross's horses."

"Can we go play in the jumping games?" Olivia pointed toward the inflatable games set up across the field.

"Yeah, Uncle Ross, can we?" Jared joined in.

Sally looked back at the crowd in line for food. Were Kody and Lucy here yet? She didn't want Ross to think he had to entertain her as well.

"Sure we can." Ross started that way with Jared and Olivia on either side of him. He glanced over his shoulder. "Sally, you coming?"

"Sure." She hurried after them. If he didn't mind, it would be nicer than just standing around waiting on Kody and his daughter to show up.

As Jared and Olivia played in the inflatable game with the net sides, she and Ross stood outside watching them dive and roll through the small multicolored balls.

After a few minutes of uncertain silence, she said, "Jared and Olivia are really sweet."

"Yeah, I think they're pretty great. Their mom and dad are raising them right."

"Is your sister older or younger than you?" She was more curious than she should be about Ross.

"I'm older, but sometimes she treats me like I'm the younger one. She worries about me being a fireman, or not being married. I know she cares but it does get old."

"I know the feeling. Kody likes to worry over me. My father encourages it as well. I don't know what I'd do without Kody though. He's the one who encouraged me to move out here. Best thing I've ever done."

Kody had told her that she needed to get away from the memories. More than once he had talked about how much he and Lucy liked living here. He'd even tried to get their parents to move out west as well.

"That's right, y'all aren't from around here. You moved out here from North Carolina, isn't that right?"

"Yeah, after my divorce Kody told me there was plenty of work for a paramedic out here. So I decided to come."

"Kody said something about you having been in a bad marriage. I'm sorry."

Sally was too. She didn't take marriage lightly.

"Hey, Aunt Sally."

She turned to see Lucy running toward her with Kody not far behind. Lucy reached her and wrapped her arms around her for a hug. Sally loved her niece. On Sally's days off she often helped Kody with Lucy. Occasionally he needed Lucy to stay over at Sally's while he worked his shift. Sally didn't mind. She enjoyed spending time with her niece. "Hey there. I was starting to wonder where you were."

Kody joined them. "Sorry, the birthday party Lucy was at went longer than I expected." He reached out a hand and spoke to Ross. "Hey, man."

Ross gave Kody's hand a hardy shake. "Glad you made it. Have you tried the ribs yet? They're great."

"Yeah, we just ate, then saw y'all down here. Thanks for taking care of my sister."

Heat went through Sally. She didn't need taking care of. She gave her brother a quelling look. "Kody!"

He acted as if she hadn't said anything as Ross said, "We saw each other and I invited her to eat with us. No big deal." Ross made it sound as if he was trying to explain keeping her out too late to her father.

"Daddy, can I jump?" Lucy pulled on Kody's hand.

"Sure, honey."

Lucy kicked off her shoes and entered the box. Soon she was busy having fun with Jared and Olivia and the other children.

A few minutes later the man monitoring the game told the children inside that it was time to give others a chance. The kids climbed out, put their shoes on and joined them.

Sally put her hand on Lucy's shoulder. "Lucy, I'd like for you to meet Jared and Olivia. Jared and Olivia, this is Lucy. She's my niece."

"Like Uncle Ross is our uncle," Olivia chirped.

Sally smiled at her. "That's right."

A man announcing over a microphone the relay games were about to begin interrupted their conversation.

"Can we go watch, Uncle Ross?" Jared asked.

"Sure. You guys going?" He looked from her to Kody.

"Why not?" Kody responded for them both.

They walked toward the field that had been set up as a relay course. A crowd was already lining up along each side of the area marked with lanes.

"The first race is the egg carry. Children only. Get your spoon and egg and line up."

All three of the kids wanted to participate.

Jared and Olivia were in lanes next to each other. Ross stood behind them. Lucy, with Kody doing the same, was in the lane next to them. Sally stood on the sidelines to cheer them on. The children put the handle of a plastic spoon in their mouth and sat the boiled egg in the other end.

The man said, "You have to go down and around the barrel with the egg in the spoon. First one back wins. Go on three. One, two, three."

The children took off. Olivia only made it a short distance before her egg fell out. She hurried to pick it up and place it in the spoon again. Lucy and Jared were already at the barrel. Not getting far, Olivia lost hers again. She looked at Ross, her face twisted as if she was about to sob.

With what looked like no hesitation, Ross hurried to her.

He went down on one knee and said something to Olivia. He offered her the spoon. She looked unsure but placed it in her mouth. Ross added the egg, then wrapped his arms around Olivia's waist and lifted her. He walked with a slow steady pace toward the barrel. Sally's heart expanded. Ross Lawson was a good uncle. They were way behind the others but the crowd cheered as Ross and Olivia rounded the barrel and headed for the finish line.

They were the last to cross the line but the people acted as if she was the first. Ross placed Olivia's feet on the ground and went down on a knee. The little girl dropped her spoon and egg, and turned around, beaming at Ross. She wrapped her arms around his neck and gave him a hug. What could have been a horrible memory for his niece, Ross had turned into one of joy.

Ross and Olivia joined their little group once more and they watched more of the races, cheering on people they knew.

A little while later the man with the microphone said, "Okay, it's time for the three-legged race. We're going to do something a little different this year to start out with. We need a male and female to represent each fire station. We're going to have a little friendly house-to-house competition. Pick your partner, and come to the line."

"Uncle Ross, you and Sally need to go," Jared said.

"Yeah, you need to," the girls agreed.

"I don't think so." Sally looked around for an excuse not to participate. She received no help from Kody, who just grinned at her.

"Someone does need to represent our station." Ross studied her.

"Go, Aunt Sally." Lucy gave her a little push.

She returned Ross's assessing look. Surely he wouldn't want to do it.

He said with far more enthusiasm than she felt, "Come on. Let's win this thing."

It figured Ross was competitive.

They hurried to a lane. Ross quickly tied the strip of cloth lying on the ground around their ankles. The entire time she tried not to touch him any more than necessary. She wasn't very successful. They met all the way up the length of their legs. Her nerves went into a frenzy when Ross's arm came around her waist. He felt so solid and secure. What was going on with her?

"Put your arm around me," Ross commanded.

With heart thumping harder than normal, Sally did as he requested. Her fingers clutched his shirt.

"Not my shirt, *me*." His words were teasing almost, but demanding, drawing her gaze to his face, which was fierce with concentration and determination. She bit back a laugh as her fingers gripped the well-founded muscle of his side.

"You really do want to win?" she murmured.

He glanced at her with disbelief. "Don't you? We start with our outside leg. You ready?"

"Uh, yeah?" She wanted to run for her car.

The man asked, "Runners ready?"

"Okay, here we go." Ross's voice was intense.

"Go!" the man said.

Ross called, "Outside, inside…"

They were on their way. He was matching the length of his stride to hers. Ross continued to keep the cadence as they hurried up the lane. She tried to concentrate on what they were doing but the physical contact kept slipping in to ruin it. When she tripped, his grip on her waist tightened.

"Outside, inside…" He helped her to get back in sync.

As they made the turn around the barrel, he lifted her against his body as if she weighed nothing. After they had swung around, he let her down and said, "Inside."

Her fingertips dug into his side. Ross grunted, but didn't slow down. His ribs must still be tender. She eased her grip and concentrated on their rhythm again.

The crowd yelled and Ross held her tighter, plastering her against him. They picked up speed.

Between breaths Ross said, "Come on, we're almost there."

Sally put all the effort she had into walking fast. They were near the line when Ross lifted her again and swung her forward with him. The crowd roared as they crossed the finish line. They stumbled hard and went down. Ross landed over her. They were a tangle of arms and legs and laughter.

Ross's breath was hot against her cheek. Her hands were fanned out across his chest. His arms were under her as if he had tried to protect her from the fall. As he looked at her, his eyes held a flicker of masculine awareness. Her stomach fluttered with a feminine response.

"Stay still. I'll untie us." His breath brushed over her lips.

"Well, folks, that was a close one," the man said.

"Aunt Sally, you won! You won!" Lucy's voice came from above her.

"We did?" she grunted as she and Ross worked to untangle themselves from each other.

Ross finally released their legs and stood. He had that beautiful smile on his face again as he offered her a hand. She put hers in his. He pulled her up into his arms and swung her around. "We sure did!"

"Oh." Her arms wrapped around his neck as she hung on. Just as quickly, he let her go. It took her a moment to regain her balance.

Lucy hugged her and Kody slapped Ross on the back. Jared and Olivia circled them, jumping up and down.

"You were great." Ross grinned at her with satisfaction.

She brushed herself off. "Thanks. You did most of the work."

"Okay, everyone," the man said. "There's ice cream for everyone before we have the stations' tug-of-war events."

"I don't know about you guys but I think Sal and I earned some ice cream," Ross said to their group.

"It's Sally, Uncle Ross," Olivia corrected him.

Ross looked at her. "Sally and I, then."

"I've always called her Sweet Pea," Kody quipped.

Sally groaned.

Ross glanced at her and beamed mischievously.

Sally started walking. The three kids joined her. She might never live this day down.

Ross spooned another bite of ice cream into his mouth. He, Kody and Sally were sitting at a table finishing their food while they watched the kids playing on the park playground equipment. The kids had become fast friends.

He looked at Sally. Her concentration remained on her bowl. She'd really been a trouper during their race. Yet by her expression he'd gathered she hadn't wanted anything to do with it. Was her silent objection to the race or running it with him?

His reaction to having her bound to him had been unexpected. That response had grown and hung like a cloud over them when they had been tangled in each other's arms. There had been a smoldering moment when she had looked at him with, what? Surprise? Interest? Desire? He was male enough to recognize her interest but smart enough to know that she was off-limits, for a number of reasons.

Sally was the sister of a friend. She worked with him. From what he understood she wasn't yet over her divorce and had no interest in dating. More to the point, she didn't strike him as someone who would settle for a fling. As for himself, he couldn't afford to have his mind or emotions anywhere but on his job right now. A real relationship would be a distraction, and something about Sally made him believe that she would be the definition of distraction.

Then there were his scars. More than once they had turned a woman off. A number of women he'd dated had expected a big, strong firefighter would be flawless, would look like a subject of a calendar. They had been disappointed by him.

Thankfully Kody asking him a question directed his mind to a safer topic. A few minutes later the announcer called the tug-of-war teams to the field.

Ross said to Kody, "Well, it's time for the fun to begin. We need to win this thing. I've heard about all I want to about how strong the Twos are." He raised his voice. "Come on, Jared and Olivia, it's time for the contest."

The kids stopped playing and started toward them.

Sally chuckled. "You're really looking forward to this, aren't you?"

"Oh, yeah. All I've heard from Station Two is how they won last year. I'm ready for payback. Do you mind watching Jared and Olivia while I'm pulling?"

"Not at all."

"Lucy too?" Kody added.

"Sure. I've got them all. You guys go on. I'll bring the kids."

He and Kody loped across the field to join the other members of the station. When they reached the part of the field where the tug-of-war would take place, Ross raised his hand. "House Twelve. Here."

Other station captains were doing the same. There was

a great deal of commotion as everyone located their fellow companies.

The announcer came on again. "Firefighters and first responders may I have your attention?"

The crowd quieted.

"This is how the competition is going to work. We've set up brackets by pulling station numbers out of a hat. Those will pull against each other. The winner will continue on to the next bracket until we have a winner. Now each house needs to huddle up and decide which six people from your station will be pulling. There must be at least one woman on the team. If your house doesn't have enough people present, then you may recruit from your family members. If you have any questions you need to see Chief Curtis up here. As always, he's our final word."

Using his "at a fire" voice, Ross spoke to the people around him. "Okay, Erickson, Smith, Hart, Kody and me. Rogers, you'll be our designated woman. Does that work for everyone?"

"Ten-four, Captain!" they cheered.

"Great. Now, get into position and get ready to give it all you've got."

Those who weren't chosen went to join those lining the tug-of-war area. Ross and his team moved to the large-diameter rope lying on the ground. A piece of cloth was tied in the middle of it. A chalk line had been drawn across the pulling area.

He glanced over to see Sally and the kids standing near the line. There was excitement on their faces. They all hollered, "Go, Twelves!"

Each team member picked up a section of the rope. Ross anchored at the back where a knot was tied.

The announcer said, "We have our first two teams. The Twelves and the Thirty-Fives. On the word *go* I want you to start pulling. You must keep pulling until the last man is over the line. Is everyone ready?"

"Ten-four!" both teams shouted.

Ross called, "Dig in, firefighters. Let's win this thing." He grabbed the rope tighter.

When the announcer yelled, "Go!" Ross pulled as hard as he could. The grunts of the others ahead of him joined his as they slowly walked backward. The shouts of the crowd encouraging them grew louder. Suddenly there was slack in the rope and he staggered to keep himself upright. They had won. The crowd cheered as his team turned to each other, giving each other high fives.

He would be in pain before the day was done with that much exertion. His ribs had objected when Sally had gripped his side during the three-legged race. With the pulling, they had spoken up loudly again. Still, he was going to do his part to win the tug-of-war. His team needed him. The key was not to let on he was hurting.

Sally and the kids joined him and Kody, giving them their excited congratulations.

Sal said, "Hey, kids, how about helping me get some bottled water for our team?"

"Okay!" all three of the kids agreed.

Sally and the kids hurried away and soon returned with arms filled with bottles. Those standing around took one. Ross finished his in two large gulps. With the next competition about to begin, they moved to the side to watch as the next two teams took the field.

Soon it was time to compete again. They won the next three pulls and were now in the final facing Station Two.

Ross lined up again with his team.

"Go, Uncle Ross, go!" Olivia yelled.

"Go, Twelves! You can do this!" Sally called.

Ross's heart pounded in anticipation as the announcer

said, "Go!" On that word he dug his heels into the ground and pulled with all of his might. His hands, arms and shoulders strained. The muscles in his legs trembled with the effort to move backward. Sweat ran into his eyes and still he pulled. His side burned. Clenching his teeth, he tried not to think about it. Concentrate was what he had to do.

The crowd shouted, voices mixing into a roar of encouragement.

Despite the pain he continued to tug. His legs quivered from the effort. Once, twice, three times the team was pulled forward. Only with strength of will did they remain steady and reverse the movement.

He dug deep within himself and called, "Let's take these guys."

With a burst of energy, Ross pulled harder. The others must have done so as well. They made steady steps backward.

Not soon enough for him the announcer said, "And the winner is Station Twelve."

A cheer went up. Ross put his hands on his knees and gulped deep breaths. The other members of the station surrounded them. A bottle of water appeared before his face. He looked up. Sally held it. She gave him a happy smile that made his already racing heart thump harder. All his efforts were worth it for that alone.

"You were great." Her voice was full of excitement.

Ross returned her smile. "Thanks. It wasn't just me. We did it as a team."

"Yeah, but you got them to give their all."

His ego expanded. He had to admit he liked her praise.

Others coming to congratulate him on the victory separated him and Sally.

As everything settled down, the announcer said, "Well,

that's all for this year's picnic, folks. We look forward to seeing you next year. Be safe on your drive home."

Everyone slowly drifted off. Their party started toward the parking lot.

"Can I ride piggyback, Uncle Ross?" Olivia asked.

He didn't think his body could tolerate it, but didn't want to disappoint her.

Before he could say anything, Sally suggested, "How about holding my hand?" Lucy already had one of them. "I think your uncle Ross is tired after all that pulling." She gave him a knowing smile.

"Okay." Olivia took it.

Thank you, he mouthed to her.

She nodded.

"We're down this way." Kody nodded, indicating the other end of the parking lot. He gave Sally a quick hug. "See you soon."

Lucy did the same. "Bye, Aunt Sally."

"I better head to my car too." Looking unsure, Sally let go of Olivia's hand. "It was nice to meet you, Olivia and Jared. I enjoyed the day." She started off.

"Hey, wait up, we're going that way too," Ross called.

Sally paused. Olivia took her hand again.

"We'll walk you to your car." Why he'd decided that was a good idea, he didn't know. Sally was fully capable of getting to her car by herself.

"Uh, okay."

He grinned. "You thought you'd get rid of us easier than that, didn't you?"

"I'm not looking to get rid of you." She glanced at him. Her cheeks were pink. "You know what I mean."

He chuckled, then immediately winced.

Her face turned concerned. "Are your ribs still bothering you?"

"You're not going to get all up in my face if I tell you yes, are you?"

Her lips drew into a thin line. "I might."

"Yeah, today's activity didn't help much." He didn't like people seeing weakness in him and for some reason it really mattered that she didn't.

"Have you been taking it easy, until today, that is?" She studied him.

He couldn't meet her gaze. "Well, I've been trying. How's that for an answer?"

She quirked her mouth to one side in disappointment. "When you get home, run a hot bath and soak. It'll help. You do know someone else could have taken your place in the tug-of-war?" There was a bite to her words. She wasn't happy with him.

He grinned. "Yeah, but what fun would that have been?"

She shook her head. "Men. Here's my car. Bye, Olivia and Jared. See you later, Ross."

He and the kids called goodbye and continued on.

Why did he miss her already?

As he was about to start the truck, there was a knock on his window. He jumped. It was Sally. She motioned for him to roll down the glass.

"Hold out your hand."

He did. She deposited some capsules.

"These'll help with the pain. Bye, Ross." She said the last softly.

Something sweet lingered as she walked away. Something better left alone.

# CHAPTER THREE

Two DAYS LATER Ross was in his chair in the office doing paperwork when the ambulance backed into the bay. He watched out the window as Sally came around to the rear of the ambulance. She looked tired. They had already made twice as many runs as the fire side had during the shift.

His company had spent the last few hours washing the trucks, checking the supplies and making sure the station was in pristine order. Now some of the men were in the exercise room working out while others were watching a movie in the TV room.

One of his men stopped at the open door and looked in. "Hey, Ross, it's your turn to cook tonight. Do we need to make a run to the grocery store or do you have what you need?"

Each shift shared kitchen duty. Some stations had one person who liked to do the cooking, while others had a revolving schedule and the crew took turns. His station shared the duty. They assigned two people per shift to handle the meal. His turn had come up. He wasn't a great cook but he could produce simple meals. Mostly he hoped to have someone more skilled than him as his partner.

"I'll check. Who's on with me?"

"Sal."

He'd planned to stay out of her circle as much as possible, spooked as he was by his over-the-top reaction to their time together at the picnic. Cooking a meal with Sally wouldn't accomplish that, but how could he get out of it without causing a lot of questions or hurting her feelings? No solution occurred to him, so he resigned himself to spending time with her. Surely he was capable of that.

During the last few weeks it seemed as if they had seen more of each other than they had in months. In spite of their one day on and two off schedules, he was aware she often worked extra hours in order to have extended time off. What did she do during that time? Why that suddenly mattered to him, he had no idea. He huffed. It wasn't his business anyway.

Ross again glanced into the bay, then back to the man. "They're just rolling in. I'll give her time to clean up, then go see what she thinks. They've already made a couple of runs this afternoon. I don't know for how much I can depend on her."

"Ten-four."

A few minutes later Ross crossed the bay to the door of the medical area. Sally was going through a drawer. "Hey."

She turned. "Hey."

"Tough shift?"

"You could say that. Two big calls back-to-back." She shrugged. "But you know how that goes."

She was right, he'd had those days as well. "I hate to add to it but we have KP duty tonight. I'd say I'd handle it, but I'm not a great cook."

Sally grinned. "You're not one of those stereotypical firemen who has his own cookbook?"

Ross chuckled. "No, Trent who works over at Tens does. I bought his cookbook to be supportive but that doesn't mean I know how to use it. I could see if one of the other guys wants to help."

"What gives you the idea I'm not any good either?"

He wasn't used to people putting him on the spot and gave her a speculative look. "Are you?"

Her eyes twinkled. "Yeah, I'm a good cook."

Ross wiped the back of his hand across his forehead. "Woo, that's a relief. If we need something, my crew can make a run to the grocery store."

"I have a couple more things to do here, so I'll meet you in the kitchen in a few minutes and we'll see what we've got available. Surely you can open some cans if I'm called out."

"That I can do." He left and headed toward the kitchen.

This was the first time they'd been partnered in any real way. They had each done their jobs during runs but had never really interacted until the picnic. He rather liked Sally. She challenged him even at creating a meal. He wouldn't have thought he would appreciate that kind of confrontation but he did.

He was already in the kitchen area when she showed up. "Any ideas?"

"Let's see what's in the pantry." She opened the over-size door off to the side and propped it open with a crate, despite the fact the closet was large enough to hold both of them with ease. Was she fearful of being in a closed space with a man, with him in particular, or was there something else? It was just as well he wouldn't ever take a chance on being caught in a suggestive situation with a female at the station. Having that on his record would ruin any chance for advancement. This promotion was important to him, his opportunity to make a real difference.

It had been while he was in the hospital after the fire that he'd decided one day he would help people as that firefighter had helped his grandpa. As soon as Ross had graduated from high school, he'd joined the same volunteer fire department that had saved them. He'd continued to do so while he was in college. After that, he'd joined the Austin Fire Department. He loved everything about being a fireman.

In some odd way, he was determined to outdo fire. To be smarter than it. Learn to anticipate its next move. He wanted to control, conquer it so no one else would ever have to live through those moments of fear he'd had.

Sally ran her fingers down the canned goods stacked on a shelf. "Yeah, I think we have enough here for vegetable soup. Corn, beans, chopped potatoes and tomato juice. Two tins of each should do it and we can always make grilled cheese sandwiches."

He pursed his lips and nodded. "That sounds good."

Ross stepped to the doorway but didn't enter. Their meal would have to feed six firefighters and two medical support techs.

"Is there any ground beef left over, or roast beef in the freezer or the refrigerator?" she asked as if she'd been thinking along the same chain of thought.

"I'll check." As he walked across the kitchen, he could hear the clinking of cans being shifted.

After rummaging through the freezer for a moment, he announced, "Yeah, there's two or three pounds of ground beef."

"Pull it out to thaw. It can go into the soup," she called from the closet before she appeared with her arms full of cans. She dumped them on the counter as he placed the beef in the sink.

"There's a couple more cans in there. Do you mind getting them?"

He went to the closet and retrieved the cans sitting off by themselves. "Are these them?"

"Yeah."

With his foot, Ross pushed the crate back into the pantry and let the door automatically close before going to the counter. He put the cans beside the others. "What now?"

Sal looked at him with her hand on a hip. "This is a partnership, not a chef/sous chef situation."

"I prefer the chef/sous chef plan." Ross grinned.

"You act as if you don't do this often."

He leaned his hip against the counter. "I don't, if I can get out of it."

"Okay, since you've designated me to be the chef, I'm going to put you to work. Start by opening all the cans. You're qualified on a can opener, aren't you?"

"I can handle that. It's electric, isn't it?"

Sally laughed. "Yeah. It is." She turned her back to him. "And they let him be captain of a company."

Ross pulled the opener out from under the counter. "I heard that."

Pulling a large boiler out from under the cabinet near the stove, she put it on a large unit and turned it on. Ross opened cans and set them aside as he covertly watched Sal uncover the still-frozen meat and place it in the pot. She worked with the same efficacy that she used in her medical care.

"So you just have that recipe in your head? Carry it around all the time?"

Sally glanced over her shoulder. "I made it for my family all the time growing up." She tapped her forehead. "I keep it locked away right here."

"Well, I have to admit I'm impressed. I had no idea you had such skills."

"I'm not surprised. We really haven't worked together much."

Ross sort of hoped that would change even as he sternly told himself, yet again, he wanted no interferences in his life right now. Socializing with a female he worked with would definitely qualify as that.

"It's nothing but meat and a few cans of vegetables." She turned serious. "But the secret ingredient is Worcestershire sauce. Would you mind checking the refrigerator door and see if there's any there?"

He did as she requested. "There's half a bottle."

"That'll be enough." Her attention remained on what she was doing. "We'll make it work. Is there any ketchup, by chance?"

Ross opened the refrigerator door again. "Yeah, there's some of that."

"Then bring that too."

"Ketchup?" He'd never heard of such a thing.

"It'll add a little thickness to it and also a little sweetness."

"You really are a chef."

"It takes more than ketchup soup to make you a chef."

A loud buzz followed by a long alarm then three shorts indicating it was their station being called ended their conversation. Ross was already moving as Sally turned off the stove and put the pot into the refrigerator along with the open cans.

As they ran down the hall toward the bay, the dispatcher's voice came over the loudspeakers. "Two-car accident at the intersection of Taft and Houston. One car on fire."

Moments later Ross was sliding his feet into his boots next to his crewmates. He jerked up his pants and flipped the suspenders over his shoulders. It took seconds for him to pull on his turnout gear that had sat ready on the bay floor. Grabbing his coat, he swung up and into the passenger seat of the engine, while the other firefighters got into their seats behind him. He secured his helmet with the strap under his chin.

One of his men was assigned the job of pushing the buttons to open the huge overhead door. The driver hopped in and they wheeled out of the station with the siren blaring. His company worked like a well-oiled machine. They were out the door in less than a minute. They had four to get to the scene. This economy of effort was another of his leadership qualities that hopefully would get him an edge on that promotion.

Sally and her crewman were right behind them. The traffic pulled to the side and stopped, allowing them to go by. At the lights they slowed then continued on. The goal was not to create another accident in their speedy effort to get to the first emergency.

As they traveled, Ross was on the radio with dispatch, getting as much information about the accident as possible. His heart rate always rose as the adrenaline pumped and thoughts of what to expect ahead raced.

They pulled up to the accident but not too close. Sally and her partner did the same. Ross's stomach roiled. The driver's-side door of one car was smashed. It had been the center of impact. The passenger door behind it was a mangled mess but standing open. A child-size jacket hung halfway out the door and a doll lay on the road.

Smoke bellowed from the hood of the other car and oil covered the area. His job was to get the fire contained and put out. Thankfully there was no gas spreading.

"We need a fire extinguisher up here. Spread for the oil."

As his men worked with the fire, he could see that at least the car seat remained intact inside the first car and the child was gone. Looking about, he could see Sally's partner assessing the kid, who looked about four years old. The bigger issue now would be getting the woman who was still wedged in the front out.

Another ambulance arrived.

Ross continued to give orders and his men moved to follow them without questions. They knew their duties and went to work. He moved closer to the car to see Sally climbing into the back seat.

"What do you need?" he asked.

She didn't look at him. "We're going to need the Jaws of Life to get her out. The car is crushed so badly the front doors won't open. I suspect the driver has internal injuries. We need to get her out right away."

Using the radio, Ross said, "Rob, we need the Jaws of Life. Jim, you help him."

The men rushed to the supply truck. Ross looked at Sally again to see her securing a neck brace on the woman. All the time she was reassuring her patient she would be fine, and her child too. He walked away long enough to see that everything was under control with the other car. The driver was sitting on the curb, dazed but otherwise looking uninjured. One of the EMTs from the second ambulance was seeing to him.

A couple of his firefighters were rerouting traffic along with the police.

He rejoined Sal as his men with the heavy-duty machine returned to the car. They inserted the mouth of the instrument into the area where the doors met and the machine slowly pushed the two apart. It took precious minutes. The metal creaked as it bent and groaned as it shifted. Finally, the firefighters were able to separate the doors.

"We need the gurney over here," Sally called, then said over her shoulder to Ross, "We'll need some help getting her on it."

Ross and another firefighter moved into position, while she and another EMT stood across from them.

"I want us to slowly move her out, scooting her along

the gurney." This was Sally's area of expertise and he would follow her lead.

Minutes later the patient was in the box with Sally in attendance and sirens blaring, headed toward the hospital. Ross and his company went to work seeing that the vehicles were loaded on wreckers and debris was cleared from the road.

By the time Sally finally made it back to the station kitchen, she found Ross stirring the soup, which bubbled gently on the stove. He was more talented than she had given him credit for.

"Hey, I'm glad you could join me. I thought I was going to have to take all the glory." He grinned at her. The kind that caused a flutter in her middle. Why him? Why now? He was a nice guy. The kind she might be able to trust. She shook her head. If it was another time in her life, she might be tempted.

She smirked. "Like I was going to let that happen."

"You were right. Looks like I can brown meat and dump cans of vegetables." He sounded pleased with himself.

"Turns out you have more talent than you let on."

"Some say that about other areas as well." His comment sounded offhand but she suspected there might be more to it. Was Ross flirting with her? No, that wasn't possible. What if it was? She had to stop thinking like that. There was nothing but trouble down that road.

Suddenly self-conscious, she cleared her throat. "So where were we before we were so rudely interrupted?" She pulled the loaf of bread that was sitting on the counter toward her. "I'll get the grilled cheeses ready. Everyone must be hungry." She started buttering bread.

"What're you doing there?"

"Making fast and easy grilled cheese sandwiches. Pull

out one of those large sheet pans, please." Sally kept moving the knife over the bread as she spoke. "Then get the sliced cheese and start putting it on the bread. We'll slip it into the oven, put it on broil, and we should have grilled cheeses in no time."

Ross went to work without question. Soon they had the sandwiches browning. "I'll get the plates, bowls and things while you go tell everyone soup's on."

"Are you always so bossy?" Ross asked as he exited the kitchen.

Did he really think she was dictatorial? She never thought of herself as being that way. Yet Wade had complained she was always on his case. Toward the end of their marriage, she guessed she had been. Wade hadn't ever been at home. More often than not he'd been between jobs; either it wasn't the right one or he was too smart to work with the people around him, or some other excuse. His parents had raised him to believe he could do no wrong.

She'd dreamed of being a doctor all through high school but after she and Wade had married he'd not wanted his wife going to school. He'd said school took up too much of her time. Time she could be spending with him. He'd never been a fan of her working as a paramedic, but she'd refused to give up volunteering when she'd been needed so badly by their rural community. That was the only thing she had defied him on. She had wanted their marriage to work.

Looking back, she could see how selfish Wade really was. That had certainly been brought home when she'd learned he was having an affair. But where she'd really messed up was not seeing through Wade before she'd married him. Her judgment had been off, so caught up in the fantasy rather than the reality. Next time, she'd be more careful about who she opened her heart to.

Ross returned with the other firefighters on his heels.

Over the next hour the company shared a meal, told stories and laughed. When the meal was over, she and Ross cleaned up, each thankful that most of the dishes went into the dishwasher.

Ross was washing the last of the pots when his phone rang. He shook off his wet hands and pulled the phone out of his pocket. He moved away from the sink and Sally stepped into his spot. She was tired and still had paperwork to take care of. Hopefully they wouldn't be called out anytime soon.

As she rinsed off the pan, Ross said with a disappointed note in his voice, "I'll work something out." He paused. "No, you can't help it," he said, before saying his goodbyes and hanging up the phone.

Sally hesitated to say anything, afraid it might be wrong, but didn't want to appear unsympathetic. "Everything all right?"

"No, not really. The lady I have watching Olivia and Jared while I work? Her mother has had an accident and Marcy has to go help her. That leaves me having to find someone to help me out."

"Would swapping shifts help?"

He was scrolling through the numbers on his phone. "Naw, I've got a meeting with the Chief. One I can't afford to miss." Ross spoke more to himself than to her.

"What day are you talking about?" Sally dried her hands on a dishrag.

"This Friday." He still wasn't giving her his attention.

"I'm not on the rest of the week. I have too much overtime. I'll watch them. If you don't mind Lucy joining us."

"Hey, if you'd do that it would be great. Jared and Olivia would love to have someone to play with."

"There's only one problem." She paused until she had his attention. "I don't think three kids are going to be happy overnight at my place. It's too small. I guess I could ask Kody if we could go there."

"Y'all can come to my place. There's plenty of room there. A lot of space outside to play. Plus, Jared's and Olivia's stuff is already there."

"Are you sure?"

He took the pot from her and put it under the cabinet. "Of course I am. You're doing me a favor."

Sally wasn't sure that going to Ross's house was a good idea. It seemed as if they were getting too friendly. Yet her place was so small and Kody's would be a little tight for three active kids as well. She didn't see another good choice. "That would probably be best."

He studied her a moment. "I'll owe you big-time for this."

"Don't worry about it. It sounds fun. The kids and I'll have a good time together."

"If you could come out around eleven, that should give me time to show you around then get to town in time to start my shift. I'll text you my address." He headed out the door.

"Hey, don't you need my number?"

He looked bashful. Cute, in fact. "I guess that would be helpful."

"You don't arrange childcare often, do you?"

"Nope." Ross grinned. "It's a fine art I'm just now learning."

She gave him her number. He punched it into his phone, then he was gone.

# CHAPTER FOUR

SALLY HAD MADE a serious mistake by agreeing to watch Ross's niece and nephew. Doing so was another step into further involvement in Ross's life. Being together at the picnic had revealed she was far too attracted to him. An attraction she neither wanted nor needed. She must stay focused. Still, she liked the guy. The last time she'd been this enamored with a man, she'd been devastated. That mustn't happen again. She wouldn't allow it. The upside to the day's arrangement was that Ross would be at work the entire time.

And she would be with the kids…

In his home. His personal space. She hadn't thought that through either. She would be where he lived. Touching, sitting and sleeping among his personal belongs. No, she hadn't considered that part of this agreement at all. She should have done so before she'd blurted out her willingness to help. Yet helping out a fellow firefighter went with being a member of that family. It was just what a team player did in an emergency situation.

Ross had texted her his address as promised. Sally had picked up Lucy from Kody's house on her way to Ross's. Lucy had been so excited about seeing Jared and Olivia again she couldn't get in the car fast enough. The idea of an overnight stay had heightened her anticipation. She'd chatted most of the way about all the fun they would have. Sally certainly hoped so. The closer she came to Ross's house, the tighter Sally's nerves knotted. She hadn't acted this way over seeing a man in a long time. Control—she needed to get some over her wild emotions.

The drive was ten miles out of town to where the land rolled gently, the trees were tall and the fields green. When she had moved to this part of the country, it hadn't taken long for her to fall in love with Texas. Even though she liked her apartment, she wished she could find a place with more outdoor space.

The day was beautiful with the sun shining in a blue sky as she turned the car off the two-lane highway onto a dirt lane. On either side were fenced pastures with a few trees here and there. The lane ended at a white clapboard house with a porch along the front. Large oaks shaded one side and the lawn surrounding the house was neatly mown. Behind it there was a small red barn with a couple of horses in the corral.

She sighed. When she got her medical degree, this was just the type of place she would look for. There was something restful, comforting about it. A place someone could find contentment. She loved everything about it, immediately.

When she'd taken Kody up on his suggestion to move to Texas, she'd realized how right he'd been. She'd had no trouble getting a job and there had been something cathartic, cleansing, about leaving all the ugliness of her marriage behind and starting over again. It had taken some time, but she'd finally settled in, had decided on a plan and was now focused on seeing it through.

Soon after arriving in Austin, she'd enrolled in college and finished her degree. Sally smiled. To think she was studying to take her MCAT now. If she did well enough, she hoped to enter medical school in the fall, while continuing to work part-time at the firehouse when she could. She wasn't going to let anyone or anything divert her this time.

As she climbed from the car, Ross stepped out of the beveled glass front door.

A warmth washed over her. Especially not a man with striking blue eyes and a hunky chest.

He came to stand beside a wooden post of the porch. He wore his usual fire station uniform of navy pants and T-shirt with the department logo on one breast. Practical work boots completed his attire. He appeared healthy and fit. His welcoming smile made him even more handsome than she remembered. Her stomach quivered. She had to get beyond this fascination with Ross. Still, couldn't a girl enjoy a moment of admiration for a man?

He drawled, "I see you found us."

Returning his smile, she gathered her purse. She'd bring in her MCAT study books after he'd left. Lucy had already hopped out of the car and gone to meet Jared and Olivia, who were in the side yard.

Ross came down the wide steps. His agile movements reminded her of a panther she'd once seen in a zoo. "Are you ready for this?"

"What if I said I wasn't?" She glanced at him as she gathered Lucy's and her overnight bags.

He grimaced. "I don't know what I'd do."

She grinned, looking at the kids. "I'm going to be fine. We'll all be fine."

"Here, let me get those for you." He reached for the bags.

"Thanks." His hands brushed hers and she quickly pulled away. The physical contact had intensified her growing nervous tension.

They walked side by side to the house. Happy laughter from the kids filled the air. Ross moved ahead of her and hurried up the steps. Tucking Lucy's bag under his arm as he reached the door, he opened it and held it. She strode by him, making sure they didn't touch. If they had, would he have felt the same electric reaction she had when their hands had met?

The room Sally entered was dim and it took a moment for her eyes to adjust. Only a few feet inside the door, she looked around the large open space. The high ceiling was supported by dark beams. The walls were a cream color complemented by a gleaming warm wooden floor. It was furnished with a brown leather sofa and two armchairs along with an old chest she assumed he used as a coffee table. A TV hung over the mantel of a stone fireplace.

In the back of the house was the kitchen. A large bar separated it from the living area. A table for four sat to one side. Windows filled the corner, giving a beautiful view of the barn, trees and the fields beyond. Everything was neat, but masculine.

This was a man's abode. Ross's. Sally shivered. She had truly entered the lion's den.

Ross set the bags down beside a door to a small hallway and walked farther into the house. "Come on in. Let me show you around. As you can see, this is the kitchen." He pointed toward the hallway. "Over there are two bedrooms. Jared and Olivia are in them. Olivia has the one with the twin beds so there's an extra bed for Lucy. On the other side of the house is my room. The sheets on the bed are clean. Ready for you."

Her breath caught. Her eyes widened. Finally she blinked. "I, uh, think I'll just sleep on the sofa. That way I'll be closer to the kids in case one calls out." Spending the night in Ross's bed would be far too...personal? Uncomfortable? Nerve shaking? Lonely? Whatever the word was, she wouldn't be doing it.

"I want you to be comfortable. I think you'd be happier in a bed. It's the only one I have that's available." He shrugged. "But all that's up to you." She made no comment and he continued, "You can find all kinds of movies and games in the cabinet beside the fireplace. The kids know where everything is."

She nodded.

"I've already ordered pizza for dinner tonight. It should be delivered at six. Right, here's the tip." He tapped some bills on top of the counter. "My number is on this pad if you have any questions, anytime."

Sally moved closer to look.

"There should be plenty of sandwich fixings in the refrigerator. I also have peanut butter and jelly. Chips. And drinks."

Her smile widened as she softly laughed.

His look turned serious. "What's so funny?"

"You are."

"How's that?" He watched her too close for comfort as if he didn't want to miss any change in her expression.

"Firehouse Captain turned Mr. Mom."

He chuckled. One that started low and rough then slowly rolled up his throat and bubbled out. "I do sound a bit that way, don't I?"

"You do, but it's nice to know there're supplies, I'll give you that. Thanks for taking the time and thought to make it as easy as possible for me."

"You're welcome." He picked keys up off the counter. "I'd better get going."

She followed him out onto the porch.

"Oh, I forgot. Could you see that the horses are fed tonight and in the morning? Jared knows what to do." He moved to the porch railing and called, "Jared and Olivia."

Both children stopped playing and looked at him. "I don't want you giving Sally any trouble. If she needs help, you do so. No argument about bedtime either."

"Yes, sir," they called in harmony.

He smiled and nodded. "Good. I'll see you tomorrow."

"Bye, Uncle Ross." Olivia waved.

"Yeah, bye," Jared said as an afterthought as he ran for a ball.

Ross turned to her. "I really appreciate this."

"You've already said that."

"I know, but I do." He walked to her, stopping just out of reach. His gaze met hers. A spot of heat flushed through her middle that had everything to do with his attention. "Well, I'll see you tomorrow around one." He went down the steps.

"Okay."

He hadn't made it to his truck before he said, "Call if you have any questions."

"I will." Sally wrapped her arm around the post he had stood beside earlier and leaned her cheek against it. She watched him leave. Ross put his hand out the window and waved. She stayed there until he was out of sight.

What would it be like to have someone who wasn't eager to leave her? That she could say bye to who would look forward to returning to her. At one time she'd believed she had that. Instead Wade had acted as if coming home to her was a chore. Why had he married her if he hadn't really wanted her? In less than a year he had been off with someone else.

She wanted a man who desired her. That she was enough for. Maybe one day she would try again, but that wasn't going to happen anytime soon. She had plans, dreams.

That was what she should be thinking about. She was better off without the obstacle of a man in her life for the time being.

Yet here she was seeing to Ross's niece and nephew. At his house. When he'd driven away, it had seemed as if they were husband and wife and she were seeing him off to work. But that wasn't reality. She was the babysitter and nothing more. And she didn't want anything but that.

Lucy interrupted her troubling thoughts with, "Aunt Sally, we're hungry."

"Well, it's about lunchtime. Come on in."

The kids stomped up to the porch.

"Let's go see what we can find in the kitchen."

After lunch they returned to playing. The pizza Ross had promised arrived just as he'd said it would and they ate it picnic style under one of the oak trees.

The sun was low as they finished then went to feed the horses. Jared took the lead. First, he turned on the hose to add water to the trough. Sally grinned at his puff of importance as he went into the barn to get grain. He returned with a gallon tin can full and let each of the girls dump a part of the feed into two buckets for each of the horses.

As Lucy took her turn, she hit the rail with the end of the can. It went flying and landed in the water trough. She gasped and tears filled her eyes.

Sally placed a hand on her back. "It's okay, hon. We'll get it."

"I'll do it." Jared started pulling his shirt off.

Sally looked at him in dismay. "What're you doing?"

"It'll get wet if I don't take it off." He handed her his shirt, then leaned into the trough far enough that his head almost touched the water. When he straightened pulling the can out, the water inside spilled all down his front.

Sally laughed. "Obviously you knew what was going to happen."

Jared grinned, dropped the can on the ground and took his shirt from her. "Yeah, we drop it in almost every time we visit."

"How come a boy can take his shirt off and a girl can't?" Lucy asked.

This wasn't a discussion Sally wanted to get into, especially with other people's children. She just had to keep the answers simple. "Well, because boys and girls are different. Especially when they get older."

"Uncle Ross is a boy and he never takes his shirt off," Olivia announced. "Not even when he's swimming."

What was she to say to that? "Guys don't have to take their shirts off if they don't want to."

"When it's hot I like to take mine off." Jared picked the can up and headed for the barn.

Olivia's statement left Sally curious. She'd have thought a man with Ross's physique should be proud to show it off.

Lucy took Sally's hand. "Sometimes when I'm playing with the water hose, I take mine off."

It was time to change the subject. "Let's go get a bath and have a snack before bedtime."

By just after dark, Sally had all the kids in bed. She wasn't sure who was happier, them or her. She'd had less active days at work. Plopping on the couch, she stretched out her legs, letting her head rest on the pillowed leather behind her. Sally closed her eyes and sighed. She and the kids had had a nice day. They were a good tired and she was as well. While she was trying to convince herself to get up and do some studying, her phone rang.

Digging in the back pocket of her jeans, she fished it out.

"Hey, how's it going?" Ross's rich voice filled her ear.

Her heart did a little pitty-pat. "We're doing great. Have you been worried about us?"

"More about you. Two kids can be a handful so I can imagine three's more difficult."

He had been thinking about her? "Everybody's fine. They're all in bed now." She yawned.

"I bet you're thinking about going as well." The timbre of his tone suggested ideas better left locked away. She sat straighter. "I'll be up for a little while longer."

"I really thank you for this."

It was nice to feel useful to a man to whom she was attracted. For so long she'd felt unworthy. In the end duped and rejected. "You don't have to keep saying that. How did your meeting with the Chief go?"

"Really well."

He'd asked her some personal questions, so she felt entitled. "Do you mind if I ask what's going on?"

"No. It's just that I'm on the shortlist for Battalion Chief. I've been trying to make a good impression. Not being there when the Chief's making his rounds wouldn't have been good."

"You'll make a great Battalion Chief." Of that she had no doubt.

"I don't have the job yet."

"Maybe not yet, but you'll get it." He was good at his job and others noticed. She certainly had.

"The competition is pretty strong. I've worked with all of them at one time or another."

"I can't imagine anyone being more qualified than you." And she couldn't.

"Thanks, Sal, for that vote of confidence. It means a lot." Ross's voice held a note of gratitude.

She couldn't stem her curiosity about him. "Have you always wanted to be a firefighter?"

There was a pause. "Yeah, ever since I was a little boy."

"That's a long time." Her amazement rang in her voice. They shared something in common. They both had known what they wanted to do since they were young.

"I'm not that old." He chuckled.

"You know what I mean. What made you want to be a firefighter?"

This time he didn't falter before answering her. "I saw firefighters at work when I was a kid and I decided then that I want to help people like they did."

She almost said *aww* out loud. "That's very admirable. Was it a bad fire?"

"The worst. My grandfather's house was a total loss." His voice had grown rougher with each word.

She could tell that it had been a life-changing event for him in more than one way. "Oh, Ross. I'm sorry. I hope he was all right."

"He was. He rebuilt. You're sitting in his house now. He left it to me when he died a few years ago. I've made some updates."

Sally looked around. "I like your house. I want something like it one day."

"I'm happy there." There was a pause, then he said, "Tell me something, are you going to sleep in my bed tonight?"

Heat flowed hot and fast throughout her body. Her mouth went dry. Ross coming on to her. She liked it.

The buzz of the fire station alarm going off, then the dispatcher speaking, was all she could hear for the next few seconds.

"Gotta go," Ross said. "See you tomorrow." More softly, as if a caress, he finished with, "Take care, Sweet Sally."

"Bye," she said into an empty line. Sweet Sally? She liked the sound of that coming from Ross.

* * *

Ross neared the end of the drive to his home with keen anticipation. He was coming home to someone. Was his life really that isolated? Not until this moment did he realize how much he liked the idea of having someone waiting on him at home. He'd looked forward to seeing Sally and the kids. Hearing how their time together had gone.

He grinned. Maybe now he'd get an answer about where she'd spent the night. It still shocked him that he'd dared to ask. Had called her Sweet Sally. After all, she was doing him a favor and he'd hit on her. He hoped things wouldn't be strained between them now. He should have kept that question to himself. In a twisted way he was relieved to have been out on a run most of the night. At least he hadn't had time to think about her in his bed—without him.

He'd put taking a real interest in a woman on the back burner for so long his reaction to Sally was unsettling. Did he dare take a chance on her? Gambling on how a woman would respond to his scars, he'd kept most of them at arm's length. He'd let Alice in but that hadn't ended well either.

Maybe it was time for him to think about more than his job. Still, the idea of living through major rejection again struck him with fear. Was it Sally in particular or just that it was time for him to try again that had him thinking this way?

He parked his truck next to Sally's car, then grabbed his duffel bag.

The kids were playing right where they had been when he'd left the day before. They called hello as he climbed the steps. A fireman's schedule with the staggered hours had always seemed like a difficult schedule for a family to live around but there was something nice about the idea of having children. What had caused that idea to pop into his head? He'd been satisfied with Jared and Olivia's visits and hadn't thought of having his own children in a long time.

These days he was having all sorts of odd thoughts.

As he entered the house, he was tempted to call, "Honey, I'm home," but he didn't think Sally would appreciate his humor. An amazing aroma filled the air. There was food cooking in the oven. Sally's back was to him as she chopped something.

Her hair was pulled up in a messy arrangement, yet it suited her. She wore a flowy top of some kind and jeans. There were sandals on her feet. There was nothing special about her clothes, yet the combination made her appearance fresh, simple and disturbingly sexy.

Music played softly from the radio. She swayed and hummed along. It was strangely erotic. His blood heated. He wanted to walk up behind her and pull her back against him. Leave her in no doubt of his need for her. How would she react to him kissing her neck?

Not a good idea. At all. Tamping down his desire, Ross cleared his throat. "Hey."

She turned and smiled. "Hey. I didn't hear you come in."

He walked toward her, sniffing. "I'm not surprised. What's that wonderful smell?"

"My father's favorite meat pie. I thought since we've had sandwiches, pizza and cereal that we should have a real meal. We voted to wait on you."

He could get used to this. "Are you saying what I left wasn't nutritious enough?"

She shrugged. "I'm not complaining. I like to cook and it's nice to do it for more than just myself."

"You're welcome to cook for me anytime." He met her look and held it.

Her gaze turned unsure as she said, "Will you call the

kids in and tell them to wash their hands while I get this on the table."

"Sure thing. Let me put my bag up first." Yes, he liked coming home to Sally, the kids and a meal. He sure did.

Picking up his bag, Ross went to his bedroom. Sally hadn't slept there. Nothing had been moved and he had no doubt that her scent would have lingered. For some reason these days his body picked up on every detail of hers despite his best effort not to notice. The idea she had slept on the sofa bothered him. She should have been comfortable at his house.

Stepping to the bath, he saw that she hadn't been in there either. He didn't know much Shakespeare, but he did think maybe the woman did "protest too much." He grinned. Maybe she was more affected by him than she wanted to admit.

He went outside to call the kids. After a good deal of noise and shuffling around, including adding a chair to the table, he and the kids were seated. Sally placed a bowl of salad on the table and joined them.

He looked at Sally. Her face was rosy from being in a warm kitchen. Tendrils of her hair had come free and fallen across her cheek. She pushed at them with the back of her hand. She was lovely. "It looks wonderful, Sweet Sally."

Olivia giggled. "It's just Sally."

He waved his hand over the table. "Don't you think she's sweet? She did all this for us. I sure do."

The kids chorused their agreement.

Sally giggled and her color heightened. "Thank you."

This was a real family moment. The type of thing he'd not given a thought to having in a long time. He liked it. Found himself wanting it more often.

The kids spent the rest of the meal talking about all they had done while he was gone. Sally remained quiet, listening and smiling. Not once did she make eye contact with him, despite the fact he was sitting across from her. Was she afraid of what she might see or what he might find in her eyes? He'd have to give that more thought.

After their meal was over, she said, "Kids, please carry your plates to the sink, then you may go back out and play. Lucy, we'll need to be leaving soon."

They did as she asked without an argument, which Ross couldn't believe. When they were gone, he turned to her. "How do you do that?"

She stood and picked up her plate. "Do what?"

He gave her an incredulous look and pointed with his thumb over his shoulder. "Get them to do something without back-talking?"

She shrugged and carried the plate to the sink. "I'm a woman of many talents."

"I don't doubt that." Some of those he'd like to explore.

Sally began filling the dishwasher. Ross brought the rest of the dishes off the table to her. They finished straightening the place together.

"We make a pretty good team in the kitchen." Ross returned the dishrag after wiping the table off, trying to keep his mind off the other things they might be good at together.

Sally dried her hands and hung the dishcloth on a knob. "Seems that way."

Ross noticed a stack of books at the end of the bar and walked over to see what they were. He placed a hand on them. "Are these yours?"

"Yes." Sally picked them up and hugged them against her chest as if protecting them. "I don't want to forget them."

"This says MCAT on it. Are you studying to take the

test to be a doctor?" He didn't even try to keep his surprise out of his voice.

"Yeah. I'm trying to get into medical school."

He leaned a hip against the counter. "I'm impressed. I had no idea." How had he not heard talk at the house? "Is it a secret?"

Sally shook her head. "No."

Apparently, he'd been so caught up in his wish of being Battalion Chief he'd not noticed that about her. What kind of boss would he be if he didn't see more outside of his own world? He needed to do better. "So, when's the test?"

"Two weeks from today."

"Good luck."

"I'm afraid I'm going to need it."

"I doubt that. I think you'll make an amazing doctor." And he did. The more he knew about Sally, the more captivated he was by her.

Her eyes were bright. "Thanks for that. I hope I do."

He gave her his best encouraging look. "I've no doubt you will."

"Thanks, that's nice to hear. I've always dreamed of being a doctor."

"Is this your first time taking the test?" Ross was far too interested in her life, but he couldn't stop himself from asking.

"Yes."

"Why haven't you done it before now?"

"My husband didn't want me to go to school. He wanted me to be there when he came home."

Something close to anger boiled within Ross. The dirtbag hadn't even supported his wife's dreams. Kody had said he was a jerk, but Ross had had no idea how big of one.

Ross heard the laughter of the kids. "I'm sorry. I'm sure you didn't get much study time here."

"I did some this morning while the kids were playing. When I get home, I'll go at it hard. Only thing is that they're replacing the siding on my apartment complex, so I'll have to work around that. Speaking of going, Lucy and I need to be doing that."

Ross was reluctant to see her leave. He found he really didn't like that idea.

"You're welcome here anytime. I mean, it's quiet here. You can come out anytime, whether or not I'm here."

"I don't know..." She looked uncertain.

He raised a hand. "Hey, just know the offer's there if you need it."

"Thanks. That's kind of you." She gathered her books and left them at the front door before she stepped outside and called, "Lucy. We have to go now."

"Do we have to?" Lucy whined.

"Yes. Your daddy's expecting you, and I have studying to do."

Ross joined her with her bags in hand.

She grinned at him. "So much for my talents."

He laughed. She reached for their belongings. "I'll carry them to the car."

The kids came up on the porch.

Olivia pointed her small finger toward the rustic star nailed over the door on the beam above his and Sally's heads. "Look, Uncle Ross, you and Sally are standing under the Texas star. You have to kiss her!"

Ross had forgotten about the star. It was a game he'd been playing with Olivia since she was a baby. Before she left from a visit, he gave her a kiss under the star.

"When you're standing under the star, you have to kiss the one you're with. Isn't that so, Uncle Ross?" Olivia gave him an expectant face.

Sally's eyes had grown wide. "What?"

Ross spoke to Olivia. "Yeah, but that's between you and me. It's not for everyone."

"But you kiss Mom and Grandma under it," Olivia insisted.

"I, uh, don't think that's necessary." Sally took a step away.

"That's not what you said, Uncle Ross," Jared said. "You said you must always tell the truth."

"I did say that." He was caught in a trap and he was afraid Sally was as well. He looked at her. "You wouldn't want me not to be a man of my word?"

"It seems I have no choice." She didn't sound convinced. In fact, she acted as if she'd like to run. Yet she put the bags down and placed her books on top of them.

He took her hand and led her back to where they had been standing under the star. She must have been in shock because she offered no resistance. He placed his hands on her waist. Their looks met. He said softly, "You do know it won't be a fate worse than death, don't you?"

"I'd like to think so."

He kissed her, stopping any further words with his mouth. Her lips were soft and warm. Everything he had imagined and more.

Sally's hands came to his waist and clutched his shirt as if she needed him as a stabilizer. After the first seconds of indecision, she returned the kiss. His body hummed as his hands tightened with the intention of pulling her closer. This kiss was too sweet, too revealing, too little. It had quickly gone from an intentioned friendly kiss under the star to one of passion.

"Ooh."

"Ick."

"Ugh…"

The sounds coming from the kids made him draw back.

Ross looked into Sally's eyes. She appeared as shaken as he. He registered the shiver that ran through her. Sally broke from his hold and he didn't stop her.

"Lucy, we need to go." There was a quiver in Sally's voice as she grabbed her books.

He reached for the bags before she had time to pick them up and followed her to the car. She opened the door and without looking at him said, "You can just throw those in the back seat."

"Will do. Thanks again for helping me out."

"You're welcome. Lucy, buckle up." Seconds later she and Lucy were ready to go.

Ross stood out of the way as Sally turned the car around and headed down the drive. He watched her go with his body still not recovered from their kiss. By the way Sally had acted, she'd been as affected as he had been. One thing was for sure, he wanted to kiss her again. If he had anything to say about it, it would happen again—soon.

# CHAPTER FIVE

FEWER THAN THREE days had passed but that wasn't enough time for Sally to erase the memory of Ross's lips against hers. In fact, she'd relived those moments over and over to the point where it had disrupted her study schedule. Yet another example of how letting a man into her life again could derail what she really wanted. She had to put an end to the daydreaming.

Doing well on the MCAT was too important. Instead of focusing on questions and the correct answers, she had been thinking of the tingling sensation having Ross's arms around her had generated and the throbbing in her center as he'd kissed her. She'd been aware of their attraction but had had no idea how electric it was until his lips had touched hers.

Would Ross try to kiss her again? She had to stop thinking about him.

She had to focus on her studies, work around her emotions as well as the construction being done on her apartment complex. With air hammers going off constantly and the banging of siding falling, she'd quickly learned she couldn't get any studying done at home.

She'd tried waiting until the workmen quit for the day but that had left her studying well into the night. Once, she'd gone to a coffee shop but even there she had become too distracted. The library had been her last resort, but the chairs weren't comfortable after an hour or two. She needed her own little nest, a place to spread out her books. What she wanted was for the work on her apartment complex to be completed, but that wasn't going to happen anytime soon.

Now she was dragging her books into the fire station, hoping it would be a slow shift so she could get some studying time in. Pulling her bag out of the car, she headed inside. She groaned long and deep. Ross's truck was in the parking lot. He was working today. She took a deep breath, trying to settle her heartbeat.

Unfortunately, he was the first person she saw. The living, breathing diversion in her life. To make matters worse, she ran straight into him as he circled the back of the engine while she walked between it and the rescue truck. He grabbed her shoulders, but quickly let go and stepped back. Even that brief touch was enough to set her blood racing.

"Are you okay?" His eyes searched her.

"I'm fine," she answered around a yawn.

He studied her closer. "You sure? You look tired."

"Thank you. That's what every woman wants to hear." Her voice was overly haughty.

"Hey, that wasn't a criticism, but concern."

She shifted her bag. "I'm sorry. I'm just a little on edge. And tired. It's not your fault. I shouldn't take it out on you." Though some of it *was* his fault.

His voice turned sympathetic. "What's the problem?"

"I've been trying to study and they're working at my apartment complex. It's so noisy during the day I've been staying up late at night. I've taken all next week off to study but I don't see things getting better. I've got to find someplace quiet to concentrate."

"I told you you're welcome out at my place."

Sally's breath caught. What was he suggesting?

Ross must have seen her look of astonishment because he hurriedly raised a hand. "Hey, it's not what you're thinking. I have to be at the training center all next week. So I'll be working eight to five. The kids are with my parents now. You'd have some peace and quiet to study. By the time I come home in the evenings, they should be done for the day at your place."

It did sound like a doable plan. An exceptional one. "That's really nice of you. But I can't put you out like that."

"You won't be putting me out. I won't even be there. How could you disturb me?"

Ross made it sound as if she would be stupid not to agree. It'd be better than skipping around from one place to the other trying to get some real studying done. Just the thought of sitting on Ross's porch swing as she worked had its appeal. Yet...

She shook her head. Things between them were already too... She couldn't put a word to it. Didn't want to. Going to his house again would only make them more involved. "I don't know. I'm sure I'll figure out something."

"This is what I'm going to do. I'll leave a key under the mat. If you want to go, go—if you don't, don't. Just know you're welcome."

One of the firefighters called out to him.

"See you later, Sally."

He didn't give her another look, as if they were two old friends and didn't have that kiss hanging between them. Maybe it hadn't been as big a deal to him as it had been to her.

After doing her usual shift routine, she managed to get in a few hours of study before the intercom buzzed and the station was called out on a run.

She and Ross shared no conversation outside of what

was essential during the accident. She left at noon the next day and returned home to find the construction trucks parked in front of her building. She ground her teeth. This just wasn't the time in her life for this. She had to find some quiet. It would be another week of bangs and clangs but now they would be right outside her walls. Her test was only four days away. She'd taken time off work to cram all she could into her brain but how much of that could she get done here?

The idea of sitting on Ross's swing with a breeze blowing and the horses in the pasture popped into her mind. The image was too sweet. She might ace the test if she studied there.

When Ross had suggested she go to his house, she'd had no intentions of doing so, but with the men working on her building in particular it seemed silly not to. If she timed it right, she could arrive just after Ross left for the day and leave before he came home. The worst that could happen was that he'd come home early. Then she'd make an excuse and leave.

The next morning Sally loaded all her books and notes into the car and headed out of town. She needed quiet and Ross's place offered that. If it meant she had to push away her anxiety over using his place to get quality time in her books, then she'd manage it. The bigger picture was more important. Just turning up his drive eased her nerves.

His home looked just as inviting as it had before. She climbed out of the car. More than that, it sounded as serene as she had hoped. The only noises were from chirping birds and the occasional snort of a horse. Filling her arms with books, she climbed the steps to the porch. She placed her armload on a small table near the swing.

Going to the door, she glanced at the star hanging above and refused to give it any more thought. Doing so would waylay her plans for the day. She didn't have time for *what ifs* and *maybes*. All her plans, dreams and hopes were concentrated on what would happen on Saturday. She must be prepared.

Just as Ross had promised, the key was under the mat. Unlocking the door, she filled a large glass with water, returned outside and set the glass on the table. She picked up a book and settled on the swing. Using the big toe of one foot, she gradually started it to moving.

Time passed quickly and it was soon lunchtime. She'd brought her food and enjoyed it on the porch. Needing to do something to give her mind a rest, she decided to cook Ross dinner in appreciation for giving her this great place to study.

She found enough in the pantry to put together a small chicken casserole and a dessert. Leaving a note of thanks for Ross on the counter, she made a list of items to buy on the way home for tomorrow's meal and returned to studying.

The next days passed much as the first one. By Friday afternoon, Sally felt confident about the test ahead. She'd managed to get a great quantity of quality studying done. She'd be forever grateful to Ross.

His truck came down the drive as she was on her way to the car to leave. Her breath caught and her heart beat a little faster. He was early.

Ross pulled up beside her, his window down. "Hey, I was hoping I'd see you before you left. I wanted to wish you luck."

"Thanks. I could use all I can get. I really appreciate you letting me come out here. I don't know what I'd have done if I hadn't."

He put his arm on the window opening and leaned out.

"Hey, I'm the one who should be thanking you. The meals have been a nice treat. I'll miss them."

"You're welcome. It's the least I could do." She opened her car door.

"How about sharing dinner with me tonight?" His words didn't sound as confident as she would have expected them to.

Sally considered it for a moment. She was tempted, but she needed to keep her focus. Get a good night's sleep. Be prepared for tomorrow. Not be distracted. And Ross was undoubtedly a distraction. "Thanks, but I'd better not. I need to get home. Get ready for tomorrow. I have an early morning and even longer day and I still have notes to check." Now she was overselling her decision.

"I understand. Maybe another time." There was a note of disappointment in his voice.

"Maybe." She couldn't afford to give him encouragement. Or herself any either. She moved to get into the car.

"Good luck tomorrow. I know you'll do great."

She gave him a tight-lipped nod as she climbed into her car. "I sure hope so."

He called, "Hey, Sweet Sally, I have faith in you."

She liked that idea. Wade had never encouraged her or made her feel confident. That Ross did bolstered her spirit. She felt special. Something she hadn't experienced where a man was concerned in a long time.

Ross had spent the day doing chores around the place and wondering how Sally was doing on her test. Why it mattered to him so much, he had no idea. Possibly because he knew it mattered to her. He was beginning to care too deeply for Sally. The last time he'd let someone in it had ended badly but for some reason he couldn't seem to resist Sally's pull.

He was glad that he could help her by giving her a place to study. The meals had been a pleasant surprise each evening. It had been fun to guess what would be waiting on him next. He feared he could get too accustomed to having a hot meal waiting on him. He'd probably gained five pounds over the week. Because of Sally his home seemed warmer and more inviting.

More than that, knowing Sally had been thinking about him had gotten to him on a level he didn't want to examine. Damn, he had it bad. He was starting to think like a sappy teenager.

What he should be doing was thinking about being Battalion Chief, planning what he wanted to say at his interview. He would tell the review committee that he wanted to use the position to help implement new and innovative firefighting techniques. He knew personally what fire could do to a person's life and he wanted to make positive changes where he could. For Austin to become a world-renowned department who used cutting-edge practices. As a member of the higher ranks, he could help make that happen. Maybe help keep a boy and his grandfather from ever being hurt in a fire. He hoped to help change the department for the better and, more important, save lives. That was what getting promotions had always been about for him since he'd started working at the fire department.

Finished with all he had planned to do for the day on the ranch, and thinking through his ideas for the interview, Ross still couldn't get Sally out of his mind. That afternoon he cleaned up and drove into town. He went by the farm supply store to pick up a few items. After making a couple more stops, he ended up at the fire station. Kody was working. Maybe he had heard from Sally. Just how long did one of those tests last?

He and Kody leaned against Ross's truck talking about

nothing and everything. More than once Ross was tempted to ask him about Sally but stopped himself. He didn't want to be that obvious about how involved he was in her life.

"Lucy had a great time at your house the other day. Sally said she enjoyed it as well. I had no idea you were such a family man." Kody grinned.

He'd enjoyed their time together too but he wasn't going to let Kody know that. "I don't know about that. I'm pretty sure Sally got the short end of the stick. She did all the work. Three kids to watch is a handful."

"From everything she said, she had fun. She couldn't say enough about how much she liked your place." Kody sounded as if he were making casual conversation but for some reason Ross questioned that.

"Yeah, she came out this past week to study while I was at the training center."

Kody gave him a speculative look. "She didn't tell me that."

Ross shrugged. "She said she needed a quiet place to study, and I offered."

Kody's eyes narrowed. "She didn't say anything to me. Didn't ask to use my place."

It was Ross's turn to grin. "You don't expect her to tell you everything. You do know she's a grown woman?"

"Yeah, but I'm her big brother. It's my job to know what's going on. She's had a hard time of it."

"Little overprotective, are you?" Ross would be as well if Sally belonged to him. That wasn't going to happen. He couldn't let it. Still…

Kody huffed. "She says the same thing." He gave Ross a direct look. "I'm just concerned about her. She's been hurt badly in the past. I'd hate for her to go through that again."

Ross held up a hand. "Hey, you're jumping the gun here. We're just friends."

"I'm just sayin'—" Kody's phone rang and he pulled it out of his pocket, looking at the number. "Speak of the devil." Into the phone he said, "Sweet Pea." There was a pause, then, "Yeah." A pause. "Really? Call the auto club and have it towed in. Can you get a taxi home? I hate it but I'm at work."

"What's going on?" Ross asked. He sounded more concerned than he should have.

Kody studied him a second. "Sally's car won't start."

"I can go." He was already heading to the driver's door.

Kody looked a little surprised. "Okay." He said into the phone, "Ross is coming after you." There was quiet. "No, he offered. He's right here. He should be there in about twenty minutes. You get in the car and lock it. Don't open it for anyone except the tow driver or Ross."

"Tell her to stay put. I'm on my way. You text me the address." Ross hopped into his truck.

Ross shouldn't have been as happy as he was that Sally was having car trouble but it gave him an excuse to see her.

He made the drive in less than twenty minutes. Sally's car was parked near a walkway into a large glass-and-brick building on the Austin State University campus. There were only a few other cars in the lot. She was waiting in the car just as Kody had told her. When he pulled up, she got out. Wearing a light blue button-down shirt, jeans and ankle boots, Sally looked younger and more vulnerable than he knew she was.

She gave him a weak smile. "I appreciate you coming."

"Not a problem. I was at the house when you called. What seems to be wrong?" Sally looked exhausted, as if she had been through the mental mill.

"I don't know. It just wouldn't start. I've called the auto club and they're on their way but it'll be another forty minutes or so."

"Do you mind giving it a try?"

"Okay." She turned the key. The engine just made a grinding noise.

Ross opened the hood and moved the battery cables. He leaned around and called, "Try it again."

The car acted as if it wanted to come to life, then nothing.

Ross closed the hood as he shook his head. "You just got all my mechanical knowledge."

This time she grinned. "I guess it's a good thing the tow truck is on the way."

"Come on over to my truck and we'll wait there." He held the passenger door open for her.

Sally acted reluctant for a moment but gathered her purse and joined him in the truck.

Once inside he turned so he could see her face. "So how do you think you did on your test?"

She sighed deeply. "It was harder than I thought it would be. I don't know how I feel about it. I guess all that's left to do is cross my fingers."

He crossed his. "Mine'll be as well."

Sally rested her head back on the seat and closed her eyes. "I'm just glad it's over. I'm exhausted."

"When was the last time you had something to eat or drink?"

She opened her eyes to slits. "We had a lunch break, but I was too nervous to eat much."

"You stay put. I'm going to that convenience store across the road to get you a drink and something to eat. When we've taken care of your car, we'll stop and get you something more substantial." He opened his door and climbed out. "Lock the door while I'm gone. I'll be right back."

Sally murmured something but he suspected she was already half-asleep.

Ross made a quick walk across the parking lot to the store. When he returned, Sally was just as he'd assumed she would be—sound asleep. Her chin hung to her chest and she softly snored. Climbing in as quietly as possible, he gently put an arm around her shoulders and brought her head to his shoulder. She settled against him. Everything about the moment seemed right.

He pushed his disappointment away when all too soon the tow truck arrived. "Sally, wake up. The tow truck is here."

She moaned and burrowed closer to him, all warm and sweet.

"Sweet Sally, come on, wake up."

"What?" She blinked, looking perplexed.

"The tow truck is here."

She quickly sat up and shifted away. "Oh, yeah. Sorry."

"No problem."

She scooted out her door. He stepped out, joining her and the tow driver.

Half an hour later they were back in his truck and on their way.

Ross glanced at Sally. "I'm going to get you something to eat. Do you have a preference?"

"I want a big juicy burger." Just as she answered, thunder rumbled. The sky had been slowly darkening.

"Consider it done."

Ross pulled into the first fast-food place he came to and into the drive-thru line. While they were waiting for their food, the wind picked up. Thunder rolled and lightning flashed in the sky off to the west.

"Sally, I know you've had a tough day but would you mind if we run out to my place for just a moment before I take you home? The horses are out and in this weather they get nervous. I hoped it would go north of us but it doesn't look like that's going to happen."

He handed her their bag of food as she answered, "I don't mind. With a nap and a burger, I'm ready to go. If I'm not, I need to learn to be, if I want to be a doctor."

She'd already finished her sandwich by the time they were on the outskirts of town. Ross glanced at her and grinned. "Good?"

There was no repentance in her smile. "I was starving."

He chuckled. "Would you like to have my other one?" Ross held up a second burger, still in its wrapper.

"No, that's not necessary," she said in a sassy tone. "But I'll have some of your fries if you aren't going to eat them."

"Well, that figures." He placed his container on the seat between them.

"What do you mean?" Her complete attention was on him. He liked it that way.

"They're the best thing you can order at that place. I like my fries super crispy."

"I do too." She plopped the last one of hers into her mouth and reached for his.

As they turned onto his drive, large raindrops hit the window shield. Angry lightning split the sky.

"Looks like it's going to be an ugly one," Sally said. "These are the kind of days that go by so fast at the house you don't know if you're coming or going. More traffic accidents than you can count."

Ross laughed and pulled the truck to a stop. "I've had more than my share of those days too. This shouldn't take long. The key is still under the mat. Make yourself at home. I'll be back in just a few minutes."

Sally watched Ross sprint off around the house toward the barn. The rain was coming down harder. Thunder and lightning were filling the sky in a regular rotation as she ran to the porch. She opened the door, going in and turning on a light. Stepping to the large picture window at the back of the house where the table was located, she searched for a glimpse of Ross at the barn.

She continued to look out the window as the storm grew. The rain fell hard enough to make it difficult to see. Minutes ticked by, enough she started to worry something had happened to Ross. Just as she was about to go out after him, he came through the back door in a burst of wind and water.

Grabbing a dish towel, she hurried to him and handed it over.

"Thanks." Ross took it and wiped his face.

"A tree came down on the fence. The horses are out. I've got to go after them and fix the fence. I'm sorry about this. You're welcome to stay here, or I can call you a taxi?" He pulled a kitchen closet door open. Rubber coats hung inside it. On the floor were mucking boots. Ross grabbed a jacket and boots, then went to a chair and started putting on the high-top rubber shoes.

Sally picked up a pair as well.

"What're you doing?" Ross gave her an incredulous look.

"I'm going with you." She sat at the table and started removing her shoes.

Ross returned to gearing up. "You don't need to do that. You've already had a long day."

"I'll survive. You don't even know where the horses are. You're gonna need help."

Ross opened his mouth.

"I wouldn't even bother arguing. I'm going." She pulled on a boot. It was too large but she would make do.

He grinned. "Figures."

As he shrugged into his coat, she picked out one and did as well.

"Ready?" Ross took two large flashlights off the shelf in the closet.

Sally pulled the cap up over her head. "Ready."

He nodded and opened the door.

She could hardly see with the storm blocking what little of the sun was still up. The angry sky made what light there was a spooky haze of yellow green. At least it wasn't completely dark. She didn't want to go crazy in front of Ross. Her silly childhood fear wouldn't impress him. At least having the flashlight would help her keep her sanity.

The rain blew sideways as she braced herself against the wind. It didn't take long for it to blow her cap back. She would just have to get wet. Ross headed toward the barn. She followed. As they went, she saw one of the giant limbs from the oak in the side yard had fallen on the fence.

"What're we doing in here?" Sally shook her coat as she entered the barn, relieved to get out of the wet for a moment. Her hair was drenched and the front of her jeans soaked.

"I wanted to get a couple of halters and leads." Ross went into a small tack room.

"Where do you think we'll find them?"

He called out to her as he moved around in the room. "I don't know. If the fence was up, I'd say in the trees out in the pasture. With the fence down, I'm not sure. I'm going to try out by the road first. I can't afford for them to cause an accident. In this weather cars can't see them."

Ross's concern was evident in his voice. He soon joined her again, carrying what he had come after. He handed her one of the halters. "This won't be a fun trip."

"I've done un-fun things before. Ready when you are."

She wasn't going to let him stop her from helping, especially after he'd done so much for her.

"Hopefully they didn't go far." He had a resigned look on his face as he lowered his head and left the barn.

Sally joined him. He led the way down the drive. The wind let up some but the going was still difficult as they trudged along with their flashlights moving in a back-and-forth pattern in the hopes of seeing the animals. As they came to the paved road, there was still no sign of the horses. She could sense, by the hunch of his shoulders, Ross's frustration and concern. He moved the beam of light wider.

"I'm going to check those trees across the road," he shouted.

"Okay." She joined him and pointed her flashlight that way. There, standing under the trees, were the horses.

They sidestepped as if nervous as she and Ross approached.

Ross put his hand out, indicating she should hang back. He slowly approached them.

Sally could imagine him speaking softly to them. She'd bet he did the same when he made love. Ooh, she needed to concentrate. Thoughts like that did nothing to keep Ross in the friend slot where she had placed him.

Ross waved her forward. He handed her a lead attached to the halter on Juliet and took the halter she carried. She'd been right. He talked to Romeo the entire time he worked. It was solid and reassuring. Something she missed in her life.

"Ready?"

She nodded.

"Hold the halter and the lead." He demonstrated. "If there's more lightning, they may balk. They're pretty skittish."

Sally made sure to place her hands in the same position that Ross used. She'd been around horses some but never under these conditions. As Ross had suspected, the sky did light up again. Both Romeo and Juliet jumped and flinched but she managed to keep Juliet under control. Romeo reared but Ross soon calmed him.

"Let's get them in the barn." He started toward his place and she kept pace.

They made it to the barn without any more mishaps. Being in the dry again was like heaven. Slinging her wet hair out of her face, she looked at Ross. He was every bit as wet as she and it only made him look sexier.

He grinned. "Well, I'm glad that's over."

Sally couldn't agree more.

Ross led Romeo into a stall. She waited. He soon joined her and took Juliet to another stall.

When he returned this time he said, "I'll still have to go out and see about the fence. Do you mind giving them a couple of cups of oats? You'll find it in the tack room."

"I'll take care of them." Sally pushed at her hair but a strand stuck to her cheek.

Ross, using a finger, moved it away from her eyes. Their gazes met. "You were great out there, Sweet Sally." His hands went to her waist and he pulled her to him. "What would I do without you?"

For a second she thought he might kiss her. Thought how it would warm her from the inside out as a hot drink did on a cold night. This close, Ross smelled of rain, earth and healthy male. Alive.

But instead he let her go and left the barn, leaving a honeyed heat coursing through her veins.

Ross had expected Sally to go to the house when she'd finished with the horses but instead she stayed outside to help him. He had pulled the truck over so he could use the headlights to work by. Thankfully the rain had eased.

As he used the chain saw to cut limbs off the tree branch that had broken the fence, Sally pulled the debris out of the way. Wet and with the high pitch of the chain saw ringing in their ears, they worked side by side. They soon had the worst of it off the fence.

Ross cut off the saw. "Why don't you go on in the house and clean up? I have to get some tools and get this fence back into place. I'll finish the cleanup later. I'll be in soon."

"I can help you." She kept pulling limbs.

Was there anything that Sally couldn't do or wouldn't do? She was a special person. He put the saw in the shed and found the tools he needed to repair the fence. When he returned, she was still cleaning up the area.

Ross started removing the broken barbed wire.

Sally came to him. "What can I do to help?"

He picked up a tool. "Do you know how to handle a claw hammer?"

She lifted her chin. "I sure do."

He'd given up on encouraging her to get out of the weather. "Then go to the next post and start taking out the staples."

While he worked on replacing the wire on his post, Sally went to the next one. He joined her and she moved on to the next one. She was good help but he wasn't surprised by that, though he was thankful. Because of her he wouldn't be out all night repairing the fence.

An hour later she held the wire as he hammered the last staple into place.

"That'll do it until morning." Ross picked up his tools.

"Give me those. I'll put them away while you move the truck." Sally reached for the toolbox.

Ross let her have it and off she went to the shed. He

found her again just inside the kitchen door, struggling to remove her boot. "Hey, let me help you with that. Hold on to the counter and I'll pull it off for you."

"It has been winning." She leaned her butt back against the counter, held on and lifted her foot.

Ross tugged and the boot slipped off. "Okay, the other one."

Sally lifted her other foot. He pulled that boot off as well and dropped it on top of the first one with a thump.

"You want help with yours?" she asked.

"No, I can get them." He started working his boot off. "What I'd really like is for you to head to the shower."

"I know you're used to giving orders—"

"All I want is for you not to get sick. I'll bring you some warm clothes to put on."

She put her hands on her hips and gave him an indignant look. "I'm made of stronger stuff than that."

He grinned. "I've no doubt of that, but just so I don't have to worry, humor me. Please? You're welcome to my shower or you know where the spare one is."

Sally glared at him for a second, then turned and walked toward the guest bathroom.

Disappointment jolted him. He wished she'd chosen his—with him in it.

Ross shucked off his clothes in his bathroom and pulled on a pair of shorts and a T-shirt. Going to his chest of drawers, he found a T-shirt and sweatpants for Sally.

He knocked on her bathroom door. The sound of running water reminded him that the only thing between him and a naked Sally was the door. He swallowed, then called, "There's some clothes on the floor for you."

"Okay, thanks."

Ross returned to his bathroom, turned on the shower to cold instead of hot.

\* \* \*

When he came out to the living room again, he didn't expect to find Sally lying on his couch asleep. He shouldn't have been surprised. She'd had an emotionally hard day taking a life-changing test, then to have car trouble, wrangle horses and fix a fence in a storm. She'd withstood more than most and remained in a positive mood as she'd done them all. She had the right to fall asleep.

He quickly checked the station schedule on his phone to make sure she wasn't on duty the next day, then went to the spare bedroom to turn back the covers. Back in the living room, he lifted Sally into his arms, noting how slight she was for a woman with such a strong will. He carried her to the bed, covered her up and tucked her in. After a moment of hesitation, Ross placed a kiss on her forehead. "Thanks for all your help, Sweet Sally."

Ross had had hopes for a more satisfying kiss tonight. He had to admit he was disappointed. But Sally needed rest. He went to the kitchen looking for a snack. Opening the refrigerator, Ross searched it for some ideas. As usual, there was little there but he did have one more plateful of the last casserole Sally had made for him. He dished it out, warmed it in the microwave and sat down to watch a sports show.

Between shows he started their dirty clothes in the washing machine. He rarely had women's clothes joining his. There was something intimate about his and Sally's clothes comingling. Erotic and right at the same time.

Before going to bed, he went out to check on the horses. They were secure but thunder rolled in the distance. They were in for another round of bad weather. Inside again, he looked in on Sally. She was sleeping comfortably on her side, her hands in a prayerful manner under one cheek. Leaving the door ajar, Ross went to his room. He climbed into bed. Would he be able to sleep knowing Sally was just steps away?

Sometime later the sound of screaming jerked him awake. For a moment Ross was disoriented until he remembered that Sally was across the house. His eyes darted to the alarm clock on his bedside table. It was blank. The electricity was off. A scream ripped the air again. This time he had no doubt it came from Sally.

Rushing across the living room, he worked his memory not to stumble into the furniture. Too late he realized he hadn't paused long enough to pull on shorts or a shirt. He was only wearing his boxers. There was no time to turn back. Sally needed him.

Another shriek caused ripples down his spine. She sounded terrified.

Lightning flashed and he could see her huddled against the headboard. Her head was down in the pillow she clutched to her chest. She was sobbing and shaking in panic like a wounded animal.

He took a few steps into the room. "Sally, it's Ross." He kept his voice low so as not to scare her further. "I'm right here. Everything's okay. You're at my house. The electricity is off."

Lightning lit the sky once more.

Her eyes opened. There was a wild look there. They remained unfocused. She didn't recognize him. He moved to the bed. "It's Ross. It's going to be okay. I'll get some candles."

She gripped his forearm, her fingers digging in. "Don't go! Don't leave me."

The fear in her voice went straight to his heart. This was a side of Sally he'd never seen. He suspected few had. "Sweetie, I'm just going after candles. I'm coming right back."

"No." Her grip tightened. He'd have fingernail marks in the morning.

Ross sat on the bed and pulled her into his arms. Rocking softly, he said soothing nothings to her just as he had to the horses earlier. Sally seemed to ease. "I won't leave you."

Why was Sally so scared of the dark? She'd always acted so invincible.

He couldn't leave her, but they couldn't stay here all night. The bed was too small for both of them. If either one of them was going to get some rest, they had to go to his bed.

"Sally, I'm going to get up now. I'm going to carry you to my room. Hold on."

She made an unintelligible sound as he stood and lifted her into his arms. As she clung to him, he picked his way to his room without any missteps. He placed her on the side of the bed he'd been on and tucked the covers around her. Even in the darkness of the room he could see that her eyes were shifting from side to side with distress. "I'm going after candles. Just into the bath. I'll be right back."

In a weak voice she whined, "You won't leave me?"

"Sweetie, I'd never leave you. I'll be right back."

He hurried to the bathroom to gather the fat candle and matches he kept there for power outages. Placing the candle on the bedside table, he lit it. That little bit of light in the dark room removed most of the fear from Sally's eyes.

"Hold me." The words were low and sad.

She didn't have to ask him twice. He slid under the covers beside her and pulled her close. She shifted into him, sighed and her breath soon became warm and even against his neck.

# CHAPTER SIX

SALLY WOKE TO the sun shining through the window of a room she didn't recognize. Her back was against a solid wall of heat. She moved her hand. Her palm brushed across coarse hair on the muscled arm around her waist.

A shiver of panic ran through her. Slowly glimpses of waking in the dark, terror absorbing her, Ross coming to her, then him carrying her to his bed settled in her mind.

Oh, heavens, she'd begged him to hold her.

Could she have embarrassed and humiliated herself more? She was a grown woman afraid of the dark. At her house she was prepared for events like the one last night. She always had a flashlight next to her bed and one in the kitchen and living room. In an unfamiliar place, she had come undone. How was she ever going to face him?

The mattress shifted beneath her. It was going to happen sooner rather than later. She moved to slip out from under Ross's arm.

"Sally, are you awake?" His voice was rusty from sleep, making him sound terribly sexy. Worse, he sounded worried about her.

How was she going to explain her bizarre behavior?

She continued to slide across the sheet until she was out of touching distance and as far away from him as the bed would allow. She was grateful it was king-size. She put her feet on the floor and turned from the waist to face him. At least she was still wearing the T-shirt and sweatpants he had loaned her. That gave her some armor in this uncomfortable state of affairs.

Ross quickly pulled on a T-shirt. The bedsheet covered his lower half. He was decent, yet she was too aware that moments earlier she had been in his arms, against his bare chest. He lay on his side with his head propped on his hand, waiting and watching her.

"Mornin'," he drawled, as if it were a regular occurrence to have her in his bed.

"Good morning." Sally paused. She must be the one to address the elephant in the room. Adjusting her position for comfort while searching his face, she reluctantly added, "Thanks for helping me last night. I guess you're wondering what happened."

"I'd like to hear the why, but right now I'd like to know if you're okay." He watched her too closely. As if he was gauging her emotional stability.

"Yes, yes, I'm fine, except for being extremely embarrassed." She glanced out the window to the side of the house. From here she could see the damaged part of the fence and the barn. The sky was clear. It all looked so peaceful now. A complete one-eighty from the upheaval in her.

"I'm sorry I had to bring you to my bed. I hope you haven't taken it the wrong way. We both wouldn't fit in that smaller bed and you wouldn't let me go. We needed someplace to sleep."

Heat washed through her. The best she could tell, the section of his bed they had been sleeping on was approximately the same size as the bed in the other room. Had she moved next to him? Or had he stayed close to her? It didn't matter now. What did matter was that it should not happen again. Even if it had been nice to wake up to.

"It's okay." She tried to make it sound far more insignificant than it was to her. "You don't owe me an explanation. I know I was acting crazy."

He lifted a corner of his mouth. "I'd go with 'out of character.'"

Sally winced. "You're being kind. I think *crazy* is accurate."

"I'd like to know what happened, but only if you want to tell me." Curiosity was written all over his face as he waited, his eyes not leaving her.

She crossed her legs and settled more comfortably on her side of the bed. Ross had a way of putting her at ease even when she didn't like the subject.

"When I was a kid, a group of us were playing hide-and-seek. I hid in a trunk. One of the kids thought it would be funny to lock me in. I was stuck there for hours before my mother found me. Now I'm terrified of the dark and small spaces. Silly, I know. My ex-husband used to make fun of me all the time."

A dark look covered his features. "I don't think it's silly. Everyone's scared of something. They may not show it, but it's there anyway."

"Yeah, right. Like you're afraid of anything. I've seen you run into a burning building."

His look was unwavering. "I assure you, I am."

"Like what?" It was suddenly important that she know. Ross seemed invincible to her.

He shifted, acted unsure, not meeting her eyes. It was as if he had said more than he'd intended. But sharing her own fear had made her realize how important it was for him too. "So tell me. What're you afraid of?"

"You aren't going to let this go, are you?" His words were flat.

"No. You know my secret. I promise not to share yours."

"Turn your head."

It was an order but she did as he requested. The mattress lifted, letting her know Ross had stood. What was he doing?

"You can look now." Ross was wearing a pair of shorts and walking toward the window on his side of the room. He spoke to the windowpane. "I don't make a habit of telling this. In fact, I don't ever tell this."

Sally moved around the bed to sit where he had lain. It was still warm.

"Remember I told you about the fire that took my granddaddy's house?"

"I do." She'd thought of that boy many times.

"There was more to the story."

She held her breath. This wouldn't be good.

"As I was coming out of the door of the house, part of the ceiling fell on me. My shoulder was burned."

Sally sucked in her breath.

"I have some ugly scars as reminders of that night." His shoulders tensed.

She wanted to reach out to him. "So that's why you always wear a shirt. I'm sorry, Ross, I had no idea."

"Few people do. Like I said, I don't share this with everyone." There was an emotion in his voice she couldn't put a name to. Disappointment? Fear? Uncertainty?

"Why're you telling me?"

"Because you wanted to know, and I didn't want you to think you were the only one with hang-ups."

Goodness, he was a nice guy. Sally had forgotten that there were men who had compassion for others. She arose and went to him, placing a hand on his shoulder. "Thank you for trusting me with your secret."

He flinched.

Sally took a step back. She shouldn't have touched him. Especially his back.

Ross said something under his breath and turned to meet her gaze. He reached for her. She stumbled against him. Seconds later his lips found hers. His kiss was hungry, igniting something long dormant in her. Her arms reached around his neck and pulled him tight. She would have crawled up him if she could. She couldn't get close enough.

They were two hurting souls who carried secrets that had found release by sharing with each other.

Ross teased the seam of her mouth and she opened to him. Her tongue greeted his like a long-lost friend. His danced and played with hers until her center throbbed with need.

"Sweet Sally," Ross whispered against her jaw as he kissed his way up to nibble at her ear. She shivered. "I always want you to touch me. Please touch me."

How could she resist such a tempting invitation? Her fingers found the hem of his shirt and she ran her hands upward over his chest. It was as firm with muscles as she remembered. The little brushing of hair was soft and springy. Her hands traveled to his waist then on to his back.

"It feels so good to be touched by you. I've dreamed of this too many nights." Ross kissed behind her ear.

He'd been dreaming of her? Her heart picked up a beat. She brought his mouth back to hers and kissed him with all the desire that had been building for days. He was the kindest, most caring and charming man she knew. A hero in every way.

While she kissed him, his hand pulled at her shirt. Lifting it, he drew it off and dropped it to the floor as his mouth floated over the top of one of her breasts. She shuddered from the pleasure. He stepped back and looked at her for a moment. "So perfect."

Ross lifted a breast as his head bent and his wet, warm mouth slipped over her nipple. The throbbing in her core pounded as her blood ran red hot. He slowly sucked and worshipped first one breast then the other. She closed her eyes, absorbing the pleasure of having Ross touch her as she ran her hands through his hair, savoring every tantalizing movement of his tongue. She'd found another of his talents.

When Ross broke the contact, she sighed in disappointment. He gave her an intense look, desire blisteringly strong in his eyes. Swinging her into his arms, he carried her to the bed and laid her gently on it. "I want you, Sweet Sally. I desire you with everything in me. What happens between us is up to you. You have the control."

She opened her arms to him.

"Say it, Sally. Say you want me. I need to hear it."

Her gaze met his. "How could I not want you, Ross? Of course I want you. Please."

He tugged his borrowed sweatpants off her, leaving her bare to him. She grabbed for the sheet but his hand stopped her.

"No, I want to see you in the morning light. You're so amazing."

He studied her with such intensity that she blushed all over. Sally looked away but not before she saw the length of Ross's manhood pushing against the front of his shorts. He desired her. After learning she wasn't enough for Wade, it was exhilarating to see visual evidence of Ross's need for *her*.

"This is unfair. You need to take your clothes off." She almost whined.

There was a swish of material and her eyes jerked back to him. His manhood was even more impressive without covering. Ross put a knee on the bed as if he were coming down to her.

She placed a hand on his chest. "Shirt too. I want to touch, see you."

"But…"

Her heart went out to him, but she wouldn't let him think he wasn't good enough in every way. "Ross, I trusted you and you need to trust me."

His face showed pain seconds before he murmured. "Others have been disgusted."

She rose so that she could cup his face. Turning it back to her, she gave him a long kiss. "I'm not those others. You're more than your scars to me."

His earnest eyes found hers. "I want you too badly. I can't take the chance."

"Sit down." She patted the bed beside her. He stepped back, looking hesitant. She sat up, trying to appear more assured than she felt, especially since she was naked in the daylight in front of Ross. She needed him to decide what the next move would be.

Slowly, Ross sat next to her. She kissed his arm at his shoulder. "I want to see. After this first time, it won't matter ever again between us. I want to admire all of you. I don't want just part of you."

Moments passed. Finally, he removed his shirt in one quick jerky motion. He put his elbows on his knees.

She didn't look at his back right away. Instead she ran her hand lightly across his shoulders. He flinched but settled. Her fingers gently touched each dip and pucker. "Such strong shoulders. You have to remember I've seen what they're capable of. Felt them hold me."

Some of the tension in him eased away.

Sally looked at his back. Covering one entire shoulder blade were wrinkled, reddish marks and twisted skin. She drew in a breath, not from the ugliness of the sight but from the horror of the pain Ross must have experienced. Moisture filled her eyes. Her heart broke for him.

Ross moved to stand. Her fingers wrapped his biceps, stopping him as she laid her head against his arm. "I'm so sorry you had to go through that. It must've hurt beyond words."

He eased back to the bed but there was still stiffness in his body.

Sally moved so she was on her knees behind him. She placed her lips on his damaged skin. Ross hissed. His skin rippled.

"You don't want to do that." His voice was gruff.

How had other women acted when they saw him? What had they said to this amazing man to make him feel so unworthy, ashamed of himself? Her tears fell. Didn't he know how special he was? She placed her hands on his shoulder, keeping him in place. She gently kissed the scarred area, then worked her way to the nape of his neck.

She wrapped her arms under his, pressing her breasts against his bare back. Her hands traveled over his chest as she continued to kiss him. First the back of his ear, then his cheek. Her hands dipped lower, to tease his belly button, then to brush his hard length.

With a growl that came from deep within his throat, Ross twisted and grabbed her, flipping her to the bed. His mouth found hers in a fiery kiss.

Ross's length throbbed to the beat of his racing heart. When had a woman made him feel so wanted, needed?

Undamaged? Ross couldn't get enough of Sally. Of her tenderness, concern, her compassion. It had taken his breath away when she had kissed his scars. As if she had peeled away all the hurt associated with them. No one had ever understood what it had been like for him as a boy or a man to carry those scars. Until Sally. She had cried for him. He'd seen her eyes.

He would make it his mission to give her all the pleasure she deserved, in and out of bed. Her breasts had been silky against his back when she had pressed against him. It had been years since he'd allowed a woman to see his deformity, to remove his shirt. To know all of him, even the broken parts. The wonder of being so close heightened his desire for Sally.

He cupped her breast and swept his thumb across her nipple until it rose and stiffened. His mouth surrounded it, his tongue swirling. Sally moaned and lifted her hips against him.

"Easy, Sweet Sally, we've all day, if you wish."

He left her breast to place a kiss on her shoulder blade. Her hands flexed on his back in a begging motion. His lips took hers as his hand glided over her waist, along her hip to her thigh. It circled to the inside of it, then returned to her hip. He was rewarded by her legs parting in invitation.

Ross accepted it. His hand fluttered near her heat. Asking, then begging, before he ran a finger over her opening.

The purring sound that came from Sally increased his hunger to a consuming need.

He dipped his finger into her hot center. She squirmed. Slipping it in completely, he then pulled it out. Sally trembled. Her tongue, entwined with his, mimicked the movement of his finger. Lifting her hips, she pushed toward him. Holding her tight, he entered her again and increased the pace. She arched against him, her body tensing before she broke their kiss and eased to the bed. Her eyes drifted closed on a soft sigh.

Ross was gratified by her pleasure. But he wanted to give her more. She deserved it. He rose over her and kissed her deeply. Her arms circled his neck. She returned his kisses with her own. Her lips went to his cheek, his temple, to his neck, then down to his chest. Her hands ran over him with abandon. When they went to his shoulders, he faltered, but Sally didn't slow her movements. He forgot his apprehension and concentrated his thoughts on the feel of Sally's hands touching him, bringing him closer.

Ross captured her hands and gave her a gentle kiss before he rolled away from her. Fumbling with his bedside-table drawer, he located the package he was looking for. He looked down at Sally. She looked beautiful and bereft at the same time. Opening the package, he covered himself. His gaze met hers. "Are you sure?"

"Oh, yes, I'm sure." She drew him back to her.

Ross settled between her legs. His tip rested just outside her heat. Supporting himself on his forearms, he leaned down to give her a long slow kiss. Slowly he entered her. And with a final push he found home.

He almost pulled out completely before he drove into her again. His mouth continued to cover hers. Sally lifted her hips to his, meeting and matching his rhythm until they created their own special tempo. She quivered as her fingers dug into his back. He pushed harder, his pleasure growing.

On a cry of ecstasy, Sally stiffened and relaxed against the bed. He groaned and followed her into a joyous oblivion he'd never known before.

Ross woke to the sound of water running in the bathroom. Sally came into the room, wearing her own clothes. Apparently, she'd gone looking for them in the dryer. Her hair was pulled back and damp strands framed her face. His chest expanded with pride. She had the looked of a woman recently fulfilled.

"You're awake."

He frowned as she didn't meet his eyes. He didn't want any uncomfortable moments between them. He smiled. "I am, but I missed you when I woke."

She blinked. "You did?"

"I did." Ross sat up. "You could've woken me. I would've liked that."

Sally gave him a perplexed look. "Really?"

They watched each other for a moment. What was she thinking? Had he said something wrong? "Yeah. Who wouldn't want you beside them?"

The worried look across her features disappeared, then she smiled. "Thank you. That's not what I'm used to. My ex-husband didn't like for me to linger in bed. He always wanted me to get up and get a shower."

Ross wanted to hit something. "Look at me, Sally."

She did.

Hopefully she could see the sincerity in his eyes. "You're welcome to stay in bed with me as long as you want or you're free to leave whenever you want. It's up to you. I want you to understand this next part. It's very important that you do." He paused. "I promise I'm nothing like your ex-husband. I don't, nor will I ever, control your actions. You can always trust me, and I'll always be honest with you. Inside and outside of bed."

"Oh."

"Yes, oh. And by the way, right now, I'd like to have your sweet lips on mine but if that isn't what you want, then that's fine."

Her eyes opened and closed a couple of times before a

smile came to her lips. She came to him. Placing her hands on his shoulders, she leaned down. Her kiss was hot and suggestive, setting him on fire again. When he tugged her toward the mattress, she stepped away.

Looking down at him, she teased, "Hey, I need some food if I'm going to keep up with you."

"Okay, let me get a shower and I'll take you out to eat." Ross flipped the sheet back. He didn't miss the sparkle of interest in her eyes as she looked at him.

"Uh...you don't have to do that. I'll see what I can find in the kitchen." She stepped toward the door.

Ross headed toward the bathroom, chuckling. "Good luck with that."

It wasn't until the water was running over him that he realized that he'd been completely naked in front of another person without being self-conscious. And Sally's look had been an admiring one. What miracle had she performed on him?

Done with his shower, he found Sally busy in the kitchen. "I see you found something. It smells wonderful." He walked up behind her, giving her a kiss on the neck. "What're you fixing?"

"I found enough for an omelet and some toast. That work for you?"

"It does. As usual, I'm impressed. Your cooking is one of the many things I like about you." He turned her to give her a proper kiss. "What can I do to help?"

"How about getting a couple of plates for me and setting the table while I finish up these eggs?"

He did as she requested. She plated an omelet and started on another. He took the bread out of the toaster and added it to the plates. She carried those to the table while he filled her glass with water and poured himself a cup of coffee. At the table, Ross sat beside her instead of across from her. He wanted her within touching distance.

They ate for a few minutes, then Sally said, "I called about my car. It's going to be Monday or Tuesday before they can get to it. I know you've a lot of things to do around here so I hate to ask you to take me home." She looked away from him. "But I'd really rather not have Kody come get me. He'd ask a bunch of questions I don't want to answer."

Ross understood that. Kody was protective, even making his position clear to Ross. He didn't want the third degree from him either. "Do you have any plans for today?"

Sally shook her head. "No, other than I'd planned to sleep and not open a book."

"You could do that here, if you want. I'll be glad to run you home, but I first need to check on a few things around here after the storm."

"Do you mind if I help?" She leaned forward as if eager to do so.

The women he knew were generally more interested in their fingernails than doing manual labor. He couldn't keep his surprise out of his voice. "Sure, if you want."

"If you don't want me to…"

He reached across the table and took her hand. "I'll take any help I can get, anytime, especially if it's yours."

That put a smile on her face.

"I need to see about Romeo and Juliet. They need to be let out into the pasture. Then we need to check the fence—since I did the work in the dark there may be more repairs. Next is the tree. You sure you're in for all that?"

"I'm sure." Sally smiled as she cut off a bite of omelet and forked it into her mouth.

After eating, they cleaned up the table and kitchen together. With that done they once again pulled on the high boots and headed outside.

"Horses first." Sally walked beside him toward the barn.

"Yep." They took a few more steps before Ross asked, "Do you mind telling me about your ex-husband?"

She was quiet for a moment. Ross feared he might be ruining things between them, but he needed to know about the man who had clearly done Sally so much hurt.

"There's not much to tell. We were only married for a little over a year. He was the Mr. It in our part of the world. The football quarterback from a prominent family, the good-looking guy, the one with the best car. Why he looked at me, I have no idea."

"I know why. Because you're great," Ross assured her. She was an amazing person. Why wouldn't she recognize that?

"Thanks. That's always nice to hear but harder to believe after being married to Wade."

"Based on what you said earlier I'm guessing your ex was pretty controlling." Ross glanced at her, measuring her reaction to his statement.

"It turns out he was. I didn't realize it at first. Maybe it was there all along and I just didn't want to see it. I was already working as an EMT when we married. I have always dreamed of being a doctor. Wade knew that, but he didn't want me to go to school. I gave it up for him. It turns out that he didn't give up anything for me. Including his girlfriends."

Ross stopped short and looked at her. "What're you talking about?"

"Kody didn't tell you?"

"Tell me what?" For those who knew him well, they'd have recognized his ominous tone.

"Wade ran around on me. He started about six months

into our marriage. I tried to make it work. Crying, begging, counseling—nothing worked."

Ross blurted a harsh word before bringing her into a hug. "You deserved better than that. It's a good thing he doesn't live in town or I'd beat him to a pulp with my bare hands."

She gave him a watery grin and started walking again. "That's close to what Kody said. I guess I just wasn't enough for Wade."

"Enough?" Ross followed her. He couldn't believe what he was hearing.

"Of course you were, and still are. You're *more* than he deserved." He gave her a look he hoped showed her just how sexy and desirable she was. "I should know."

They entered the barn.

Her smile was appreciative, but her eyes still said she didn't totally believe him. "Kody encouraged me to move out here because he didn't want me facing people every day who knew the truth. At first, I wasn't brave enough to make the move, then I decided I had to."

Ross cupped her face. "You're brave in every way I can think of."

"That's nice of you to say."

Ross lifted her chin with a finger. "Hey, I'm not being nice. I'm telling you the truth."

Putting her hands flat on his chest, she backed him against the wooden stall gate and kissed him with a passion he'd only dreamed of. His hand slipped under her shirt and found the warm skin there. Her finger curled into his jean loops and brought his hips tightly against her. His body became rocket hot. He was going to have her right here on the barn floor.

Only the whinny and nuzzle of a horse's nose against

his head brought Ross back to reality. He and Sally chuckled and patted Juliet.

"She must be jealous." Sally grinned.

"Or just hungry," Ross quipped as he opened the stall door and brought the horse out. He ran his hand over her coat and looked at her legs.

"Is anything wrong?" Sally asked, standing nearby.

"Nope. Just making sure she didn't get hurt in the storm." He then let the horse wander out of the barn into the pasture. He gave Romeo the same care before letting him go. "Now to the fun stuff."

They went to the shed, collected his tools and headed for the fence.

"You want to do fence work again? Worse, stack wood?" Ross still couldn't believe Sally was choosing to do that type of work.

"Sure. You could use the help, couldn't you?"

"It would be nice to have." And it would.

She shrugged. "I'm a captive audience."

"I can take you home first." Ross was really hoping she would stay. He enjoyed her company. Sally looked unsure for a moment. Did she think he wanted her to leave? "Hey, you're welcome here for as long as you want. I'm glad to have you anytime."

Her expression eased. "I like it here. I just don't want to overstay my welcome."

He stepped to her and took the tips of her fingers in his, not daring to bring her any closer for fear he'd never get the work done. "That could never happen. Stay all day..." his voice lowered "...all night too."

She looked at him and gave him a soft smile. "I'd like that."

His heart soared. "Then it's settled. Now, let's get to work. When we get the fence and tree taken care of, I'll cook you the best steak you've ever eaten and show you the stars."

That put a teasing smile on her face. "You're cooking?"

He tapped the end of her nose. "You just wait and see."

Over the next few hours they worked together making the fence stronger and cleaning up the limb that had fallen. Ross couldn't have asked for better help. Sally seemed to know what he needed done before he had to ask.

"You've done this kind of work before," Ross stated as he stacked firewood from the truck at the back of the house.

"More than once. My father believes that every woman needs to be prepared for what comes along. Kody and I were expected to help out the same."

"Smart father."

She smiled. "I think so. For me to do things like this used to drive my ex-husband crazy. His idea of work was to call someone on the phone."

Ross had heard enough about her lousy husband. He didn't want to hear any more. "You're welcome to do as much or as little as you want. I'm happy for the company."

She looked off toward the grazing horses in the pasture. "This is such a great place. How could you not like working on it?"

"I feel the same way." Ross threw the last log on the pile. "Let's clean up and go pick out our steaks."

"I was thinking, since I have limited clothes and these are dirty again, I'd stay here and take a nap and let you pick mine out."

He walked into her personal space and looked into her face, flushed from vigorous activity. "You trust me that much?"

"And more."

Ross raised a brow. "More?"

"Sure. Let's see, I've seen you run into a burning building and save a man's life, watched you care for your niece and nephew, and you saved me when my car broke down. You're a hero. All you're missing is a cape. I think I can trust you with a steak."

He swaggered his shoulders. "Put that way, I do sound pretty impressive. But you forgot one thing."

Her brows grew together in thought. "What's that?"

"How good I am in bed."

Sally's cheeks turned pink. "That goes without saying."

Male satisfaction swirled through him and he leaned into the heat of her. "It does, does it?"

She slapped at his arm. "Don't get too full of yourself. Now you're fishing for compliments."

Ross wrapped an arm around her waist and pulled her tight against him, kissing her soundly. He wiggled his eyebrows wickedly. "I'm even better in the shower. Want to find out?"

Hours later Sally stretched like a cat in the summer sun. The sound of Ross's truck returning had woken her from a nap on the swing. She smiled. He was right, he did have talents under running water. They'd made love in the shower and then on the bed before he'd dressed and left for the store. Made love? Was she falling in love?

She sat up. What was she doing playing house with Ross? She had plans that didn't include him. She'd temporarily lost her mind. But she couldn't deny that she liked being around him. He was fun, interesting, exciting. All the things she'd been missing in her life for too long. Just seeing his smile made her happy.

No, she wouldn't go down that road anytime soon. She had her life planned out and she wasn't going to deviate, not even for someone as wonderful as Ross. But why couldn't they be friends? Enjoy each other's company for a while? After all, it had only been a couple of days. What she had to do was see that things between them stayed fun and easy. Nothing messy. She'd had messy and wasn't going there again.

Sally stood to meet Ross. He stepped out of the truck with both hands full of grocery bags. He was so handsome that it almost took her breath. What made him even more appealing was that he had no idea of how incredible he was.

His smile was bright and sincere. He appeared as glad to see her as she was him. She liked that. Now she could see that her husband had never looked that way when he'd returned to her.

"Hey, sleepyhead, I can see you've been hard at it."

She leaned against the porch rail. "You told me to take it easy."

He started up the steps. "I didn't say that."

"That's what I heard."

Ross chuckled. The sound was rough but flowed like satin over her nerves. That was him. Metal on the outside and cotton on the inside.

"You need help?" She reached for the bags.

"Not with these but there's a couple more bags in the truck." He gave her a quick kiss.

Sally held the door open for him, then went to the truck. She returned with two more bags and a bundle of flowers.

Ross was unwrapping a steak from white butcher paper when she joined him. "The flowers are beautiful."

"I thought you might like them."

She narrowed her eyes at him but grinned. "Are you romancing me, Ross Lawson?"

He gave her a kiss. "Would it be all right if I were?"

Her heart skipped a beat. She loved the concept but she had to make sure things didn't get too serious. "You do know that for both of our sakes we have to keep this un-complicated?"

"I do, but that doesn't mean I can't give a friend flow-ers, does it?" He pulled out a couple of baking potatoes then a loaf of bread from one of the bags.

When he put it that way it was hard to argue with him. "Can I help you do anything?"

He continued to sort items. "Nope. Tonight's your night off. I'm gonna cook for you, if you don't mind?"

"I don't mind at all." In fact, it was sweet of him. She wasn't used to people doing things for her.

Ross turned on the oven and put the potatoes in. "It'll be about an hour before it's ready. You're welcome to keep me company or go back out to the swing."

"Do you mind if I pick out some music?"

"No, as long as it's country and western." He gathered some spices.

"That figures." She went to his stereo beneath the TV and found a radio station. "I'm going to at least set the table."

"Okay. And do you mind seeing to the flowers? They're *not* my thing."

Ross prepared them a lovely meal that included flow-ers in the center of the table. While they ate, they talked about music, movies and TV shows they liked.

It was just what Sally needed, relaxed and enjoyable. Ross was good company. Why didn't he already have a special someone? "Have you ever been married?"

His head jerked up from where he'd been cutting his steak. "That came out of the blue."

She lifted a shoulder and let it drop. "You're such a good guy I was just wondering why you aren't taken."

"I think there was a compliment in there somewhere but, to answer your question, I was engaged once."

Somehow it hurt her that he'd had someone he'd cared enough about to ask to marry him. "You were?"

He nodded. "Alice. She's a local Realtor."

Sally knew who she was. "She's the one with her picture on the billboard."

"Yep, that's the one."

Sally stopped eating and rested her chin on her palm, watching him. "So what happened?"

He put down his fork and knife. "It turns out she hated my job. And my scars were a constant reminder of the danger. After a while she just said she couldn't do it anymore. To make her happy I was going to have to give up being a fireman, and that I couldn't do. She couldn't get past her fear, so we broke it off."

"I'm sorry, Ross." She understood the pain of knowing you weren't what the person you loved wanted.

"I have to admit it took me a while to get over her, but we would've been miserable. I could've never made her happy. I know that now."

Sally reached across the table and squeezed his hand.

They finished their meal and cleaned up.

When the last dish was put away, Ross said, "Dessert will be under the stars. It'll be dark soon. I have a few things to get together. While I do that, would you look in my closet and find something to keep you warm and bring me that sweatshirt hanging on the chair in my room? I'll meet you at the truck."

She did as he asked and was waiting beside the truck when he came out of the house with a basket in hand. Under his other arm was a large bundle. He put both in the back of the truck.

He held the door open for her. "Hop in."

Ross turned the truck around and started down the

drive. He drove about halfway and stopped, turned off the truck and got out, leaving the door open. "Stay put. I'll be right back."

She leaned out the door. "Is something wrong?"

"Nope. This is where we were going."

She laughed as she watched him through the rear window. He climbed into the truck bed and unrolled the bundle. With it flat, he returned to the cab and plugged a cord into the electrical outlet. Seconds later an air mattress started to fill.

The pump was so loud she couldn't question him until the mattress was full. She called out the door once more, "Hey, Captain Lawson, this is starting to get a little kinky."

He came to the door and gave her a suggestive grin while he removed the cord. "Normally, I would've driven out into the pasture but with the storm last night it's too wet. So I'm improvising. Give me a few more minutes and I'll have everything ready. Don't look."

It was hard but she did as he asked.

Moments later he returned and offered her his hand. "Okay, come with me." He guided her around to the end of the truck. The tailgate was down. There was a sleeping bag spread out over the air mattress and another lay along the tailgate, making a cushion. Off to the side was the basket.

"What's all this?"

"Dessert under the stars like I promised." Ross looked proud of himself.

"Looks nice." She was impressed with the thought he'd put into doing something nice for her. Sally smiled at him. "I'm not sure about your plans for that mattress."

"Have you ever lain on a metal bed of a truck?"

"No."

He grinned. "Trust me, you'll like the mattress better."

His hands went to her waist and he lifted her to sit on the tailgate. He joined her, then reached for the basket. "Would you like a beer?"

"Sure."

He opened the basket and gave her a long-necked bottle with a Texas Star on the label.

Sally took a swallow. "It's good."

"I have a friend who microbrews this." Ross took a long draw on his before he reached into the basket again and pulled out a prepackaged chocolate cake with a filling. He offered it to her. "Dessert?"

A laugh bubbled out of her. She took it. "My favorite. Thanks."

He pulled his own out. "I aim to please."

They ate while swinging their legs, occasionally intertwining them as they watched the sun set. When the stars started to pop out, Ross put their empty bottles in the basket along with their trash.

"It's time to climb on the mattress. You go first, otherwise we might bounce the other one over the side."

Sally giggled and scrambled onto the mattress. When Ross joined her, she floated up, then down as if she were on a trampoline as he settled beside her. He pulled the sleeping bag they had been sitting on over them.

"Come here." Ross reached for her. She settled her head on his shoulder.

Over the next hour they lay there huddled in their own cocoon of warmth and silence watching the black sky fill with sparkling stars that looked like diamonds thrown across velvet. It was the most perfect hour of her life. One that she didn't dare hope to repeat.

Ross rolled toward her. His hand slipped under her shirt

and traveled over her stomach as his mouth found hers.
They made love beneath the stars.

She was wrong. It was the most perfect night of her life.
So perfect Sally was sorry it couldn't last forever.

# CHAPTER SEVEN

ROSS GLANCED AT Sally as he pulled into the auto-repair place Monday afternoon. The last couple of days together had been wonderful, but it had to stop. What was going on between them was surely nothing more than hot sex between two ambitious workaholics. She would be going back to work tomorrow. Him the next day. One day soon they'd be sharing the same shift. What then? He wasn't that good of an actor.

For them to date, or whatever they were doing, was against department policy even if they did somehow find time for it. Sally was bent on becoming a doctor. He had the promotion to think about and nothing could get in the way of that. If the word got out…

They hadn't said much on the ride in. It was as if Sally was working through what the last few days had meant just as he was. Could she be as uncertain of what was developing between them as he?

After pulling into a parking spot, he turned off the truck and took a moment to gather his thoughts, then looked at Sally. Her attention seemed focused on something out the front windshield.

"Sally—"

"Ross—"

They both gave each other weak smiles.

"You go first," Ross said.

"I'm not sure how this is supposed to go. I've not been in this position before." Her words were slow and measured.

This didn't sound like something he wanted to hear. But he couldn't disagree with her.

"Ross, I had a wonderful weekend."

Now he was sure it wasn't something he wanted to hear. "Why do I think there's a 'but' coming?"

She shrugged. "Because there is. I think we need to chalk this up to just that, a nice weekend. We need to just be friends."

"Ugh, that's the worst thing a woman can say to a man." Still, he couldn't argue with the wisdom of what she was saying.

Sally touched his hand for a moment, then withdrew it. "I really like you. But I can't be distracted from what I'm working toward."

"I'm a distraction?" He rather liked that idea.

She offered him a real grin then. "Yeah, you're a big distraction. I just think we need to stop this before it gets out at the house, or we get too involved. I don't have time in my life for this…whatever it is. It was a great weekend. Let's leave it at that."

Now she was starting to talk in circles. Yet those were the same thoughts spinning in his head.

She continued. "I think all we'd be doing is complicating each other's lives."

That was an understatement. She'd already gotten further under his skin than any woman since Alice. Yet being in a relationship with a person he worked with could only mean disaster.

"Besides that, I promised myself after my divorce I wouldn't be sidetracked from what I want ever again."

That statement didn't sit well with him. He didn't want

her to change her dreams for him. "You think I want you to give up what you want?"

"No, I just think I'd eventually do it for you. I have before."

Ross didn't like that statement any better, but he could understand it. "I want to be Chief one day. Us seeing each other could be a problem. A big one."

She waved her hand. "See, that's just what I'm talking about. It makes sense that we just remain friends, no more. It would make life too complicated for us to date."

"I think you're right." So why did it seem so wrong? He reached and took her hand. "Good friends."

She squeezed his hand. "Very good friends."

"May this friend give his best friend one more kiss before she goes?" Could he survive if she said no?

She gave him a sad smile. "I'd like that. You're a fine man, Ross."

"You're really sweet, Sally."

He brought her to him and gave her a kiss that quickly turned from friendly to hot.

Sally broke away. "See you around, Ross." She opened the door and was gone.

Why did he feel as if he'd just agreed to something he might regret?

The next few days were long. He missed Sally. Wanted to see her, talk to her, touch her. Even being at his place didn't feel the same. He went into work for the first time with little enthusiasm simply because she wouldn't be there. He didn't like this arrangement and he was going to tell her so. There must be another way.

As soon as his shift was over, he would go to her place and talk to her. See if she felt the same.

Ross was walking in the direction of his truck the next

day at the end of his shift, just after noon, when Kody called his name. He turned.

"Hey, man, you want to play some hoops for an hour or so? I don't have to pick up Lucy until three."

"No, not today. I've got something I need to take care of."

*Like convincing your sister to come back to my bed.*

"Well, okay. Talk to you later."

"Yeah." Ross climbed into his truck. Kody was a hurdle he'd have to face one day soon. Maybe he and Sally could keep their relationship from him and the department until it fizzled out, which it surely would. In the meantime, he wasn't ready to give up on Sally. Hopefully, she was of the same mind-set.

Ross pulled up in front of her apartment building ten minutes later. The work crew had moved on to the next building but they still made it difficult to find a parking place. Sitting with his hands on the steering wheel, Ross studied Sally's front door. What was he going to do if she wasn't home? Worse, if she didn't want to talk to him? He hated to appear desperate to see her, but he was. What if she rejected him? He'd been dodging that emotion for years. It didn't matter. He needed to see her, talk to her. Tell her how he felt.

Climbing out of the truck, he walked to the door with determination. He raised his hand to knock and lost his nerve for a moment. Then he knocked.

Sally had done most of the talking last time. Now he was going to do it. Maybe he could change her mind. He wasn't going to know until he tried.

He didn't hear any movement. Fear she wasn't home swamped him. He thought of returning to his truck, but then the latch moved. Moments later the door opened.

Sally's questioning expression quickly turned to one of pure joy.

It filled him too. He smiled and opened his arms.

She squealed and jumped into them. Hers circled his neck. He chuckled, stepped inside and kicked the door closed with the heel of his shoe. She rained kisses over his face as he backed her against the wall.

"I know we shouldn't be doing this but I missed you." Desperation filled her voice.

He chortled with pleasure. "I guessed that." His mouth took hers in a hot, hungry kiss. She could have missed him only half as much as he'd missed her. It was heaven to have her body against his again.

"What're you doing here?" Sally asked between breathless kisses.

"I wanted to talk to you."

She pulled at his shirt. "Is that all you wanted?"

"Hell, no," he growled, returning his mouth to hers as he worked at the snap of her pants.

Sally had been longing for Ross, but hadn't known how much until she'd seen him in her doorway. Her heart had almost flown out of her chest with excitement. Her neighbors would have thought she had lost her mind if they had seen her acting like a kid at Christmas.

As she and Ross lay in bed, she scattered kisses on top of his chest as her hand roamed his middle.

She was in trouble. Once again she'd gone over the line into the land where her heart was becoming involved. The problem was she didn't know how to step back to safe ground. What she had to guard against now was making the mistake of changing what she wanted for Ross.

He groaned. "You keep that up and you'll get more than you bargained for."

She shifted so she could see his face. "Who said I didn't want more?"

Ross smiled indulgently down at her. "Mmm… That's the kind of thing I like to hear." He leaned in to kiss her.

"Ross, what're we going to do?"

The look in his eyes turned devious. "You don't know by now?"

She gave him a little pinch. "You know what I mean. We agreed to be friends."

"You don't think I'm being friendly?" His hand traveled over her bare butt.

"You're just not going to listen, are you?" Her voice held a teasing note.

Ross kissed her neck. "Who said I wasn't listening? I heard every word you've said."

"Ross, we can't do this."

"I think we did 'this' just fine. Great, in fact." His lips traveled lower.

"We have to stick to the plan." Her voice had turned sharper than she had intended.

He captured her gaze. "Look, why can't we just enjoy each other while it lasts? We don't have to make a big deal of it. We can keep it between us. We can be friends and still see each other when our schedules allow."

"I guess that'll work." She wasn't convinced. The more she saw Ross, the harder it became to give him up. Hopefully, one day soon she would have medical school to think about. There wouldn't be any time for a relationship. But she'd miss him desperately if she gave him up right now. Maybe if they just saw each other until she started school…

Over the next few weeks she and Ross fell into a routine. If they both had extended days off, then Sally would go to his place. They would work around the ranch, go out for dinner in a small town nearby. They couldn't afford being seen together by someone in the fire department, so they made sure to stay out of Austin. When their schedules had them working back-to-back days, then Ross would come to her apartment. She'd never been happier. Or more worried about her heart being broken.

It was exciting to know Ross would be waiting on her when she came home or be coming to her after his shift. Against her better judgment, she was caring for him a little more each time they were together. Still, one day soon it would all have to end, but that wasn't today.

Sally was leaving his place to go to work when Ross said, "I promised Jared and Olivia when they got out of school, I'd take them tubing on the Guadalupe River. We're going Saturday. Wanna come?"

"I wish I could, but I told Kody I'd watch Lucy. He's scheduled to work. He's started asking me what I'm doing with my time. I haven't seen much of either of them since you've been keeping me busy." Her look was pointed, yet she grinned.

"And I like keeping you busy." His smile grew. "Lucy's welcome to go. I know Jared and Olivia would have a better time with her along."

Sally's heart lightened. She would've missed seeing Ross. Her feelings for him were like trying to stop a runaway train. She was doing everything she'd promised herself she wouldn't do. "I'll talk to Kody and ask Lucy and let you know."

"That sounds like a plan. I'll get the tubes together."

"Can I do something?"

"No. I think I can take care of the sandwiches for lunch. All you have to do is get you and Lucy here in your bathing suits." He came in close, moving to stand between her legs where she sat on his kitchen counter. "I especially like that idea."

She grinned. "I thought you might." Then she kissed him.

Kody gave his okay that also included a suspicious look when she told him Jared and Olivia had requested that she and Lucy came tubing with them and Ross.

"You've lived here for over a year and had nothing to do with Ross Lawson. Yet in the last month or so you've spent the day with him at the picnic, watched his niece and nephew, studied at his house and now you're going tubing with him. Is something going on I should know about?"

"There's nothing going on. We're just friends. Aren't I allowed to have friends?"

"Yeah," he said, but gave her a narrow-eyed look implying he was unconvinced.

Early Saturday morning Sally picked up Lucy. This time Sally was the one the most excited about going to Ross's. She hadn't seen him in a couple of days because he had worked a double shift. He'd worked his regular shift, then gone to the Fire Department Office for a meeting the next day. There was something off in her day when she didn't get to see him.

She didn't know how much longer they would be able to keep their relationship a secret. It was getting more difficult every day. Sometime soon they'd have to work together. In fact, she was going to get to find out sooner rather than later how good of an actor and actress they were because the new schedule had come out the day before and they were to share a couple of shifts next week.

What then? Would someone notice the looks between them? Or that one knew more than they should about something the other did on their days off? It would be so easy to slip up. It could damage Ross's career and she didn't want that.

He deserved the Battalion Chief position. As a dedicated firefighter, a great leader and someone who had a vision for the future of the department, he was a perfect fit. More than that, he had a passion for fighting fire. It wasn't just a job to him. Ross completely believed in what he was doing.

As she and Lucy traveled closer to Ross's house, Sally's heart beat faster in anticipation. She smiled to herself. This was what happy felt like. It had been a long time since she'd been that. She'd counted on medical school to give her that feeling again. Then along had come Ross.

He and the kids were waiting on them beside his truck. He wore a T-shirt and swim-trunks along with a pair of tennis shoes. There was a ball cap on his head and his eyes were covered by aviator sunglasses. He had never looked better. She banked the urge to run into his arms, reminding herself to remain cool in front of the kids.

Lucy started waving before Sally stopped the car. The kids returned it, and Ross offered one as well.

He was at her door before she opened it. Was he as happy to see her as she was him? As she climbed out, he stepped toward her. Sally had no doubt he planned to kiss her. His intent was obvious. She stopped his movement with a hand to his chest and a dip of her head toward Lucy. Ross looked past her shoulder. With the sag of his shoulders and dimming of his smile, he nodded and backed away. Lucy would no doubt enjoy telling her father the moment she saw him again that Ross had been kissing her aunt Sally. She certainly wasn't prepared to field Kody's questions about that.

In an odd way, sharing a clandestine relationship with Ross was exciting. Fun like she hadn't had in a long time. She didn't have to share him with anyone. Yet some part of her wanted people to know this amazing man belonged to her. But did he?

"Come into the house. I've got to put our lunch into a

dry bag, then we'll be ready to go." Ross started up the porch steps.

"Dry bag?" Sally followed him.

"It'll keep things dry. I'll tie it to my tube." He held the door for her.

"Great idea." She went inside.

"I'm full of those." He called over his shoulder, "Kids, we'll be right out. Make sure you've got your towels and anything else you need in the truck."

As soon as they were inside out of sight of the kids, he hauled her to him and kissed her. There was hunger there, yet tenderness as well. He'd missed her too. "I'm not sure how I'm gonna make it all day without touching you. With you just being an arm's length away."

Sally giggled. She seemed to do that often lately. It was empowering to her bruised self-image to be considered so desirable by such a remarkable male. Ross made her feel as if she was enough. That was something Wade hadn't done, ever.

Ross pursed his lip in thought. "Maybe it was a bad idea to invite you along."

She pulled away, pouting. "I could always get Lucy and leave."

"Over my dead body." Ross pulled her back to him. She liked being against him. "I'll take my chances on having you around. I'll just have to work on my self-control today."

"That's more like it. You're just gonna have to restrain yourself, because I can promise you that Lucy will catch on pretty quick. I don't think either one of us wants to face Kody quite yet."

"I can handle Kody. You and I are adults. Now, how about one more quick kiss for the road?" Ross's lips found hers.

Too soon for Sally they went to the kitchen. Ross already had the sandwiches in individual plastic bags. He placed them in a heavy rubberized bag. "Do you have anything you want to put in here?"

"My phone?"

He carefully put the food in the bag. "I'll take mine, so why don't you leave yours in the truck?"

"Okay. I don't guess we need two of them."

"Roger that."

Ross locked up, and they joined the kids at the truck. The tubes were already loaded and secured by straps.

"Climb in, kids. Buckle up," Ross called.

They scrambled onto the back seat. Sally climbed into the passenger's seat and Ross got behind the wheel. The kids chattered for the hour it took to drive to the river. Ross pulled into the makeshift dirt parking lot.

When the kids climbed out, Ross put his hand over hers. "I'm sorry we didn't have a chance to talk, catch up."

She smiled at him. "I don't mind. I'm just happy to be with you."

He gave her a bright smile. "That was certainly the right answer."

"Come on, Uncle Ross. Let's get on the river," Jared called with impatience.

Ross unloaded the tubes, handing one to each of the kids then her. After passing out the life vests, he took a moment to secure the bag to his tube. "Okay, kids, huddle up."

The three of them circled in front of him. Sally joined them.

"What're the rules on the river?" Ross gave them an earnest look. He was such a good leader. He would one day make an excellent head of the fire department.

"Stay together," Olivia said.

"Wear your life jacket at all times," Jared added.

"Then we'll have fun," Ross finished. "Got it?"

In unison, they all said, "Yeah!"

He led the way to the riverbank. She helped the kids put on their life vests and get into their tubes and soon they were all floating down the river. The day was warm and the water cool. They leisurely rode the current, letting it take them at its speed. The kids laughed and splashed each other, then turned on her and Ross. A few times other people or groups passed them.

Once the kids were ahead of them enough that Ross came up close to her. His look remained passive and focused on the kids while the hand closest to her went beneath the water.

She jumped as his hand ran over her bottom. "Oomph."

"Easy," he said in an innocent voice. "You don't want to make a scene in front of the kids." As he said this, one of his fingers dipped under the leg opening of her bathing suit and worked its way around to the crease of her leg before it was gone. That was all it took for her center to start throbbing. With a teasing smile on his lips, he floated away.

"Not fair, Lawson."

He gave her a wicked grin over his shoulder.

Not much farther along, Ross called a halt, telling the kids to pull over to the sandbar where the water was placid. It was time for lunch. They brought their tubes out of the water and found a log to sit on. Sally pulled the sandwiches, health bars and bottled water out of the bag along with napkins and a small package of wet wipes. Ross had thought of everything.

It didn't take the kids long to eat. Soon they were asking to go swimming.

"You can go but stay close to the shore," Ross told them.

She and Ross watched as they headed for the water.

"This tube floating is fun. I've never done it before.

I'm really glad I came. Obviously, this isn't the first time you've gone." Sally looked at Ross and bit into her sandwich.

"It was a regular pastime when I was growing up. Jared and Olivia have been a few times before."

"This won't be my last time either." With or without Ross, she intended to do this again. The only thing was that when she did, she'd always think of Ross. It would take some of the joy out of it.

"I'm glad you're having a good time." His attention remained on the kids.

Again, the thought he'd make a good father entered her head. And the fact that such a thing would never involve her left her a little sad. Shaking it off, she sighed. "There's nothing more refreshing than a day on the river when it's hot."

"I can think of at least one other thing." Ross's suggestive remark was accompanied by a heated look. Placing his palms on the log, he leaned back.

Sally took a swallow of water, set the bottle down in front of the log, then leaned back in the same manner as him. She placed her hand over Ross's, intertwining their fingers. Ross looked at her and smiled before his attention returned to watching the kids.

"I'm going to miss you tonight," Ross said in a mock whisper.

Sally tried to act unaffected, but her heart was already picking up speed. "You think so?"

His eyes flickered with burning need as he looked at her. "I know so. Lean over here. I want to kiss you."

"The kids—"

He glanced at them. "Aren't looking."

Her lips met him for a quick kiss.

With a sigh, Ross called, "Let's go, kids. Come clean

up your trash and put it in the bag. We have to carry everything out we bring on the river. Then get your tubes."

Within minutes they were back on the water.

They had been floating for about an hour when they reached a bend in the river and heard, "Help, help, help."

In seconds Ross was off his tube. He shoved it toward her and started swimming. As he passed the kids, he ordered, "Stay with Sally."

He disappeared around the bend as she and the kids picked up their pace. As they rounded the curve, she could see Ross stepping out of the water at a calmer area up ahead. She directed the kids that way.

When they reached the spot where Ross had exited, she told the kids in a stern voice, "We're getting out here. I want you to pile your tubes here beside the river and go over there to that spot and sit." She pointed at a log. "Do not take your life preservers off. Stay put while I see if your uncle Ross needs my help. I'm trusting you to do as I say."

Ross was kneeling over by a woman lying on the ground in a small grassy area. There was another woman sitting on the ground beside her. Sally hurried to them.

"What's wrong?" she asked, coming up beside Ross.

Ross shifted and she could see that the woman had a compound fracture just above her knee.

"How did this happen?" Sally asked.

Ross said to the women, "This is Sally. She's a paramedic. She'll help you."

"We got out of the river to look at a flower and stupid me got my foot caught in a hole and fell," the injured woman said between tight white lips.

Ross could handle burning buildings or automobile wrecks, but he wasn't good at physical emergencies. He had EMT skills, which he rarely used. The woman had severely broken her leg and he was more than happy to turn her care over to Sally's excellent knowledge.

He went to where the kids sat. As he reassured them, Ross searched the dry bag for his phone. Finding it, he punched in 911 then returned to Sally, who was talking to the injured woman.

"I've got 911 on the phone. What do I need to tell them?"

"Thirty-four-year-old female," Sally stated in a firm voice. She was clearly in paramedic mode. He relayed the message. "Compound fracture of the right femur. Treating for shock."

Sally already had the woman lying down with her uninjured leg up.

"Heart rate steady. Pulse one-twenty. Moderate pain. Splinting now."

Ross repeated everything to the dispatcher. He said to Sally, "A medivac can't get in here. The tree canopy is too heavy. We'll need to get her downriver to the takeout spot. It's about a mile away."

Sally spoke to the injured woman's friend. "Please see if you can find at least three pieces of wood or straight sticks that can be used as splints. They must be sturdy." As the woman moved away, Sally asked him with worry in her voice, "What's the plan?"

"I'm going to lash the tubes together and float her down. We're too far from the road for the ambulance, and the helicopter can't get in here."

Sally nodded. "Okay, I'll have her ready. Have one of the kids bring me the towels. I've got to manage shock if we're going to do this."

"I'll get started on the raft now." He hoped it went as smoothly as he had it planned. Ross went to the kids and issued orders for them to hunt for long sticks but to stay within eyesight of him. He sent the towels by Jared to Sally.

Pulling four of the tubes close to the river, Ross put them side by side. Without thinking twice, he jerked his T-shirt over his head. He then pulled a knife out of the dry bag and cut and tore the shirt into strips. He glanced at Sally to find her struggling to do the same with her shirt. Ross went to her. Taking the shirt out of her hands, he began tearing it as well.

"Thanks," Sally said.

He pointed. "I'm going to need one of those towels."

"Okay. I'll put my life jacket over her."

"You can have mine as well." He took it off. "I'll need any of your leftover strips."

The woman's friend came back with some sticks. Sally's attention returned to splinting the woman's leg.

The kids had found some sticks. Some he could use, others not. He sent Jared back out to look for more and had the girls hold things in place as he tied the tubes together with the strips of his shirt. He then tied the sticks on to give the woman a platform to ride on.

The whop-whop of the helicopter flying in could be heard in the distance.

"You ready, Sally?"

"Ten-four."

"Okay, kids, we're going to get this lady on the raft. Then I want you to each get in your tube. I'm going to tie you to the raft. Sally and I'll be swimming. Understand?"

The kids spoke their agreement.

"Stay here until we get the woman settled," he told the kids and then joined Sally.

She had the woman's leg secured in a splint of branches and strips of T-shirt. The leg was evenly supported on the bottom and the top. Sally had made sure it wouldn't move.

He spoke to her. "I've been thinking about the best way to move her. I could pick her up while you support her leg."

"I can help," the woman's friend said.

Sally looked down at the woman. "I don't see that we have a choice." She then said to the injured woman, "What happens next isn't going to be fun. Hang in there and we'll have you at the hospital in no time." She smiled. "And on pain medicine."

The woman nodded, her mouth tight. "That sounds good."

Sally turned her attention to the friend. "Take the towels and life jackets to the raft. Lay one towel over the sticks. We'll cover her with the others again."

The woman did as Sally instructed and removed a towel and the life jacket lying over the injured woman and hurried off.

She soon returned, and she and Sally helped Ross get the injured woman into his arms by supporting her hips and legs. His thigh muscles burned as he strained to lift her. She cried out in pain but there wasn't anything they could do for her except be as gentle as possible. That he was already trying to do. It was a slow process walking over the rough ground, but they finally made it to the raft. Ross placed her on it. Sally quickly checked to make sure the woman's life jacket was still secure. She then covered the patient with the towels and her and Ross's jackets.

"Let's get the raft in the water," he said to the woman, then, "Kids, get your tubes."

It took the three adults to lift and scoot the raft out until it floated not to jostle the woman.

"Sally, will you take one of the front corners? You." He spoke to the friend. "Will you take the other? I'll take the back. Kids, get on your tubes. I'll tie you on."

Everyone did as he instructed. "Okay, let's get this show on the river."

Slowly they moved out into the current.

"I'm looking for slow and steady," Ross called. "No sudden moves."

It took them almost an hour to get to where the helicopter was waiting on the slow winding section of the river. As they came into sight, the medivac crew went into action. They had a gurney and supplies waiting at the river edge when they arrived. Sally gave a report while he saw to the kids.

As they watched the helicopter lift off, Sally said, "I'm glad you were there with me on this one."

His fingers tangled with hers for a moment. "I was just thinking the same thing about you."

She smiled up at him. "You do know you aren't wearing a shirt, don't you?"

"Yeah."

"You okay with that?" Sally gave him a concerned look.

"I'm a little antsy, but handling it."

Her fingers found his again. "I'm proud of you."

Ross squeezed her hand, then let it go. "Couldn't have done it without you."

"Oh, yeah, you could. I've no doubt you would've done whatever was necessary to get that woman to safety whether or not I had come along. That's just the kind of guy you are, Ross Lawson. You're made of hero material. Scars and all."

When Sally thought he was a hero, he felt like one.

"Thanks, you were pretty heroic back there too."

She laughed. "Now that we've told ourselves we're wonderful, how about let's go home?"

Ross laughed. "Let's go."

They gathered the kids and caught the next shuttle back to the truck. The other floaters riding with them asked questions about the incident and offered their appreciation for a job well done.

At the truck Ross turned to the kids and said, "I think we've all earned pizza and ice cream. Who would agree?"

The kids cheered. Sally smiled.

"Okay, I'll order in and stop and buy the ice cream. Since we don't have enough clothes on to get out anywhere."

It wasn't until then that he registered he'd not given a thought to riding the shuttle or being around the kids without a shirt on. They hadn't even noticed. Maybe he made more of a deal of his scars than they were. There was something freeing about that knowledge.

The kids climbed in the back seat of the truck. Ross hadn't driven far when he looked in the rearview mirror to find them all asleep.

"Hey," he whispered to Sally.

She looked at him. He nodded toward the back seat. "Don't you think you're too far away?"

Sally glanced behind her and grinned before she slid over against him. He put his arm around her shoulders and pulled her close. She kissed his cheek. "You were my hero again today. The raft was brilliant."

Ross kissed the top of her head. "No more than you."

He glanced at Sally. What had happened to him in the last few weeks? He'd changed. Sally had made all the difference.

# CHAPTER EIGHT

SALLY PULLED INTO the fire station parking lot two days later with a grin on her face. She was going to see Ross. Her smile grew as she remembered how unhappy she'd been at the idea of seeing him just weeks before. It had been four days since she'd truly been in his arms and she missed him terribly. She could understand where his ex-girlfriend had been coming from about odd schedules. Working around them was difficult but she would never give Ross up just because of that.

The day was coming soon when she would have to. But even as she thought it, she wondered if she did have to give him up. Couldn't they work something out? Did she want to? It was already happening. She wanted to make changes in her life to accommodate Ross. But if she did, could she trust he would always be there for her? His job was important to him. If it came down to her or his job, he'd take his job every time, wouldn't he?

When she entered med school—make that *if* she entered med school, as she still hadn't heard back from her test—she could only imagine how difficult it would be to make time for a relationship. Would they be together that long? No, she wouldn't let things get that far. At the beginning, she wouldn't have thought she and Ross would have lasted this long but now she couldn't imagine not having him in her life. For now, she'd just have to enjoy the time they did have while it lasted.

There had been a particularly sad look in Ross's eyes when she and Lucy had left his house after they had gone tubing. It was nice to have a man so disappointed to see her go. To show it so honestly. After her husband's betrayal, her self-esteem had suffered greatly. Ross's attention had gone a long way in restoring it.

The day they'd tubed the plan had been for Lucy to stay the night with her, so Ross couldn't come over that evening. Kody had asked her to join him and Lucy for supper the next evening. All of this made it seem like an eternity since she'd had personal time with Ross.

She was beginning to believe they might have something special. She'd never felt this way before. That low-level hum of need for Ross was always there. That jump of excitement when she saw him always thrilled her. The anticipation of his touch made the prospect of seeing him more rousing.

Now she was thinking in circles. Not making sense. One minute she was thinking of when their time together would end and the next she was dreaming of a future with Ross. She had to stop thinking with her heart and focus on what her mind was telling her or she was going to get hurt, badly.

It had become tedious, even nerve-racking to keep their relationship to themselves. She was tired of it. Two grown people had every right to see one another. She wasn't ashamed of Ross and she didn't think he was ashamed of her. At least letting Kody and Lucy in on her and Ross's secret would help.

She pulled her bag out of the back seat of her car and headed into the station. Inside the engine bay, she turned toward the paramedic side of the building. She saw Ross on the other side with his hands in his pants pockets talking to one of the firefighters. He glanced her way. Even from that distance she could see the glimmer of awareness in his eyes. His body language changed, as if he wanted to drop what he was doing to come to her. Her heart did a skip and a jump.

Sally entered the paramedic supply room and walked on into the locker room to put her bag away. She sensed more than saw someone enter behind her. Glancing behind her, she found Ross. He stood with his back to the door, blocking it. If anyone tried to enter, they couldn't unless they pushed him out of the way.

"Ross, what're you doing?"

"Come here." The words were low and forceful.

She narrowed her eyes. This wasn't like him. "What?"

"Please come here, Sally." His voice was solemn but had a pleading note, as if he physically hurt.

That warm spot in the center of her chest that grew when she was around him heated. Now she understood. She walked into his arms. Ross's hands cupped her butt and he pulled her up against him as his mouth found hers. His searing kiss was sensual and stimulating, leaving her in no doubt where his mind was.

Ross soon set her at arm's length. "I keep that up and everybody'll see what being around you does to me."

She giggled.

He grinned. "You like that idea, don't you?"

"It does have its appeal." She gave him a nudge. "Now, Casanova, move out of the way and let me see if the coast is clear." He stepped to the side. She opened the door and looked out. "You're good to go, Captain Lawson."

As he went by her, she brushed his cheek with her lips.

* * *

The shift was a busy one. There were no fires but a number of auto accidents. One of them required the Hazmat team. Ross was especially trained for Hazmat so his crew was out cleaning up past the end of the shift. Sally didn't see him before she left. They hadn't discussed their plans, so she decided to go home. Disappointment washed over her as she drove out of the parking lot.

It was early evening when she settled down to read her mail. She still hadn't heard from Ross. She suspected he'd had a large amount of paperwork to do but she would've thought he'd have called or texted by now.

There was a knock at the door. Her heart started racing with hope.

Ross stood on her stoop. He didn't say a word. Just scooped her into a hug and kissed her. Her soul went wild with joy. She clung to him, wrapping her legs around his hips.

"Happy to see me?" He sounded pleased.

He pushed the door closed with his foot, held her with one arm and locked the door. Starting down the hall, he continued to kiss her as he found her bedroom. There he rolled them onto the bed with a bounce.

Sometime later, still in bed, they snacked on popcorn and watched a comedy show.

Ross fed her some corn. "After our shift I know the definition of hell. It's having you so close yet being unable to touch you."

Sally giggled. "I kind of like the idea. It's flattering."

"That may be so, but it's not much fun for me." He kissed the corner of her mouth.

"You can touch me all you want to right now." She gave him a suggestive smile.

His hand skimmed the inside of her thigh. "Now, that sounds like an excellent idea."

Ross started his shift two days later feeling rather good about himself. He looked out of his office window to see Sally standing beside the ambulance talking to her crew member. She glanced over her shoulder and made eye contact with him.

Heat washed through him. He was acting like a lovesick male horse that hung its head over the fence hoping the female horse in the next pasture would notice him.

*Focus, Lawson. You have that promotion on the line.*

He attempted to turn his attention to his paperwork. Instead his mind went to memories of his last few days off. A short while after the comedy show had ended, Sally had accompanied him home and they'd spent the time at his place. She seemed to thrive there. Which gave him a warm feeling deep inside that he didn't wish to analyze. She was becoming ingrained in his life, as necessary as the air he breathed.

He not only appreciated her body, he enjoyed being with Sally. She had a sharp wit that kept him on his toes. She thought nothing of working right next to him, even when the job included mucking out the barn. She was game for anything. More than that, she made him feel like the hero she said he was. Not once had he seen her flinch when he removed his shirt, which he'd started doing regularly when he worked on the farm. She treated him as if he were whole and flawless. With her, he was.

They didn't talk about the future. Ross worried if they did it would change things between them. He didn't want that. Giving up Sally would already be far harder than he had originally thought. He'd ride this wave of happiness for as long as it lasted. It was too wonderful to let go of.

Sally was a partner both outside of work and at work as well. Today, she'd be sharing the shift with him, then they would have another few days together. For him life was good. The only thing that could make it perfect would be to earn the Battalion Chief position. Hopefully he'd know about that any day now, after his interview a week ago.

The company made a few runs during the early evening but managed to have dinner in peace. He and Sally sat next to each other around the large table with the rest of the people at the station. They made an effort to appear as normal as possible, yet under the table he slid his foot next to hers and Sally pressed her lower leg against his.

The alarm beeped and the dispatcher came on over the intercom just after sunrise the next day. Rush hour almost always meant an accident and this one was no different. Ross hurried to the bay and suited up with his crew. He climbed into the truck and the driver flipped on the lights and siren.

Ross swung into emergency mode, already thinking through the possibilities of what was ahead for him and his firefighters. Dispatch told him it was a four-car accident. His team had to work their way through and around the traffic. The ambulance was right behind them.

As they arrived, Ross assessed the situation. Apparently, a car turning left in the intersection ran into the side of an oncoming car. The other two cars had hit their rears. The car that had been going straight took the worse of the crash. Gas covered the ground. A few people sat on the curb off to the left.

Ross was on the radio issuing orders before he climbed out of the truck.

"We need fire extinguishers out just in case. Make sure that gas doesn't spread. Don't let the medics in there until we know how many we have involved and the area is secure." He wouldn't put anyone in danger, especially Sally.

The ambulance pulled up next to his truck with the help of the police directing other cars out of the way. One of his firefighters led a woman to the ambulance. Sally took care of her while the other EMT checked on those on the curb.

"Are all the people in the cars accounted for?" he asked into the radio.

"Ten-four," one of his firefighters came back.

Ross's attention returned to the scene. His firefighters had the situation in hand. He glanced at the box to see Sally taking care of a man who looked as if he was in his thirties.

Into his radio he said, "Let's get traffic moving and clean up this mess."

"Ten-four," came back from his men.

Ross directed the wrecker into place, then started toward Sally, who had a different patient sitting on the back bumper of the box now. She stood in front of the man, tending his head wound.

The man started to stand, but Sally put a hand on his shoulder and eased him back down. In a flash her patient slung his hands high, one of his fists hitting Sally in the face. Her feet came off the ground and she landed on her butt.

Ross roared her name. Something inside him that he didn't recognize roiled to life. Bile rose in his throat. Raw heat flashed over him.

He ran toward Sally. Reaching the man, Ross curled his hands into his shirt. He didn't think—just reacted. Jerking him around and away from Sally, he lifted the scumbag to his toes and shook him. How dared he touch Sally?

Ross growled with fury. "You sure as hell better not have hurt her."

"Stop, Ross! Stop!" Sally's voice penetrated his anger. Her hands pulled at one of his arms.

The policeman took the moment to capture an arm of the man and Ross let go. Seconds later, the policeman had the man's hands secured behind his back.

"What're you doing?" Sally demanded in a loud voice despite the fact she stood in his personal space.

"Helping you!" Ross's heart pounded as if he'd been in a race for his life. The man had knocked Sally to the ground. She could have been seriously hurt.

Sally glared at him. "I could've handled him."

Ross studied her, making sure she had no major injuries, then ground out, "Yeah, I can see that by the shiner you're going to have."

Sally's partner joined them. "He's right. You took a hard shot. You're going to need to be seen at the hospital."

Sally shook her head. "I'll be fine."

"Do as you're told, Sally," Ross snapped and stalked off. Didn't she understand she could have really been hurt? His heart had constricted when she'd gone down.

Ross had been shocked at how quickly he'd reacted to Sally being hit. He was known for his calm demeanor and even thinking during an emergency. Emotions didn't enter into his decisions—ever. But where Sally was concerned, he stepped out of his norm.

His heart still slammed against his chest as he walked back to his post. Slowly he calmed down. Started thinking straight, but the damage was already done.

Sally had only been doing her job. Surely she'd been pushed and hit before by a crazy patient. The difference was it hadn't happened in front of him. Something primal had fueled him. He was going to protect his woman. In seconds, he'd shifted into defensive mode.

One of the firefighters handed him his radio. Ross

hadn't even realized he'd dropped it. His lieutenant gave him an odd look when Ross joined him. Ross didn't acknowledge it. Instead he started issuing orders.

Who had seen his over-the-top reaction? Would they put two and two together and figure out he and Sally were seeing each other? Worse, would his loss of professionalism get back to the bosses?

Sally went to the hospital emergency room against her will even though she knew it was necessary. It was company and fire department protocol that it be done. Thankfully, X-rays indicated there were no broken bones, but she had to admit her face throbbed. It had already started turning dreadful colors just as Ross had said.

She'd been told not to return to the station. Someone had been called in to replace her. A policeman had given her a ride home.

Ross had broken their professional relationship. In two. She could've handled the situation. He had overstepped his bounds. His reaction had been way over the top. She'd never seen him act that way. Part of her appreciated him caring enough that he was that concerned about her, but it wasn't good for either one of their careers for him to go ballistic, particularly where she was concerned. It was just an example of why they should not be seeing each other. What if the higher-ups got wind of what happened? It might hurt Ross's record.

Yet she kind of liked the idea he'd ridden to her rescue. Chivalry wasn't dead. Once again, he was her knight in shining armor.

There was a knock at the front door. That would be Kody. She'd called him and asked if he and Lucy could come over for the night. She had to have someone with her. With a bag of frozen peas over her eye, she opened the door. Instead of Kody and Lucy, Ross walked in without invitation, carrying a white bag. She watched, bewildered, as he made his way toward the kitchen.

"Hey, you do know I'm mad at you?" she called to his back.

He glanced at her with concern on his face. "Are you all right?"

She followed him to the kitchen. "You know I am. You called twice while I was in the ER. All I have is a black eye. I'm under a concussion watch for the next twelve hours because of the bump on the back of my head, but I'm fine. About your behavior…"

In one swift move he put the bag on the table, turned to her and grabbed her shoulders, looking deeply into her eyes. "Let me make this clear right now. For the rest of my life whenever I see somebody hit you, I'll react the same way. No apologies." He pulled her to him and held her as if she were a new duckling. Tender, but reassuringly safe.

Had he been that scared for her?

Finally, he released a deep breath and let her go. "Have you eaten?"

"No."

"Great. I brought us Chinese takeout." He started removing small white cartons out of a bag.

Just like that they were moving on.

"You need to put those peas on that eye. It looks painful. By the way, why doesn't a paramedic have a disposable ice pack in her own apartment?"

"I'm not a paramedic *all* the time," she said in a huff.

He took her hand and kissed the palm. "I know that. I even like it. A lot." He kissed her and she returned it. "It hurts me to know you were hurt."

This type of attention she could learn to love. In fact, Ross would be easy to love. She was halfway there anyway. Her chest felt heavy. This was just what she'd been afraid would happen. Could she go back? Pretend those feelings didn't exist? Ross coming along wasn't part of her grand plan. "I'm all right, Ross. The guy was on drugs. Those people are always unpredictable. Next time I'll have a policeman secure their hands before I see about them."

"Next time? There better not be another one where you get hurt." He hugged her again. "For somebody who has dedicated their life to caring for people like you have, then have somebody do you that way…"

She cupped his face. "You do know it comes with the territory sometimes."

"Yeah, but that doesn't mean I have to like it." He suddenly looked tired. As if his emotions had gotten the best of him.

"Says the man who runs into burning buildings." She could well remember how she had felt when he had run into the burning house.

"Let's eat before it gets cold."

It was as if Ross couldn't stand to talk about what had happened anymore. As if his emotions were too open, fresh. She'd focused on her feelings and not enough on his. Ross was being so sweet she couldn't be mad at him anymore. He really had been scared.

They had just finished their meal when there was a knock at the door.

"That'll be Kody."

Before she could get up, Ross rose and went to the door. "I'll get it."

How was Kody going to react when he saw Ross at her place? He'd already started asking questions.

"Come on in. She's in here," she heard Ross say.

Lucy came down the hall. Ross and Kody were still at the door. What were they saying to each other?

"Aunt Sally, are you okay?" Lucy asked, making it impossible to hear the men.

"I'll be fine. You don't need to worry about me." Sally patted the cushion beside her.

Lucy plopped down.

A minute later Kody, flanked by Ross, came into the living room.

"So how're you doing, Sweet Pea?" Kody stood above her, studying her.

"A black eye and a bump on the head, but I'm fine. I should be good by tomorrow."

Kody dropped his bag with a thump. "So..." he glanced at Ross, then focused on Sally "...we're here to watch over you."

"That won't be necessary," Ross said from where he leaned against the wall. "I'll be here." His wooden tone implied his mind wouldn't be changed.

Sally's heart tapped as she looked between the two men.

Kody's head whipped around in Ross's direction. "Really?"

"Yes." Ross didn't miss a beat as he gave Kody a steady look. These were two bulls marking their territory of protection.

Abruptly Kody looked at her. "So it's like that?"

Sally nodded.

Kody looked at Ross, who flatly said, "It is."

Sally watched her brother's face harden. "I'm sorry to have bothered you. I didn't know Ross was coming when I called you."

"Lucy, honey, there's been a change in plans. We won't be staying tonight." Kody waved her toward him.

"But I wanted to stay," Lucy whined.

Sally put her arm around Lucy's shoulders. "When I'm feeling better you can come back."

Ross walked Kody and Lucy to the front door. Sally listened from where she was.

"Lucy, go wait in the truck. I'll be right out," Kody told her. The child obediently went. Sally held her breath.

"You break her heart and I'll break you."

Ross returned with a firm "Ten-four."

# CHAPTER NINE

ROSS STOOD NEXT to the fire engine two days later, working on his monthly equipment inspection, when he noticed the Battalion Chief's truck pulling into the station parking lot. It was Battalion Chief Marks.

He and Chief Marks had been friends for some time. Ross had been in his company when he'd first joined the fire department. Chief Marks had been a mentor to him, even encouraged Ross to put in for the Battalion Chief position. What made this particular visit interesting was that he wasn't Battalion Chief over Ross's station. Was this good news or bad news?

Anxiety filled Ross. Did Chief Marks have news about the selection?

"Hey, it's nice to see you." Ross walked toward him with a hand extended as his friend entered the station.

"Ross." Chief Marks shook Ross's hand.

"How's Jenna and the kids?" Ross asked.

"Doing great."

"Good. What brings you over to my side of town?"

Chief Marks's expression turned serious. "I wanted to talk to you about something that has come up."

"That sounds ominous," Ross said a little more casually than he felt.

"Why don't we go into your office to talk?"

"Okay." Ross led the way. In his office, he dropped his clipboard on the desk and sat in the seat behind it. Chief Marks took the chair across from him. "So what's up?"

"I'm not going to beat around the bush on this, Ross. I heard something happened the other day during a run that had to do with a female paramedic."

Ross didn't try acting as if he didn't know what Chief Marks was talking about. "I was just taking care of my company."

Chief Marks's look held steady. "You sure there wasn't more to it?"

Ross knew there was more to it. However, what he was having trouble determining was just what "more to it" meant. He wasn't going to lie. That would come back to haunt him. This man was his friend. Had his best interests at heart. "Yeah, we're seeing each other."

Chief Marks leaned back in his chair, crossed his fingers over his belly and pursed his lips.

Ross returned his direct look. Sally had been upset with him. Apparently, she'd been right, if the Battalion Chief's question was any indication. It might have been unprofessional for him to have grabbed the man, but Ross was a human first and he had been scared for Sally. Seeing her hit had made him roaring mad. He'd be that way again where she was concerned. That was the problem. He couldn't ignore his feelings for her. Now he had to deal with the fallout of his actions.

"I'm going to shoot you straight here. This isn't good for your promotion. I don't think the Chief has heard about it, which is in your favor. Only time will tell on that. If he does, it very well may be the end of your chances for Battalion Chief. I'd hate to see that. You're a good firefighter. Are you in love with her?"

Was he? Ross wasn't sure. He did care—a lot. His performance the other day proved how much he cared. But love? That meant forever for him. He'd been concentrating so hard on not examining his feelings that he wasn't sure. "I think I am."

"Then I suggest you think things through carefully. What you decide may mean your career." Chief Marks stood.

Ross did as well.

"I hope I get to see you in the Battalion Chiefs' meeting soon." With that, Chief Marks left.

In his own way, he had told Ross what he should do. But could he?

He and Sally had started as a fling, a weekend together. Then it had stretched to a few weeks. Yet as the days went by he wanted more. She seemed to as well. They'd not spoken of ending things in weeks. Now that the time had come he didn't want to. What he felt for Sally was real. Something special. He couldn't just throw it away. They needed to find a way to make this work. Wasn't there some design where he could have both? He couldn't just walk away from her.

He desperately wanted that Battalion Chief job. He'd worked all his professional life to earn this promotion. He'd done the schooling, taken the additional classes and been the best captain he could be. The only hiccup had been this period with Sally. Why should the Battalion Chief position hang on his personal life? If he got the job and didn't have Sally, what would he really have? When had she become the most important? It didn't matter, just that she was.

The problem would niggle at him until Ross spoke to her. Surely together they could work something out where they could both have what they wanted. She would return to work the next day, but he had to talk to her before then.

They couldn't share another shift until they'd had the conversation. He called her and she agreed to meet him at his place instead of him going to hers.

Ross didn't remember the drive home. All he could think about was the upcoming discussion. He needed a solution. Sally would be going to medical school soon, of that he had no doubt, and that would improve the situation greatly. If she'd moved, then they wouldn't be working together even between semesters.

His chest tightened. What if she didn't care as much as he did? They'd never spoken of their feelings. He had to jerk the truck back to his side of the road before he was hit. Was he planning for something that didn't even exist? A fling was their agreement. Now he was wanting to change that. There had been no promises between them. What if she didn't want any? He and Alice had made promises and nothing had come from them—what if that happened again with Sally? Panic started to build. Suddenly the promotion seemed a small concern.

When Ross arrived home, Sally was waiting on the porch swing. He would always think of her that way. She loved the swing. It was her favorite place. His heart quickened. Sally was nice to come home to.

She came to the top of the steps and waited. He took her into his arms, kissing her with all the care he felt. She returned his kiss with equal enthusiasm.

Afterward she giggled. "I see that Texas star is still working for you."

"Yeah, and I'm going to use it every chance I can get." He kissed her again.

She reached for his bag. "Let me have that and I'll put it up while you go see to the horses."

He let her take the bag. Their talk would come soon enough.

\* \* \*

Sally found Ross under the large oak tree a few minutes later. He stood beside the fence looking off into the horizon.

"Hey." She placed her hand between his shoulder blades and rubbed his back. "Something bothering you? How were things at the house today? Anything exciting happen?"

He didn't answer immediately while his attention remained on something out in the pasture. "Chief Marks came to see me."

She grabbed his arm. What did that mean? Had Ross gotten the Battalion Chief position? She wanted it for him so badly. She knew it meant as much to him as her doing well on the MCAT did to her. Excitement bubbled in her. "He did? Is it good news?"

Ross gave her a sad shake of his head. "Sweet Sally, I hate to disappoint you. No, what he came to tell me was that he'd heard about what happened at the accident the other day."

The colorful balloon of delight at the chance he might have the job deflated with a whoosh. Her stomach tightened.

"He wanted to know if I was seeing you. What the situation was."

She moved away just far enough she could see his face. "And...you said?"

He turned to look at her. "I told him the truth." Ross didn't say anything more for a few moments, then, "He thinks what happened at the accident site could affect my chances for Battalion Chief. The committee looks for any little thing to make a difference between candidates."

Sally bit her top lip. The day had come. "I see."

Ross turned to her. "Sally, help me find some way

around this. Together we can come up with a plan. Maybe you could transfer? You're going to school sometime soon anyway. It could be temporary, then you could move back if I make Battalion Chief. I'd be over stations that didn't include Twelves."

She couldn't, wouldn't, be the reason Ross didn't get his dream. That had been done to her by Wade and she wouldn't be the one to do it to Ross. He deserved better. But to transfer? She'd told him once that she wouldn't do that. But what if she did and he didn't get the job? Or she didn't get into med school? She helped Kody with Lucy. If they were in the same station, they could work out the schedule easier. She lived nearby the station house. More than all that, she'd promised herself she'd never rearrange her life again for a man.

Ross had said nothing about his feelings. What if she upended her life for him? What if Ross never made a real commitment? What if all he wanted was what they had now? She couldn't take chances with her life like that. Too much damage had been done to her dreams and herself by her relationship with Wade and she refused to let that happen between her and Ross.

Sally shook her head. "Ross, I won't be the reason you don't get the job of your dreams. I've been in your spot before. I know what it's like to push your dreams away to make room for someone else's. Please don't ask me to."

He searched her eyes for something she couldn't identify before saying, "We knew all along that this day was coming. One way or another." His voice had become firm, taken on his captain-in-charge tone.

"Yeah, if it wasn't you, it would be me. Hopefully I'll know something about med school soon. It's been a nice ride while it lasted."

Ross sighed heavily. "It's just that I've worked toward

moving up the ranks my entire career. This is my chance. Higher-ranking jobs don't come along often. I believe I can make a difference in Austin's fire department. That I'm the kind of leader they need."

Sally put a hand on his arm. "Hey, you don't have to sell me on the idea. I believe that about you as well. We agreed to keep it between ourselves for just that reason."

Ross was still focused on his job, she could understand that, even hoped the promotion was his, but still it hurt that he wanted it more than he needed her. That even after what she had told him about her marriage, he still had the nerve to ask her to transfer without any mention of his feelings.

But Ross hadn't led her to believe anything different about what he wanted in life. Had never mentioned the future, or wanting more. She shouldn't be upset. If the table was turned, wouldn't she give him up if it meant missing out on med school? She'd let Ross get too close. "This wasn't supposed to be this hard."

He faced her. "No, it wasn't. But we can remain friends."

Sally shook her head. "No, we've tried that before. Co-workers, yes—friends, no. It would never work."

"I guess you're right." His voice was flat.

She looked out at the green pasture with the sun shining across it. Ross's ranch had felt more like home than any place she'd been in a long time. But it had never really been hers. It was a part of that pretend world she'd let herself be drawn into once again.

"I better be going." She went up on her toes and kissed his cheek. His hands came to her waist and he brought her to him. Sally gently pushed him away. "Please don't. It only makes it harder. Please don't come in the house until I'm gone. Have a happy life, Ross."

She held her tears until she reached the front door. In a blurry haze, she gathered her belongings. Stuffing them haphazardly into a bag, she headed out of the house. Ross had honored her request, but he now waited at the bottom of the porch steps.

His lips formed a thin line on his handsome face. Maybe one day he would find the right woman for him, and the timing would be right. The thought made her heart feel as if it were being squeezed to death. If only they were different people.

"Can I help you?"

She shook her head and kept going. He didn't move as she threw her bag into the car, got in and drove away. Yet she was aware that his eyes didn't leave her.

Hours later Ross hit the fence staple another time despite it already being secure in the post. After Sally had left, he'd gathered his fence-repair bag, saddled Romeo and ridden as if the devil were after him to the remotest point of his property. There he'd started checking the fence that was already in good repair.

He was doing anything he could to drown out the voice that poked and prodded that she hadn't been willing to help him find a way around the situation. Hadn't wanted to fight for them.

He didn't like her decision at all, but he really couldn't give a good argument against it. Maybe she was right. Their relationship had been a diversion. If he got the Battalion Chief position, then he would start working on the Assistant Chief position. Yes, this was for the best. If they had waited till later on to break up, it would have just been harder.

So why did he feel as if his heart had been ripped out? Worse, something about the situation made him think he'd treated her far more badly than her husband had.

Maybe when this Battalion Chief stuff was over they could try again.

He shook his head.

No, as long as she was working in the same station as he it would never work. If she didn't get into medical school, she'd have to keep her job. And even if she did, she still wanted to stay on at the station for part-time work. One of them would have to give up something they greatly wanted in order for them to have a relationship.

Ross hit the post even harder.

What they'd had was all there would be.

He jerked his shirt off and used it to mop the sweat off his face. Afterward, he looked at it and groaned. Just a few weeks ago, he wouldn't have even done that. Even when he was alone. Sally had changed his world in more ways than one.

Ross didn't return to the house until just after dark. He wasn't looking forward to going inside where he'd shared such wonderful moments with Sally. She had permeated every aspect of his life. The thought of climbing in his bed without her drove him to sleep on the sofa.

The next few days weren't much better. Everything in his world had been turned upside down and not for the better. If he'd been miserable before, it came nowhere near the pain he experienced now. What he had to do was learn to live with it.

He hadn't even gotten to the hard part. Working with Sally and knowing he couldn't touch her.

Sally had gone home and flung herself on her bed to sob until there were no more tears.

With Wade it had all been make-believe, and now with Ross… The only difference was that she'd known this was how it would end from the beginning. Still, she couldn't stop her heart from being involved. It was breaking.

Ross hadn't demanded she make changes. He'd suggested it as an idea. She'd known how important the promotion was to him from day one. Ross didn't deserve any comparison to Wade. Had she been putting that on every man she met? Ross had proven trustworthy over and over.

Still, what if she'd been the only one to make concessions and their time together had run its course or Ross had become so caught up in his job their relationship had died? What would she have then? She just couldn't take that chance.

Done with her crying, she climbed into the shower, ordered her thoughts and put her emotions on autopilot before she dressed for work. At least there she would be distracted until she and Ross had to share a shift. That she wasn't looking forward to.

She returned to the station to great fanfare, but her heart was heavy. She put on a brave face, with the intention of not letting on how broken she was. Thankfully everyone was focused on her bright purple eye. It looked worse than it felt. Her heart was far more battered.

Her fellow shift members made fun of her, along with shadowboxing when they walked past her. A couple of them made jokes about Ross's over-the-top reaction to one of his company getting hit. None of them asked any deeper questions about why Ross had acted the way he did. She was glad. Not being honest with them would have bothered her. Talking about him would have made her cry. It would all be out if she let that happen.

She dreaded the day she and Ross shared the same shift. When she'd first become involved with him, she'd known that when they stopped seeing each other their working relationship would be strained. Now they were going to have to deal with just that. It wouldn't be fun, but she would keep moving. She couldn't give up her job just because it was difficult being around Ross.

Her fear came true a week later. The new schedule was posted and there along with Ross's name was hers on the same day. She came to work determined to keep her thoughts on her job and not let the fact she was just feet from Ross for a full twenty-four hours affect her work. She'd have to learn to deal with the reality that she couldn't talk to him on a personal level or touch him on an intimate one. Those thoughts almost caused physical pain. She understood in her head that their being apart was necessary, but her heart wasn't convinced.

Managing to make it to the locker room without running into Ross, she put away her bag. When she returned to the bay, she saw him standing beside one of the trucks talking to the captain of the outgoing shift. She stopped dead still. Her heart drummed against her ribs.

This situation was more excruciating than she'd anticipated. With a fortitude she didn't know she had, she picked up her clipboard and headed for the ambulance to do her routine shift check of the supplies. Ross looked in her direction. She nodded and kept moving. The rest of the shift she stayed on her side of the building. Despite that she was well aware of where he was at all times.

The only time her brain shut him out was when they were on a call. Thankfully it was a relatively busy shift. By the next day and shift-change time, she was more mentally than physically exhausted.

Ross had spoken to her a couple of times to give her directions during a run. There was never anything but professional interaction between them, which was as it should be, yet she longed for more. She'd put a bag of his things that he had kept at her place in the back of his truck before she'd left the station. That was the last of anything personal between them.

The next time they shared a shift, only a few days later, it was better. She kept to herself and had as little inter-action with the firefighters as possible. What she feared would happen when she became involved with Ross had. Now she was reaping what she'd sown.

She'd been hurt when she'd found out Wade was cheat-ing on her but none of those feelings compared to what she was experiencing now. It was like walking around as a shell of a person. Ross had become essential to her living and breathing, and not having him was slowly killing her.

She had to get out of this funk. Her grade on the MCAT should arrive any day. When she found out how she'd done, then she could really move forward, make plans. Her focus would be on school and what was happening at the hospi-tal. Still, she would need to do part-time paramedic work to pay the bills and keep her certificate up to date. That would mean working with the fire department and pos-sibly Ross, if he didn't get the Battalion Chief's position.

Somehow she'd get beyond this. Or would she?

It had been a couple weeks since she'd stopped see-ing Ross when Kody started asking questions. She was at one of Lucy's school functions when he pulled her off to the side.

"What's going on with you, Sweet Pea?"

She wasn't going to tell him that she was heartsick. "I told you not to call me that."

"Don't evade the question. I know something's going on. You didn't look this bad when you divorced that jerk you married."

"I'm fine. I'm just anxious about my MCAT grades." Or she could tell him she hadn't slept a full night since the last time she was in bed with Ross.

Kody huffed loud enough that a couple of people looked at them. "I was on Ross's shift today."

"What does that have to do with me?" She didn't meet his look.

"It's just interesting that he has the same look."

She said softly, "We're not seeing each other anymore."

Kody bared his teeth. "I told him he'd have to deal with me if he broke your heart."

Sally placed a hand on Kody's arm, giving him a pleading look. "Please don't say anything to Ross. We both agreed it was for the best. His actions when I got my black eye were noticed by the bosses. I don't want him to lose his chances for advancement because of me. I'd never want to be responsible for that. I'm going to medical school, I hope, and I won't have time for a relationship. It's for the best. It's not Ross's fault."

"I just hate to see you hurting."

"I'll get over it."

Kody studied her. "Will you?"

Lucy's program was starting so Sally didn't have a chance to answer. If she said yes, she was afraid she would be lying to him as well as to herself.

# CHAPTER TEN

ROSS TURNED IN his chair so that he could look out the window into the bay for a chance glimpse of Sally. He did that too often on the days she worked. His time was spent figuring out a way to get through those days in particular and life in general without her. He missed having her as part of his real world. Just seeing her at work wasn't enough. Then again, if he never saw Sally, maybe he'd get over her. Either way, he wasn't sure how to survive. What he was currently doing wasn't working.

Right now, she stood beside the ambulance grinning at her crew member. She hadn't smiled at him in days. Not having her happiness directed at him was a physical hurt in his chest.

Sally kept a low profile, staying on her side of the building as much as possible. The first couple of weeks, that had been fine with him, easier in fact, but now it made him angry, sad. This wasn't a way for either one of them to live. His days had turned tedious and challenging, in not a good way.

The last time they'd worked together he'd scheduled a station meeting that included the medical side before an inspection. He and Sally hadn't been in a room together in weeks. She'd sat in the back keeping as much distance between them as possible. As he'd spoken, a couple of times his glance had met hers. There had been a gloomy aura in her eyes. He'd stammered over his words. It was his fault it was there.

But wasn't it Sally who had agreed they'd just have a good time together? That she wanted no attachment because she didn't want a relationship to interfere with her plans? She'd known what they were doing wouldn't last. So why did she act as if she were taking it so hard? Did she care for him more than she'd let on? More than he'd realized?

At dinner that evening they made sure to sit on opposite ends of the long table where it wasn't easy to interact, yet he was aware of every move she made. Her laugh skated down his spine. It should be him sharing that with her. Something had to give soon. He couldn't continue to live like this.

They were just finishing eating when the alarm sounded. Relief washed over him. Was it wrong of him to be grateful for a call? At least on those he would focus on something other than Sally.

Everyone jumped into action, leaving their plates on the table.

The dispatcher called out: "Three-year-old. Stuck in storm drain. Fifth and Park."

Despite his desire to be elsewhere, this was a call Ross didn't want to hear. A sick feeling filled his stomach. He'd trained for this eventuality, but it was one he'd never been involved in and had never wanted to have to oversee either. He'd heard more than once at seminars that it was the most difficult, emotionally and physically.

To make matters worse, a storm was on the way. And it was getting dark. The clock was ticking on two levels. Could the situation be grimmer?

Ross was out of the truck the second it stopped at the

scene and striding toward the policeman standing beside a sobbing woman.

"What's the situation?" he asked the policeman.

"This woman's child climbed in the drain after a ball and fell in. He's been in there for about ten minutes now. We've heard him crying."

"Ma'am…" Ross placed his hand on her arm briefly, to get her attention "…I need you to talk to him. Tell him someone's coming to get him. Reassure him. Can you do that?"

She nodded.

Ross said into the radio, "I need a blanket over here."

Seconds later one of his firefighters brought it to him.

"Put the blanket down in front of the drain and have the mother talk to the child."

"Yes, sir," the policeman said.

Ross assured the woman, "We'll get him out." As he walked away, he said into the radio, "I need a plan of the drainage lines along here, asap."

"Copy that," his lieutenant replied.

"Have the policeman in charge meet me at the truck," he said into the radio.

"Ten-four. He's right here and on his way," the engineer came back.

Ross talked as he walked, surveying the area. "We're going to need rope, the tripod, and have medical on standby."

"Medical here." Sally's voice came across the air.

At the truck, he told the policeman to see that people stayed back and to reroute traffic. This rescue wasn't going to happen fast.

Ross spoke into the radio. "Remove your turnout gear. Put vests on. We're going to be here for a while. I need three men to meet me at the drain. We've got to get that cement cover off so we can see what's going on." Ross removed his gear. He was wearing a T-shirt, pants and his regular shoes, and added his reflective light coat. He put on a yellow hard hat.

When he joined his firefighters at the drain, the policeman guided the mother away so Ross and the other three men could flip the cover over and out of the way.

"These things are supposed to have a grate," one of the men said.

The policeman offered, "Yeah, but they get missed or rust out. This one doesn't have one for whatever reason and now there's a kid to save."

"Flashlight," Ross said.

Sally handed him hers. He shined it into the hole. It was about twenty feet deep and three feet wide. At the bottom he could just make out the top of a child's head where the drain fed into the larger cross drain. The boy wasn't saying anything now. However, there was an occasional whimper so they knew he was alive.

The problems were mounting. Rain was coming. The sun was setting. The boy was going into shock. Now the narrow drain.

One of the men stated the obvious. "Captain, none of us are small enough to go down."

Could the situation get any more challenging?

"I'll do it." Sally's voice came from behind him.

*It could!*

She was the slightest on the shift. To punctuate the need to hurry, thunder rolled. Rain would be here soon. The child could drown if they didn't get moving.

Ross's first instinct was to say no, knowing Sally's history. Plus, it was against regulations because Sally wasn't a firefighter, and she hadn't been trained for this situation.

But there was no choice. If they didn't move now, the child would certainly die. Ross had to think about the bigger picture. Now that included putting Sally's life in danger.

"Get us some light here. Secure the tripod over the hole. Triple-check the rope and pulley. I'll get Sally into the harness," he told the men. "Sally, come with me."

He led her to the rescue truck. After making sure no one could hear him, he said in a low voice, "Are you sure about this?"

Sally gave him a firm nod. "I'm sure."

"It's everything you hate."

She gave him a determined look. "If I don't go, the child will die."

"We could look for another way." Yet he knew of no other way. He wanted to take this burden away from both of them.

"You and I know there isn't one, so help me with the harness." Her voice indicated she wouldn't discuss it further.

Resigned, Ross pulled the harness out of the storage box on the side of the truck. He helped her step into it, pulled it into position over her jumpsuit and around her leg before buckling it at her waist. "If I could have it any other way, I would."

She gave him a thin-lipped nod. "I know that."

He took out a helmet with a light on the front, placed it on her head. His gaze met hers as he buckled it under her chin. There was a flicker of fear in her eyes that pulled at his heart. Sally was the bravest woman he'd ever known. She was facing her fears head-on. Could he say that about himself?

"You know, to make this even worse, we're going to have to send you in upside down. The space isn't wide enough for you to turn around to put a harness on the kid. You'll have to go down headfirst, secure him in the basket, come up and we'll pull the kid out. You'll have a headset. I'll be right there with you the whole way."

After what had passed between them over the last few weeks, did that reassure her? Ross hoped it did. He wanted her to trust he was there for her.

"I understand. I can do this."

He grabbed a pair of leather gloves and handed them to her. "These may be a little too large, but they'll be better than nothing."

"Thanks." She pulled them on.

"Okay. Let's go," Ross said.

She called to her crew member to bring the child-size basket. "What's the boy's name?"

Ross asked into his radio, "What's the boy's name?"

"Mikey."

"Ten-four."

When they arrived at the hole, Ross said to Sally, "Don't take any chances. If you think something isn't right, come up."

"Ten-four."

Ross asked one of the firefighters for his radio head unit. He positioned it around Sally's neck. "You don't have to push anything, just talk. I can hear you and you can hear me." He set the channel so that it would only be the two of them on it. Flipping on the light and securing the basket to her chest, he said, "You ready?"

Their eyes held for a moment as the rain started to fall. Sally nodded and he clipped the rope onto the harness. She went down on her hands and knees. As she put her head into the hole, Ross and one of the other firefighters each took hold of one of her legs and guided her in. Another two firefighters manned the rope, slowly letting it out.

Ross's chest tightened to the point he couldn't take a full breath as he watched Sally's feet disappear into the blackness.

Fear clutched her heart as Sally slid into the tight space. The only thing that kept her going was the knowledge that if she didn't do this a child would die. It could have been Lucy, or Jared or Olivia.

By inches, she was lowered. Her head hurt from the blood rushing to it but soon eased as it adjusted. Either way she had to just not think about it. Using her hands, she guided her way down. She was thankful for the helmet light. Without it she wasn't sure she could remain sane.

"Sally, talk to me." It was Ross's deep, calming voice, yet there was still an edge to it. He was afraid for her. Ross knew her fear too well.

"I'm about halfway down. I see the child. He isn't moving."

She continued downward as her clothes began to get wet.

"It's really raining now, isn't it?"

"Ten-four." Ross hadn't even tried to keep his concern out of his voice that time.

"Okay, I've reached him. Hold me here." She hung just above the boy. He was sitting on the mush made of old leaves, grass clippings and garbage with his head leaning against the wall. "Mikey? I'm here to help you."

There was no reply from the child. A chill went through her. She pulled off a glove and used her mouth to hold it. Reaching down, she checked the boy's neck for a pulse. She blew out a sigh of relief. "He's alive, but in shock."

"Ten-four. Now get him in that basket and we'll get you up here."

Water poured in a steady stream around her and over

her as she released the basket. It was growing higher in the shaft because the child plugged part of the cross-drain hole. She needed to get the boy out of the way to let water flow into the larger drain before it came above his head. If she could get the basket flat enough to get the child into it, she could move him out into the larger drain long enough for her to go completely down. The water was rising by the minute.

"Sally, talk to me!"

She spat out the glove and took off the other one. They were just in the way now.

"I'm thinking down here!" At least her frustration with Ross's demands was taking her mind off how dangerous all of this was. "Water is getting higher down here."

"We're diverting all we can."

"Lower me another foot." She went down. "Right there."

She needed to lay the basket down beside the boy, but she couldn't have him float away on the water rushing down the larger drain.

"Send the other line down."

Seconds later another rope came down beside her.

"What're you doing?" Ross demanded.

"I'm having to do some repositioning."

"Repositioning?" Ross's voice wasn't as steady as it usually was.

She clipped the line onto the basket, then laid it next to the boy.

Placing her hands under the child's arms, she used all her strength to lift him into the basket. She pulled the blanket in the basket over him the best she could and clipped him in. Water was beginning to wash over him.

"Give me some slack in the second rope."

"Ten-four," Ross came back.

"Now in mine." She went down. "That's good. That's good."

Sally pushed the basket out into the larger cross drain, making sure the boy's head stayed well above the water, then angled the basket against the wall.

"Let me down some more."

"What?" Ross all but screamed in her ear.

"Do it, Ross."

Seconds later she had her head in the larger drain. She was glad to see that it was about five feet wide. Her knees hit the bottom of the small drain. A moment of panic washed through her when she feared her feet wouldn't quite make it but they soon slid down the slick wall. Cold water poured around her. It was rising. Her teeth chattered. She was soon lying on her stomach, with her head raised in the cross drain as water flowed down her sides. Rolling over, she grabbed the boy and pushed the basket back through the opening.

The increasing pressure of the water current made it difficult to maneuver. She braced her feet against the wall to hold her position and held her head up to the point she strained her neck to keep it out of the water.

"Pull him up. Slowly. I can't see him or guide him. I'm having to do it all by feel."

Ross gave the order. The basket started moving. Soon it left her fingertips.

"What've you done? You're supposed to be coming up." Panic filled Ross's voice.

"There was a change in plan. It's a swimming pool down here."

She hoped with everything in her that she could get back into the other drain without any trouble.

"Uh, Ross, it's going to be a little tricky down here for

the next few minutes. You mind talking to me and keeping my mind off it while I figure things out?"

"Aw, Sweet Sally, you're killing me. We have the kid. The EMT is checking him right now. He'll be on the way to the hospital soon."

Sally tucked her head back through the hole into the smaller down drain. So far so good. "How're Romeo and Juliet doing?"

"They're great." His voice lowered. "I think they miss you. I know I do."

If she hadn't been concentrating so hard on what she was doing, she would've reveled in that statement. Sally continued to snake her way upward into the drain.

"Tighten the rope."

Ross gave the order.

"Now pull me slowly. I'm not sure I'm going to make it through this way."

Ross's groan sounded as if he was in agony, then he gave the order.

With the help of the tension on the rope to support her and performing an extreme back bend, she slid through until she was on her knees. She'd have scrapes on her back from that maneuver. Her jumpsuit had been torn. "Stop."

The rope didn't move. She came to her feet. The water came to her calves. She needed to get out of here.

"Is everything all right?" Ross's voice held a note of panic.

"Ten-four. I just needed to stand up." Seconds later she said, "Hey, Ross, would you mind pulling me out of here?"

He snapped. "Let's get her out, guys."

She was halfway up when she said, "I've missed you too."

"You're going to be the death of me." The words were almost a caress.

Her head had hardly popped out of the hole before Ross's hands were under her arms and she was hoisted against him. "I don't know what I'd do if I lost you."

"Stop, Ross," she whispered, pushing against his shoulders. She looked behind him to see the Battalion Chief watching them. "Don't do this. How do you think it looks?"

Thankfully others grabbed her, so that it looked as if everyone was taking their turn in congratulating her, making Ross's embrace look as if it weren't anything special.

She wiped the dirt on her face as she stood in the heavy rain. To her great amazement Ross dropped his coat, pulled his shirt over his head and started cleaning her face. Embarrassed at his attention, she took it from him and used it to finish the job.

The shirt was soaked yet still warm from Ross's body. The musky smell of him clung to the fibers. Sally inhaled. It had been so long since she'd been close enough to enjoy his scent. She clung to his shirt.

Someone handed her a blanket. Ross pulled his coat back on.

She winced when someone touched her back.

"Are you hurt?" Ross asked with concern as he pushed people away.

"My back."

He spoke into the radio. "I need a medic over here."

"I've just scraped my back. I'll be fine."

"Maybe so, but you'll be checked out." He handed her off to the paramedic. "Now go."

Ross didn't want to live through anything like the last eight hours ever again in his life. Sally going into the drain had been bad enough but those moments when he'd feared she couldn't get out had almost been more than his heart could take. He'd actually thought he was going to lose her.

He'd been such a self-serving piece of human debris. He'd never once considered Sally's feelings. He'd acted as if it had all been about him, his job. Not once had he questioned if what he was doing was right for them both. He'd encouraged her to have a fling with him when she'd not wanted to out of fear he would act the way he had. Sally had known herself too, known how invested she would become in their relationship.

It hadn't taken him long to learn that she didn't give by half measures, yet he'd pushed her into seeing him when she'd known full well what would happen. The worst part was that he knew her history and had done it anyway. As much as he would like to think that he was better than her ex-husband, he wasn't. He'd treated her the same way. As if her needs and dreams weren't as important as his.

He'd even asked her to make concessions for him. He'd not once considered doing that for her. What kind of person was he? Was he even good enough for Sally? With every fiber in his being he wanted her, loved her. If she would take him back, he'd do everything in his power to be worthy of her.

After they had cleaned up and returned to the house, he'd requested that all the company be allowed to go to the hospital and check on Sally. They went in as a group. Sally had been asleep most of the time. He was sure that she was exhausted from coming off an adrenaline rush, the cold of the water, the physical exertion she'd endured and the fear she'd had to control. The doctor said she would be fine. She only had bumps, bruises and some major scrapes on her back. They were going to keep her for observation until morning.

"Okay, guys, we need to get back to the house," Ross reluctantly announced. He'd have stayed if he had a choice. Instead he lingered behind the others. Reaching for Sally's hand that lay on the hospital bed, he found it warm, which was reassuring. He kissed her lips before whispering, "I love you."

"Captain…" His lieutenant stopped short at the door.

Ross looked at him as he straightened.

The man grinned. "It's about time you admitted it."

"You knew?"

His lieutenant shrugged. "Heck, we all do."

Ross was shocked. "How?"

The man chuckled. "By the way you look at her, or don't lately. But the real clue was when you called out her name during the night."

Ross rolled his eyes. "I'm not going to live it down, am I?"

The man squished up his nose and mouth and shook his head. "I doubt it."

With one last look at Sally, Ross left. Tomorrow he'd start eating humble pie and begging her to take him back. Promotion or not, he wasn't giving her up. If she'd have him. He was afraid that would be a huge *if*.

Kody would be caring for her. Ross had called him to tell him what had happened and asked him to take care of Sally until he could get off his shift.

"I thought you weren't seeing each other anymore," Kody said.

"That's going to change."

"It is, is it?" Kody asked with humor in his voice.

"Yes."

"Then I suggest you bring flowers and chocolate because she's going to need convincing. She'll never agree to play second best to anyone or anything else again." Kody's voice held a firm note.

"I know that. I already feel guilty enough without you piling it on. I don't plan for her to ever be second best again. She'll always be the most important to me. She'll come first."

"Then I'd make that clear and keep that promise."

"That's what I plan to do. Now, will you pick her up at the hospital and get her home until I can get there?"

Kody huffed. "Come on, Ross, I've been watching over her all her life. I can handle this."

"After this time, it'll be my job." Ross hung up.

The station had made the morning TV news and the newspapers. A picture of him embracing Sally was on the front page. Everything he felt for her was there for the world to see. Everything he hadn't wanted the fire department's higher-ups to know. Sally was being hailed as a hero, as she should be. His leadership hadn't gone unnoticed either, or the abilities of the other firefighters.

By the time shift change came around, Ross was anxious to get out of the station. He wanted to see Sally, hold her and reassure himself that she was really okay. He'd called the hospital a couple of times to check on her after they had arrived back at the house. On the last call he'd been told she'd gone home. She would be with Kody.

Ross drove straight to Sally's house from the station. He all but ran to her door. Once again he hesitated there. Would she want to see him? What would he do if she didn't? Beg. Yes, beg was the plan. Somehow, he had to get through to her. He took his courage in hand and knocked. She didn't answer. He tried again. Nothing. He tried calling her on the phone and there was no answer. Slowly he walked back to his truck. Where was she?

Maybe she was at Kody's. He tried phoning him. There was no answer. He went by Kody's house. He wasn't home either. Where were they? Could they be at the station picking up Sally's car? Ross made a circle back by there. Sally's car was gone. He tried her phone. Still no answer.

He'd just have to go home and keep calling. After he saw to the horses, he'd put on his best shirt and pants, buy some flowers and chocolate, and try again. Fear gripped him. Was she nowhere to be found because she didn't want to see him?

Sally hoped what she thought she'd heard Ross say at the hospital was true. That he loved her. Maybe she'd just imagined it because she wanted his love so desperately. She loved him with all her heart. She was admitting it by coming out to his place unannounced.

He had acted as if he'd been relieved, as if she was his world and he'd gotten it back when she'd come up out of the drain. She was afraid that he was going to lose it again with the Battalion Chief standing right there. Ross hadn't seemed to care. It had been wonderful being in Ross's arms again. Having him hold her always made things better.

She glanced at the letter that lay on the swing next to her. It might not solve all their problems, but it might help.

Her heart picked up its pace when she saw Ross's truck coming down the drive. She went down the steps to meet him. Would he be mad or happy to see her?

He pulled the truck to a jerking stop, hopped out and ran to her. "I've been looking everywhere for you." He stopped just short of pulling her into his arms.

"I told Kody to let you know I was coming out here."

"He didn't, but then, he was probably punishing me for being such a jerk," he all but growled.

She shrugged. "You could be right."

Ross studied her for a few moments. "Are you okay? Really okay?"

The concern in his voice touched her heart. Why didn't he touch her? "I'm fine. Really. I just don't want to have to do anything like that again."

"I don't want you to have to either. It almost killed us both." His gaze held hers. "I would've died if you had. I love you."

"You do?"

"I do with all my heart." The intensity of his voice filled her with joy. "You might not have seen much evidence of it lately, but I do."

"I had hoped what I'd heard at the hospital was true."

Ross stepped closer, almost touching her chest with his. "Does that mean I have a chance? To straighten up, strive to be worthy of you? I don't care about promotions anymore, if I can't have you. I can go to a smaller fire department and work. But I won't live without you. I can't."

She placed her hand on his chest. "You're my hero. You've always been worthy enough. I've never doubted that I could trust you, or that you would protect me or be there if I needed someone. Even if we were just friends. But to have your love is so much more."

Ross scooped her into his arms and kissed her as if he would never let her go. She wrapped her arms around his neck and returned his kisses with equal devotion.

When he set her on her feet again, he looked into her eyes. "I love you, Sweet Sally. I will always."

Sally cupped his face with her hand. "And I love you with all my heart."

He kissed her so tenderly that she was afraid she would cry.

"May I show you just how much I love you?" Ross took her hands.

"I thought you'd never ask."

He led her up the steps and into the house.

Ross lay with Sally snuggled beside him. There had been days he'd thought he would never have this again. And never again would he take moments like this for granted. They were too precious. Life was too precious. What mattered was he and Sally being together.

"Hey, handsome. What're you thinking up there?" Sally looked at him from where her head rested on his chest.

"I was thinking what a lucky man I am."

"That was a nice answer." Her fingers trailed over his skin. "I consider myself pretty lucky too. Oh, that reminds me." She hopped out of bed and pulled on his firehouse T-shirt.

Ross watched as her beautiful body with its back marred by long scratches left the room. He winced. They were a reminder of what could have been. He heard the front door open. "Hey, where're you going?"

"I'll be right back. I have something to show you."

Seconds later the door opened again. Sally came into the room with an envelope in her hand.

"What do you have?"

She sat beside him. "This came in the mail yesterday. I didn't get it until I got home today. You were the first person I thought of sharing it with."

"What is it?"

"My MCAT score."

He sat straighter. "How did you do?"

She grinned at him. "Well enough to get into any medical school I want."

Ross gave a whoop and hugged her to him. "That's my Sweet Sally." He gave her a kiss.

"So, where're you thinking of going?" Could he stand it if she went far off? No, anywhere she went there would be a fire department. He'd just have to follow.

"I was thinking of staying here and going to Austin Medical. Kody has a doctor friend who could probably help me get a job afterward."

"Now, that sounds like a good plan. I'm so proud of you." He hugged her.

She met his gaze. "You know, it means a lot to me to have you in my corner."

Ross took her hand and kissed her palm. "You can always count on that."

"I've been thinking that now I know I'm going to medical school soon that maybe I should transfer to another station or maybe go to a private company."

He shook his head. "You don't have to do that. I won't ask you to."

She cupped his cheek. "You're not asking. Or demanding. If that's what it takes to help you, then I'm willing to do it. What matters most to me will always be you."

His heart swelled with love. "And you'll always come first with me."

"I love you, Ross."

His lips brushed hers. "And I love you."

# EPILOGUE

THREE DAYS LATER Ross was about to walk out the door of the station when he got a call from Chief Marks. He wanted Ross to come by his office and see him that afternoon. Ross hesitated. He and Sally had plans to celebrate her medical school acceptance with Kody and Lucy that evening. She was cooking dinner for them at his place.

He grinned. It was his and Sally's place now. He loved knowing she would be there when he came home.

"Can we do it right now? I've plans this evening."

"Sure, come on over," said Chief Marks.

A short drive later, as Ross entered the office Chief Marks stood. "I hear you had an exciting shift the other night?"

"Yeah, the house did."

"You know, most firefighters go an entire career and are never involved in a child rescue like that."

"I know." Where was he going with this? It could have all been said over the phone.

Chief Marks's look turned serious. "I also heard the paramedic did an outstanding job as well."

"Yes, Sally was amazing."

"She's the one, isn't she?" The Chief watched him closely.

Ross sat straighter in his chair. "Yes, sir, she is. She's

also the one for me. I plan to marry her if she'll have me. I appreciate all you've done for me but if I have to choose between the promotion or her I'm always going to pick her."

Battalion Chief Marks smiled. "I don't think you'll have to do that. The Chief was very impressed with the reports he received about the rescue. Some of it wasn't by the regulations but the end result was excellent. The boy will make a complete recovery. The decision on the new Battalion Chief had pretty much been made, but your leadership during the rescue sealed the deal. The Chief gave me the honor of telling you myself. You'll be our newest and youngest ever Battalion Chief." He stood and offered his hand. "Congratulations. You earned it."

With a huge grin, Ross took his hand. "Thank you, sir."

"The Chief plans to announce it when you, your house and the paramedic, uh, Sally, are awarded a citation in a couple of weeks. But he wanted you to know about it now."

Ross left the Chief's office feeling on top of the world. He wouldn't ruin Sally's celebration of her success tonight. It should be all about her. Instead he would tell her his news while they were alone later in bed so they could have their own special celebration.

He touched his injured shoulder. Life was good. Especially now that he had Sally in it.

Sally was at her apartment with Lucy, packing up the last of the small things to take to Ross's. It hadn't required much persuasion on his part to get her to agree to move to the ranch. She loved it there. Almost as much as she loved him. The last few weeks had been a whirlwind. Between her acceptance to medical school, Ross getting his promotion to Battalion Chief and them both receiving citations from the mayor for their work saving the boy, her life and heart were full.

Tomorrow, after Ross and Kody's shift ended they and a few of the other station members would load up the furniture she wanted to keep and move it out to the ranch. One of the firefighters at the station was moving into her apartment and taking over the lease.

"Here, Aunt Sally." Lucy handed her an empty box she'd sent her after.

"Thanks. I think this should almost get it." Sally pulled a stack of books off a shelf in her living room.

The flash of red lights through the window and the sound of a large engine that she knew well drew her attention. What was going on? Was an apartment burning? Someone hurt? She hadn't heard a siren. But they usually turned them off when they entered a neighborhood.

"What's happening?" Lucy asked.

"I don't know but whatever it is the firefighters will take care of it, I'm sure."

The roar of the heavy truck sounded near as if it had pulled to a stop in front of her building. The emergency lights coming in from the windows reflected around the blank walls of the apartment. Sally hurried to the door. Lucy was at her heels. She opened the door to find the large red engine parked in front of her building. In the near darkness, the lights flashing made a real show.

Ross climbed out of the front passenger seat. He was wearing his usual firehouse uniform. This was his last shift before he started his new job, which would require a white shirt and black pants.

Sally walked toward him. "What's wrong? What're y'all doing here?"

Lucy ran past her. "Daddy!"

She looked beyond Ross to see Kody's truck parked behind the engine. The other firefighters on the shift stood by the engine with smiles on their faces.

"Ross, what's going on?" Sally asked.

He came to stand in front of her. "As my last official act as Captain at Station Twelve, I ordered this crew of firefighters to bring me here to ask you something."

She looked at the men at the truck, including her brother, whose smile had broadened, and his daughter, then around at her neighbors, who had come out of their apartments to see what was going on. "You couldn't have done it over the phone?"

He shook his head. "This isn't the kind of question you should ask over the phone."

Sally started to tremble. Her gaze met his.

Ross took her hand and went down on one knee.

Her heart beat wildly.

"Sally Davis, will you marry me?"

Her eyes filled with moisture, making Ross's handsome face blurry. She blinked. Nodding, she said, "Yes."

With a whoop, Ross came onto both feet and grabbed her, twirling her around.

There was clapping and cheers from those around them.

Ross set her feet on the ground before he gave her a kiss so tender she almost started tearing up again.

She looked at him with all the love she felt. "You know, Battalion Chief Lawson, I think Dr. Sally Lawson will sound perfect."

Ross smiled. "As long as we're together, life will be perfect for me."

Sally came up on her toes and kissed him. "For me too."

\* \* \* \* \*

# SECRET INVESTIGATION

**ELIZABETH HEITER**

For my mom, who gets to be surprised by this book
(even though there are no aliens).

# *Prologue*

The sandstorm came first. Then came the bullets.

Training had been going well. The locals wanted to take the lead in the fight on their land, and US Army captain Jessica Carpenter was more than willing to let them. Leave behind the ninety-degree heat—and that was before she loaded herself up with fifty pounds of gear, which made it feel a million degrees hotter. Leave behind the sand that swept up out of nowhere, got into your eyes and nose and mouth until everything was gritty. Leave behind trudging for miles up mountainsides, where one wrong step sent you on a downward slide over nothing but sharp shale and deadly rocks.

Go home to her kids. Her oldest was starting middle school this year. He was getting into gaming and skateboarding, and losing interest in talking to his mom over satellite phones when his friends were down the street waiting. The youngest was about to start kindergarten. Her baby, who'd never met her dad and cried every time her mom left for another tour. Ironic that Jessica, who ran headfirst into firefights, was still here and her unassuming engineer husband had been taken from them with a simple wrong turn in a thunderstorm and a head-on collision with a telephone pole.

"What was that?" The young soldier at her side jerked,

his weapon coming up fast, sweeping the space in front of him even though there was no way he could see anything.

Jessica slapped her hand over the top of the weapon, forcing it toward the ground. "Don't fire unless you can see what you're shooting."

It was going to be nearly impossible. She tried to ignore the hard *thump-thump* of her heart warning her something was wrong. Sandstorms came hard and fast here, with the ability to shred away the top layer of skin. They reduced visibility to almost nothing, and the sound—like high-velocity wind—meant she could barely hear the soldier screaming beside her.

She put her hand on his shoulder, hoping to calm him, as she strained to hear over the wind. Had she imagined the gunshots? Maybe it was a local, startled by the ferocity of the sandstorm. More likely it was one of the newer members of her team, still not used to the violence of it.

The sand whipped up from her feet, stinging every inch of exposed skin like a thousand tiny needles. Times like these, she was grateful for the uniform that stuck to her skin in the heat and the full body armor she and her team had donned. Yes, it was a training op, but they'd chosen to take the locals into a dangerous pass, practice tactical approaches. Out here, you could never discount an ambush.

Yanking her goggles down over her eyes, Jessica blinked and blinked, trying to get the grit out. No matter how much her eyes watered, the sand wouldn't clear. Her vision was still compromised. She hunched her shoulders upward, trying to protect the exposed skin on her face, but it didn't matter. If this kept up, it would be raw in minutes.

Time to bug out. She lifted her radio—her best bet of them hearing through the storm—to tell the team to get back to the vehicles when another shot rang out.

Instinctively she ducked low, forcing the soldier beside

her down, too. Her MP4 carbine assault rifle was up without conscious thought, but she couldn't see a thing. Was there a real threat? Or was someone panicking in the storm?

"Report!" Jessica yelled, but her voice whipped away on the wind.

Even though it would make her a target, Jessica flipped the light on her helmet, trying to illuminate the space in front of her. Her hand brushed the camera strapped to her head, reminding her she'd been taping the training session. Little good it would do them now, even if the camera wasn't ruined.

She didn't expect the light to make a bit of difference, but it actually helped. Or at least that's what she thought until she realized it was just the storm dying down as fast as it had come. She had a moment's relief until movement caught her eye. An insurgent, darting from an outcropping in the mountain above, the muzzle on his rifle flashing.

"Take cover," Jessica screamed as she took aim.

The insurgent ducked into a mountain crevice, but as the howling wind abated, the heavy *boom-boom-boom* of automatic fire took its place. He wasn't alone.

Toggling her radio, Jessica told base, "We're taking fire. Sandstorm moving out. Insurgents..." She paused, glancing around and trying to gauge numbers. Dread sunk low in her chest, bottoming out as she saw her soldiers racing for cover. "At least twenty, maybe more. Send—"

The radio flew out of her hand before she could finish and Jessica swung her weapon up, ignoring the way her other hand burned. She didn't dare look to see how bad it was. First she had to assess her team. At least she'd made them wear their body armor. Brand-new and the best the army had, it was lightweight but ultrastrong. It could stop a bullet from anything short of a .50 caliber. And her soldiers were wearing full-body plating today.

It wouldn't save them from a shot to the face or a lucky hit that found its way underneath the plates, but she had faith in their training and their gear.

Then the soldier next to her—the new recruit who'd been on her team for less than a week—let out a wail that made her stomach clench. He hit the ground hard, head thrown back at an impossible angle.

Still, Jessica dropped next to him, reaching for a pulse beneath his neck guard. That's when she saw the bullet holes. Straight through the chest, five of them in an arced line. She slammed a hand down over them, furious at him for not wearing his vest, and pain ricocheted up her arm. Not just from the bullet that had nicked the fleshy part of her thumb, but from the hard plating that should have protected him.

Her dread intensified, a new panic like she'd never felt in the almost ten years she'd dodged bullets for the army. Her head whipped up, surveying the scene. The locals, diving for cover or already down and not moving. Her soldiers, taking hits that should have knocked them down but not taken them out, crumpling under the fire of the insurgents.

Too many of them.

The panic worsened, tensing all her muscles and dimming her vision even more, a tunnel within the specks of sand. She didn't want to die seven thousand miles from home. Didn't want to fail her team. Didn't want to leave behind the kids who meant everything to her. The kids she'd taken this job to support, back when her husband was still studying for his degree. The job she'd discovered she loved enough to keep even after he was gone.

But she didn't want to die for it.

Fire seared through Jessica's arm and the force of the bullet made her stagger backward. She'd been hit. She shifted her MP4 to the other hand, blood from her thumb smearing across the trigger guard as she returned fire. The next shot knocked her back. She slammed into the ground, gasping for breath.

Bullets hitting your body armor always did that. Ripped the air from your lungs and left a nasty bruise.

But this time the pressure wasn't lessening. It was getting worse. Jessica gasped for air, trying to raise her MP4 as she saw another insurgent taking aim at her. She couldn't lift it, so she went for her pistol instead, strapped to her side and much lighter than the assault rifle.

Her fingers closed around it even as her vision began to blur. Then the whole world went dark.

# Chapter One

"I assume everyone's seen the news coverage." Jill Pembrook, director of the FBI's Tactical Crime Division, didn't bother to wait until her team was settled in the conference room. She stood at the front of the long table, arms crossed over her tailored navy blue skirt suit. On a large screen behind her, a video was paused, frozen on the terrified face of a soldier.

Pembrook was petite enough that even standing while most of the team was sitting didn't give her much clearance over those assembled. But she didn't need it. Pembrook had been with the Bureau for almost forty years, meaning they'd opted to keep her on past the regular mandatory retirement age. With her pale, lined skin and well-coiffed gray hair, she might look like someone's sweet yet chic grandma, until you locked eyes with her. Then you knew exactly why the FBI had handpicked her to lead TCD—a rapid response team that could activate quickly and take on almost any threat.

Davis Rogers was still amazed he'd made the cut to join the team. He looked around the room at the other agents, with backgrounds ranging from the military like him to hostage negotiation and profiling to missing persons and computer hacking. He'd only been here for a few months. But they'd welcomed him into the fold fast, with the kind of camaraderie he'd only felt with his family—in and out of the military.

Normally he'd sit back and take the assignment the director gave him. He'd be willing to bide his time and prove himself, without any of the hotshot antics that had motivated many an army ranger. But not today. Not with this case.

He gritted his teeth as Hendrick Maynard stepped up beside Pembrook. Hendrick was their resident computer genius. With his tall, lanky frame and a face that was still battling acne, he looked young enough to be in high school, but that facade hid a genius mind and mature outlook.

Hendrick seemed more serious than usual as he pressed the handheld remote and started playing the video on the screen behind the director. The clip he played was one Davis had seen last night on the news and again this morning in slightly more detail on the YouTube version.

It started suddenly, in the middle of a firefight, with gunshots blasting in the background and sand whipping everywhere, the sound intense even over video. The soldier who'd been frozen on screen finished his fall and didn't get up again. The camera made a quick scan of soldiers and Afghan locals going down, all of it hard to see through the sand that shot up from the ground like a tornado. Then everything suddenly cleared as the camera dived in for a close-up of a young soldier, eyes and mouth open with the shock of death. The camera panned down, a hand slapping against his chest as the bullet holes became visible.

The average American probably wouldn't have realized from the brief footage that the soldier had been wearing full body armor. But somehow the news station had known. They'd also known who'd been running the camera: decorated US Army captain Jessica Carpenter. Widow, mother of three, and as of 6:52 a.m. Tennessee time, a confirmed casualty.

Davis pictured her the way she'd looked a decade ago, the day he'd met her. Only a few inches shorter than his own six feet, with gorgeous dark skin and hair she'd had twisted up and away from her face in braids, she'd worn that army uniform with a confidence he'd envied. She'd been five years older, and with two months more military experience, it had seemed like much more. If she hadn't been happily married, with a toddler and a new baby at home, he might have taken his shot with her.

Instead, they'd become friends. She'd even trained him early on, back before she'd become a captain and he'd headed for Special Operations. If he wasn't sitting in this conference room right now, waiting for the chance to go after the people responsible for her death, he'd be flying to Mississippi to attend her funeral this weekend.

Davis squeezed the underside of the table to keep himself from slamming a fist on top of it. As he refocused, he realized Hendrick had turned off the video screen and taken a seat. Around him, agents were nodding thoughtfully, professionally. Only fellow agent Jace Cantrell—JC to the team—showed a hint of anger on his face. But JC had been military too. And once a soldier, always a soldier.

As in the Bureau, dying in the field was a possibility you accepted. You did whatever you could to prevent it, but if it happened, you knew you'd be going out doing something you believed in. But not like this. Not the way Jessica had died, trusting the military, trusting her training, trusting her equipment.

"I want to take the lead on this case," Davis blurted.

Gazes darted to him: from profiler Dr. Melinda Larsen, silently assessing, suspicion in her eyes, as if she somehow knew he had a history with one of the victims. Always buttoned-up Laura Smith was quiet and unreadable, but her Ivy League brain was probably processing every nuance of his words. JC, staring at him with understanding, even though he didn't realize Davis knew Jessica personally. No one on the team did.

"Is your personal investment in this case going to be a hindrance or a help?" Pembrook asked, voice and gaze steady.

Davis's spine stiffened even more. She was talking about his army background. She had to be. But if she thought he was going to fidget, she underestimated the hell he'd gone through training to be a ranger for the army. "A help. I'm familiar with how the army works. And I'm familiar with the product. I've worn Petrov Armor vests."

Petrov Armor had supplied the body armor Jessica and her team had been wearing during the ambush. That armor—supposedly the newest and best technology—had failed spectacularly, resulting in the deaths of all but three of the soldiers and one of the locals. In his mind it wasn't the insurgents who had killed Jessica and her team. It was Petrov Armor.

He didn't mention the rest. He'd more than just worn the vests. He'd had a chance to be an early tester of their body armor, back when he was an elite ranger and Petrov Armor was better known for the pistols they made than their armor. He'd given the thumbs-up, raving about the vest's bullet-stopping power and comfort in his report. He'd given the army an enthusiastic endorsement to start using Petrov Armor's products more broadly. And they had.

"I'm not talking about the armor," Pembrook replied, her gaze still laser-locked on his, even as agent-at-large Kane Bradshaw slipped into the meeting late and leaned against the doorway. "I'm talking about Jessica Carpenter." Her voice softened. "I'm sorry for your loss."

The gazes on him seemed to intensify, but Davis didn't shift his from Pembrook's. "Thank you. And no, it won't affect my judgment in the case."

Pembrook nodded, but he wasn't sure if she believed him as she looked back at the rest of the group and continued her briefing. "Petrov Armor won a big contract with the military five years ago. The armor this team was wearing is their latest and greatest. It's not worn widely yet, but their earlier version armor is commonly used. The military is doing a full round of testing across all their branches. They've never had a problem with Petrov Armor before, and they don't intend to have another.

"Meanwhile, they've asked us to investigate at home. We got lucky with the news coverage. We're still not sure how it was leaked, but not all of it got out. Or if it did, the news station only played a small part. And somehow they don't have the name of the body armor supplier. *Not yet,*" she said emphatically. "Rowan, we don't have to worry about PD this time. I'm putting you on the media. Hendrick can lend computer support if you need it."

Rowan Cooper nodded, looking a little paler than usual, but sitting straighter.

Since the TCD team traveled all over the country and abroad, they regularly had to work with police departments. Sometimes their assistance was requested and cooperation was easy. Other times the local PD didn't want federal help at all, and it became Rowan's job to smooth everything over. Davis had never envied her that job. But he envied her dealing with the media even less.

"What's our initial read on the situation?" JC asked. "Did Petrov Armor just start sending inferior products or are we talking about some kind of sabotage?"

"At this point, we don't know. The army hasn't had a

chance to begin evaluating the vests yet. They're still dealing with death notifications and shipping home remains."

The clamp that had seemed to lock around Davis's chest the moment he'd heard the news ratcheted tighter. Jessica had lost her husband a few years earlier. Davis had met him once, when he and Jessica happened to rotate back home at the same time. He'd never met her kids in person, but he'd gotten to talk with them once over a ridiculously clear video chat from seven thousand miles away. They'd been funny and cute, jostling for the best position in front of the camera and all trying to talk at once. They were orphans now.

Davis took a deep breath and tried to focus as Pembrook continued. "Petrov Armor has recently gone through some big changes. About a year ago, founder and CEO Neal Petrov retired. He passed the torch to his daughter, Leila Petrov, formerly in charge of the company's client services division. One of the biggest changes she's made has been to shut down the weapons side of their business and focus entirely on the armor. But you can bet Neal Petrov was the one to convince the board of directors to agree to that decision. He had controlling stock share and a lot of influence. He stayed involved in the business until three weeks ago, when he got caught up in a mugging gone bad and was killed."

"You think the new CEO is cutting corners with dad out of the picture?" Kane asked, not moving from where he'd planted himself near the doorway.

That strategic position was probably in case he wanted to make a quick getaway. The agent-at-large had known the director for a long time, but he was one of the few members of the team Davis couldn't quite get a read on. He seemed to flit in and out of the office at random, more often away on some secret assignment than working with the team.

"Maybe," Pembrook replied. She looked at JC. "I want you to bring her in. Take Smitty with you."

Laura Smith nodded, tucking a stray blond hair behind her ear as Davis opened his mouth to argue.

Before he could, Melinda jumped in, sounding every bit the profiler as she suggested, "Make it a spectacle. Do it in front of her people. We don't have enough for a formal arrest at this point, but Leila Petrov is only thirty, pretty young for a CEO. Technically, she's been in charge for a year, but we have to assume her father has been holding her hand until recently. Almost certainly he convinced the board of directors to let her take the helm when he retired. If we shake her up from the start, get her off balance and scared, she's more likely to cooperate before contacting a lawyer. And she's more likely to slip up."

Pembrook nodded and glanced at her watch. "Do it in an hour. That should give her employees plenty of time to get settled in before you march her out of there."

Davis squeezed his hands together tighter under the table. He could feel the veins in his arms starting to throb from the pressure, but he couldn't stop himself any more than he could prevent blurting angrily, "Director—"

That was all he got out before she spoke over him. "Davis, I think your military background will come in handy, too. I'm going to let you run lead on this."

Shock kept him silent, but his hands loosened and the pain in his chest eased up. "Thank—"

"You're dismissed, everyone. Let's jump on this." Pembrook turned toward him. "Follow me, Davis. Let's have a chat." Before he could reply, she was out the door.

Davis was slower getting to his feet. As he passed Kane in the doorway, the other agent offered him a raised eyebrow and a sardonic grin, but Davis didn't care. Not about Kane's opinion and not about whatever warnings Pembrook was about to level at him.

He was on the case. Whether it was new CEO Leila

Petrov to blame or someone else, he wasn't stopping until he brought that person down.

He glanced skyward as he stepped through the threshold of the director's office, saying a silent goodbye to his old friend. Promising to avenge her death.

"THE SOLDIER YOU see died at the scene. Army captain Jessica Carpenter, who took the video, also died when she was shot through her bulletproof vest. The army is looking into the circumstances. Keep watching for updates on this story and more. Next up—"

Eric Ross turned off the TV and Leila Petrov had to force herself to swivel toward him. She tried to wipe the horror and disbelief she was feeling off her face, but Eric had known her since she was a lonely thirteen-year-old. He'd been her first kiss two years later. Three years after that, he'd broken her heart.

He read her now just as easily as he always had. "Maybe it's not our armor."

"Maybe it is." Petrov Armor had supplied the military with millions of dollars' worth of guns and armor in the past thirty years. Their accounts had started out slow, with her father barely showing a profit in those early years. Now, the military not only kept them in business with their big armor purchases, but those sales also allowed her to employ almost two hundred people. It was her father's legacy. But it was now her responsibility.

The numbers said there was a good chance those soldiers had been wearing some version of Petrov Armor. But logic said they couldn't be. Petrov Armor was serious about its testing. Any tweak, no matter how minor, was checked against every bullet and blade in its testing facility. Every single piece of armor that left its building was inspected for quality. If the armor was damaged, it went in the trash. The company could afford the waste; it couldn't afford to screw up.

Leila breathed in and out through her nose, praying she wasn't going to throw up. Not that she had much in her system to throw up anyway. She'd barely been eating since her dad had stood up to that mugger instead of just handing over his wallet. In a single, stupid instant, she'd lost one of the only two close family members she had left. Tears welled up and she blinked them back, not wanting Eric to see.

Maybe once he'd been her first confidant, her closest friend, and her lover, but now he was her employee. The last thing she needed was for anyone to doubt her strength as a leader.

It had been an uphill battle for a year, getting her employees to take her seriously as CEO. She thought it was working until her dad died. Then she realized just how much resentment remained that she'd succeeded him. She'd come in every day since, not taking any time off to mourn, in part because she'd known her father would have wanted her to focus on work. And in part because work was the only thing that could take her mind off her crushing loss. But it was mostly to prove to the staff that she'd earned her position. She couldn't afford to lose her cool now, not when so much was at stake.

Leila took a deep breath and tipped her chin back. She spotted the slight smile that disappeared as quickly as it slid onto Eric's lips, and knew it was because he recognized her battle face. Ignoring it, she said, "We need to get ahead of this. Start making phone calls. Anyone you've made a sale to in the army in the past year. Find out if it's ours, so we can figure out what happened. And we'd better see if we can track down the actual shipment. If there are any other problems, I want to find them first."

"Leila—"

"I need you to start right now, Eric. We don't have time to waste."

"Maybe you should call your uncle."

Joel Petrov, her dad's younger brother and the company's COO, hadn't come in yet. If somehow he'd managed to miss the news reports, she wanted to keep him in the dark as long as possible. He'd handled so much for her family, keeping the business afloat all those years ago when her mom died and her dad had been so lost in his grief he'd forgotten everything, including her. Her uncle had picked up the slack there, too, making sure she was fed and made it to school on time. Making sure she still felt loved.

Right now, she could use a break. Hopefully they'd find out those devastating deaths weren't due to their armor. She'd worked hard to transition the company from producing both weapons and armor to solely armor. She wanted Petrov Armor to be known as a life-saving company, not a life-ending one. This incident put that at risk.

Maybe the panic Leila was feeling over the whole situation would be a thing of the past before her uncle climbed out of whatever woman's bed he'd found himself in last night and she'd be able to tell him calmly that she'd handled it.

"We're looking for Leila Petrov."

The unfamiliar voice was booming, echoing through Petrov Armor's open-concept layout, breaching the closed door of her office. Even before that door burst open and a man and woman in suits followed, looking serious as they held up FBI badges, she knew.

Petrov Armor was in serious trouble.

She stepped forward, trying not to let them see all the emotions battling inside her—the fear, the guilt, the panic. Her voice was strong and steady as she replied, "I'm Leila Petrov."

"FBI," the woman announced, and the steel in her voice put Leila's to shame. "Agents Smith and Cantrell. We have some questions for you. We'd like you to come with us—"

Eric pushed his way up beside her, taking a step slightly forward. "You can't possibly have warrants. What kind of scare-tactic BS—"

"Stop," Leila hissed at him.

The other agent spoke over them both, his voice raised to carry to the employees behind him, their heads all peering over their cubicle walls. "We can talk here if you prefer."

Leila grabbed her purse and shook her head. "I'll come with you."

"And I'll contact our lawyer," Eric said, his too-loud voice a stark contrast to her too-soft one.

She kept her head up, met the gazes of her employees with confident, "don't worry" nods as she followed Agents Smith and Cantrell out of Petrov Armor.

She prayed that slow, humiliating walk wouldn't be the beginning of the end of everything her father had worked for, of the legacy she'd promised herself she'd keep safe for him.

# Chapter Two

Despite its location in a nondescript building on the outskirts of Old City, Tennessee, the Tactical Crime Division had an interview room that would be the envy of most FBI field offices. Maybe it was a result of working with a profiler who believed in setting the stage for each individual interview. That meant sometimes the room looked like a plush hotel lobby and other times it was as stark as a prison cell. It all depended what Melinda thought would work best to get the subject talking.

Today it leaned closer to prison cell, with uncomfortable, hard-backed chairs pulled up to a drab gray table. But what Davis was most cognizant of was the video camera up in the corner, ready to broadcast in real time to the rest of the team everything he was doing.

*Don't lose your cool*, he reminded himself as the door opened. He could hear Smitty telling the CEO of Petrov Armor to go ahead in.

He'd read Leila Petrov's bio. Even with her undergraduate degree in business with minors in communications and marketing followed by an MBA, thirty years old was awfully young to be the CEO of a billion-dollar company. Then again, nepotism had a way of opening doors that little else could.

He'd seen her picture, too. She was undeniably gorgeous,

with shiny, dark hair and big brown eyes. But she looked more like a college student getting ready for her first job interview than a CEO. Still, he wasn't about to underestimate her. He'd seen what that could do on too many missions overseas, when soldiers thought just because someone was a young female meant they couldn't be strapped with a bomb.

But as she came through the door, he was unprepared for the little kick his heart gave, sending extra blood pumping to places it had no business going. Maybe it was her determined stride, the nothing-fazes-me tilt of her chin in a room that made hardened criminals buckle. He felt her reciprocal jolt of attraction as much as he saw it in the sudden sweep her gaze made over his body, the slight flush on her cheeks.

She recovered faster than he did, scowling at the setup. "If you're trying to intimidate me, it's not going to work. I'm here voluntarily. I want to help, but I don't appreciate being bullied."

He debated rethinking the whole interview plan, but decided to trust Melinda. He'd never worked with a profiler before coming to TCD, but in the short time he'd been here, he'd become a believer. "If you think this is being bullied, you have no business working with the military. Take a seat."

Instead of following the directive, she narrowed her eyes and crossed her arms over her chest. Her stance shifted, as if she was considering walking right out.

Silently Davis cursed, because the truth was, she could leave whenever she wanted. But he'd picked a course and he refused to back down now. So, he crossed his own arms, lifted his eyebrows and waited.

A brief, hard smile tilted her lips up, and then she pulled one of the chairs away from the table and perched on the edge of it. Rather than looking poised to run, with her perfect posture and well-tailored black suit, she managed to look like she was in charge.

Never underestimate someone who'd made CEO by thirty, no matter the circumstances, he told himself. Then he pulled his own chair around the table and positioned it across from her. Settling into the seat, he leaned forward, reducing the space between them to almost nothing.

If he couldn't intimidate her with this room and his job title, maybe sheer size would work. She was tall for a woman—probably five foot ten without the low heels she wore—but he still had a few inches on her. And a lot of breadth with muscles he'd earned the hard way in the rangers.

Her eyes locked on his without hesitation. They were the shade of a perfect cup of coffee, with just a hint of cream added. This close to him, he could see how smooth and clear her skin was, with deeper undertones than he'd first realized. The flush on her cheeks was still there, but now it was darker, tinged from anger. And damn it all, she smelled like citrus, probably some expensive perfume to go with the designer clothes.

Clothes that hung just a little looser than they should suggested she'd been skipping meals. Despite her appeal, he didn't miss the heavy application of makeup underneath her eyes that couldn't quite hide the dark circles. He didn't miss the redness in those eyes either, as if she'd been up late crying. Most likely still grieving the father she'd lost unexpectedly three weeks ago.

"I'm Special Agent Davis Rogers. I'm sure Agents Smith and Cantrell told you what this was about—assuming you didn't watch the news this morning." Davis knew Smitty and JC wouldn't have given her much in the way of details. They wanted to keep her off balance by having different agents bring her in than the one questioning her. But so far, nothing seemed to faze her much.

He didn't want to respect that, but it was a trait that was crucial in Special Operations. He couldn't help admiring it in a civilian CEO facing a massive investigation of her company and possible jail time.

"The soldiers who were killed in an ambush," Leila replied. "Reporters say they were wearing armor. I'm guessing, since I'm here, that the army thinks they were wearing Petrov Armor?"

He could see the hope in her eyes, the wish that he'd correct her, say it was all a mistake or she'd just been brought in for her expertise. He actually felt bad for a nanosecond, then he remembered hearing the news about Jessica—over the television as her family had since the video had leaked before notifications could be made. "They don't *think* it. They've confirmed it."

She sighed heavily, then nodded. Her gaze stayed serious, no trace of panic, just sadness lurking beneath determination. "I want to see the plates."

"Excuse me?" Was she joking? "They're evidence in an open investigation."

His words should have made her blanch, but instead the hardness in her gaze just intensified. "They're not ours."

He couldn't stop the snort of disbelief that escaped. *This* was her spin?

She rushed on before he could figure out how to respond to that ridiculousness. "We have a lot of checks and balances in place. My dad joined the military when he was eighteen. He stayed in four years and watched three fellow soldiers die in a training accident. It stuck with him, made him want to do something to prevent it. He decided to dedicate himself to making better gear and weapons. The army paid for his tuition, helped him get the knowledge and skills to start Petrov Armor. It mattered to him—and it matters to me—that what we make saves lives. From the beginning, most of our gun and armor sales were to the military."

The words out of her mouth were passionate, but Davis had been an FBI agent in white collar crime for four years before getting recruited to TCD. He'd learned quickly that one of the most valued qualities in CEOs of crooked companies was being a good liar. He'd also learned that when things got dicey, those same CEOs would throw others under the bus as fast as they could. So, he leaned back and waited for it.

Leila leaned forward, closing the gap between them again.

He hid his surprise at her boldness, trying not to breathe her subtle citrusy perfume.

"Nothing leaves our facility without being inspected. Furthermore, we don't make changes without testing them with every kind of weapon we promise to protect against. There's no way our products were breached by the kind of weapons the news reported were being used. So, either the bullets the insurgents were using changed or those soldiers weren't wearing Petrov Armor."

Since she was sticking with her story and he had no idea how long she'd hang around, Davis decided to help her out. "What about the person in charge of inspections? Or the people in charge of testing? Isn't there a possibility that corners were cut without you realizing it?"

If she had any brains, she'd agree with him, give herself a little distance in case the whole thing blew up in her face—which he was pretty sure it was going to do.

Instead, the fury in her gaze deepened. "You really think I'm going to sell out one of my employees? No. That's not possible. Anyone in a key role like that has been at Petrov Armor a long time. We don't concentrate power without unannounced checks by other members of the team. It was my father's rule long before he took the company public and the board of directors and I stand by that to this day."

Davis felt himself frown and tried to smooth out his features. She was either a better liar than she seemed or she actually believed what she was saying.

The problem was, he believed the army. Jessica had been wearing Petrov Armor when she died. Which meant someone else was lying.

He had a bad feeling it might have been Leila Petrov's father, longtime CEO of Petrov Armor and as of three weeks ago, dead. If Davis was right, then he'd already missed his chance to throw the bastard in jail. If he was right, there'd be no way left to truly avenge his friend's death.

MELINDA LARSEN HAD seen some of the best liars in the country during her twelve years with the FBI. Before that, while doing her graduate thesis in psychology, she'd talked to incarcerated serial killers. They'd woven the most convincing tales she'd ever heard about their innocence with almost no body language tells that contradicted what they were saying. They'd also scared the hell out of her, with so much evil lurking beneath calm or even neighborly exteriors.

It had all been practice for her role at TCD, where she didn't have the luxury of months-or years-long investigations, but had to make assessments almost on the spot. It was a near impossible task, but Melinda had discovered she thrived on the challenge.

It was also the best distraction she'd found in the past decade to keep her from thinking about the losses in her own life. Because no matter how much she'd thrown herself into her cases before TCD, there was always one unsolved case at the forefront of her mind. But here, that case was starting to fade into the background. She was starting to finally accept that she might never know the truth about the most important case she'd never been able to officially investigate. At TCD, she was finally starting to move on with her life.

Leila Petrov hadn't presented much of a challenge. But Melinda still gave her standard disclaimer as she stared at Davis and Pembrook. Because no matter how good she was—and she knew she was one of the best—she wasn't immune from mistakes. "One interview isn't enough time to form a complete assessment."

Jill Pembrook gave a slight smile as she nodded, half amusement and half encouragement. It was a look Melinda had come to expect in the year she'd worked for Pembrook. Davis just crossed his arms over his chest, looking pissed off in what Melinda thought of as his civvies—well-worn jeans and a dark T-shirt that emphasized the strength in his arms and chest. But she knew Davis's anger wasn't directed at her. It was for the high-priced lawyer who'd shown up in the middle of his interview with Leila Petrov and pulled her out of there.

"I think she's telling the truth. She doesn't know anything about it."

At Melinda's proclamation, Davis seemed to deflate. "I agree," he said. "And let's be honest, Petrov Armor isn't small, but it's not exactly a huge company. Unless it was pure sloppiness—which I doubt, given their history supplying the military—there's something unusual going on here."

"Cutting corners," Melinda suggested. "Maybe these checks she thinks are in place aren't being followed. Or she's too distracted grieving her father to notice they messed up a big shipment. Or we could be talking about sabotage."

Davis looked intrigued. "Cutting corners could suggest

her father knew about it and was just trying to make more money from substandard, cheaper materials, and maybe less vigorous testing, too. Sloppiness would suggest one or more of her employees are taking advantage of her grief to be lazy. Or maybe they're all grieving and distracted, too. But sabotage? Are you thinking someone inside the company or out?"

"Given what I've read about their process, sabotage from someone who doesn't work there seems unlikely. So, I'd say inside. If that's the case, it could be someone with a grudge against the military."

"That's unlikely too, considering what Leila said about the people in charge of anything important being there for years," Davis cut in. "If this had been happening a long time, what are the chances the military wouldn't have already found out?"

"I agree," Melinda said. "So, if it's sabotage, it's probably someone who wanted to discredit Neal Petrov himself. But honestly, I think the most likely motive is the most obvious."

"Greed." Davis nodded. "They produced inferior products to save money, get a bigger profit. Well, it sure backfired. But if that's the case, we're back to Neal Petrov. As CEO and biggest shareholder, he'd be in the most likely position to profit. With him dead…"

"JC has been on the phone with the army while you were interviewing Ms. Petrov," Pembrook said. "He's confirmed that the shipment of armor the soldiers who were killed were wearing went out after Neal Petrov was killed. It's possible he set it up before he died, but I think there could be an accomplice."

"It makes sense," Melinda agreed. "If there are really as many checks and balances as Leila Petrov claimed, it might be hard for one person to pull this off, even if he was the CEO. Two, on the other hand..."

Davis nodded, anticipation back on his face that told Melinda how badly he wanted to put someone behind bars for his friend's death. The case was probably too personal for him. It could lead to mistakes. But it could also be exactly the dogged determination they needed.

"Melinda and I have been talking about sending someone inside," Pembrook said, staring at Davis.

"Undercover?" He sounded frustrated as he said, "Well, Leila Petrov knows me, JC and Smitty, so we're all out. Who were you thinking about sending in?"

"I think you should do it," Melinda said, before Pembrook could respond. They hadn't had a chance to talk about who might go undercover before Davis had come into the room.

Before the interview, Davis would have been the last person she'd have suggested. But the more she'd watched him and Leila, seen the sparks practically flying between them from both anger and attraction, the more the idea had grown.

Davis stared at her like she'd gotten into the head of one too many criminals and finally cracked. "What would I do undercover that—"

"This." Melinda cut him off, holding up her cell phone. She'd found an advertisement for a job as an office assistant to Leila Petrov. "We lucked out."

"How?" Davis demanded, glancing from her to Pembrook as if their boss would set her straight—or suggest Melinda get her own head checked. "Leila Petrov is never going to go along with this."

"I think she will," Melinda contradicted as Pembrook just watched them, her mind probably running through a million scenarios at the speed of a computer.

"And why's that?" Davis demanded, even though he had to be dying to be the one to go in.

"Attraction," Melinda said simply.

As she spoke, Kane Bradshaw walked past the open doorway. He didn't pause, just lifted an eyebrow at her, looking amused.

Forcing herself to ignore him, Melinda told Davis, "There was an immediate physical attraction between you two."

When Davis frowned, she added quickly, "It's my job to catch these things. I'm not saying you were unprofessional. But you can play on that attraction to gain her trust."

"She's in charge of the company," Davis argued. "There's no way she's going to go along with this."

"I think she will."

"Because she thinks I'm cute? Come on. This isn't high school, Melinda."

She couldn't help a wry smile in return. The six-foot tall, broad-shouldered African-American agent *was* cute. That would probably influence Leila Petrov, whether she wanted it to or not. But it wouldn't get Davis into the company; it would merely stop the door from being slammed in his face before he could make his case to her. "No, but we both agree she's probably innocent. I think she wants to find the truth. You can help her get it."

That quieted him down, but only for a minute, before he frowned and shook his head again. "Believe me, I want to be the one to find whoever's responsible. But this seems like a crazy risk. It's not worth it."

"How sure are you about this?" Pembrook asked Melinda.

Her heart beat harder at the possibility she was suggesting the wrong course of action and it could blow up an important investigation. But as she mentally reviewed Davis's interview with Leila, her gut insisted this would work. "Davis needs to convince her the only way to save the company her father founded is to get ahead of this. Which means she needs to think they're on the same side. If that happens, I'm very sure."

Pembrook turned her steely gaze on Davis, who stood at attention like he was undergoing military inspection. Finally she gave a curt, final nod. "You're going in."

# Chapter Three

"There's been a mistake. The FBI is investigating, and they'll track down who's really responsible soon enough. In the meantime, we need to focus on getting our next shipments ready."

Those were the words Leila had used to rally her employees when she'd finally returned to the office. They'd all nodded and smiled back at her. Tight, worried smiles that led to whispers as soon as she went into her office.

Hopefully, there'd still be next shipments to deliver. Eighty percent of their business was with the military. The rest was domestic law enforcement and private companies, usually civilian security firms. They'd already absorbed a significant revenue loss by closing the weapon side of the business. Now that armor was their only product, the military's business and their reputation were crucial. But it would all dry up if the tragedy overseas came back to them.

Leila shut the door to her office because she was tired of pretending not to hear the whispers. Then she let out the heavy sigh she'd been holding in since first thing that morning, when FBI agents had taken her to their oddly nondescript office to be questioned.

When Eric had sent the company lawyer to haul her out of there, she'd been half relieved and half annoyed. Relieved because as hard as she tried not to let it get to her, that stark office and that muscle-bound federal agent with the too-intense stare had started to raise her anxiety. Annoyed because the more she thought about it, the more certain she was there'd been a mistake. No way had their armor failed.

She'd bet her reputation on it. Sinking into the plush chair behind her desk, she opened her laptop, ready to get to work. Because it was more than her reputation that would be destroyed if she didn't figure out what had really happened—and fast.

The question was, how? With the FBI unwilling to let her see the armor the soldiers had been wearing, how could she prove it wasn't theirs?

She should have started working on that question as soon as the lawyer had gotten her out of the FBI office, but she'd been too unnerved to come directly back to work. So, she'd gone to her father's gravesite first, spent a long while talking to him the way she used to. Only this time, the conversation was one-sided.

It was the first time she'd been there since she'd had to dump a shovelful of dirt over his coffin, watch it slowly disappear from view. She hadn't been ready to see his name on that sleek granite headstone. But after too long sitting there battling her grief, she'd started to feel his presence. Started to feel his love. It had helped her focus on what she needed to do.

The knock on her office door startled her, and Leila called out a distracted "Come in" as she pulled up the latest military invoices. She'd already charged Eric—the company's head of sales—with reaching out to his contacts, but maybe she should be doing the same. Between the people she knew and her father's connections, maybe someone would be able to get her more details about the armor the soldiers had been wearing.

"Leila, I know today has been a little crazy, but I've got some good news."

Leila glanced up at their head of HR. Ben Jameson was young and new, but anxious to prove himself. So far, he'd been efficient and always full of energy. "I could use some good news."

"I found you an assistant."

"Oh."

He frowned at her lack of excitement, but with everything else going on, the last thing she wanted to deal with was a new employee who needed training. Glancing back at her laptop screen, she debated how she could put him off for a while. Just until she could deal with the disaster with the FBI.

"We got his résumé a few hours ago," Ben continued quickly. "Normally, I'd do more of a formal process, but he was available for an immediate interview and he's exactly what we've been looking for. I called his references right away and figured we should scoop him up before someone else does. He said he could start today, so I thought, why not let him get the lay of the land?"

When she didn't reply, he added, "I mean, I thought if the FBI stuff has blown over…"

Finally she looked up and nodded, hoping her CEO face hadn't slipped. "Great. I could use the help."

Ben's face lit up. "Perfect! Let me introduce you." He turned back toward the door and called, "Davis!"

No way. Two men named Davis in one day?

Leila got to her feet, anxiety already tensing the back of her neck before Davis Rogers entered her office.

This morning, he'd looked more like the brawny owner of a night club in jeans, and a T-shirt that clung to a muscled chest and arms. He'd even had a layer of scruff on his chin. Definitely not what she'd expected for an FBI agent.

Now, he was clean-shaven in dark dress pants and a blazer. He should have looked less appealing in clothes that hid his physique. Instead, it made her focus more on his face. On hypnotizing dark brown eyes made even more intense beneath heavy brows. On unlined brown skin she wanted to run her hands over, feel for the last traces of this morning's scruff. On generous lips she wanted to kiss.

The thought startled her. She wasn't the type to lust over men she barely knew. Putting it down to too many emotions near the surface—stress, grief and anxiety mixing together and messing with her head—Leila straightened her blazer, trying to focus. "What do you think you're—"

"It's nice to meet you," Davis spoke over her. "I'm so excited to join Petrov Armor. I can provide any assistance you need," he added, only a hint of sarcasm there, probably so small Ben wouldn't notice.

But Leila sure had. She felt her face scrunch up with disbelief as Ben looked back and forth between them. But before she could toss Davis out of her office, one side of those lush lips lifted in a slow grin. It was a smile half full of amusement and half full of confidence, like he knew exactly what she was thinking.

What kind of game was he playing? Did he honestly think she was going to let him screw with her company, with her employees?

She smiled too, but infused hers with enough warning that he should have taken a step back. It was a trick she'd learned long before rising to CEO, back in university when walking home from the library at night meant passing drunk guys who thought it was acceptable to follow. It never failed to drop the smirks off people's faces.

But Davis stepped closer, held out his hand. "I think we can work well together to do what needs to be done."

Nervy. She should have expected it from an FBI agent.

And he should have expected her to immediately call his bluff. But as she looked past that cocky grin into his steady gaze, she saw something she hadn't expected, something that looked like honesty.

"Thank you, Ben." She flicked her gaze to her young head of HR, who opened and closed his mouth like he was trying to figure out what to say. Then he nodded, stepped backward out of her office and shut the door behind him. Leaving her alone with Davis.

"I'm letting you stay out of pure curiosity," she told him, crossing her arms over her chest. "But you've got about two minutes to explain why I'd let you run this charade. Then, I'm tossing you out and my lawyer will be back down at your office, asking questions about the FBI's ethics."

Instead of looking worried, Davis stepped closer, his gaze locked on hers in a way that made the hairs on the backs of her arms stand up and each breath come faster. Then, he was holding a folder up between them, almost in her face.

She frowned and stepped back, taking the folder. One glance and she understood the cocky grin he'd given her. It was a close-up of a piece of body armor. It had been pierced by three bullet holes. And there, stamped on the edges in their trademark, was the Petrov Armor logo and a rating that should have stopped the kind of bullet that had made those holes.

Her gaze returned to his, as dread rose from her gut and seemed to lodge in her throat.

"We've tracked this to a recent batch of armor. I don't believe you know anything about this or I wouldn't be telling you. So, right now you have two choices—keep my cover and let me figure out how this defective armor got out, or blow it and bring the rest of my team down here to tear apart this place until we find the truth. We're getting warrants right now."

Leila looked at the photo again. It could have been faked. Or the bullets could have been some new form of armor-piercing technology that their armor didn't protect against. But deep down, she knew something was very wrong in her company.

A recent batch probably meant it had happened on her watch. The way the company was set up, this wasn't a sloppy error. It was intentional, someone trying to destroy what her father had spent so much of his life building.

She lifted her gaze back to Davis's, suddenly understanding that he—and the FBI—might be her best bet to find the person responsible. That letting a stranger try to tear apart her company could very well be the only way to save it. A secret investigation might find a single person responsible, might allow her a chance to save Petrov Armor. A public one—no matter the outcome—would destroy them.

"I want you to keep me updated on everything you do here. If I agree to this, you let me be involved in the investigation." She held out her own hand, the way he'd done before. "Agreed?"

That smile returned, smaller and more serious this time, as he put his big hand in hers and shook. "Agreed."

With that single touch, Leila hoped she hadn't just doomed her company.

ULTIMATELY, IT DIDN'T matter if Leila Petrov was unaware that defective products were being delivered to the military. As the CEO, she was responsible for what happened here.

Ultimately, she was responsible for every piece of armor that had been sent overseas with the promise to save lives that had betrayed the soldiers who'd worn it. That made her responsible for every single death. Including Jessica's.

That truth would be easier to accept if Davis wasn't more impressed with her with each passing minute. The woman was tough. So far, as she'd walked him around the office and introduced him to her employees, he could see that she was respected. Sometimes grudgingly, but most of them seemed to genuinely like her as a boss.

Then again, most of them seemed to have truly liked her father. They kept touching her elbow or bowing their heads, sadness in their eyes as they spoke his name. Still, if Leila hadn't known about the defective products, what were the chances her father hadn't either? The more he saw of their process and security as he walked around, the lower those chances appeared. Because even though the recent shipment had been sent out after her father died, it had probably been made while he was alive.

It had become immediately obvious that Petrov Armor took its security seriously. No way were these systems ignored until the news report yesterday. They were too ingrained, too second nature as he watched employees without hesitation card in and out of not just the building, but also any sensitive areas. He'd noticed the security cameras around the outside of the building, but they were inside, too. Whoever was behind the defective products knew how to get around all of it. Either that or the company's own security would be what ultimately brought them down.

Making a mental note to ask to see some of the camera footage from when the defective armor had been made, Davis pasted on a smile as he was introduced to yet another employee.

"Davis, this is Theresa Quinn, head of research and development at Petrov Armor. Theresa, this is my new assistant, Davis Rogers."

Leila's voice hadn't wavered through any of the introductions and none of her employees seemed to have picked up on anything strange, but he could feel her discomfort. She didn't like lying to them. He hoped she wouldn't break down and tell anyone who he really was.

He'd have to stick close to her. He already needed to pretend to work with her if he wanted to keep his access to Petrov Armor. But a CEO with a conscience was both good and bad. Good because if he was right and she really wasn't involved, then Melinda was right, too. Leila would want the truth, even if she didn't want it to get out. Bad because lying obviously didn't come easily for her.

"What happened with those FBI agents?" Theresa demanded, with the tone of someone who'd been around a long time and held a position of power. It was also a tone that held a bit of irreverence, as though she was Leila's equal instead of her employee.

Davis looked Theresa over more closely. Wearing jeans and a blouse with the sleeves rolled up past her elbows and reddish-brown hair knotted up in a messy bun, Theresa's attire made her seem younger than the crinkles around her eyes suggested. Davis pegged her at close to fifty. He wondered if the aura of confidence and authority she radiated was just age and position, or if she had more sway at Petrov Armor than the average head of R and D.

Leila visibly stiffened at Theresa's question, and Davis made a mental note that the two women didn't like each other.

"Like I said earlier, everything is fine," Leila answered.

Theresa's eyes narrowed. "Just like that?"

"Just like that. It wasn't our armor."

"Do we know whose it was?" There was still suspicion in Theresa's voice, but it was overridden by curiosity. "Because that's going to take out some of the competition."

Davis tensed at her callous comment, but he kept his body language calm and eager, like he imagined a new assistant would act.

"The FBI isn't going to share that kind of thing," Leila replied. She turned toward Davis. "Let me introduce you to our head of sales." Then she called across the open concept main office area. "Eric!"

The man who turned toward them looked about his and Leila's age. With blond hair gelled into perfect place and dark blue eyes almost the exact shade as his suit, he looked like a head of sales. But as he walked toward them, his gaze landing briefly on Davis before focusing entirely on Leila, all Davis could see was a man with a crush.

Probably betraying her company wasn't the way to win the woman over. Unless Leila hadn't returned his affection and Eric wanted revenge.

As Eric reached their side, his attention still entirely focused on Leila as if no one else was there, Davis stuck his hand in the man's path. "Davis Rogers, Leila's new assistant."

Eric's eyes narrowed slightly with his assessing gaze, but he offered a slightly less than genuine smile and held out his hand. "Eric Ross. Head of sales." His hand closed a little too tightly around Davis's as he added, "I'm glad Leila finally got an assistant. She works too much. You make sure she takes it easy."

Before Davis could reply—or even figure out how to reply to that—Eric had dropped his hand and turned his attention back to Leila. His voice lowered slightly as he added, "Your dad was just like a father to me, too, Leila. You know you can talk to me." He put his hand on Leila's upper arm, comforting but a little too familiar. "No one is going to think less of you if you take time off to grieve."

Leila shrugged free with a stiff nod and a slight flush.

She cleared her throat, ducking her head momentarily. Her voice wavered just slightly as she answered, "I know he was, Eric. Thank you."

Davis glanced between them, wondering at their history, as Theresa interjected with less emotion, "We all miss your father. He was a great CEO and a great guy." Then she walked away, leaving Davis to wonder if her comment had been meant as sympathy or a subtle dig at Leila's leadership.

Based on the way Eric scowled after Theresa, he thought it was a dig. Davis studied him a little closer. His history with Leila and her family obviously went back a long time. If Neal Petrov was like a father to Eric, maybe the man had let him in on his secrets. Or had him help make a little more money off the books.

Before Davis could ponder that, a man came hurrying across the office, making a beeline for Leila. Probably mid-fifties, with dark brown hair and light blue eyes, he looked like a younger, more handsome version of the man Davis had studied in pictures just that morning. It had to be Neal Petrov's younger brother, Joel.

As soon as he reached them, the man gripped Leila by her upper arms, staring intently at her face. "Are you okay? I heard the FBI pulled you in for questioning about this military disaster."

Leila's gaze darted to Davis, then back to the man who had to be her uncle. She didn't quite look him in the eyes as she replied, "I'm fine. It was a mistake. Don't worry."

"Don't worry? You know I always worry. With your dad gone…" He sighed, gave Leila a sad smile, then let go of her arms. "I'm sorry," he said more softly. "We should have talked in private. But I wish you'd called me right away. Eric said—"

"Everything is okay," Leila said, cutting him off. "Uncle,

this is my new assistant, Davis Rogers. Davis, this is Joel Petrov, our COO."

Joel's attention shifted to him, and the intensity of the man's scrutiny was like a father inspecting his teenage daughter's first date. Fleetingly Davis wondered why Neal Petrov hadn't convinced the board of directors to make his brother CEO instead of his daughter.

Then Joel's hand closed around his. "Davis. Nice to meet you. I'm sure you'll like it here." Just as quickly, Joel let go, dismissing him as effectively as if he'd left the room.

"I'm glad it was all a mistake," he told Leila. "But if anything else comes up, let me help you handle it. You've got enough to deal with right now." He squeezed her hand, then headed off into a private office on the edges of the open space and closed the door.

"Let's finish our tour," Leila told him, all business as she strode past her uncle's office and toward the testing area.

Davis hurried after her, his mind spinning. Neal Petrov's brother was COO of the company and yet, when Neal had stepped back, he'd talked the board into putting his twenty-nine-year-old daughter in charge instead. And even after leaving his CEO role, from what his employees had said, Neal Petrov was still in the office all the time. As founder and biggest shareholder, he still profited. Maybe stepping back protected him from liability if things went sideways. Maybe he hadn't pushed to have his young daughter in charge because of nepotism, but because he thought she was too inexperienced to realize what was happening under her nose.

He frowned, remembering the sadness in her eyes when Eric had talked about her father. If Davis's suspicion was true, her father hadn't really cared about her. Because by using her inexperience and trust against her, he was also putting her in the position to be the first one law enforcement came after if it all unraveled. He was making her his scapegoat.

Davis was a long way from proving any of it, but if he was right, he wished more than ever that Neal Petrov was still here, so he could truly make the man pay.

"Let me show you the area where we do testing," Leila said, her tone strong and confident, as if showing him their process would prove there was no way for someone to have sabotaged the armor. "We used to have a separate section of the building for gun testing, but that closed last year and we're in the process of converting it into another R and D area for our armor." She used her security card to key through a new doorway, holding it open for him.

As he followed, his phone dinged and Davis glanced at it. A message from Hendrick lit up on his screen.

This case is much bigger than we thought. Turns out Petrov Armor's name has come up in Bureau cases before—a LOT of them over more than a decade. But nothing panned out.

Frowning, Davis texted back a quick question: Military cases? Defects?

The response came back fast and made Davis swear under his breath.

No. Supplying guns to known criminals.

# Chapter Four

Kane Bradshaw hated being stuck inside an FBI office, digging through old case files. He especially hated doing it with Dr. Melinda Larsen.

He snuck a glance at her, head bent over her laptop, wearing her default serious expression. She looked more like an academic than an FBI agent, with her small frame and that dark hair she always wore loose around her shoulders. Her Asian heritage had given her skin warm undertones and along with how perfectly unlined her face was despite her job, she looked a decade younger than the early forties he knew her to be. But one glance into those deep brown eyes and he could see every year, every tough case.

She was one of the Bureau's foremost experts on body language and a damn good profiler. He'd worked with her peripherally over the years, but had hoped to avoid being teamed up with her at TCD.

He'd seen her around the office, quick to offer her opinions on cases and silently studying anyone else who spoke. Profiling them, he was sure. She'd done it to him, too. If her reputation was deserved, she'd seen way too far into his mind, into his soul. He had no intention of letting her see any more.

He'd prefer to keep his secrets.

If anyone else had asked him to work with Melinda, he

would have refused. But he owed Jill Pembrook more than he could ever repay her. So, if she wanted him to partner with the too-serious profiler to look into Petrov Armor's connection to criminals, he'd keep his mouth shut and do it.

"I've got another one," Melinda said, angling her laptop so he could see the most recent case she'd pulled up.

They'd been at it since yesterday, when Hendrick had found Petrov Armor listed in a number of Bureau cases. Their computer expert had flagged all the files, but Pembrook had assigned him and Melinda to go through each one, since Petrov Armor had never been officially charged.

So far, most of the mentions were offhand and too small to be useful. Like a single Petrov Armor pistol found at the scene of a mass killing. Although the man had been a convicted felon before that incident, he hadn't bought the gun himself. A friend without a criminal history had purchased it and lent it to him, so Petrov Armor hadn't done anything wrong.

He and Melinda had read and eliminated more than a dozen cases like that. Small numbers of guns, purchases traced back to someone with no criminal record, even if they ultimately handed it off to a criminal. But no indication that Petrov Armor had facilitated an illegal sale.

But every so often, a case would pop up with more guns—boxes of them rather than a single piece. They'd be sitting in the attic of a known gang member's house. Or on the scene of a large, coordinated armed robbery. Although the guns were Petrov Armor's, the serial numbers had been filed off, so investigators hadn't been able to trace any back to a sale. It was why Petrov Armor had been investigated, but never charged.

It was legal for them to sell guns to civilians; they just couldn't sell to convicted felons. Since that was a crime the ATF investigated, most of the cases Hendrick had tagged for them were joint FBI-ATF files. Which meant there could be more.

"What have you got?" Kane asked, leaning closer.

Like she did every time he got too close to her, Melinda twitched slightly, then stilled. She probably didn't want to work with him, either. Although the director never talked about it, the role Kane had played in the death of Pembrook's daughter was common knowledge.

Kane gritted his teeth and tried not to let Melinda's reaction bother him. It was part of the reason he liked to work alone. But Pembrook had insisted she wanted both Melinda's ability to read people's intentions—even from a case file—and Kane's extensive experience in the field, undercover with criminals, on this case review. So far, he had to admit, they made a good team. When she wasn't flinching at his nearness, anyway.

"Convicted murderer, released on early parole. About a month after he got out, he strapped on some Petrov Armor body armor, took out a Petrov Armor pistol and killed five people in his old workplace, including the guy who turned him in. He bought the armor directly from Petrov Armor, which isn't illegal. But the gun is a different matter. ATF could never figure out where he got the pistol, but his friend, who was also a convicted felon, told FBI agents that buying the gun was even easier than buying the armor. Then he shut up and wouldn't give us anything else. But it sure seems like he could have gotten them at the same time, one on the books and one off."

Kane leaned back in his chair, letting it tilt so he was staring up at the ceiling as he stacked his hands behind his head. "Maybe he just means it's easy to get a friend to buy a firearm for you legally and then lend it. Happens all the time."

Even though he could see her only from his peripheral

vision, the way her lips twisted in disbelief wasn't hard to picture. "Come on. Why does the average person need body armor and a gun? If this was your friend and you knew he was a violent criminal who'd just bought body armor, would you lend him a gun?"

Kane shrugged. Melinda could see through people better than anyone he'd ever met. But she'd never spent time undercover. Kane had spent so much of his career pretending to be someone else that his own identity sometimes felt nebulous. Which wasn't such a bad thing, as far as he was concerned.

It had taught him just how much people wanted to believe those they loved, even when all the evidence warned them they were making a big mistake. Lending a criminal a gun and lying to yourself that they were just afraid—maybe of a system you'd also convinced yourself had railroaded that person—didn't seem like much of a stretch.

"Well, maybe this one is less convincing than some of the other cases where we've got big boxes of guns. But add all these cases up and there's something here."

"I don't know," Kane argued. "There's a huge black market for guns. It doesn't mean Petrov Armor is involved in the sales."

Melinda sat up straighter, folding her hands in front of her on the table, in a move Kane recognized. She was ready to make an argument.

He hid his smile as he gave her all his attention.

"Selling guns off the books means a huge markup. Criminals will pay more because they need to go through back channels. But a year ago, Leila Petrov shut down that part of the business."

Kane let his chair tip him forward again as he wished he'd realized the connection sooner. "So, now whoever was making those backdoor deals—if that was happening—

could be sending out inferior armor at the same prices as the good armor, pocketing the money left over from using cheaper materials."

"Yes," Melinda agreed, finally smiling at him.

It was probably the first real smile she'd given him since they'd been working together at TCD, or even in all the years before when he'd cross paths briefly with her. The hair on the back of his neck stood up as he noticed how much it changed her face. Not that she wasn't always pretty, but academic and too insightful had never been his type. But a smiling, proud Melinda was someone he needed to avoid even more.

"We need to find a way to get a look at Petrov Armor's finances," Melinda said.

"They've probably got double books," Kane argued, putting his brief, ridiculous burst of attraction aside. "But maybe we need to try and set up a sale. Pretend to be a criminal and buy from them. An undercover op like this is a piece of cake. I've done a million of them."

If he was trying to buy guns from someone at Petrov Armor, he wouldn't be stuck in a tiny office with Melinda Larsen, pretending not to care that she could read anyone with a single glance. Pretending not to care if she did it to him.

"No," Melinda insisted. "We've got to do more legwork first or we could blow the whole case and make whoever is doing this suspicious of Davis."

Kane clamped his mouth shut over the argument he wanted to make. He was dying to get back in the field, put on a new persona like a new pair of clothes. Get away from Melinda's scrutiny. But he knew she was right.

He'd have to wait to jump into the action and the danger he craved, the chance to go out in a hail of bullets like his old partner—Pembrook's only daughter—had done.

The chance to die doing something worthwhile. The way he should have done years ago, beside her.

DAVIS HAD BEEN undercover at Leila's company for a day and a half. To Leila, it felt like he'd been there for a week.

She was overanxious, having to watch every word around him, resist sending him suspicious glances that her employees might notice. Most of them would likely just attribute it to her overprotectiveness of the company and everyone and everything inside it. But Uncle Neal or Eric would have probably known something was off. She was amazed they hadn't realized it already.

Then again, she never lied to either of them.

She and Eric had once shared a bond she thought would never break. He'd been the friend who'd pulled her out of a deep depression three years after she lost her mom. The first boyfriend she'd ever had a year after that. Once their relationship had ended, they'd eventually returned to friendship. It would never be the same as when they were kids, but Leila couldn't forget what he'd done for her or how much he'd meant to her family.

She and her uncle were close. They didn't do much together outside of the office, but mostly that was because they were both so busy with work—and in her uncle's case, with the women he seemed to attract with a single smile. It was a skill she'd never mastered with the opposite sex and, after the way Eric had broken things off with her, had never really wanted to.

The thought made her glance sideways at Davis as he walked alongside her out to her car. Eric was on her other side, making too-fast small talk about his latest sale that told her one thing he *had* noticed: her attraction to Davis.

Eric knew her too well. He'd probably spotted that she glanced at Davis a little too much. Eric wouldn't know only part of that was attraction and the rest was worry because of why Davis was here. All he'd see was that Davis intrigued her.

Eric was jealous. Frustration nipped at her, and with it, a little bit of anger. He'd given up his right to be jealous a long time ago, when he'd broken her heart.

"Oh, you've *got* to be kidding me." Leila sighed as they reached her car in the lot. The front right tire was completely flat. "Damn construction. That was my spare tire."

Davis leaned closer to the wheel, frowning. "I don't suppose you have another? If you do, I can change this for you, no problem."

"Yeah," Leila said. "So could I, but I don't have a second spare. I probably ran over another nail."

She ignored the little voice in the back of her head suggesting one of her employees had done it. She knew quite a few of them weren't happy she'd assumed the role of CEO when her father retired. But they had to be expecting it. Since the day she'd started at the company five years ago, she'd put in more hours than anyone besides her dad. This had started out as a family business, and the board of directors had seen the benefits of keeping it that way. No one could begrudge her that. Especially not with something this juvenile.

"I'll drive you home," Eric said, putting a hand on her arm.

"Not a problem. I can do it." The curiosity on Davis's face told her he hadn't missed Eric's jealousy either.

Before Leila could tell them she'd just call for a car, Davis added, "I am her assistant, after all. Might be a good time for us to talk about how I can help Petrov Armor."

"It's your job to support Leila on the job," Eric said. "Not—"

"That's a good idea," Leila cut him off. "Thank you."

She told Eric a quick good-night, then pivoted to follow Davis to his vehicle.

She swore she could feel Eric's unhappy gaze on her as she climbed into Davis's black SUV, but she didn't look back. Instead, she sank into the surprisingly comfortable bucket seat of what she assumed was his FBI vehicle and closed her eyes. The past two days had been stressful, the past three weeks some of the worst of her life.

No matter how hard she threw herself into work, how much she tried not to think about her dad, he was all around her. Not only had he built the business up from nothing, but he'd also been involved in every decision when they'd moved into their building. He'd picked the furniture and artwork in the lobby, designated the office right next to his for her. When he'd retired, they'd changed the label on his door from CEO to Founder, but he'd kept the office since he was there so often, consulting. She hadn't been able to bring herself to go inside since his death.

Thinking about that terrible moment when she'd gotten the call, the back of Leila's throat stung and she knew tears weren't far behind. Swallowing the pain, she opened her eyes and blinked back the moisture. Realizing Davis had already left the parking lot and was navigating the streets of Old City, she forced her attention back to the one thing she could still control: her father's legacy. "So, what have you found?"

Her heart pounded faster as she waited for his answer, both hoping for and dreading the news. True, she didn't personally know every one of her nearly two hundred employees. But she did know the ones in key positions, roles that would give them the kind of access required to pull this off. And every one of *those* employees, she trusted. Maybe even more telling, her dad had trusted them. He'd had thirty-four years of experience either owning Petrov

Armor or—once he'd taken it public—being the largest shareholder. For all but the last five, he'd run it. Even after he'd turned it over to her, he'd been there to guide her every step of the way.

"Your security is solid," Davis responded, not taking his eyes off the road. "But tomorrow, I want to take a look at your security video for the days connected to the armor being built and shipped out. I want to look at your security card access logs, too. See who went in and out of sensitive areas who shouldn't have been there or who was there at odd hours."

"Sure." Her mind rebelled at the idea of letting an outsider sift through their security footage, but better Davis find the truth than some big, public FBI investigation. Assuming she really could trust him to keep her in the loop and let her manage the betrayal without a huge media fallout.

She wasn't naive enough to think the press wouldn't eventually get the story. But better it came from Petrov Armor than in the form of an FBI statement.

"What about suspects? Who do you think did this? Is it possible it was a switch that happened after the armor left our facilities?" As she said it, the idea gained traction in her mind and gave her hope that she hadn't massively misjudged someone crucial inside her company.

A switch along the delivery route still meant a Petrov Armor employee was probably involved. But it wouldn't be someone she'd known well for years. It wouldn't be the same level of betrayal to the company or to her father's memory.

"I've been inside for a day and a half," Davis answered, still not looking at her. "Right now, everyone is a suspect."

"You want me to work with you, Davis? I need you to work with me, too. I can't give you insight into anyone if I don't know who you need to check out."

His head moved just slightly toward her, his gaze sweeping over her face like he was looking for something. Then he focused on the road again, probably training drilled into him at the FBI. Never take your eyes off the task ahead.

"Tell me about Eric Ross."

She choked on nothing, on air, on the ridiculousness of that statement. Eric, a traitor? "I've known him since I was thirteen. He was almost as close to my dad as I was. Trust me. He had nothing to do with this."

"Are you sure you can be impartial? The man obviously has a crush on you."

"He doesn't…" She let out a heavy sigh. "That's ridiculous. Look, I get it. I misjudged someone at the company. But it's not Eric."

She shifted in her seat so she could see him better and got distracted by the way he looked in dress pants and a blazer. The bulge at his hip under his seat belt caught her attention, and she realized what it was. "You're wearing a gun."

He gave her another one of those quick, searching gazes, then replied, "Always. Even if the FBI didn't require it, I was an army ranger before I joined the Bureau. I like being prepared."

A ranger. Leila let that image fill her mind—Davis in an army uniform, wearing that revered tan beret that identified him as a member of the elite Special Forces unit. It was easy to imagine him parachuting out of a plane, steering a small boat full of soldiers through a jungle river, or rappelling down the side of a mountain. Something about the quiet confidence in his gaze, the outright cockiness of his grin and the muscles that his blazer seemed barely able to contain.

Forcing the image out of her head, she joked, "So, if

you're always prepared, what's in the back? An inflatable boat and a parachute?"

He gave her that quick look again, but this time there was laughter in his eyes and that sexy, amused tilt to his lips.

He'd probably already put her in a box in his mind: serious CEO determined to live up to her father's example. Not a real, rounded person who went home to a too-quiet house, couldn't sleep without background noise and liked to dance by herself in the living room.

Leila instantly regretted letting him see her ridiculous sense of humor. She shifted her left leg back to the floor, no longer facing him as she tried to focus. But it was hard not to think about that smile, those lips. It made her belly tighten with awareness, and she wondered if this was part of his arsenal.

How often did he use sex appeal undercover in order to get what he wanted?

And what exactly did he want? He'd implied that he suspected Eric, made the absurd suggestion that Eric had a crush on her. But surely he'd looked into her past before coming into her company. Did he know she and Eric had dated for four years? Did he know how badly Eric had broken her heart? Or how hard it had been to come into a company where Eric already worked, to try to treat him like any other colleague?

As Davis pulled up in front of her house and Leila realized she'd never given him the address, dread sank to the bottom of her stomach, replacing any twinges of lust.

Of course he knew all of those things. Probably a lot more, too. Even worse, he hadn't told her a single real thing about his investigation.

She didn't know if he'd done it on purpose. Or if he planned to let her in only when he needed her.

But one thing was certain: she couldn't trust Davis either.

# Chapter Five

"You do realize I could blow your cover whenever I want, right?"

Leila Petrov stared at him with narrowed eyes. Her lips pursed tight, and the muscles in her forearms and biceps twitched as she crossed them over her chest. She'd pivoted in her seat again, this time snapping off her seat belt. But she'd made no move to get out of his vehicle and disappear into her house.

As furious as she looked, Davis knew none of his own worry showed. He'd spent too many years running or parachuting into enemy territory with only as much gear as he could carry and no backup that could reach him and his team for days. He was well practiced in faking confidence in moments of doubt. If his fellow soldiers couldn't see through it, neither would the young CEO heir of Petrov Armor.

"Well?" she demanded when he was silent too long.

A smile threatened and Davis fought to hide it. She was nothing like he'd expected when he'd first opened her file. Whether or not she'd gotten her role as CEO because she was the founder's daughter, she knew the company inside out. She wasn't afraid to call him on things, no matter the FBI's involvement. He definitely hadn't expected her dry sense of humor.

A laugh bubbled up thinking about her comment about the inflatable boat he probably kept in his SUV. If she only knew how often an inflatable boat had come in handy in his previous job.

"Are you *laughing* at me?" Leila demanded. "Because if those vests are truly ours, I plan to figure out who was behind it. I'm going to do it with or without your—"

"I'm not laughing at you," Davis cut her off. He leaned closer, saw her chest rise and fall faster in response. "Why would you want to blow my cover?"

"You're not holding up your end of the deal. I don't appreciate you trying to manipulate me with flirtation, with… this." She gestured in front of her, indicating their nearness.

This time, Davis knew his surprise showed. He leaned away from her, trying to regroup.

Leila pivoted even more in her seat, getting into his personal space the same way she had in that interview room. Going on the offensive when most people would do the opposite. "Is this your thing when you go undercover? Try to seduce your contacts?"

"I'm not…" Davis blew out a breath that ended on a laugh. "This is my first time undercover."

He wasn't at all comfortable with it. Sneaking into enemy territory as a ranger or doing dangerous raids as an FBI agent was far more his speed than pretending to be someone he wasn't. Manipulating people into giving him information or access felt foreign and vaguely wrong, even if those people had criminal intentions.

"You've never gone undercover before? Oh." She sat back fast, facing the windshield and giving him a chance to study her profile.

She looked nothing like Jessica Carpenter. Leila's file said she was Russian and Pakistani, while Jessica was African American. Leila had a delicate, almost dainty profile, while Jessica had the bearing of a soldier. But there was something similar underneath the surface, something about the balance between a serious exterior and a softer, goofier side they both tried to hide.

Except Leila was still here, protecting a company that had killed Jessica.

The fact that she hadn't known about it didn't matter. The fact that he liked her more with every moment he spent in her company didn't matter. All that mattered was using whatever means necessary to keep her trust and find the person responsible.

So, he forced a slow, knowing smile and added, "I can't help finding you attractive."

Her lips parted like she was going to say something, but he didn't give her a chance. Instead, he continued. "I *am* keeping up my end of the deal. I told you I wanted more information on Eric Ross."

Her head swung toward him, a frown already in place that told him he'd guessed correctly: she and Eric had a history that went way beyond the company. His plan had worked, to distract her from the real issue—whether he was telling her everything. Because of course he wasn't. And he never would.

The jolt of jealousy at her reaction surprised him, but he ignored it and pressed on. "Unless that's what this is really about? You don't want me digging up dirt on your ex?"

She sputtered for a second, then frowned harder. "Just how involved is your file on me? You know who I dated when I was a teenager?"

Davis hadn't known anything about it, but sensing that her anger might lead to answers, he shrugged, gave a vague answer. "We're the FBI. We try to learn everything we can about suspects in active cases."

"Suspects?" Leila said. "I thought we were past that."

"We are," Davis said, drawing his answers out, long and slow, the opposite of her fast-paced words. "But we had to start at the top, Leila. We know a lot about you."

A flush rose high on her cheeks. "Does that mean you know how Eric befriended me after I pushed everyone else away after my mom died? How he got me help before I really hurt myself? How he dropped out of my life with no explanation when I graduated from high school? Or how he's been calling me every night since my dad died just to make sure I don't fall back into that same depression?"

The jealousy shifted, turned into appreciation that Eric had been there when Leila needed him, despite their history. Davis had seen her strong mask crack, seen how much she missed her father, how she was quietly grieving him. But he couldn't imagine Leila depressed or self-destructive. The thought actually made his stomach hurt.

Leila's voice wobbled just a little, then anger came through again. "Why does the FBI need to know about the hardest things in my life? Is it so you can use it all against me?"

Instantly regretting his tactics, Davis resisted reaching out for her hand. "We don't have any of that in a file, Leila."

Not really, anyway. The file had told him her mother died twenty years ago, but he hadn't known anything about Eric. "I just guessed that you'd dated Eric from the way he talks to you, the way he looks at you."

"Oh." She stared down at her lap, then back at him. There was confusion on her face, but something else, too, something that looked too much like hope.

His gut clenched in response, a mix of guilt and nerves. It was one thing to take on an enemy who was an obvious threat, someone aiming a weapon back at him. It was totally different to try to earn someone's trust when he knew he might have to betray that trust in the end.

But this was the job. His colleague Kane did it all the time. The agent seemed to thrive on it. If it meant getting justice for Jessica, it was what Davis had to do too.

Trying to hold the guilt at bay, Davis unhooked his seat belt and shifted so he was facing her more fully. "How are you holding up since your dad died?"

Her forehead furrowed, like she was trying to gauge his sincerity. Then she sighed and said, "My dad and I are— were—like best friends. In some ways it was just the two of us. My mom died when I was ten. I've never met her family except for a few cousins over video chat. They're all back in Pakistan. My mom moved here for my dad and mostly lost touch when she did. They never really forgave her for leaving. His family is...not so great. Except for my uncle. My uncle is wonderful. He helped get me through losing my mom back then, and he's helping me get through losing my dad now."

She heaved out another sigh and leaned back against the seat. "I can't believe he's gone."

"I'm sorry."

"Of course he had to stand up to that mugger." She let out a bitter laugh. "That's my dad. Never give in to anyone."

Davis's chest constricted at the pain in her voice. He understood Neal Petrov's response. The police report said Neal had been armed, carrying a small Petrov Armor pistol hidden at the small of his back. Apparently, it wasn't unusual, and he had a concealed carry license. He'd probably thought the mugger was no real threat. Probably figured he could pull the gun, warn the guy off. Instead, he'd gotten shot. "He sounds tough."

"Yeah, I guess so. Not with me. He was..." She shrugged. "A softie."

"You were his only daughter."

Still not looking at him, she nodded. "When my mom

died, he lost it. Just withdrew from everything and everyone—including me."

Davis frowned. No wonder she'd sunk into depression. At ten she'd lost her mom, and her dad hadn't been there for her. "I'm glad you met Eric then."

She looked over at him, surprise on her features. "I didn't meet Eric for another three years. But my uncle stepped up. Before that, Uncle Joel was…" A wistful, amused smile tilted one side of her mouth, then dropped off. "Flighty, I guess. He was always off chasing women and fun. Not that he ever stopped that. But when he saw how checked out Dad was, he stepped in. Practically raised me for a few years, practically ran the business too, until Dad got it together. That's when my dad and I really got close. Right before my dad got it together was when I met Eric."

"Your uncle ran the business for a while?"

"Yeah. He spent so much time dealing with Dad's job that he lost his own."

"What do you mean?"

"He didn't work for the company before that. He was a sales rep at a pharmaceutical company. But when my dad got himself together, he gave Uncle Joel a job."

Davis nodded, trying to sound casual when he asked, "After all that, why didn't your dad convince the board of directors to appoint your uncle as CEO when he stepped down?"

Leila frowned. "What makes you think my dad talked them into that decision?"

"Are you telling me he didn't? He was the largest shareholder, wasn't he, before he died?" Before those shares had been split up between Leila and Joel.

"Yes," Leila admitted. "But—"

"So why not push for your uncle to take on the role?" Was there any lingering resentment on the uncle's part?

Maybe enough to sabotage the business, even all these years later?

Leila laughed. "Uncle Joel, CEO? No way. I mean, obviously he was the de facto CEO for a few years when I was a kid. He can do it. He even grew the business. But he doesn't want to. Never has. He likes being COO. Gives him security and a say in the company's direction, but not all of the responsibility."

"How does he feel about reporting to you?"

She shrugged. "Fine. It's a little weird. He is my uncle, after all. But he's great about it. A lot better than some of the others."

"Like Theresa Quinn?" The head of Petrov Armor's R and D had struck him as less than thrilled about Leila's leadership.

"How'd you guess?" Leila sighed. "She's not the only one. But they all know me. They all know how much I care about the business, about my father's legacy." She gave him a hard look. "They know how hard I worked for this position. They'll come around eventually."

There was less confidence in her last words, so Davis said, "I'm sure they will."

Her expression turned pensive. But as she stared at him, the worry in her gaze slowly softened. Her lips parted and he could hear her swallow, and suddenly the vehicle felt way too hot.

Then she was leaning toward him, her eyes dropping closed.

He felt his body sway forward in response, and his hand reached up to cup her cheek as his own lips parted in anticipation of touching hers. But sanity returned before the distance between them disappeared.

Jerking away, Davis couldn't quite hold her gaze. "I

should probably get going. Call me if you need anything or if you have any thoughts about the case, okay?"

She blinked back at him, confusion and embarrassment in her stare. Then, she blinked again and it was gone, replaced with a hard professionalism. "Good night, Davis."

She stepped out of his vehicle, walked up the stone pathway to her house and let herself inside without a backward glance.

HE WAS AN IDIOT.

Leila Petrov had been inches from kissing him and he'd backed away. Now, not only had he missed out on the chance to taste her, he'd blown the tenuous trust they'd been building. But that was a professional line he couldn't cross.

Besides, she'd been vulnerable. And he'd been lying. Every moment he spent with her was a lie, because even though she knew he was there to find out the truth about the defective armor, she had no idea how badly he needed to see someone punished for it. She had no idea that regardless of whether she'd been involved, he would always hold her responsible, since she ran the company.

He liked her. Too much, probably. He didn't want to use her. Not even to help the investigation. Not even to avenge Jessica's death.

Davis slammed his fist on the top of the steering wheel as he drove away from Leila's house. His body was telling him to turn around, knock on her door and come clean with her. His mind was telling him he needed to do the same thing, for the sake of the case.

But he couldn't do it. She'd had too much loss and betrayal in her life already. He wasn't about to add to it.

His cell phone rang and Davis hit the Bluetooth button on the steering wheel, eyes still on the road. He glanced at the dashboard screen, an apology already on his lips. But he swallowed it as he realized the name on the display. Melinda Larsen was calling him. Not Leila.

The surge of disappointment he felt surprised him as Melinda asked, "Hello? Davis, are you there?"

"Yeah." His voice didn't sound quite right, so he cleared his throat. "Yeah, what's up?"

"Kane and I have been looking through Petrov Armor's potential illegal gun sales, as you know."

That was quite a partnership. Even though they sat in the same briefings all the time, Davis couldn't imagine quietly confident Melinda Larsen and now-you-see-me-now-you-don't Kane Bradshaw working a case together. "Did you find anything?"

"Maybe. We've got photos from a joint FBI-ATF gang case. Illegal arms sales were only a peripheral part of the case, but we were running anything we could find, no matter how small. One of those things was a partial plate on a Lexus that showed up in a photo. The driver isn't visible and we've only got part of the vehicle, but the partial matches up to Theresa Quinn, head of—"

"Research and development at Petrov Armor," Davis finished. "But a partial plate? How partial?"

"It's not a slam dunk, not even close. Hundreds of red Lexuses match this partial. But in Tennessee? On the edge of a gang meeting?"

"What do you mean by the *edge* of a meeting?" Davis asked as he changed lanes, heading toward the TCD office instead of home.

"It's possible it's not connected. But again, a Lexus in this part of town? Right near where a gang member was meeting up with someone for a gun sale?"

"Who made the sale?" Davis asked.

"We don't know. They never showed. ATF said they

think the guy got spooked. Or the gal, if this vehicle really does belong to Theresa Quinn."

"Anything else?" Davis asked hopefully. It did sound like a potential lead. Theresa definitely didn't seem to respect Leila, maybe a result of working with her father for years in illegal sales without the young CEO realizing it?

"I'm coming into the office," Davis told Melinda.

"Good. Kane and I are still wading through case files, but we'd love to hear how you're faring on the inside."

"Having a lot more fun, I'm sure." Kane's voice carried from the background.

"Not really," Davis muttered. Before Melinda could ask, he said, "I'll be there in two," and hung up.

He made it in one minute, and found Kane and Melinda sitting on opposite sides of the long conference table where the team had its morning briefings. Each had a laptop open, and Davis wondered how many hours they'd managed to work together without actually talking.

"There's a reason Petrov Armor has never been charged," Kane told him. "If they're selling guns on the side to criminals—which I think they are—they're savvy."

A hard ball of dread made Davis's stomach cramp. It should have been good news—not that Petrov Armor was talented at avoiding prosecution, but that there was another route to try to collect evidence. But all Davis could think of was the conviction in Leila's face when she'd told him it wasn't their armor. The hope in her eyes when she'd suggested maybe the armor had been switched after it had been shipped out of their facility.

She truly believed the core of her company was good. It looked like she was very, very wrong.

"Undercover work is tough, isn't it?" Melinda asked, making Davis realize she could probably read every one of his emotions.

Suddenly Kane's attention was fixed on him, too, and Davis forced a shrug. Tried to push Leila out of his mind. "It's a big company. But the number of people who could have pulled off both illegal gun sales *and* defective armor shipments is probably pretty low. Assuming we think it's the same person."

"Someone in power," Kane agreed. "Possibly more than one person, since we still think it's pretty likely Neal Petrov was involved when he was alive. Who's on your short list for his partner in crime?"

"Obviously Theresa Quinn is on our list," Melinda said, then looked at Davis. "What about Neal's brother, Joel?"

"Maybe," Davis hedged, not liking the idea that both Leila's father and her uncle might be criminals. But he tried to think objectively. "Neal and Joel could have been in it together all along. After Neal's wife died, Joel managed everything for a few years, so maybe he handled the criminal side for his brother, too. Maybe that's why Neal kept his brother on after he was ready to return to work."

Melinda's eyebrows rose. "That's promising. Although that red Lexus still seems awfully coincidental."

"Who else?" Kane asked. "What about the head of sales?"

"Eric Ross." Leila's ex. A man who'd broken her heart years ago, but had called her every night for the past three weeks to make sure she was okay after her father's death. "Also possible. He's got access to everything, and his job takes him out of the office a lot. It probably wouldn't raise eyebrows if he took samples with him, saying they were for sales calls demos. Maybe he used that as a way to get bigger quantities out. He was really close to Neal Petrov, so they could have definitely been partners."

"Even though the most obvious answer initially looked like Neal's daughter was working with him, Leila seemed genuinely shocked in that interview," Melinda said. "A year ago, she was the one who initiated the shutdown of the gun side of their business to focus on the armor. No way she'd do that if she was making tons of money from guns off-book."

"Leila's not involved." The words came out of his mouth before he could pull them back, but Davis knew they were true.

Kane lifted an eyebrow, but all he said was, "Have you considered that her dad put her in charge because she'd never suspect him of wrongdoing? That she'd be easier to fool? Seems like it backfired when she shut down the gun part of the business, but he still had a tidy fall girl."

Melinda frowned. "That's pretty heartless."

"Yeah, well, have you read the guy's file?" Kane shoved a manila folder across the table, and Davis snagged it.

"What is this?" Most of the FBI's files were computerized, unless they were so old they hadn't been transitioned over. But this looked like a PD file.

"Police file on Neal Petrov's mugging is in there somewhere. I just skimmed that. But there's also a really old file from a welfare check. A neighbor called it in twenty years ago, saying a ten-year-old girl—Leila—had been on her own for a week. Police checked it out, and even though the girl claimed everything was fine and her dad had just run out, the state of the house said otherwise. They were going to call Children's Services, but the girl's uncle showed up and smoothed things over."

"Neal's wife had just died," Davis said, his shoulders slumping as he read the details of a dirty, hungry Leila, alone and trying hard to be brave when police had arrived.

Knowing things had turned out okay and feeling like he was spying on a part of her life she hadn't given him permission to see, Davis turned to the report on the mugging.

It was brief, but this report had ended much worse. Davis started to close the file when a small detail caught his eye. He swore, sitting up straighter, and read it again.

"What is it?" Kane asked.

"I don't think this was a random mugging." Davis looked at Kane, then Melinda. "I think Neal Petrov was murdered."

# Chapter Six

"Neal Petrov was murdered?" Kane asked. "That's not what the report said."

"The official story is that someone tried to mug Neal, he went for his gun and the mugger shot him. But they never caught the mugger," Davis said.

"So what?" Kane demanded. "He was in an area that had seen a rash of muggings. It was inevitable that it would get violent eventually. If he was trying to pull a gun, probably the mugger panicked and shot first."

"Neal Petrov holstered his gun at the small of his back." Davis skimmed the report once more to be sure he hadn't missed something, then swore under his breath. He was right. "According to this report, his right arm was positioned under his back, like he was reaching for the gun when he fell."

"All consistent with a mugging gone wrong," Kane said, but he was leaning forward now, his tone suggesting he was waiting for something inconsistent.

"Neal Petrov had no damage to that arm. No broken fingers from landing on them. No scraped-up arms when he hit the pavement. It's as if—"

"His arm was positioned that way after he fell," Melinda finished, looking pensive.

"Exactly."

"Well, this case just took an interesting turn," Kane said, settling back into his chair.

It *was* interesting. Because if it wasn't a random mugging and the scene had been staged, that suggested someone Neal knew. It seemed likely the murderer was connected to the faulty armor coming out of Petrov Armor. That potentially put a completely different spin on what was happening at Petrov Armor and who was involved.

But all Davis could think about was the sadness in Leila's voice when she'd talked about losing her mom, the grief in her eyes when her employees had talked about missing her dad. He didn't want her to face more hurt. He definitely didn't want to have to tell her that someone she knew might have murdered her dad.

"So, who might have wanted Neal Petrov dead?" Melinda asked.

Davis forced himself to focus, but he couldn't quite get Leila's sad eyes out of his head as he replied, "Potentially a lot of people if he was involved in illegal gun sales and defective body armor sales."

"Or even if he wasn't, and he found out what was happening at his company," Kane added. "Though I'm betting he was part of this, probably the instigator. My guess is that he was making a lot of money off the illegal gun sales, letting him retire at sixty. With a partner inside, that person still had the necessary access. So did Neal, since he was still at the office all the time as a consultant and member of the board. This way, Neal could focus on the illegal side of the business. I bet he put his daughter in charge because she'd never suspect him of this. Right?" Kane stared questioningly at Davis.

He nodded reluctantly. "Leila loved her dad. She'd never suspect him of anything illegal or immoral. But honestly, she still doesn't think it's anyone at the company. She's convinced a switch happened after the shipment left Petrov Armor."

"Well, that might have been plausible—if unlikely—when we were talking about one defective armor shipment. But she doesn't know how big this case has gotten, including all the illegal arms sales," Kane replied. "So, he helps get his daughter put in charge, thinking she'll be clueless. Then, she shuts down the gun business, so Neal switches to defective armor. As the biggest shareholder, he's still getting plenty of the company's profits. So, he's swapping out the materials for cheaper stuff and pocketing the balance. That would suggest he was working with Theresa."

"And then she had him killed?" Melinda interrupted. "Why?"

"Maybe she wanted more of the profits for herself," Davis suggested, able to imagine the determined head of R and D paying someone to kill Neal. Or even pulling the trigger herself. "She resented Leila being put in charge. Maybe she blamed Neil for putting her there and giving her a chance to shut down the gun side of the business."

"Or it wasn't Theresa who killed him at all," Melinda suggested. "Maybe it was someone who learned what he was doing and took their own revenge."

"But the faulty armor only caused deaths after Neal was already murdered," Davis said.

"At least as far as we know," Melinda contradicted. "But what if it was someone internal? Someone who learned about the gun sales and wanted them stopped? Maybe they sent the faulty armor to get him investigated and when that took too long, they had him killed instead."

"There are easier ways of dealing with that, though. Anonymous tip to police, for one. Sending out bad armor to trigger an investigation seems pretty drastic and complicated. Too many variables the perp can't control," Davis argued.

"Yeah, but what revenge murder do you know of that's not drastic?"

"Point taken. If it's revenge. But I don't think it is. It seems more likely he was killed by his partner in the illegal gun sales, doesn't it?" Davis glanced at Kane, wondering about his take. Melinda might be the profiler, but Kane had spent most of his career undercover. He'd worked with the CIA repeatedly. He understood the underhanded dealings of criminals better than most, because he'd seen them up close. Rumor had it that sometimes he'd even participated to keep his cover intact.

"Maybe," Kane said, but there was uncertainty in his tone. "It's the timing I'm interested in. What happened three weeks ago that got Neal Petrov killed? It's interesting that it's close to the timing of that faulty shipment. Then, there's the fact that the gun side of the business shut down last year. My gut says all those things are somehow connected."

"Leila has agreed to give me access to the security camera footage and logs from the time the latest batch of armor was made," Davis told them. "Hopefully that will give us some insight."

"In the meantime, you need to continue to act like you're just there about one shipment of defective armor," Melinda said. "Leila can't suspect her father was murdered or she might just blow open this whole investigation."

"I know," Davis answered, not quite meeting her gaze. He had no intention of telling Leila the truth, at least not until they had someone in custody. But lying to her even a little bit made him feel terrible. How was he going to keep something this huge from her?

IT WAS SEVENTY degrees and the sun was shining, but Kane Bradshaw was tucked into a dark corner beneath an underpass. Fifty feet away, a low-level drug deal was taking place. A hundred feet beyond that, a cluster of cardboard boxes and blankets housed more people than should have been able to fit in the tight space.

Kane ignored all of it. He kept his back to a pillar and swept the area with his gaze until he spotted his confidential informant. Dougie Zimmerman sauntered over with his typical cocky attitude, hiking up pants that never seemed to stay above his bony hips. With what little hair he had on his head shaved close and a goatee hiding some of his pockmarked face, Dougie looked like he was more arrogance than real threat.

The truth was somewhere in between.

Dougie had dropped out of high school and started driving trucks full of illegal goods when he was seventeen. By the time he was nineteen, he'd done two short stints in jail, but hadn't turned on anyone. It had earned him trust among the criminal element and more illegal jobs. A year after that, he'd been caught again, this time with enough drugs to send him away for a long time.

Instead of going to jail, Kane's then-partner at the FBI had made the arrest disappear and turned Dougie into a confidential informant. That had been eight years ago. Since then, Dougie had become one of Kane's best CIs. Kane had helped disappear multiple drug possession charges, an illegal gun charge and even an armed robbery charge to keep Dougie on the streets. Because he always delivered more than the damage he caused.

Still, Dougie had become a CI to stay out of jail and for the way the thrill of double-crossing boosted his ego. At the end of the day, Dougie was still a criminal. And Kane was still FBI.

Although he kept his hands loose at his sides, Kane was ready to react if Dougie showed any sign of a double-cross. Kane had one of the quickest draws at TCD. He'd never had a meeting with a CI go sideways, but he'd had plenty of undercover operations turn bad, so he was always prepared. Usually with multiple weapons hidden on his body.

Only once had his preparedness not been enough. Back then, his partner had paid the ultimate price. Which was why Kane was standing beneath the underpass alone and hadn't even let Melinda know where he was going. If Pembrook was going to force him to work with Melinda, she could handle the parts of the investigation that involved reading case files in an air-conditioned office. He'd manage the rest.

"What have you got for me?" he asked Dougie, giving him a quick scan. But Dougie's ill-fitting clothes didn't leave a lot of good places to hide a weapon. Kane doubted he had backup of his own. Although the man had made contacts with a ton of Tennessee's criminal elements, he rarely liked to work with anyone long-term. As far as Kane could tell, their relationship was the longest one Dougie had ever had.

Dougie's head swiveled slowly left and right, looking more like a slow-motion dance move than a scan of his surroundings. Then he gave Kane a quick nod. "Word is that if you want guns on the down low, you can get some Petrov Armor pistols around here. I asked as much as I could without making people suspicious, but no one seemed to know exactly who the contact was. Least not anyone I know."

Kane frowned. Dougie knew everyone. Then again, if someone had been illegally selling Petrov Armor guns to criminals for more than a decade, they were good at hiding both the activity itself and their identity.

"What about recent sales?" Officially, the gun side of the business was shut down, but that didn't mean Petrov Armor didn't have excess weapons or that someone wasn't still secretly making them and selling them at a huge markup to criminals.

"I don't know how recent these sales are, but…" Dougie glanced around once more, then leaned closer and dropped his voice to a whisper. "Supposedly BECA has been buying up a lot of guns lately. Word is they've got a whole room full of Petrov Armor pistols."

Dougie's words sent an electric current along Kane's skin, the rush of a new lead that his gut said was real. The Brotherhood of an Ethnically Clean America—BECA for short—was a nasty zealot group that specialized in equal-opportunity hate. The FBI had been watching them ever since they'd popped onto the radar four years earlier, but so far, none of the attacks by members had been connected strongly enough back to the group to make a large-scale arrest.

"How do you feel about making an introduction?" Kane asked.

Dougie shook his head. "No way, man. Those guys are all crazy. I don't want to work with them."

"You don't have to. Just tell them I want to."

Dougie's lips twisted upward, making him look even more unattractive. "I don't have connections there, but I know a guy who does. He's the one who told me about the guns. I can get you in with him, but I'm gonna need some cash."

Usually Kane played up the fact that Dougie wasn't in jail to keep the man from asking for too much cash for information. It helped keep Dougie honest, prevented him from making things up for money. But today, he just nodded. "How fast can you do it?"

"Maybe tomorrow?" Dougie glanced around once more, then started walking away. "I'll call you."

Kane waited another few minutes before he left in the

opposite direction. Protocol said he was supposed to let his partner—for this case, Melinda—know about the information. But Melinda would fight him on his plan to get close to BECA. She'd argue that it was too dangerous. She'd want to do more legwork first. Or worse yet, she'd want to go with him.

Kane shuddered at the very idea of Melinda Larsen in the field. The idea of working beside her undercover sent deeper fear through him.

But something had to be done. They couldn't wait for Davis to find the perpetrator. Not when he was getting more attached to Leila Petrov with every minute he spent undercover. The fact that his connection to her was more than just physical had been apparent last night at the office when he'd talked about her with admiration and empathy and an unwillingness to put her on the suspect list.

Davis was a nice guy. He was formidable in close-quarters battle or a firefight, and Kane would choose to have the guy next to him in most dangerous situations. But undercover? It wasn't his forte. He was too straitlaced military, too honest and straightforward. He didn't know how to inhabit a persona like a second skin.

And that was a mistake that could be fatal.

# Chapter Seven

For what felt like the hundredth time today, Leila glanced at the closed door to her office. She'd barely spoken to Davis since he'd come in to work this morning. He'd offered to pick her up, but she'd risen early and taken a cab so she'd have an excuse to avoid him.

She couldn't believe she'd tried to kiss him yesterday. He hadn't said a word about it, but considering how fast he'd backed away, there was no need. Apparently, even though he'd been using flirtation and attraction to get information for his investigation, she'd crossed the line with him by acting on those feelings.

She should be glad he hadn't let it get that far. She'd been overemotional, looking for comfort in the wrong way. If he *had* let her kiss him, she probably would have been even more embarrassed today. Yet, a part of her wished she'd still been able to press herself against that broad chest and lose herself in his kisses. For even half an hour, to take a break from the reality that her dad was gone and her company—the biggest part of her dad she had left—was in serious trouble.

Closing her eyes against the rush of tears threatening, Leila focused on taking deep breaths in and out until she got control of her grief. When she opened them again, Davis was standing in the doorway, quietly closing the door behind him.

Just her luck that he'd seen her break down. She forced a smile, hoping to mask her sadness. "How did you do with the security card log and the videos?"

That morning, she'd given him access to the computer program that tracked who had been in and out of which areas at which times. She'd also handed over all their internal and external security video footage. The internal footage was automatically erased every week unless it was tagged for saving, but they held on to their external video for months. Letting Davis access all of it had been her attempt at getting their mutual goal back on track.

He frowned at her, the expression on his face telling her he was going to ask if she was okay.

"Well?" She was finished getting personal with him. From this point forward, she needed to remember that they were unwilling partners in an investigation to uncover the truth about what had happened to those soldiers. That was it.

Even if they were working together, even if she respected his intelligence and investigative experience, ultimately, they were going to end up on opposite sides. Yes, right now, they wanted the same thing. But once they found the perpetrator, he was unlikely to care whether Petrov Armor went down with the culprits. She couldn't let that happen. Not only because of her dad, but also because of all the employees who counted on the company for their paychecks.

"I found something."

Her heart seemed to plummet to her stomach. Leila clamped her hands on her desk for stability as she got to her feet. "What did you find?" Or rather, who? Who had been betraying her father, the company and their country?

Who at Petrov Armor didn't care if soldiers died thinking they were protected by body armor?

"Nothing on the external video. Not really, anyway."

Davis stepped around to the back of her desk. She could smell his morning-fresh scent and feel the brush of his arm as he shifted her laptop toward him.

He leaned past her, typing away as he said, "I don't know exactly when to look, so it's a little tough to sort through all that raw footage. But you do have some gaps. I don't know if it's a system error or someone erased footage. What I didn't find was anything obviously suspicious, like a truck being loaded with crates at night."

"Well, I still think someone could have swapped out that armor after it left our facility," Leila said, peering around him to see what he was doing on the laptop.

His fingers stalled and his whole body went unnaturally still. It couldn't have been more than a few seconds before he was straightening and shrugging, but Leila's mouth went dry. There was something he wasn't telling her.

Before she could figure out what, he spun the laptop toward her. "This is a bit more interesting."

Leila peered closer, recognizing their security card access logs. Every time someone used their security card to key into the building or any of the secure areas, the system logged it.

"Theresa Quinn was here late at night during the time you said that shipment of armor was being made."

Leila sighed. "That's not really a smoking gun, Davis. Theresa lives for the work. She's here on weekends sometimes."

"But these super-late-night visits don't seem to happen except during this time period."

Leaning in again, Leila scrolled through the dates in question, realizing he was right. "It still might not mean anything."

She and Theresa had never gotten along. Maybe it was because the head of Research and Development had been part of Petrov Armor since Leila was a kid. Although her father had never told her about it, Leila had overheard Theresa arguing with him about recommending the board put Leila in charge. Theresa hadn't seemed to want the CEO spot for herself, just thought Leila hadn't earned it and wasn't capable of running the company.

But Theresa was a professional. Once Leila had been given the job anyway, Leila had never heard a word about it from her head of R and D. They might not like each other personally, but it had never gotten in the way of work. Leila couldn't imagine Theresa betraying the company she'd spent the last twenty years helping to build. Not even if that company was handed over to someone she'd called "the person who's going to destroy Petrov Armor."

"You and Theresa don't get along," Davis said.

"You noticed," Leila said dryly. "Look, I've known Theresa since I was ten years old. My uncle brought her in while my dad wasn't functioning after losing my mom. But when he got back to work, Dad said finding Theresa was one of the best things his brother had done. She can be prickly, but she wouldn't betray this company. She helped make it what it is today."

"So, how did she feel about you shutting down the firearm side of the business?"

Thrown by the topic change, Leila sank into her chair, wheeling it away from her desk to put a little space between them. "She wasn't happy about it. Honestly, no one at the top was. But I'd been thinking about it for a long time. I didn't do it right away, but last year, the timing seemed right. The ultralight body armor the military had been testing was a big success, and they finally started ordering in massive quantities. It was time to stop splitting our focus, and armor seemed like the way to go."

"That's why you did it?" Davis pressed.

"Mostly, yeah. But on the weapon side, we just made pistols. Honestly, I've just always been more comfortable selling to the military. Protecting soldiers by providing them with solid armor seemed like the best way to spend our company's resources. Plus our armor was profitable. It seemed right, since it was where my dad started the business anyway."

"So that was it? What about the excess?"

Leila shrugged. "Most of the excess was destroyed. Yes, we lost money at first, but we got the board of directors to wait out the slump, so we could move our focus completely to armor." She stared up at him, captivated by the intensity that was always on his face, even when he was giving her one of his slow, cocky grins. "Why do you want to know about the shift in our business plan?"

"I'm just surprised, that's all. Your dad was really okay with it? He spent a long time building up weapons sales."

"Then he and the board entrusted the future of the business to me. It wasn't what he would have done. My dad and I didn't always agree, but he always supported me. He knew I was already in an uphill battle with the employees over being named CEO." She frowned down at her lap. "I think he knew if he didn't support me on this, my leadership would be in trouble."

"He was a good dad," Davis said, but Leila wasn't sure if it was a statement or a question.

"Yes," she stressed, standing up and facing him. "He was the best."

She could practically see his mind working, going over what she'd said about her uncle looking after her when her dad had checked out after her mom died. But it had been a long time ago. Her dad had grown up with parents who'd abused him. It had been just him and Uncle Joel for so long, only counting on each other. He'd once told her that when he'd met her mom overseas when he'd been there on business, a single glance from her had changed the entire trajectory of his life. Leila knew it was the fanciful memory of a man who'd loved his wife deeply and then lost her too young, but the idea always made her smile.

"Yeah, my dad took a while to get over losing his wife. That's pretty normal, I think. Especially when you have no one to lean on besides your brother—who's busy running your company and watching your ten-year-old daughter."

Davis didn't say anything, but she could tell he wanted to, probably about her own care in that time.

"Anyway, once he dealt with his grief, you couldn't ask for a more involved father." She smiled at the sudden memory of the first day she'd brought Eric home to meet her dad. When she'd met Eric, she'd been thirteen and just seen him as a friend, nothing more. But her dad had probably seen that Eric—two years older—had a deeper interest.

"What's so funny?" Davis asked.

"If my dad had met you, he wouldn't let you out of his sight for a second."

Davis frowned, maybe thinking she'd meant because her dad would have known Davis was undercover.

She used a lighthearted tone, intending to be playful, make a joke out of their mutual attraction and this impossible situation. "Not for the investigation, although he probably would have figured that out. But he would have watched you closely for another reason entirely." She raised her eyebrows, waiting for him to catch on.

Finally a smile stretched his lips, starting slow like it always did. With it came a gleam in his eyes. "Is that right?"

She swallowed, resisting the sudden urge to lick her lips. She'd meant it as a joke. She'd let her serious CEO persona slip with him yet again, and oddly, it didn't feel strange. She was actually more comfortable being herself around Davis than she'd been with anyone in a long time.

Spinning away from him, she tried to get her guard back up. It made no sense to feel this normal around Davis. Not so soon after her dad had died and not considering who Davis was, why he was here.

At the end of this investigation, he'd be leaving. And he might try to take down Petrov Armor when he did it.

No matter how he made her feel, she couldn't let him in. Couldn't let him destroy the one thing she had left.

"ANY NEWS?" DAVIS asked Melinda. He'd retreated to the privacy of his SUV in Petrov Armor's parking lot to talk to her without being overheard. He felt a little ridiculous sitting in his vehicle while the sun baked him through the windows. But he couldn't take his jacket off without the possibility of his gun showing. He didn't want Leila— or anyone else—to overhear his discussion with Melinda.

"Kane is off on some meeting." Impatience crackled in her words as Melinda added, "He's been gone for a while."

"How's that going, working with Kane Bradshaw?" Davis couldn't help asking. He'd liked Melinda from the minute he'd met her. She was smart and always willing to lend her psychological expertise on a case. She was also quiet and a bit of a loner, but Davis didn't mind that. She'd gone out with the team for drinks a time or two. Although she kept her personal life to herself, she'd been friendly.

Kane, on the other hand, managed to be both a charmer and antisocial. The fact that he'd once been partnered with Pembrook's daughter—had actually been undercover with her when she'd been killed—was common knowledge. But what exactly had happened, no one seemed to know. His MO was to avoid the team as much as possible while running his own operations. Davis still wasn't sure why Pembrook let him get away with it, although it was hard to argue that the guy got results.

"Fine."

Her short answer was obviously a lie, but she couldn't see his amusement, so Davis didn't bother hiding his grin. It served him right that Eric Ross chose that moment to stride through the lot, probably returning from a sales call. He gave Davis a quizzical look, then kept going, disappearing inside the building.

Davis felt a visceral dislike toward Eric, but he tried to quell it because Eric hadn't actually done anything to deserve it, besides once date Leila.

Focusing back on Melinda, Davis told her what he'd learned that put some questions in his mind about Neal Petrov. "So, according to Leila, her dad supported her when she wanted to stop the gun side of the business. She says his support allowed her to do it without massive pushback from her employees or a flat-out refusal from the board."

"Well, that's interesting," Melinda replied. "You think she's telling the truth?"

"Why would she lie?" Before Melinda could answer, he continued, "I realize that she wouldn't want to implicate her dad, whether or not he was involved, but she still thinks this is just about defective armor. I almost blew it just now when I was talking to her about what I found on her security logs, though."

Thank goodness he'd caught himself before he'd started talking about trying to track down anomalies throughout the years. She'd definitely caught on that he was holding something back, but he was pretty sure she didn't know what.

It was a rookie mistake. Although he was a rookie at undercover work, he definitely wasn't when it came to "need to know." Most of his missions with the rangers had been highly classified. He'd had no problem keeping everything about them secret. But something about Leila made him speak without thinking.

"She probably wouldn't lie," Melinda agreed, bringing him back on track. "But maybe her father figured he didn't need to get into a fight with her over it if the rest of the company would do it for him. Push back on dropping the gun sales, that is. Or maybe he'd already planned to move over to making money illegally off of the armor and didn't need the gun sales."

"Really? I know we're talking about dealing with criminals, but in some ways selling guns illegally seems safer. At least that way, he wasn't risking a major incident with the military and a large-scale investigation. Not to mention the bad publicity."

"Well, we also don't know how many people are involved," Melinda said. "Maybe he planned to keep making guns and just hide it from Leila. Or they had enough excess that he figured he could just sell those for a while."

"Leila said the excess was mostly destroyed."

"Maybe that's just what her dad told her and she believed him. For all we know, he just moved the excess and continued to sell it."

Davis stared at the entrance to Petrov Armor. It was a huge facility, representing almost three decades of work, most of it with Neal Petrov at the helm. The FBI hadn't requested Neal's personal finances, but Davis was willing to bet he'd made millions legally. In Davis's cases, he'd seen plenty of greed that didn't make any sense to him, people who had more money than they should ever need who still wanted more. He'd come across plenty of people who framed spouses, children or friends for their crimes.

Even though Kane had described Neal Petrov as heartless, Leila spoke of him with such love. Could she just not see his faults because she adored him? Was he that good a liar? Or was the truth something more complex?

"What are you thinking, Davis?" Melinda asked, making him realize how long he'd gone silent.

He was thinking that he felt guilty for not telling Leila that he suspected her dad had been involved in killing the soldiers. That he felt worse for not telling her that her dad might have been murdered over it.

Instead of admitting to Melinda how complicated his feelings were becoming when it came to the woman he was supposed to be using to get information on the case, he sighed. "I'm wondering if her dad saw how much Leila wanted to stop selling guns and focus on the armor. I'm wondering if he supported her because he loved her."

"You think he loved her enough to sacrifice a more than ten-year-long criminal business that was probably netting him millions on top of his legal income? It doesn't seem likely, but no matter how much you break down people's motivations and the things that form them, they surprise me all the time. Love is a pretty powerful motive."

"What if he wanted to quit the illegal business altogether for her?" The idea gained traction in Davis's mind. If anyone was worth giving up millions of dollars and changing your way of life for, wouldn't it be someone like Leila Petrov? A strong, determined leader who refused to suspect anyone she trusted of wrongdoing? Who had a goofy side she tried to hide so people wouldn't stop taking her seriously? He'd laughed more than once at her silly jokes, had caught her humming popular tunes while working, and seen her bopping along to music as soon as she got into her car to head home at the end of the day.

Yet she was serious when it came to her responsibility

to the company and her employees. She held strong morals about investigating the business she ran—risking her own livelihood—to do what was right.

"So, he supported her in shutting down the gun side of the business," Melinda said. "Maybe that was his attempt at taking the company legal again. Maybe he wasn't setting her up to take a fall if things went south. Maybe he was trying to get rid of that threat for her."

"Then what happened with this armor?" Davis asked. "Could it have really been an accident?"

"I doubt it." Melinda echoed his thoughts. "What if it was Neal's partner, trying to undermine the armor side of the business? Bring the guns back?"

"It's possible," Davis said. "But that's quite a risk, purposely drawing all that attention to Petrov Armor."

"Or maybe Neal Petrov saw a new opportunity to make money off the books by using cheap armor material, and he couldn't help himself. Ten years is a long time to be involved with criminals and then just quit. It's not always just about money," Melinda reminded him. "It's also a thrill for some people."

That felt right to Davis. It even opened up a new motivation for Neal's death. "What if his partner was unhappy with the change?" Davis suggested. "Theresa—or whoever he was working with—thought he'd come around and start selling guns again. When he switched to armor, maybe she had a problem with it."

"That could be," Melinda agreed. "Selling guns to criminals is one thing. Purposely sending armor to soldiers that was defective is another. Maybe Neal's partner was afraid it was too risky. Or maybe she just drew a moral line in the sand."

"Hell of a moral line," Davis said. "I think maybe she killed him over it."

# Chapter Eight

Had Theresa Quinn—or someone else at Petrov Armor—really murdered Neal Petrov?

Davis glanced at Leila from the spot where he'd taken up residence in the corner of her office. He'd managed to avoid her for the rest of the day yesterday, but when he'd come in today, he knew he couldn't do it any longer. He needed the kind of access only she could give him.

To her credit, when he'd asked to see the company's financial records, she'd frowned but given him access. He'd been reading through them ever since. The problem was, if Petrov Armor's finances had been doctored, whoever was responsible would try to make things look legitimate. Davis might have to bring in some forensic accountants to drill down to the truth.

According to Leila, Theresa Quinn didn't have access to these records. So, if Theresa was still trying to sell weapons to criminals or pass off faulty body armor to the military, maybe something wouldn't look right in the financial records in the weeks since Neal Petrov had been killed. Of course, that was assuming he'd still had access to the finances and she'd just dealt with the production and delivery end of things.

Even if nothing looked off in the past month, maybe Neal himself would have made an error along the way.

Presumably, he'd gotten away with making illegal weapons sales for so long, he was skilled at hiding all evidence. But sometimes people who got away with something for that long started making mistakes. If Theresa wasn't involved, maybe Neal had gotten sloppy and someone else had noticed a discrepancy. Maybe they'd tried to blackmail Neal and when he hadn't paid up, they'd killed him.

Right now, everything was conjecture. Davis sighed and stretched his legs underneath the desk Leila had set up for him on the far side of her office.

For what felt like the millionth time since he'd arrived that morning, Davis glanced up at Leila. Her office smelled faintly of citrus, the same scent he'd noticed when she'd been brought into the TCD office. The same scent he noticed every time he stood close to her. He was starting to have a real fondness for citrus.

Since he'd met her three days ago, he'd only seen her wearing pant suits in shades of gray, black and dark blue. Her makeup was always subtle, her hair constantly knotted up into a bun. It was as if she dressed as straitlaced as possible to try to hide her youth and beauty. But there was only so much she could disguise. Today was no different.

Still, ever since she'd made that ridiculous joke about an inflatable boat, he'd been imagining her differently. Wearing jeans and a button-down that was too big for her, with her hair long and loose around her shoulders. Instead of her standard too-serious expression, she'd be laughing.

Except right now, she had nothing to laugh about. If he was right about her father's murder, things were only going to get worse.

He didn't even know if it was true or just a far-fetched theory and yet, he felt guilty not telling her.

*"What?"* Leila asked, a half smile lifting the corners of lips that had been so close to his just the other day.

"I didn't say anything."

"You didn't have to. You keep staring." She came around from behind her desk, striding across the room and stopping in front of him. "What is it? What did you find?"

Davis glanced down at his laptop screen again, not wanting to look her in the eyes as he said, "I haven't found anything. I'm just looking for discrepancies."

"Because the armor used cheaper materials? You think there will be a double entry for supplies somewhere?"

"Maybe," he hedged. He'd worked in white collar crime long enough to know that someone who'd been cooking the books for a decade was unlikely to make such an amateur mistake. But TCD expected him to keep the fact that Petrov Armor might have been illegally selling weapons from Leila. He closed the lid of his laptop, not wanting her to see the dates he was reviewing.

"Stop lying to me."

He finally looked up at her, surprised by the vehemence in her voice. "I'm not lying. I don't know what I'm going to find. Probably nothing. But if there's anything that doesn't seem right, it's a place to start."

"You don't know what you might find, but you're looking for something specific, aren't you?" Her eyes narrowed. "Or is there something else you're not telling me? You suspect someone besides Theresa? Don't tell me this is about Eric again."

"No, it's not about Eric." He wasn't Davis's top suspect at the moment, but that didn't mean he'd been eliminated. And since Leila had brought him up... "You said Eric and your dad were close. Was that true even after you and Eric broke up?" Realizing the time line, he answered his own question. "I guess so if he hired Eric then, right?"

"He hired Eric back when the two of us were still dating. Eric is two years older than me, so when he graduated from high school, my dad brought him on. He went to school to get his bachelor's degree at night. I was still in high school then. I didn't join the company until I finished grad school. I've only been here full-time for five years—I started a couple of years before my dad took the company public. By the time I joined the company, Eric had already been working here for nine years. But yes, my dad and Eric stayed close. Eric was the son my dad never had."

Davis squinted at her, trying to see through the mask she'd put over her features. Did she resent Eric's place in her dad's life? Did Eric resent the fact that Leila had come in only a few years ago and sailed into the CEO role, when Eric had been toiling away at the company for over a decade?

Leila let out a heavy, exaggerated sigh obviously meant for him to hear, and slapped her hands on her hips. "My dad was the father Eric never had, too, since his dad was out of the picture more often than he was in it. Believe me, Eric would never have betrayed my father. Never."

"Would he have betrayed you?" Davis asked.

She scowled down at him. "You honestly believe Eric would send out a faulty shipment of armor to hurt *me*? What for? It's been twelve years since he broke up with me. And I think the key words there are that *he* broke up with *me*, not the other way around. We're friends now. He's got one of the top positions in the company. If he wanted to bring me down by destroying the company, he'd be taking himself down with me. He's not that stupid. Or that self-destructive."

Davis nodded slowly. Her logic all made sense, and yet he couldn't stop picturing the expression on Eric's face when Leila had agreed to let Davis drive her home two days ago. No matter what Leila thought, that wasn't a man who had no romantic feelings for her.

Since talking about Eric had already put her on the defensive, Davis figured he'd get the rest of his unpleasant questions out now. "What about your uncle?"

Her hands fell off her hips as she shook her head. "Are you kidding me? You want to talk about the only person besides me who's more invested in this place than Eric? That's Uncle Joel. He gave up another career to help Dad keep this business going. He's been here ever since."

"Maybe he resents it," Davis suggested.

"I doubt it. He makes more money than he ever did before, and he sets his own hours. Dad gave him a lot of freedom, said it was only fair after everything he did for the company, for our family, after Mom died. I still do the same thing with his hours and the board doesn't care, as long as he gets the job done. He's less than ten years out from retirement—although, honestly, he could retire now if he felt like it. I think he's still here for me."

"Okay, but—"

"Davis, I get it. You don't know these people. This is nothing but another case for you. But this is my *life*. This is my *family* you're investigating."

She took a visible breath as Davis wondered whether she considered Eric part of her family.

"You're right that it looks like we've got someone rotten in our company, and I understand why you're starting at the top. But the truth is that none of the people you're asking about order the raw materials. None of them ship out the armor. We've got good security and good checks. You said it yourself. Obviously someone has found a way around them. But it's not my uncle. And it's not my ex. And honestly, even with the time stamps you found for Theresa's security card, I don't think it's her, either."

"Leila—"

"I understand that you have a job to do. Believe me, I

want to figure out who's doing this, so they can be prosecuted. But I need to keep the rest of the company intact in the meantime. When we figure out who did this, you'll be leaving and the guilty person will be arrested—rightfully so. But the rest of us are going to have to band together and push forward. I'm not letting this destroy the company my dad spent his life building. I'm not letting *you* destroy it."

"I'm not destroying anything," Davis snapped. "I'm not the one running a company and not knowing *fatally* defective products were being sent out."

Leila's shoulders dropped, the anger on her face shifting to a mix of guilt and pain.

He sucked in a breath, as a ball of dread filled his gut. He believed that the head of a company was responsible for what was happening inside of it, even if they didn't know anything about it and had no legal liability. But over the past three days, he'd found that Leila was a good, caring person. Seeing how his words had wounded her, he regretted them.

He regretted them even more when she said softly, steadily, "If you think I'm to blame for this, I'm not sure how you can trust me to work with you to find the truth. I'm not sure you should be here at all, Davis."

DOUGIE HAD COME THROUGH.

Kane smiled at the text message on his FBI-issued phone. Dougie had gotten in touch with the lowlife who'd been telling him about guns and said a friend was interested in joining BECA. Apparently Dougie had sweetened the pot by also telling the guy that Kane might have a weapons connection of his own. That part was less ideal, but Kane could work with it.

"What are you smiling about?" There was suspicion in Melinda's question.

Kane tucked his phone away as he looked up at Melinda. "I've got a date tonight."

She blinked rapidly, telling him he'd surprised her, but her eyes narrowed just as fast. "Wasn't that your work phone you were looking at?"

He shrugged carelessly, glad he had a reputation as a rule-breaker. "Yeah, well, it's another agent."

Melinda continued to stare at him with narrowed eyes.

He was a great liar. He had to be, with all the under-cover work he'd done, or he would have been killed on the job a long time ago. But apparently Melinda was an even better profiler, because she always seemed to know when he wasn't being straight with her.

Instead of trying to outstare her, he changed the subject. "I did also hear back from my CI. He's got a friend who knows someone at BECA. That person might be able to get us some more details about BECA and their connection to Petrov Armor. I want to look a little closer at BECA, see if we can find anything in our files about a possible link."

"I've already been doing that," Melinda said, her attention returning to her laptop. "The reason we've never been able to make anything stick with BECA is because it's such a loose network. We refer to them as a group, but the reality is they're not that formally organized. On purpose, I'm sure, to give each member plausible deniability if any single one gets caught."

"Which has happened plenty," Kane agreed. The group was most known for having connections to individuals who had set bombs in minority-owned businesses and even places of worship. Maybe because it was such a loosely knit group, the specific biases were different from place to place. Still, more than once, a perpetrator had mentioned that they'd learned how to make bombs from a connection at BECA. A few times, the FBI had tracked down the connection and made an arrest. But then any other local members of the network seemed to scatter.

As far as the FBI had ever found, BECA didn't keep any official books or lists of membership. Instead of connecting online like a lot of criminal organizations, they'd gone old-school and networked through word of mouth. In theory, that should have made the organization easier to penetrate. But besides being fanatics, BECA members also tended to be extremely paranoid of outsiders.

"You're thinking about trying to set up a meet with your CI's contact, the one who knows someone at BECA, aren't you?" Melinda asked.

When he refocused, he realized she was staring at him again.

"I don't think so. But if someone at Petrov Armor really is selling to BECA members, that might be how we get them."

"I don't believe you that you're not trying to set up a meet."

Melinda's words were straightforward, with no anger or frustration in her tone. Strangely, the lack of emotion made Kane feel even more guilty about lying to her. But in the end, he was doing her a favor.

"Well, believe what you want," he answered, glancing at his phone as it beeped with the notification of a new text. "Be right back."

He didn't give her a chance to argue, just slipped into the hallway where she couldn't try to read over his shoulder.

The text was from Dougie again. You're on, man. My connection says he can get you a meeting with someone from BECA. Told them exactly what you said I should. That I know you from my time in Vegas. Said you left because you were getting heat after some fires you set at businesses run by Asians and Middle Easterners. Also told them you want to buy some guns, but you've got a record. Claimed I didn't know why, but that your connection here had fallen through.

Kane smiled to himself. The bit about the fires in Vegas was something he'd given Dougie. It had really happened; it just hadn't been him. The person who'd really done it was six feet under, a casualty of a revenge plot gone wrong. Kane had come in too late to save the idiot—and put him in jail. Instead of releasing the truth about the fires, Kane had kept it under wraps, knowing one day he'd be able to use it. It had turned out to be perfect for this case. BECA was known for fostering that kind of random hate.

The bit about the weapons connection was Dougie's own improvisation, but Kane had worked with worse.

Great job, he texted back. When's the meet?

Tomorrow.

Friday. Kane nodded to himself. A weekend meet would have been better, would have made it harder for Melinda to try to track him there. But he wasn't about to complain. Getting a meet with BECA wasn't easy.

Perfect. Thanks, man.

Sliding his phone back in his pocket, Kane spun around to return to the conference room and nearly slammed into Melinda. "What the hell?"

"You setting up another date?" There was mocking in her tone.

"What if I am?"

"When's the meet?"

"There's no meet, Melinda." He tried to walk around her, but she shifted, blocking his way.

He raised an eyebrow. Yeah, she'd gone through the FBI Academy just like him, but he had seven inches and probably a good fifty pounds on her. Did she really think she could stop him from going somewhere?

Holding in his annoyance, he turned and walked off in the other direction. A meet with a dangerous group of zealots could far too easily go sideways. One thing Melinda needed to learn about him was that when it came to undercover work, he liked to go alone. No backup. No net. It was better for everyone that way.

"We're supposed to be partners," she called after him, frustration in her tone, but less than he'd expected.

Kane gritted his teeth, keeping his response inside. Images of Pembrook's daughter's broken body when he'd finally reached her during that mission gone wrong filled his head, the way they did every night in his sleep.

He was never going to have a partner again, least of all Melinda Larsen.

# Chapter Nine

Davis blamed her for everything that had happened. Blamed her for the deaths of all those soldiers.

The knowledge made her chest hurt, made each breath laborious. Because the truth was, she blamed herself, too.

How had she not seen that someone was willing to betray the company, and missed all the signs that bad armor was being produced? And for what? More profit? They were doing fine. Sales were increasing. They were looking at expanding their markets. Why would someone go to such lengths for higher numbers on their bottom line? No, someone had to be pocketing that extra cash for their own benefit, using her company to enhance their personal finances.

It shouldn't have been possible to get faulty armor out the door. Not with the security and checks in place. Her father had managed the company for twenty-nine years without a single incident. She'd been doing it without him for three weeks and there'd been a huge tragedy.

She hadn't changed anything, but had her lack of focus during her time of grief allowed this to happen? The armor wasn't made overnight. Someone had come up with this plan, introduced the cheaper materials, gotten them past testing and shipped the defective armor. At least some of that must have happened while her father was still here. But probably not all of it. Had she missed something she should have caught? Been so preoccupied trying to prove that she was worthy of being CEO even after her father's death that she'd missed what really mattered?

Leila stared at the loading area at the back of their facility where they packed boxes of armor into trucks that delivered them to military installations. It was empty now, with no new deliveries scheduled until next week.

Even those were unlikely to go out. Her employees didn't know it yet, but unless they found out who was responsible fast, she doubted the military would want this shipment— or any other. The fact was, even if they did resolve it, the incident could be the end of her company. The end of everything her dad had worked for.

*Focus*, Leila reminded herself, looking around. The loading area was hidden from the road, but visible from some of the windows at the back of the building, where they kept supplies. It was a quiet area. Not many people were there on any given day, but it didn't mean someone couldn't be. If someone had loaded defective products after hours to avoid detection, how would that work? Drivers wouldn't have a way to order cheaper materials to replace the good armor, and the people who loaded the trucks didn't have access to secure areas.

Theresa's research and development rooms were back here, too. There were no windows in Theresa's dedicated development space, but she was always wandering around; she claimed that pacing made her more creative. She often worked late. So, planning to have a truck come after hours on a certain day was dicey, too. Unless Theresa was involved.

Normally someone in a management position signed off on shipments. So, someone must have signed off on either the defective armor or good armor that had later been swapped. But if it had been swapped out, why? Was someone after the good armor rather than the money?

She pondered that for a few minutes. It didn't seem likely, but she couldn't rule it out. Maybe whoever had signed off on the defective armor was working with someone in shipping.

The potential lead gave her energy, lifted some of the anxiety pressing on her chest. She swiped her security card to go back inside and slipped into the empty testing room. Then she pulled up the shipment log from the computer there. The date was the first thing that surprised her. The armor hadn't gone out after her dad had died, when she was lost in her grief and had possibly made unforgiveable errors. It had happened before.

But it was the name in the log that made her sink back into the chair Theresa usually used.

Her father's name was beside the shipment.

Technically, as their primary consultant, he could still do that. But he rarely did, usually preferring to leave it to one of their management team.

Had he done a sloppy job of inspecting the armor? Or had the fakes been good enough to pass inspection? They'd certainly looked right in the photo Davis had shown her. Leila knew her company's products well enough to spot even small imperfections. Someone had done a good job of making them look legit.

Leila leaned close to the screen, scrutinizing the electronic copy of the signature. Could it have been faked? Her dad's signature was sloppy, probably easy to duplicate. It was impossible to know for sure.

"What's going on, honey?"

Leila spun in her chair at her uncle's voice. He was frowning at her with concern.

"You look upset. And we don't have any shipments going

out for a week." He glanced around, then added, "I know you're not back here to shoot the breeze with Theresa. So what's going on?"

Had Theresa really betrayed them? The idea left a sour taste in the back of her mouth, but it just felt wrong. Theresa was protective of the company, proud to the point of braggadocio of the armor she helped develop, rightfully so. The latest incarnation had been tested by army rangers in real battle conditions before the military had begun ordering them in bulk. They'd stood up to everything the Special Operations soldiers encountered, which was no small feat.

Theresa was unmarried, had no kids. She spoke occasionally of an older sister and a nephew, and every so often of a man she was seeing, something that had been on-again, off-again for years. But the latter always seemed more casual than a real relationship. Her life was the company. Even if Theresa was in the most likely position to betray it, Leila just couldn't imagine her doing so.

But if she had, why now? If it was anger over Leila being given the CEO position, Theresa had had a full year to take action. Or she could have quit and used her talents elsewhere. That would have been the easiest path if she was unhappy. Instead, she'd stayed, continued to innovate for Petrov Armor. Leila had continued to give her well-deserved raises.

"Leila?" her uncle Joel asked, stepping closer and putting his hand on her arm.

She blinked his face into focus and felt a bittersweet smile form. He looked so much like her dad.

She wasn't supposed to tell anyone what was really going on. It was part of her agreement with Davis. But it wasn't as if he was holding up his end of the bargain and keeping her in the loop. And her uncle was the last person who'd ever betray her father's legacy.

"Uncle Joel, there's something—"

"Leila."

Davis's voice, firm and laced with anger, startled her. She glanced toward the long hallway that led from the main part of the office and there he was, arms crossed over his chest and a scowl on his face.

When her uncle followed her gaze, Davis's expression shifted into something more neutral. "I found those numbers you wanted."

Her uncle looked back at her, and Leila tried not to let her smile falter. "Never mind, Uncle Joel. It's nothing."

His hand didn't leave her arm. "Are you sure?"

"Yeah." She turned and followed Davis back toward her office, fully aware that her uncle didn't believe her.

Even worse, Davis had clearly realized what she had been about to do. If he'd been lying to her before, what were the chances he'd give her any real information ever again?

LEILA PETROV HAD almost blown his entire investigation.

Davis tried to hold back his fury as Leila followed him into her office and shut the door behind her. As soon as it was closed, he whirled around to face her, ready to lecture her about all the reasons she should want to keep his secret. Not the least of which was keeping her out of jail.

Right before he blurted that out, he got control of his anger. Admonishing Leila wasn't going to help. He'd already lost his cool with her earlier, blaming her for what had happened. That was probably what had made her seek out her uncle in the first place. If he compounded it now, he was the one who was going to blow the investigation. Along with it, he'd blow his chance to prove himself at TCD, and his chance to get justice for Jessica.

He took a few deep, measured breaths the way he used

to do right before leaving on a ranger mission. His body recognized the cue and his heart rate slowed immediately.

"So, you found something in the ledger?" Leila asked.

Her chin was tipped up, her jaw tight, her gaze defying him to call her on what he'd overheard. On what he knew she'd been about to do.

"No. I said that to get you out of there. This is a *secret* investigation, Leila. The FBI could have sent anyone undercover here. Maybe they should have sent someone you wouldn't have recognized, someone who could dig into the company without sharing a thing with you."

Standing so close to her, he actually heard her nervous swallow, saw her blink rapidly a few times.

Good. She should be nervous.

"We didn't try to hide what we were doing from you. TCD chose to bring me in because we believed you were innocent. We believed you'd help us find the truth for those soldiers who were killed."

"You believed—" she started.

He cut her off before she could scoff at his statement about her innocence. He didn't want to get into the technicalities with her. He *did* believe she'd had nothing to do with the faulty armor and the illegal guns. But he also believed that was no excuse not to know what was happening in the company she ran.

"I understand that you trust your uncle, but then maybe he tells someone *he* trusts and that person does the same. Faster than you think, our chance to catch this person— and potentially save your company—is gone."

Leila blew out a loud breath. The proud, angry tilt to her chin was gone. So was the defiant look in her eyes, replaced by wariness and something else.

It took him longer than it should have to realize the other thing he saw was guilt.

He'd put that there. The thought made him hate himself and his job just a little. It was easy to believe that someone who ran a company should know everything that happened in it, take responsibility for all of it. It was another to see someone as honest and diligent as Leila suffer because she hadn't caught a criminal inside her organization.

Should she have really been able to do that? Or was that his job?

The unexpected thought deflated the last of his anger.

"Look, I'm sorry about what I said earlier. I was out of line." Davis wasn't entirely sure what he believed right now, but one thing he knew: Leila would never intentionally let anyone get hurt. "I knew one of the soldiers."

Leila's lips formed a small O and she blinked again, this time as moisture filled her eyes.

"She was a friend of mine," Davis continued, not sure why he was sharing this with Leila, but suddenly wanting her to know. "Jessica Carpenter. She was the one running that video footage, probably for training purposes. She was a single mom of three. Those little kids are all alone in the world now. Jessica was a great person. Strong, smart, willing to put up with all the crap that comes along with being a woman in a powerful role where too many men think it should only be for them."

He paused, realizing Leila fit that description, too.

Shaking the thought away, he continued. "I'm here right now for Jessica. Whatever it takes, I need to get the truth. No matter who you think you can trust with inside information about our investigation, if I think you're going to tell someone who I really am, that's it. I'm out and the FBI is coming in with warrants to take this place apart."

Leila stared back at him with a mixture of horror, sadness and anger, and he realized that just as he'd gotten her trust back, he'd ruined it again with a threat. Why couldn't he find the right balance with her? Why couldn't he be like Kane Bradshaw, step into whatever persona would get the job done, and to hell with real honesty? To hell with anyone's feelings?

"I don't—"

He wasn't sure what she was about to say, but he didn't let her finish the thought. There was only one way to remedy the mess he'd made of his connection with Leila. That was to be more honest with her, so she'd think she could trust him. So she wouldn't feel like she needed to go to someone else for advice.

"Your dad..." He'd planned to tell her that someone connected to the defective armor had killed her father, but what if he was wrong? What if it *was* just a botched mugging and he gave her extra grief over nothing?

"What?" Leila asked, anxiety in her voice that told him she'd recognized he was about to say something serious.

"What I was going to say is that the defective armor isn't the only problem right now. Even when your dad was CEO, there was something illegal happening."

"What?" Leila's voice dropped to a whisper. She shifted her feet, widening her stance like she was preparing for a physical blow.

"Someone at Petrov Armor has been selling guns to criminals for a long time."

# Chapter Ten

The old construction site where Dougie's BECA connection had wanted to meet was the kind of place where you shot someone and left their body to be found weeks or months later.

Adding to the ominous vibe was the sun setting, casting eerie shadows everywhere. Kane leaned casually against a half-standing wall, not putting any real weight on it in case only gravity was keeping it upright. Dougie's connection was picking his way through the abandoned pieces of building, thinking he was being stealthy. Playing along as if he hadn't spotted the guy—or his armed backup—Kane made a show of checking his watch and frowning.

It was almost twenty minutes past the scheduled meet time. Kane had been watched from the moment he'd parked his car off the side of the road and picked his way by foot down to the construction site. It was a smart spot for a meet, deserted and easy to watch all possible access points. It was the kind of place a smart agent wouldn't come alone.

As his contact finally showed himself, Kane offered a cocky grin. He'd been in worse spots dozens of times. If he had to rely on his own ability to spin a good story or someone else to keep him safe and stay out of trouble themselves, he'd choose to go in alone every time. It was probably why he was still alive.

"Guess you're Kane Bullet, huh?" the guy asked, looking him over. "What kind of name is that?"

Kane kept his irreverent grin in place, didn't step forward to greet the guy. "The kind I gave myself."

The man laughed. He was blond and blue-eyed, wearing tattered jeans and a T-shirt that read Armed and Dangerous on the front. With his overmuscular build, the guy's loose clothes still didn't hide that at least the first part of that statement was true. The bulge of a holster was clearly visible at his hip.

"So, Dougie says you had some trouble in Vegas, wanted to start over in Tennessee?"

"Yeah." Kane shrugged, stepped slightly away from the half-standing wall. He kept his hands loose at his sides, not wanting to give the guy—or his backup—any reason to get twitchy.

"I looked up those fires. Nasty business."

Kane spewed the kind of offhand hate he knew the BECA member would eat up. "If they didn't want to get burned out, they should have left on their own."

The guy laughed again, a grating sound that would have made Kane grit his teeth hard if he weren't in character. Right now, he wasn't Kane Bradshaw. That person was buried deep, beneath a layer of filth he called Kane Bullet.

So, instead he let his grin shift into something nastier, filled with determination and fury. "There was more I wanted to do in Vegas, but you know, I can't be useful if I'm locked up. So, I skipped town before they got too close."

The guy's humor dried up. "Your friend said it was a close call." His eyes narrowed, as if he was trying to read from Kane's expression whether the cops were tracking him down as they spoke.

Kane rolled his eyes. "Yeah, right. The way those pigs like to brag, don't you think it would have been all over the papers if they had a real lead? Instead, nothing but 'we're still investigating' and 'we won't stop looking' BS. I knew it was time to get out, but I did it before they could get a lead on me. Don't worry, man. I wouldn't bring my heat on you. I'm looking to make friends, not enemies."

The man visibly relaxed. "Well, that's good, because we deal with betrayal real quick."

"Not a problem. What do I have to betray, anyway? All I'm looking for is a hookup. Maybe Dougie told you, but I'd gotten a gun connection out here and it dried up." He scowled again, then took a risk. "Had myself a potential in with Petrov Armor, but ever since that idiot CEO shut down the legal side of their gun business, apparently things have been a little dry on the not-so-legal side of it, too."

The guy stiffened fast, then seemed to forcibly pull his shoulders away from his ears. He cracked his neck in both directions, then gave a tight smile. "Really?"

The hairs on the back of Kane's neck popped up, telling him he'd made a mistake. But what? Had they been wrong and Leila was actually involved? Even though Davis's judgment was clearly trashed when it came to her, Kane didn't think he was wrong about this. Had the intel about the BECA connection been bad? If so, this was a waste of time. Maybe not for the FBI, for future information, but for him with this case.

The guy reached into his pocket and Kane tensed, but when he pulled his hand out, he was holding a phone. He typed something, then tucked it away again. "Who was that contact?"

Kane tried to backtrack without raising suspicion. "Look, maybe my contact was screwing with me from the start. But I'm no rat. I can't give up his name, you know? But it sounds like he was more talk than action. I just don't know people in Tennessee the way I did in Vegas. That's why I looked up Dougie."

The guy nodded, but his eyes were still narrowed, his tone slightly off. "Hard to trust people you don't know, right?"

Kane pretended not to catch the double meaning. "Guess not. But I've heard enough about BECA to know I can trust you. Hopefully, you've seen enough of my work to know we're on the same side."

Finally the guy seemed to relax again. "So what new work are you planning? Guns are a long way from fire-setting."

Kane made his tone hard and serious. "Same goal, different method. Plus cops got too good at connecting my fires in Vegas. I figured it was time to switch things up."

"I hear you. Gotta keep 'em on their toes, right?" The guy stared for a minute, and when Kane didn't break eye contact, he finally smiled. "I think we can help you out."

"Honey!"

The too-high-pitched, feminine voice made Kane's gut clench, filling him with fear he hadn't felt in a long time. When he turned around, already knowing who it was, his eyes felt like they were going to bug right out of his head.

Melinda was picking her way through the demolition mess in a pair of heels that were dangerously high, wearing a tiny dress so skintight that no one would ever consider she could be hiding a weapon.

A million swear words lodged in his brain as she reached his side and looped an arm through his.

"I got so worried about you," she whined, her expression more vapid than he would have ever imagined too-smart Melinda could have pulled off. Maybe it was the makeup she'd plastered all over her face, disguising her natural beauty.

She was playing a role the FBI had given its female agents for decades, that of clingy, jealous girlfriend. It worked especially well in Mob cases, where the targets didn't let females into their ranks, but commonly offered prostitutes to new recruits. Saying no meant losing trust. Unless you had a girlfriend by your side. The added bonus was that particular jealous woman would be an undercover federal agent trained in close-quarters combat.

But in this case, it was the exact wrong move.

Even before he turned back to face his contact, he knew the guy had pulled his gun.

Melinda let out a giggle. "Hey, chill. I'm just checking on my man. I track his phone." She stroked his arm, making his muscles jump with anxiety.

The contact gave Melinda a quick once-over, then settled his hard gaze on Kane. "You hate Asians so much, you burn them out of their businesses, but then you date one?"

He felt Melinda's fingers spasm on his arm as she realized what she'd done.

He'd purposely misled her, focused on how Dougie's connection only knew someone at BECA, not that he could get Kane a meeting with an actual member. She probably thought she was busting in on a meet that was solely about weapons, not truly connected to the racist hate spewed by BECA.

The guy lifted his gun and aimed it at Kane's forehead. "You know what? You try to fool me?" He smiled and shifted the weapon to point at Melinda. "You can watch her die before I kill you."

*"SOMEONE AT PETROV ARMOR has been selling guns to criminals for a long time."*

Davis's words haunted Leila as she strode away from the office as fast as she could. Her low heels made a satisfying *click* with every step, giving her something to focus on, to keep her from screaming in denial or frustration.

Who had they inadvertently let into their company who'd used it for their own gain? Who'd gone against the very reason her dad had formed the company in the first place? To protect soldiers. Not to aid killing.

The feeling of anger and betrayal built up until it felt like a ball of lead in her chest and she kept walking, trying to get control of her emotions. She veered away from the route that would take her toward town, toward people who might see her or even worse, try to talk to her.

It was already dusk, the time when Old City started shifting from window-shopping tourists to evening bar-hoppers. But the other direction was quiet, peaceful. Filled with old trees and a beautiful, fast-moving river. A good place to think about all the things she'd done wrong. All the things she could never undo.

She'd left Davis with a barely coherent excuse about needing to use the ladies' room. He probably thought she was still in there, trying to get herself together. But what she'd really needed was to get out. To get away from everyone and everything.

In the past three weeks, the only times she'd been alone was at night, at home after work. Time she spent hoping to sleep, but instead all she could do was try not to weep in grief or anger over her father's death. During the day, she'd surrounded herself with the business, with reassuring the people who worked for her, with trying to keep it all going, make everyone believe she was still capable.

And what for? The whole time, someone had been betraying her. It was far worse than a single batch of defective armor, a single tragedy. For all she knew, guns made at Petrov Armor and purposely put in the hands of criminals had caused hundreds or thousands of tragedies over the years.

She was responsible. Her father, too. Neither of them had seen it. Neither of them had even *suspected* something that terrible had been happening.

*How* had it happened?

Her pace slowed until she was standing still on the center of a walking bridge. She stared out over the murky water, stepping close to the edge. There was only a low railing that looked like it should have been replaced years ago. It would be easy to just step off and let that fast-moving water take away all her troubles.

Except she wasn't that person anymore. It was still her company, still her responsibility. She wasn't going to walk away from it, even if it destroyed her. Even if it destroyed her father's legacy.

She was going to help Davis find the person responsible. She was going to make sure they paid for it.

Davis hadn't told her how long the illegal gun sales had been going on exactly, but it was more than five years, if it had been happening during her dad's time as CEO, too. Gun manufacturing had always been a separate part of the business from body armor. Yes, there was a certain overlap, but very few lower-level employees would have had access to both sides of the business. And the number of employees who'd been there long enough would dwindle, too.

Leila sighed, realizing that what was terrible for her company—and her conscience—was probably good for the investigation. It narrowed the suspect pool a lot.

It was probably someone she trusted. Someone she'd known for a long time. Someone who'd been to her father's house over the years. Maybe even someone she'd cried with at her father's funeral.

The thought made her hands ball into fists. How could someone do this to her father? To her? To all the soldiers who'd been killed and whoever else had been hurt that Leila didn't even know about yet?

The creak of the walking bridge told her someone else was there. Leila straightened, realizing she'd been so caught up in her thoughts that the person was already upon her.

The sudden, fierce pounding of her heart intensified when his hand came up, the flash of silver telling her he had a gun.

Instinct—and the self-defense training her father had insisted she take before she left for college—took over. Leila's hand darted up, swatting the gun away as he fired. The shot boomed in her ears, making them ring, as the bullet disappeared somewhere over the water.

The man who'd fired it snarled, surprise in his eyes as he stepped back slightly. Details filled in as time seemed to slow. He was taller than her. White, with brown hair and gray eyes that looked like steel. She didn't know him.

Then his hand swung back toward her and time sped up again. Instead of turning to run—and surely getting a bullet in the back—she rushed closer, getting inside his range of fire. Twisting sideways, she gripped his gun hand with both of hers, trying to break his grip.

But he was strong. His free hand came up and fisted in her hair, yanking with enough force to send pain racing down her neck.

Her feet went out from under her, but she didn't let go. She slammed onto the bridge, taking him down with her.

The back of her head pounded and her vision wavered, but she still had his wrist gripped in both of her hands. She twisted in opposite directions and he yelped, but didn't drop the gun. Yanking her body away from him, she tried to rip it out of his grasp, but he twisted, too, shifting in a different direction.

Then the ground slipped away from her as they both crashed through the flimsy guardrail and dropped into the water below.

# Chapter Eleven

Davis didn't recognize the sound that tore from his throat as Leila and her attacker rolled off the bridge and into the fast-moving water below.

He'd been too far away when the guy had appeared out of nowhere and lifted his gun. He'd been trying to keep his distance, let her come to grips with what was happening in her company without his interference. He'd let her get ahead of him, paused to text Kane and Melinda for an update. He'd spent too many minutes staring impatiently at his phone, waiting for them to reply, then checked his other messages. He'd gotten distracted, and it might have just cost Leila her life.

The thought filled his throat with an angry lump, made it hard to breathe as he ran faster, then dived into the water where Leila and the man had disappeared.

Davis was a strong swimmer. He'd had to learn when he'd become a ranger. But the current was unusually fast, probably because of the storm that had rolled through earlier in the day. It spun him under, then back up again, but he got control of himself quickly.

But someone who wasn't a good swimmer? It could disorient the person, make them swim down instead of up.

If that person was already frantic and panicked, trying

to escape an attacker? It could easily be the difference between living and dying.

"Leila!" he called, scanning the water for her as he let himself be swept forward. He didn't see her anywhere.

Taking a deep breath, he dived under, looking for any sign of movement. Silently he cursed Leila for the serious, dark clothing she always wore. Why couldn't she have been partial to red or bright yellow? Something that would have been easier to see in the dark water?

He swam with the current, hoping to spot her, until he ran out of air and popped back to the surface. Then he yelled her name again, his heart going way too fast to be as efficient as he needed it to be right now, to let him search underwater longer.

He sucked in a deep breath, almost took in river water as choppy waves rose again. But even his battle-tested method of self-calming that had gotten him through his most dangerous ranger missions wasn't working.

*Where was she?*

He couldn't be too late. He refused to believe it.

But he still couldn't see her. If she'd been underwater this long, it probably wasn't of her own choosing.

Panic threatened, but he refused to accept defeat. Then, the current swept him around a bend and there she was, fifty feet ahead of him, still grappling with the guy who'd attacked her.

Davis forced himself forward in a burst of speed, trying to get to them. Fury fueled him as his gaze locked on the man still trying to harm her. The man Davis was going to strangle if he succeeded.

It felt like an hour, but he knew it was less than a minute before he reached them. But just before he could tear the guy's hands away from Leila's throat, her fist came up, angled skyward, and smashed into the bottom of the guy's nose.

His head snapped back with a noise that made Davis cringe. Blood streamed from his nose, and he dropped below the surface of the water.

"Are you okay?" Davis demanded, reaching for Leila's arms, ready to swim her to shore.

She pulled free, sucking in unnatural-sounding breaths. "Yes," she rasped. "Get him. Don't want—" She stopped on a fit of coughing.

Davis reached to steady her again, and she slapped at his hand.

He nodded, trusting that if she was strong enough to take down her attacker while he was choking her, she could make it to shore.

Giving her one last glance, he dived underwater. Leila's attacker was sinking toward the bottom, but still being swept along by the current, too.

Davis adjusted his angle, picking up his speed so he could grab the guy before he ran out of air himself. He wrapped his arms underneath the guy's armpits, then kicked upward with all his strength, shooting them back toward the surface.

Then it was instinct taking over, the familiar feel of someone needing help in his arms as he swam for shore and dragged the man out of the water. He checked for a heartbeat and heard one, faint but there. But when he checked for breath, there was nothing.

He paused for a moment, took in Leila sitting on the ground, her knees hugged up to her chest, then returned his attention to her attacker. If he'd managed to kill Leila, Davis would have been hard-pressed not to wrap his hands around the guy's throat. But now he was no threat and he was in trouble.

Davis bent down and gave him mouth-to-mouth until the guy jerked and spit out a stream of water. Davis sat back as the guy coughed and gasped for air, not seeming to know where he was.

Finally he got control of himself and looked up. A shock ran through Davis's body. He knew this man, recognized him from files Melinda had shown him the other day.

He was connected to BECA.

ANOTHER PARTNER WAS going to die on a mission with him. Another woman he cared about, who had made a name for herself in the Bureau through so many other dangerous cases, got partnered up with him and that was the end.

At least this time, he'd go with her.

Kane tried to snap out of the fatalistic mood, return to his cocky, nothing-scares-me Kane Bullet persona. How many times had he had a gun to his head? And he'd always walked away.

But how to explain *this*?

He shoved Melinda backward, hard enough to make her stumble on those ridiculous heels and fall to the ground. He held his hand toward her, palm down, telling her to stay there as his contact's gun shifted up and down from him to Melinda and back again.

"You're screwing this up for me, man," he snapped at the guy, taking an aggressive step forward and praying he wasn't about to get a bullet in the head. Or if he was, that at least Melinda would be able to leap forward fast enough to disarm the guy after he was dead.

Of course, that wouldn't help her outrun the guy's backup, which was probably moving in closer right now.

The guy's gun shifted back to Kane, centered on his forehead. He brought his other hand up to brace it, holding it closer to his own body to make it less likely Kane could rush him. But his curiosity won out. "Screwing what up, exactly?"

"I've been using her for months to get close to her dad, get access to a big bank he owns downtown with massive security. Now, you've messed it all up for me."

The guy's eyes narrowed as he looked Melinda over speculatively.

For a few seconds, Kane thought he'd bought it. Then, the guy let out a humorless laugh. "How stupid do you think I am? You're a cop."

He was blown. Kane had been undercover enough times, in enough different situations, to know he wasn't winning back this guy's trust. But he'd agreed to this meet too fast, not set up enough precautions. If it had just been him, he probably could have rushed the guy and taken his gun. Then, Kane would have used him as a human shield, banking that the guy's backup wouldn't want to shoot their boss in order to kill Kane. But that was dicey with Melinda here, still on the ground in heels there was no way she could run in, and with the guy's backup closing in fast.

Kane could see them in his peripheral vision every few seconds, as they picked their way through the rubble.

It was time to gamble. "I wouldn't come any closer!" he called out.

His contact glanced behind him, fast enough that Kane knew it was instinct. But not so fast Kane couldn't have rushed him. He would have, too, if the backup wasn't close enough to shoot Melinda while he did it.

Kane was armed, but the gun was at his ankle. Not the most easily accessible spot right now, and there was no good way to tell Melinda where it was without alerting the contact. Even if he leaped on top of her and let himself get shot, there was no way to know what sort of bullets they were using. There was too high a chance the bullets would go through him and kill her anyway.

He cursed her in his mind as he told his contact calmly, "I'm not a cop. But you were right about the fires. That *was* nasty business. But it wasn't me. I just figured you'd like that story better than what I really want." He took another step closer, saw the guy's eyes widen with surprise and just a touch of fear.

It was exactly what he needed. Keep them guessing, make them wonder why you weren't afraid when you should be terrified. It had worked for him before. But this was the biggest gamble he'd ever taken. This time, it was more than just his own life at stake.

"I'm ex-military. Ex-ranger, actually," he added, using the first specialty that came to mind, the Special Operations unit Davis had worked with until he left the military. "My friends and I, we all got dishonorably discharged for a little…incident. We've all got rifles and pistols, things we owned before we went in, but now? After those court-martials?" He scowled, put as much anger as he could on his face, knowing it turned him from irreverent and easygoing to threatening. "Now, I can't legally buy guns. And for our plan to get even with the military? We need more guns."

The guy's gaze darted to Melinda again and he shook his head. "You really think we're going to help you now?"

Kane shrugged, tried to insert a bit of that cocky attitude back into his persona. But it felt flat this time, like he wasn't fully occupying his cover, like he was still partly Kane Bradshaw, FBI agent terrified of losing another partner. "No. But if your backup moves any closer—or you pull that trigger—my ranger brothers are going to put neat little holes in your forehead from about five hundred feet that way." He pointed behind him, in the direction where there was high cover.

His contact's gaze darted that way, and he took an instinctive step backward. Then, his lips twisted up in a snarl and Kane knew his bluff hadn't worked.

It was all over.

Knowing it was futile didn't stop Kane from spinning around and leaping on top of Melinda as the *boom* of a bullet rang out. He felt the air whoosh out of her lungs as he flattened her with his body.

Still, she was squirming under him, and as she partially shoved him off her, he realized she was holding a tiny pistol. Where she'd been hiding it, he had no idea.

He yanked the gun from his ankle holster even as he shifted, getting a look at the contact, who was lying dead on the ground. He looked beyond the guy, toward his backup, and saw they had their arms up, with agents advancing on them.

Kane looked from Melinda to the contact, then he realized the guy hadn't been shot with a small-caliber gun. He glanced back toward high cover, where he'd bluffed and said he had backup. Apparently it hadn't been a lie.

Rolling fully off Melinda, he lifted his arm in a half salute, half wave in the direction he knew Laura Smith must have been hiding with a rifle. She looked like someone who worked in some high-powered civilian firm, with her no-nonsense attitude and her affinity for suits. But she was the perfect proof that looks could be deceiving. He'd never seen anyone without military sniper training who could shoot a rifle like that.

Then, he stared back at his partner, who'd somehow figured out not only what he was up to but also where his meet was going down. Instead of talking it over with him, she'd taken it upon herself to just show up. Not only had she completely blown their chances of getting him inside BECA, but also she'd blown the CI he'd cultivated for years.

Now the FBI would have to help Dougie relocate, maybe even disappear.

The longer he stared at Melinda, the more his anger grew, until he wasn't even sure he could speak at all. When he could finally form words, he expected it to come out in a scream, so he was surprised when his voice was barely above a whisper.

"What have you done?"

# Chapter Twelve

Leila had been sitting there, shivering in the sixty-degree weather, sopping wet and staring blankly at the river that had almost swept her under, for too long.

Davis had zip-tied her attacker's hands and feet together, so there was no way he could go anywhere fast, then called in the attack to TCD headquarters. In turn, they'd contacted local PD to take the perp in for now, because apparently Davis's team was out helping Kane and Melinda, who'd run into trouble in a meeting with a BECA contact.

It was no coincidence. Davis felt it in his gut, but couldn't worry about it at the moment.

He showed his credentials to the cops who were taking in Leila's attacker, and spoke in whispered tones to them for a few minutes about holding him until someone from his team could come in and get a statement. Then, he turned his back on them, focused on Leila.

She'd already been in shock over what he'd told her about the illegal gun sales coming out of Petrov Armor. Now, she looked completely lost.

It wasn't even remotely close to being over. He still hadn't told her the truth about her father.

He needed to get her out of here. The river water had been cold, not enough to send her body into shock, but enough that he was getting worried about how long she'd sat there immobile.

He knelt in front of her, waiting for her to make eye contact. She didn't for a long moment.

Then she blinked slowly, awareness returning as she shifted her gaze to him. The dazed look disappeared, replaced by wariness and fear.

"It's going to be okay," he promised her softly. "We're going to figure this out."

His words didn't ease the fear in her eyes, but the wariness shifted into anger. Not wanting to wait to find out if that anger was directed at him, he hooked his hands under her elbows and pulled her carefully to her feet.

"Let's get you home." She let him lead her out of the woods, then he had one of the responding officers give them a ride back to her house. He'd worry about their vehicles later.

Luckily, she had a keypad at her back door, so they could get in. She seemed to be moving on autopilot as he followed her inside, waved the cop off and locked the door behind them.

As the dead bolt slid into place with a *click* that echoed in her granite and tile kitchen, she turned toward him, looking perplexed. Her mouth opened, like she wanted to say something.

Before she could, he stepped forward. He gripped her elbows with his hands, the way he had in the woods. But this time, he wasn't doing it to help her up. This time, he felt like he needed to hold her to keep *him* from falling as it hit him all over again, the fear he'd felt when he couldn't see her in that river.

"Davis," she croaked.

He lifted his hand from her elbow to her cheek, discovering it was ice-cold. "Are you okay?"

She let out a choked laugh. "Are you kidding me? Of course not. But maybe this will help."

She leaned into him and he took a step back, dropping his hands to her elbows to keep her at arm's length. "I want to," he whispered, his voice deeper, gruffer than it should have been. "Believe me, I do. But—"

"What? The smell of river water and mud isn't an aphrodisiac?" she joked, then immediately averted her gaze and moved out of reach.

A smile trembled on his lips. She wasn't the too-serious, all-business CEO with him anymore. Even if he'd messed things up repeatedly, she was starting to let her guard down. Enough to let him see glimpses of who she really was. The more he saw, the more he liked her.

Still, he couldn't believe they'd almost kissed yet again. But he couldn't cross that line. He might know in his gut that she was innocent, but the FBI hadn't truly eliminated her as a suspect. She was connected somehow to the person who *was* guilty, the person he needed to find and arrest. To do that, he had to stay impartial.

But staring at her now, her clothes sagging with water, her hair a ragged mess and her makeup smeared down her face from being in the river, he wished things were different. It actually physically hurt how much he wished that he'd met her under different circumstances, that he was free to truly pursue her. That he could really forgive her for running a business that had sent out the armor that had killed Jessica.

When she met his gaze again, he knew she could see longing there from the way her eyes dilated. Then she was back to serious, but something had changed—something important. He could see it in her eyes, could feel it in the more relaxed way she was moving. "I'm going to get in a hot shower for five minutes and then change. I don't have anything here you'll fit, but there's a dryer in the mudroom we just came through. Then we can talk."

She left the room, not giving him a chance to disagree. Not that he would have, when she'd finally decided to trust him.

When she returned downstairs a few minutes later, he'd tossed his pants, button-down, and socks in her dryer and set his gun and badge on her coffee table. He'd wrapped himself in a throw blanket he'd spotted tossed over the couch in her living room next to a paperback romance novel.

Her gaze slid over him, seeming to burn a trail across any exposed skin even as her lips quirked upward with obvious amusement. "Nice look."

Then, she sank onto the other side of the couch, close enough to talk easily but not close enough to touch.

She'd changed into sweatpants and a T-shirt, scrubbed her face clean of any makeup and pulled her hair out of the remnants of its bun. Now it fell in loose wet tangles past her shoulders, and he longed to reach out and run his hands through it, follow the trail of water that dripped down her bare arms.

Instead, he hugged the blanket more tightly to himself and told her, "Eric stopped by to check on you. I told him you were overtired, so I drove you home."

She nodded, seeming uninterested, and he waited for her to ask him what was happening.

He expected her to want more details about the illegal gun sales. Or maybe to know whether he had any idea who her attacker was, why he'd come after her. When she finally did speak, her words were soft and surprising.

"Thanks for having my back, Davis. Thanks for making me feel like I have someone I can count on when everything in my world seems to be falling apart."

SHE WAS BACK at work like nothing had happened, like someone hadn't tried to kill her yesterday.

Leila shivered in the confines of her office, where no one could see how freaked out she was. She'd already turned the heat up several times, but it was never enough.

At least it was a Saturday. Far fewer employees here to notice her acting strangely, to wonder why. She and Davis had agreed that no one in the company should know what had happened to her yesterday evening. He'd told her the attack was from someone connected to a criminal enterprise, and that group might have been sold Petrov Armor pistols illegally. He still didn't know why that person would attack *her*. Apparently, so far, the guy wasn't talking. And somehow, Davis had managed to keep the police report out of the media.

Despite the fact that she'd probably been followed from the office yesterday, she felt safer here right now than she did at home by herself. It probably didn't hurt that she'd started carrying a small pistol in her handbag. She planned to keep it there until she was sure the threat was over.

Even the idea of it made her slightly uncomfortable. Despite having sold weapons for so many years, she'd never liked firing one. The regular classes her dad had made her take, to stay refreshed in proper shooting technique, hadn't changed that. But right now, she was glad for it. She touched the outline of the gun through her bag, then locked it in her desk drawer and tried to focus.

The plan had been to distract herself with work, but instead she was distracted by Davis. He'd come in to the office today, too, both because there would be fewer people to see him looking into things an assistant didn't need to access and to stick close to her. He'd stuck close to her all last night, too, sleeping on her couch in whatever he'd had on beneath her blanket. She'd been up most of the night wondering about it.

But she'd managed to stay away from him, spent the night tossing and turning in her own bed. From the first day, she couldn't help but have a physical attraction to Davis, which surely gave him an advantage as he dug for information. But yesterday had been different. Yesterday, he'd truly seemed shocked when he'd almost kissed her. The way he'd stared at her afterward… She was starting to believe he might actually be developing feelings for her.

The idea made her stomach flip-flop with nerves, made a smile tremble on her lips. But it could never come to anything. He was investigating her company. If she and Davis got together, it would put the integrity of the whole investigation in question, maybe even throw suspicion on her, even after they found the person responsible. Unlike a fling with a handsome FBI agent with an intriguing smile and admirable ethics, that suspicion could stick. It could destroy one of the few things in her life with any permanence. Her job.

"Leila."

Her head popped up. She'd been so focused on her thoughts she hadn't even noticed the door open, hadn't even heard the knock that had probably preceded it.

"Eric."

Her head of sales was shutting the door behind him, his eyebrows lowered with a concerned expression she recognized.

She held in a sigh, because he meant well. They both missed her father desperately. Eric had taken time off to grieve after the funeral, had called her every day, pushing her to do the same. But the idea of not coming into work, of trying to find some other way to fill her days to distract herself from the fact that her father was never coming back? Even now, it made her skin feel prickly with anxiety.

"What's going on?"

She shook her head, thrown by his question. "What do you mean?"

"Something happened yesterday after you left work. You left your purse in your office. You never came back for your car. I drove all the way to your house and your assistant answered the door—dripping wet for some reason..."

He paused, like he was waiting for an explanation, then continued. "He swore you were fine, that you'd gone for a walk and realized you were too tired to drive, so he took you home. I would have pushed him aside and come in to check, but I heard the shower going upstairs. Leila, I know it's not my business, but—"

"I'm not sleeping with my assistant, Eric," she cut him off, hoping he wouldn't notice the too-high-pitched tone to her voice. Or that if he did, he would accept it for what it mostly was—embarrassment.

"Good." Eric's eyebrows returned to a normal position on his face, but his tone was still troubled as he walked around to her side of her desk. Having him in her personal space felt odd, like they'd gone back in time to when they were more than just colleagues and friends.

"Leila, yesterday when I saw your car still here when I was ready to go home and then I came back inside and saw your purse, I panicked. I was really scared. I mean, after what happened to your dad..." He closed his eyes, blew out a breath that fanned across her face and finished, "It made me realize how much I miss you, Leila."

A sudden rush of nerves and uncertainty made her feel too hot. She tried to play it off like his words weren't a big deal. "You see me every day, Eric."

He put his hands on her arms, slid them down to take her hands in his.

His touch was familiar, but still strange. Eric's hands were bigger than she remembered, the skin rougher. But they were still warm, still comforting the way they'd been the very first time he'd held her hand when she was thirteen.

"I care about you, Leila." He met her gaze steadily, his voice solid and clear. "Way more than I should, considering how long it's been since we were together."

Her heart rate picked up, but she tried to ignore how close he was standing, tried to act like it was normal for him to be holding her hands in her office. "We've been friends for a long time, Eric. We have a lot of history together. Of course you were worried."

"Maybe we never should have broken up."

She blinked back at him, speechless, as a mix of emotions surged inside her. Happiness, confusion and uncertainty. She'd waited so many years to hear those words from him. He'd been her first love, the one that got away.

But because it had been so many years ago, things had changed. Were they even the same people they'd been when they were in love? And why now? Was it just fear of losing her, grief over losing her father making him say things he'd later regret?

He knew her well enough that she was sure he sensed her hesitation, even before she said quietly, "Our time is gone."

Saying the words out loud hurt, but it had been twelve long years since he'd broken her heart without a single word of explanation. Twelve years of them growing into the people they were now. Twelve years of working to forge a real friendship, without the baggage of their relationship.

"Don't say that." Eric shook his head, stepping even closer to her, so his feet touched hers and his lips were mere inches away. "Our time never should have ended, Leila."

She blew out a breath that made him blink as the expelled air hit him. "*You* ended it, Eric. It was—"

"I did it because your dad asked me to stop seeing you."

"What?" The shock of the words made her step backward. She pulled her hands free from his, suddenly colder than she'd been before he came into the office. The serious look in his eyes, one she knew so well, told her he wasn't lying. "Why?"

Eric sighed, ran a hand through his blond hair, tousling it the way she'd loved as a teenager. "I swore to myself I'd never tell you, because I didn't want you to be mad at him. He wanted you to have a clean break when you went to college. I fought with him over it, but he felt like it was important for you to find your own way, learn to be strong alone."

He lifted his shoulders, a helpless look in his eyes. "I thought one day, he'd change his mind. But then you started working here and…honestly, it was awkward. I didn't know how to be your colleague. I tried to be your friend. We both dated other people. Then you became my boss, and it was strange all over again. But there's never been anyone like you, Leila. Never."

She shook her head, totally at a loss for how to respond. Over the years, she'd dreamed so many times that Eric would change his mind, tell her he was a fool and wanted her back. In her dreams, she'd always leaped into his arms. She'd never imagined he'd tell her that her dad had instigated the breakup. She'd never thought she'd be unsure if she wanted *him* back.

"I get it," Eric said, when she stayed silent. "This is a lot. But just think it over, okay? We can figure the company part out. I mean, this was your dad's business, his dream. Maybe you and I can cash in our stock options and start over, partners in some new venture." He smiled, his eyes hopeful. Then, he lifted her hand to his lips and kissed it.

As she continued to stare mutely at him, his smile grew, then he turned and headed for the door. He glanced back at her once more as he opened it to leave, then almost walked into Davis, who was standing in the doorway, scowling.

"Davis," Eric said, giving the agent a nod as he maneuvered around him.

Then, Eric was gone and Davis shut the door and strode toward her like a man on a mission. She stared at him, still feeling stunned from Eric's revelations. But the closer Davis got, the more she realized that he'd been in the back of her mind as she'd told Eric their time was over. The closer he got, the more all the nerve endings on her skin seemed to fire to life, the more shallow each breath became.

It made no sense. She barely knew Davis. Eric, she'd known forever.

"He's not right for you," Davis told her as he strode around her desk the same way Eric had.

"What?" He'd been listening in on their conversation? How much had he heard?

Instead of answering, he slid his hands around her waist and yanked her to him. Her body crashed into his, the hard planes of his chest stealing her breath even as she instinctively pressed tighter.

Then, his head ducked toward hers, his lips hovering a few centimeters away, actually brushing against hers as he asked, "Leila?"

She responded by pushing up on her tiptoes, wrapping her arms tight around his neck and pressing her lips to his. The softness of his lips contrasted with the hardness of his kisses, then his tongue swept into her mouth. She felt it all the way down to her toes: no matter what happened in the future, this was exactly where she was supposed to be right now.

## Chapter Thirteen

He'd kissed Leila Petrov. It hadn't been some brief passionate mistake that had burned out as fast as it happened. No, the more he'd kissed her, the more he'd wanted. If they hadn't been in her office…

His ability to look at this case impartially was blown. He needed to come clean with Pembrook, ask her to pull him out. The next logical step would be to get warrants and have the FBI go in full force, the way he'd told Leila.

No matter how quietly they tried to execute something like that, word would get out. Someone would take a video on their phone of FBI agents going into the office or talk to the press. No matter who turned out to be behind this, it would put a stain on Leila's company that might destroy it. He didn't want to do that to her.

"You're getting too close to her."

Kane's voice made Davis jerk and spin toward his colleague. He didn't need to ask who Kane meant, didn't bother to justify why he'd responded immediately when he'd felt his phone buzzing with an incoming text. Why he'd rushed right over when Kane's message said they wanted to give him a debrief on the BECA meet. He'd just pulled his lips slowly away from Leila's, skimming his hands along her skin as he extracted himself. Trying to memorize the feel of her lips and skin and hair, the dazed look in her gorgeous brown eyes. Knowing he couldn't let it happen again.

He needed to regain his professionalism. Because no matter what he *should* do, he wasn't asking Pembrook to pull him out of his cover. He was seeing this case through to the end.

Ignoring Kane's statement, he demanded, "What the hell happened out there?"

"Melinda happened." Kane pursed his lips, glanced around like he was afraid their fellow TCD agent would hear, then held open the door to the conference room.

Inside, Melinda was waiting, a laptop in front of her. She was dressed in one of her standard high-neck blouses, her hair loosely styled, with minimal makeup. There was no indication she'd overheard Kane in the hallway, but the tension on her face and the scrapes covering her arms suggested the meet had gone even worse than Davis had realized.

"We think we know what happened with Leila," Melinda said even before he and Kane were seated.

Kane scowled as she looked at him pointedly, but he spoke up. "My CI set up the meet for me. He told the BECA contact that I'd had someone here willing to sell me guns illegally, but it fell through. I probed a little, trying to see if I'd get a reaction. Said my contact was inside Petrov Armor, but it seemed like the illegal gun sales there dried up when the new CEO stopped the legal side of the gun distribution. He texted someone right after I said that." Kane cringed. "I'm sorry, man. Given the timing..."

The person Kane's BECA contact had texted was the man who'd followed Leila from her office and tried to kill her. That guy still wasn't talking, and Kane's contact was now dead.

Davis's hands fisted hard under the table and he could

feel his heart beat faster, rushing blood to those hands, ready to fight. But he pushed back the instinct, nodded tightly. It was a logical move on Kane's part. They knew someone inside Petrov Armor was selling guns off the books. Bringing it up was what any good investigator— one who wasn't blinded by a target in the investigation— would do.

"The good news is, that tells us something," Melinda said, her gaze darting from him to Kane and back again.

"The guy you were meeting with didn't know why the gun production was halted. Once he realized who was to blame, he wanted revenge," Davis stated, a million possible implications running through his mind. If BECA members really had been getting guns off the books from someone at Petrov Armor, they'd probably been feeling the pinch since Leila stopped gun production. The inside source couldn't get as many guns out without drawing attention. Typically, someone in that position would tell their customer about their pain. The fact that the seller *hadn't* told BECA the guns were drying up because of Leila probably meant that person was protecting her, didn't want BECA or any other buyers to know she'd been the one who'd shut things down.

"It seems more and more likely that Leila's dad was in charge of the illegal gun sales. And that his partner killed him because of what Leila did. Maybe he'd meant to just threaten him, try to get him to restart production, but the threat went wrong, and Neal ended up dead. It probably took about a year for their stock to run out to the point where the illegal sales would be noticed. Turning to cheap armor to bank the extra money isn't working out the way this person expected," Kane said.

"Leila said the excess guns were destroyed, but I assume that's just what she was told, and Neal or his partner simply moved the remainder to sell off books. But what if it wasn't Neal?" Davis thought of the picture Leila kept on the credenza behind her desk. An image of her and her father, sitting next to each other at some outdoor function, both of them with heads thrown back and laughing. "What if he was never involved at all?"

Kane's lips turned up in a "give me a break" expression. "Your objectivity is shot."

"Maybe," Davis admitted, because the truth was that he didn't want Leila's father to be involved. Not because of anything to do with the investigation. Simply because he didn't want Leila to feel that kind of betrayal from the father she'd loved so much and who she'd barely begun to grieve.

"But hear me out," Davis pressed when Kane looked like he was going to keep theorizing how the attack pointed even more to Leila's father being involved. "Her father has been dead for three weeks. If his partner killed him because he was angry that Neal supported Leila's decision to stop the gun side of the business, why didn't he tell his customers as soon as Neal was out of the way? If it was just Neal who was trying to hide Leila's involvement, why wouldn't his partner spill what had happened as soon as he killed Neal? Wouldn't he have bragged to BECA that he was going to turn things around, get the guns flowing again? Three weeks after Neal's death, why wouldn't they already know who was to blame, before Kane told them?"

Melinda nodded slowly and even Kane looked a little less skeptical now.

"Maybe Neal's partner is also trying to protect Leila," Melinda suggested. "It makes sense that Neal would run the illegal side of the business with someone he trusts, someone he's close to. It also makes sense that he'd want to keep his daughter out of it. But what about his brother? Or the guy he thought of like a son, but wasn't *really* his son?"

"Yeah," Davis agreed, even though he didn't like this

theory much better, because it still meant someone Leila cared about deeply was betraying her. "Both Joel and Eric would want to protect Leila. But would either of them really kill Neal? They're both taking his death hard."

"Or pretending to," Kane interjected. "You've been FBI long enough to know that the most successful criminals are two-faced. They've all got families they probably love. They're loved at the office. But deep down, it's all about number one. Anyone who's pulled this off for at least a decade—and honestly, I've got to believe it's a lot longer—is a pretty successful criminal."

"It makes Theresa less likely as a suspect," Melinda said. "She and Leila don't get along, right? She wouldn't protect Leila, try to keep her name out of it?"

"Probably not." Davis sighed. "But she was the one with the best access for swapping out the armor. Neither Joel nor Eric have a lot of contact with the raw materials."

"But they all have general access. They could go in after hours," Kane said. "Any luck with that?"

Davis shook his head, his mind still trying to unravel a scenario where Leila's father wasn't involved at all. But he'd founded the company; he was one of the few people who'd been there long enough to be behind the illegal gun sales. The only other probable scenario was if he *hadn't* known and he'd recently found out. "What if someone killed Neal because he discovered what they were doing? What if *that* person was behind both the illegal gun sales and the defective armor? What if they never had a partner?"

Both Kane and Melinda looked skeptical, but Melinda gave his theory the benefit of the doubt by saying, "Maybe. But that still means it's someone who wanted to protect Leila. To try and prevent what ended up happening when Kane inadvertently let them know she was responsible for the gun supply drying up."

"No matter how you look at this," Kane said, his gaze steady on Davis, broadcasting that he thought Davis was in way too deep, "someone Leila cares about is behind all of this. *And* they're the reason her father is dead."

"ARE WE GOING to talk about this?" Melinda demanded. She stood in the doorway of the conference room, one hand on each side of the frame, blocking Kane's exit.

Davis had left an hour earlier, not wanting Leila to leave the office alone. Melinda and Kane had dug through backgrounds on Joel Petrov and Eric Ross after he'd left, trying to find any indication one of them was making millions of dollars off-book. Then, Kane had looked up at her, the exhaustion in his eyes not doing a thing to hide the anger, and announced he was calling it quits until tomorrow.

"I'm not finding anything in either of their backgrounds," Kane said, and she knew he was purposely misunderstanding her question. "Our best chance to figure out who's behind this is the guy who needs a crash course in undercover work."

"Davis is in a tough spot." Melinda couldn't stop herself from arguing, even though she knew Kane had been egging her on, trying to get her to fight about something else. "He's got real feelings for Leila."

"It's one of the biggest dangers in undercover work," Kane told her, flicking away hair that had fallen down over his forehead. "If you're any good, you have to *inhabit* the skin of someone else. That means it's easy to become what you're pretending to be. It's easy to see the humans behind the criminals. No one is one hundred percent bad. But you cross those lines and it's hard to step back, watch them all get arrested and walk away."

"How do you keep doing it?" Melinda asked softly. It was something she'd always wondered about Kane. The profiler in her knew part of him craved the danger, craved the chance to disappear inside a persona and escape himself. Escape into the skin of others, over and over again, until maybe the things he was running from in his own life wouldn't be there anymore.

Melinda didn't know the details of what had happened with him and Pembrook's daughter. But she did know he'd never be able to run away from the guilt he felt over her death.

"Simple," Kane answered, taking her hand and pulling it away from the door frame. "I always go alone."

He slipped past her, his gaze holding hers for a brief moment before it flicked away. The man was the very definition of tall, dark and handsome. He was dangerous and mysterious in a way she would have swooned over as a foolish teenager.

But she was an adult now, with way too much education in psychology not to recognize exactly what he was doing. She turned around in the doorway, holding her ground. "You think I blew your cover."

He spun back toward her, the anger on his face so harsh she almost backed up. *Almost.*

"Yeah, I think you blew my cover. I also think you blew Dougie as my CI, as an FBI resource. I also think…" He sighed heavily, not finishing his sentence.

But he didn't have to. He thought she'd almost gotten them killed.

His judgment stung, even though she thought the same things herself. She'd had no idea that the very fact that she was Asian would be enough to bring his cover crashing down. But how could she? He'd hidden it all from her, hidden that there even *was* a meet. She'd had to follow him, sneak glances at his phone, to figure out the when and where, because she'd known from the minute he'd walked out of the room to take the call from his CI what he was doing.

"Don't you think that if you'd just been honest with me, we could have come up with a plan for the meet together? Then you would have had backup and I would have known not to go in that way."

"We didn't need to come up with a plan together," Kane snapped. "I came up with a plan myself. I work alone. I always have."

"Not always."

Melinda knew it was a risk referring to Pembrook's daughter, but she didn't expect the level of fury that lit in Kane's eyes. She had to brace her hands in the doorway again to keep herself from backing away.

"You have no idea what it's like to watch someone you care about die like that. So, don't give me your profiling BS about how I'm not a team player when *you're* the one who blew that meet."

Melinda saw the instant Kane realized he'd gone too far, the moment the raw fury in his gaze turned to regret. She also knew why.

He'd seen it on her face that she *did* know. "You're right that I've never lost a partner," Melinda agreed, stepping away from the doorway. Her hand twitched toward the ring she always wore on a necklace hidden beneath her shirts, but she resisted the urge to touch it. Her personal life was no one's business, least of all Kane Bradshaw's.

In Tennessee, only Pembrook knew she'd once had a husband, had a son, had a *life* outside of work. The chance to escape the pitying looks of colleagues who knew about her loss was why she'd accepted the job here in the first place.

An ironic smile spread across her lips as she realized in some ways, she and Kane were more alike than she'd ever expected. Both of them were running from their grief. The difference was, she'd buried herself in the intellectual puzzle of the job, whereas he'd run straight to the danger.

"Melinda, I'm—"

"You're right about something else, too, Kane. You and me? We're not partners. But right now, there's a zealot group buying up illegal guns. They think it's okay to put out a hit on the woman who dared to infringe on their ability to get those guns, intentionally or not. We're going to see this through and shut this source down. Then we can go back to the way things were before."

The muscle in his jaw pulsed, his eyes narrowed assessingly. But in the end, he just nodded. "Deal."

In the instant before he turned and walked away, she regretted all of it. She regretted giving him any hint of the loss she'd experienced when both her husband and son had been killed at the same time. She regretted showing him the way to piss her off and push her away. Maybe most of all, she regretted agreeing to keep working with him.

## Chapter Fourteen

When the doorbell rang at close to midnight Sunday night, Davis frowned and tucked his gun into the waistband of his jeans before he checked the peephole. Then he swore and opened the door wide for Leila.

She stepped inside without waiting for an invitation and he peered past her, onto the street, looking for the patrol car he'd requested to be stationed outside her house until they solved this case. Until they knew for sure no other BECA members would come after her.

A black and white was idling in front of his house. Leila's protection.

"I told the cops I was coming here. They insisted on following me over," Leila said.

He closed and locked the front door as she glanced past his entryway into the living room, curiosity on her face.

When was the last time he'd had a woman he was dating in his home? It had been too long. Not that he didn't date. But his relationships never lasted long enough to get to the "why don't you come over?" stage. A few dates in and he'd know whether it was going anywhere. Rather than hurt the woman later, he broke it off sooner. It had happened for so many years, he'd figured that long-term just wasn't for him. It was disappointing—he'd always imagined settling down some day—but he'd prefer to be alone than pretend a relationship was going somewhere permanent when it wasn't.

But Leila looked good in his house. As she strode past him and settled onto his big, comfortable couch without an invitation, he hid a smile.

He hadn't called her. He'd kissed her like he needed her as much as he needed air yesterday morning, and then he'd left for the TCD office. When he'd returned, he'd avoided being alone with her, avoided an awkward conversation or another kiss. Because when it came to Leila, his willpower was shot. But he needed to solve this case first. Needed to figure out who was behind the illegal arms sales and the defective armor before he could even begin to think about whether a relationship with Leila Petrov was possible.

Leave it to her to force the issue. He should have known she wasn't going to wait for him to decide he was ready.

He followed her into the living room, settling on the edge of the chair across from her, not trusting himself to sit beside her and not reach for her.

Her eyes narrowed slightly at his seating choice, but then she leaned forward. "Tell me about the illegal gun sales."

"What?"

She smiled slightly, but then the expression was gone, replaced by her serious, CEO face. "You thought I was going to demand answers about that kiss in my office?" She lifted an eyebrow. "Don't worry. We'll get to that."

He couldn't help it. He laughed.

Kane was right that he'd lost all focus when it came to Leila, but was it any wonder he couldn't resist this woman? If he'd met her under other circumstances, he would have long since invited her into his house.

The thought made any amusement fade fast. He was going to do everything he could to shelter her from any fallout from whoever had been using her company as a source for illegal activity. But when it was all over, he had to walk away. Had to go back to his job and let her try to pick up the pieces. Because no matter how much he wanted everything to be okay for her, it was unlikely her company would come out of this unscathed. It was unlikely *she* would come out of this unscathed.

No matter how much he wanted to separate his growing feelings for Leila from the investigation, he couldn't really do it. When this was all over, she was sure to resent him. Regardless of how he felt about her, would he ever be able to separate that from what had happened to Jessica? Could he ever truly forgive her for running the company that had caused his friend's death?

"Don't get all closed up on me now," Leila said, misunderstanding whatever emotions she'd seen on his face. "I know it's an active investigation. But we agreed that we're in this together. You told me there have been illegal gun sales coming from my company for more than a decade. So, let me help you figure this out. How much longer has it been? How many guns?"

Davis studied her, her expression intense despite the skinny jeans and long, loose T-shirt she wore. Her hair was down again, her makeup nonexistent, and he realized how much he liked her non-CEO look. The real Leila, the one people in her office didn't get to see. But she'd let him in, let him see her vulnerable, trusted him with information about the business she'd worked so hard to help build and shape. Trusted him to help her find out who was sabotaging it, without destroying it in the process.

He swallowed hard, knowing he hadn't truly earned that trust. Then he tried to channel Kane and meet her gaze with what he hoped looked like honesty. He could tell her the truth about the details: the timeline and the volume of guns. But there would always be too much he'd have to hide.

"We're on the same side," she told him softly, making him realize that he'd never be able to truly hide from her.

Nodding, he pushed his conflicted feelings to the back of his mind and focused on business. "How much longer have the illegal gun sales been happening? We're not sure. It's been at least eleven years. Possibly as many as twenty."

"*Twenty?* Almost no one has been with the company that long," Leila said, looking shocked as she sank back against the pillows on his couch.

Just her uncle and Theresa, Davis knew. But even if they could definitively say the guns had been sold illegally for twenty years, that didn't necessarily narrow the suspect pool. Because there was a strong chance her father had started the illegal side of the business as well as the legal side. He might have only brought someone else in later. Someone like Eric.

He hadn't told Leila that the FBI had narrowed the suspect pool. Now, it wasn't just those employees with high-level access who'd worked there for a while, but also those who cared about Leila enough to protect her from the BECA scum even when it was costing them huge amounts of money. But she was no fool. She'd figured out that his prime suspects were people she knew well, even people she loved.

Yet, she was still helping him. Some emotion he couldn't quite identify swelled in his chest. Pride? Attachment?

"How many guns were sold illegally?" she asked, more tension in her voice.

"A lot," he told her. "Over a decade or more, at marked up prices of course, we're talking about millions of dollars' worth."

"Millions?" She stared up at his ceiling for a long moment, before meeting his gaze again, clearly trying to absorb the information. "Petrov Armor is never going to recover from this, is it?"

His whole body tensed, wanting to jump up and sit beside her, comfort her. He wanted to tell her that she was wrong, that if it was one criminal hiding in the company, taking advantage of it, that once that person was gone, Petrov Armor could regain its reputation. But would he be lying? She'd already shut down the weapons side of the business. Now, with the investigation clearly showing the defective armor was Petrov Armor's fault, no matter why it had happened, would the military ever work with them again? He knew they were the company's main client.

"I don't know," he admitted. Then, he told her the one thing that wasn't a lie. "But if anyone can make it happen, I believe it's you."

She gave him a shaky smile, then stood and closed the distance between them.

Just as he was ready to stand, maybe to back away, she knelt in front of his chair and put her hands on his knees. The muscles in his legs jumped in response and her smile returned, this time a little more steady. She lifted her hands from his legs to his cheeks, her fingers scraping over the stubble he'd ignored shaving this morning, making his face tingle.

His breath came faster in anticipation, and he had to grip the edges of his chair to keep himself from leaning down and fusing his lips to hers. When he didn't, the small smile on her lips shifted, making the skin around her eyes crinkle as she pushed herself upward.

Her lips were inches from his when panic made him say the thing he'd been keeping from her for too long, the other thing that he couldn't continue to hide from her if he ever wanted to be with her. "Your dad's death was no accident, Leila."

HER DAD'S DEATH wasn't a mugging gone wrong. It was intentional. A murder by not just someone her dad knew, but someone he trusted. Someone who had also been using his company to sell guns to criminals and inferior armor to soldiers. All for money. Someone had murdered her father for money.

Leila tried to blink back the tears, but they were coming too fast, rushing down her face in a waterfall she couldn't stop. More than just the horror of learning it was someone she knew—someone she worked with every day—who had probably killed her father, but also the pure grief of his death. Something she'd been pushing to the back of her mind as much as possible, focusing on work, on this investigation, so she could avoid facing it.

He was gone. The person closest to her in the world.

The sobs came harder, almost violently. Then Davis was kneeling in front of her on the floor, pulling her against him. She held on tight, weeping into his chest as he stroked her hair, until the sobs finally subsided.

He lifted the bottom of his T-shirt, offering it.

She managed a laugh, then did use it to mop up the remaining tears on her face. It was something she would have done as a teenager, with Eric's shirt, when she'd been grieving the loss of her mom. Now here she was, all these years later, and it was Davis she was leaning on for support. Davis she wanted beside her.

He made her feel safe. Made her feel like she could be herself, without fearing she'd look too weak or seem unfit for her role as CEO. The ironic thing was that she probably should have feared it in front of him—an FBI agent—most of all.

She was falling for him.

The realization hit hard and sudden, even though it should have been obvious long ago. Maybe even the first day she'd met him, she should have known he was more than just a danger to her hormones, but a real risk to her heart.

She blinked at him now, kneeling in front of her, her hands still fisted in his T-shirt. His soft hazel eyes were so serious, so worried. He cared about her, too. He hadn't admitted it, but she could see it all over his face.

But he was still an FBI agent. He was still a man investigating everyone in her company. The information he'd just shared made it more clear than ever that the person they were looking for was someone important in Petrov Armor. This was no swap-out in a truck, no one-time incident. This was someone who'd been undermining the company for a long, long time. It was someone she trusted. Someone her father had trusted.

"I shouldn't be here," Davis whispered.

His words made no sense and she shook her head. "You live here."

He laughed, the tension and worry on his face fading a little. "With you, Leila. I shouldn't be here with you." His hand cupped her face, and she couldn't stop herself from leaning into it. "But I can't stay away."

Instead of reminding him that she was the one who'd come to his place uninvited, she moved her hands from the front of his T-shirt to the center of his back. Just as he was taking the hint and leaning toward her, his phone buzzed, making both of them jump.

He scowled in the direction of his phone, and she could feel him debating silently before he finally swore and said, "I need to take this."

He stood, stepped away from her and answered in a serious, all-business tone, "Davis Rogers."

His gaze was still on hers, the look in his eyes still soft, almost a caress. Then, his gaze shifted away from her and his whole face hardened. "Hang on." He moved the phone away from his ear and told her, "I'll be back in a minute."

She stood slowly as he disappeared around the corner, then used her own T-shirt to dab at the edges of her eyes. Glancing around Davis's living room—which was a lot more colorful than she'd expected given his mostly dark blue and black wardrobe—she spotted a mirror over a console in the corner. Striding over to it, she looked into the mirror and grimaced.

Her eyes were red and puffy. Her nose, too. The rest of her skin was paler than usual, and Leila realized just how much the past few weeks without enough sleep had impacted her. She'd been avoiding a breakdown ever since hearing about her father's death. She'd been afraid that once she started, she might never stop. But her outburst of tears on Davis's chest had actually been freeing. It had lifted some of her ever-present tension, made her feel less like she was moving on autopilot.

Davis had helped her feel that way, too. Just having him around—despite the reason—had forced her to feel emotions, had pulled her partway out of the numbness she'd tried to bury herself in since her father's death. She was a long way from being finished grieving, but it was a start. Hopefully, when the investigation into her company was over—no matter how it turned out—Davis would still be here.

He'd said he shouldn't be here with her now, but he hadn't asked her to leave. He'd been the one leaning in to kiss her when his phone call had interrupted. They shouldn't date while he was undercover in her company. But maybe when it was all over...

Leila felt a smile burst on her face, huge and unexpected after how hard she'd just wept. Whatever was happening between her and Davis wasn't a byproduct of her needing someone during her grief. If that were true, she would have turned to Eric, the man she'd thought she was still half-way in love with until he'd told her he wanted her back. Until his words of being together had made her think of Davis, not him.

This was real. From the things Davis had been saying to her a few moments ago, he felt it, too.

They could make it work. Once the investigation was over, they could make it work. It wouldn't be easy, especially if she had to start over again professionally, after trials and interviews over the traitor inside Petrov Armor. But he was worth it.

She followed in the direction Davis had disappeared, listening for his voice to tell her where he was. Hopefully, he was finished with his phone call. Because she needed to tell him right now that she was willing to wait until the investigation was over, but no longer. That once they figured this all out—together—she wanted *him*.

"Yes, I know Leila is still officially a suspect."

Davis's words, spoken on a frustrated sigh, made Leila freeze and her smile instantly fade.

His voice quieted even more, to a whisper Leila had to strain to hear. "Yeah, I get that, Kane. But we both know it's not her. It's someone who wants her protected, even as they steal millions from her company right under her nose. Yeah, my bet's on the uncle or the ex." A pause, then, "Yes, Theresa's still in the mix, too, but she's at the bottom of my list now."

Leila's ears started to ring and she felt so off balance she actually reached out to the wall for support. Given what Davis had shared about the gun sales, she knew the person responsible was someone in a role of importance. She'd even known the people she loved were potential suspects.

But she'd thought Davis had believed her when she'd

explained why her uncle and Eric would never, ever betray her father. She'd thought he'd trusted her judgment when it came to Theresa, too.

She backed slowly down the hall, using the wall for support, stepping lightly so he wouldn't hear her. She needed to get out of here.

Davis had feelings for her. There was no way he was that good a liar. Yet, he would still use her to get what he needed for this investigation.

This was so much worse than the betrayal she'd felt from Eric. Davis had made her believe they were working together to stop the saboteur. All the while, he was hoping to yank another person she loved out of her life.

She pulled her hand from the wall, pressed it to her chest as she spun and walked a little faster, desperate for escape. The ringing in her ears slowed, and she could hear Davis's voice, farther away now, whispering, "I've got to go."

She turned the knob on the front door slowly, pulled the door open as quietly as possible, then bolted for her car. Putting the key in the ignition seemed to take forever, but then she was speeding away from his house as fast as she could.

It was time to make a clean break from all the people who were lying to her. It was time to stop relying on the FBI to get to the truth. If she was going to prove that the people she loved weren't responsible, she was going to have to do it herself.

It was time to investigate on her own.

## Chapter Fifteen

The FBI still considered her a suspect. Not just for selling the military defective body armor, but also for illegally selling guns to criminals. Presumably even of killing her own father.

The fact that Davis didn't believe she was responsible didn't matter. He believed it was someone she loved. Despite all his promises to keep her informed, he was shutting her out.

On one hand, she understood. This was his job, and his top suspects were people close to her. But she'd given him access to everything, tried to help him find the person responsible, no matter who it was, no matter if it destroyed her career. Still, he didn't trust her with the truth.

That meant she couldn't trust him to keep her informed. She couldn't trust him to handle this in a way that would spare all the employees at her company who *weren't* guilty.

After she'd run from his house yesterday, he'd called her. She'd known if she ignored him, he would come over and check on her. So, she'd given herself a few minutes to calm down, for the ringing in her ears to fully subside, then she'd answered his call.

She'd been surprised how normal she'd sounded, how strangely calm she'd felt, as she told him that she'd needed to go home and process the news about her dad's murder. He'd expressed all the right words, even offered to come and sit with her. He'd sounded so genuine that she'd clutched the phone until her hand hurt. But still, her voice had come out even and suitably sad to convince him she just needed time alone.

This morning, she'd waited in her car until he pulled into the office, then cornered him outside when she knew they wouldn't have much time alone. She'd told him she wanted to focus on finding who was to blame for her father's murder, then figure out whatever was going on with them afterward. She'd even managed to say it with a straight face.

He'd nodded, slid his fingers along the edge of her hand and promised, "We're going to figure it out, Leila."

It had taken everything she had not to scream. She'd considered tossing him off the property, denying him access, but that wouldn't help anything. They still needed to find out who was destroying Petrov Armor, who was responsible for the deaths of all those soldiers. But she wasn't about to feed Davis details about the people she loved and let him use the information to destroy them.

He could look at the company finances and security logs all he wanted. Eventually—hopefully—those things would lead him to the truth. That someone else was responsible, someone other than Uncle Joel or Eric. Even though she wasn't Leila's favorite person, someone other than Theresa, too.

Meanwhile, Leila had started her own investigation. The first thing she'd done was put an additional alert on the security system, to notify her if anyone tried to manually override anything. If someone was trying to take armor outside the building without going through proper procedures, Leila wanted to be sure she spotted it.

Now it was time to call in backup, the person she'd

trusted with her deepest secrets since she was thirteen years old.

She hit an internal line on her phone and then asked, "Eric? Can you meet me at the loading dock? I want to discuss something with you."

She knew Eric was still on Davis's suspect list, but Eric had no motivation to wrong the company, to hurt her or her father. If he'd wanted to gain something—more money, a promotion—he could have done so easily without resorting to murder and sabotage.

She hung up before he could ask any questions, then slipped out through the front door. That morning, she'd set Davis up at a computer near where Theresa worked, giving him access to their gun database. She'd suggested he review it to see if he could figure out which gun identification numbers didn't match up to legitimate sales. Davis had told her the Petrov Armor pistols from FBI case files had their ID numbers filed off. So, it wouldn't be an easy match. But she'd suggested he look by date, see if he could come up with anything that seemed suspicious.

The truth was, she hoped he *did* find something, some evidence that would tie all of this to someone other than Joel, Eric or Theresa. The number of employees who'd been around long enough to be involved in the illegal sales for at least eleven years *and* had access to armor material wasn't large. But it was certainly larger than just her uncle, her ex and Theresa.

Thinking of Theresa made her frown. She was the only one on Davis's suspect list that Leila didn't know as well. The woman wasn't always friendly and could sometimes approach insubordinate. But she was paid well and seemed to love R and D. So why risk all of that?

No matter what, Leila knew it was a mystery that would take Davis some time. Which meant he'd be out of her way while she tried to investigate on her own. Or almost on her own.

When Eric rounded the corner of the back of their loading dock and caught sight of her, he grinned. She couldn't help but smile back. Eric had changed a lot since she'd first met him, from gawky teenager with acne to a man who looked like the head of a sales department. But his grin was exactly the same as when they'd first met. Their relationship was so different now, but she'd never forget how he'd been there for her when she'd desperately needed support.

Her uncle had done the exact same thing for her all those years ago, even moved in for a few years after her mom died. He'd made her lunches and driven her to school. Helped her with her homework and convinced her she was still loved, even if her father couldn't show it right then.

Neither of them would ever betray the company. Neither of them would ever deceive her. Most of all, neither of them would have killed her father, a man they both loved perhaps even more than they loved her.

When Eric reached her side, instead of stopping, he pulled her close, hugged her to him in a way that made her realize that unlike twelve years ago, he had no idea what she was thinking. He thought this was about the other day, about his suggestion that they give their relationship another try, maybe even leave the business and start something new together.

So much had happened since then. It was only now that she realized she hadn't actually told him a final *no*.

When she looked up to correct him, he was staring at her, his big smile shifting slowly into something more intimate.

But she couldn't. She pushed away slightly. "Eric, I have to tell you something."

"I know things have been awkward between us for years,

Leila, but I promise, it's going to change now. We can go back to how things used to be."

He dipped his head toward her and before he could reach her, Leila blurted, "Davis is an undercover FBI agent."

DAVIS HAD BARELY seen Leila since Monday. Now, three days later, he was settled in at the desk outside her office where she'd moved him, claiming he was a distraction. Initially, he'd liked the thought that his very presence could distract her from her work. But it was becoming obvious something was wrong.

She was avoiding him. Even worse, she was spending more and more time with Eric. One of his prime suspects. Of course, he couldn't tell her that. Especially since his other prime suspect was her uncle.

Joel Petrov didn't spend a lot of time at the office. As far as Davis could tell, he did his job with as much expediency as possible, then headed out with a charming smile and a wave. Living on all the overtime he'd banked twenty years ago when his brother had needed someone to handle his work and raise his daughter. He had access to everything, but based on both the offhand questions he'd asked other employees and Joel's access card records, he wasn't in restricted areas at unusual times. He was gone enough that he certainly could have been meeting contacts who needed illegal weapons, but he probably wasn't making those contacts through business channels.

Eric Ross was around a lot. To Davis's surprise, his access level was as high as Joel's and Theresa's. As high as Neal's had been before he died. Unlike Joel, he *did* have a lot of unusual activity on his access card, which Davis had somehow missed the first time he'd gone through the records. The legitimate sales calls he was often out on could have definitely also connected him to some less legitimate ones. Or they could have purely been cover for illegal meets. How simple would it be to claim he'd tried to make a sale that hadn't panned out, when actually he was connecting with criminals willing to buy the weapons at highly marked-up prices?

Was that the reason he was hanging around Leila more than usual lately, because he worried Leila knew about a traitor in the company? Or was it simply because he'd sensed the growing connection between her and Davis and he was jealous?

Then, there was Theresa. Even though he couldn't think of any reason she'd try to protect Leila from her contacts if she was the traitor, no one could have pulled off the armor switch with as much ease as the head of research and development.

Right now, he was paying Theresa a visit in her testing area at the back of the office. Other than Eric, Theresa's was the only card with particularly unusual time stamps. While Davis knew he had to tread lightly when it came to questioning Eric or Joel, because of their connections to Leila, the same wasn't true of Theresa.

When he opened the door to the area where Theresa always seemed to work, even when she wasn't testing anything, Davis realized how perfect a setup it was. No one could pass by without her noticing. Plenty of privacy to change records or swap out the material on armor.

She looked up as he entered, a mix of disdain and distrust on her face when she saw it was him. He frowned at the clipboard in his hands, pretending to read something on it, then told her, "We've got some discrepancies in the records. Leila wanted me to track down the reason."

Theresa sat a little straighter in her chair, frowned at him a little harder. But beneath the tough exterior…was that anxiety he saw?

"What kind of discrepancies?"

"Late night use of your access card," Davis said, watching her closely for a reaction.

He got one. But it wasn't quite what he expected. She looked taken aback.

"You mean weekend access? Everyone knows I sometimes work weekends," she added defensively.

"No," Davis replied, frowning. "I mean you returning to the office late at night, after you'd already left for the day."

Theresa shook her head. "That's wrong." Then she stood and crossed her arms over her chest. "I *work late* plenty. But I don't leave and come back. Sounds like a system error."

"You weren't here late at night, three weeks ago, on Friday night, about midnight?"

For a minute, he thought she wasn't going to answer him at all. But then, Theresa's eyes rolled upward and she shook her head. "No. Three weeks ago, on Friday night, I was at a concert. Here." She dug around in her purse, then pulled out her phone. She tapped something onto it, then held it toward him. "I don't know why I need to prove myself to Leila's *assistant*, but here's a picture from the concert. You see the date stamp?"

He studied it, then nodded and handed it back. She could have faked it, but how would she have known to have it ready? Unless she'd put some kind of electronic tag on the records, so she knew when the data was accessed? To give herself a heads-up if anyone ever suspected? "So, how was your card used that night then?"

"I don't know."

He stared hard at her, trying to read her, and she actually fidgeted.

"Look, I know Leila isn't my biggest fan. I'm not hers, either. Don't get me wrong—I think she's done a pretty good job as CEO. Believe me, I was skeptical. The truth is, she never would have had this job if her father didn't start the company. Everyone knows it."

"Word is that you told Leila's father not to recommend Leila her CEO," Davis said.

Theresa scowled, but nodded. "Yeah. She didn't have enough experience."

"Who did you think deserved the position? You?"

Theresa laughed, sat back down. "Maybe. If we're talking pure experience at the company. But all the boring administrative work of running a company?" She gave an exaggerated shudder. "That's not my idea of fun. I like to make things, and make them better. I'd never leave R and D."

"But at the end of the day, you don't get to make the final decisions on what gets made, right? That's Leila."

Theresa nodded slowly, studying him now as closely as he was watching her. "Like the guns? Yeah, that's true. I think it was a mistake, shutting down that side of the business. But so does everyone else here. Even her father. He just didn't say it publicly."

Davis frowned. That was what others at the company had told him, too. Which fit with the idea that Leila's father had been illegally selling guns, but willing to trade it in for the sake of his daughter's success. No matter what kind of man he'd been, he had loved her. The more time Davis spent here, the less he believed Neal Petrov had helped put his daughter in the role of CEO to be his scapegoat.

Maybe that was what had gotten him killed. Maybe he'd tried to go legitimate, to protect her, and his partner hadn't wanted it.

But was his partner Theresa? Maybe. Maybe she just hadn't had enough time to work things out with BECA if they were pressing for arms she couldn't yet deliver. According to everyone he'd talked to, it was Neal's support of Leila's plan to move solely to armor that had made it a reality. Maybe Theresa had hoped to use Neal's death to get gun production going again. That would make it easier for her to return to the illegal sales.

He frowned, not quite liking the logic or the timing. It still seemed like someone who was willing to kill to restart gun production would be willing to tell their contacts where to put the blame for it shutting down in the first place.

He must have stayed silent too long, because all of a sudden, Theresa blurted, "Look, I don't know what Leila thinks I did, or what's going on with my access card. We're not best friends, but when I told her dad that I thought she wasn't ready to be CEO, he made me promise to support her anyway. So, I'm not sure how you heard about what we discussed *in private*, but it's not common knowledge. Neal, Joel and I have known each other for a long time. Heck, I've known Leila since she was a kid. After Neal died, I committed to protecting Leila for him. And I have."

She stared at him with such intensity as she spoke, telling Davis that she'd done something she felt was big in order to protect Leila for Neal. Had she really killed Neal for letting their illegal business get screwed up and then thought she could make up for it by not selling out his daughter?

As Davis stared back at her, he realized it was a definite possibility.

Theresa Quinn had just shot to the top of his suspect list.

## Chapter Sixteen

"What if it wasn't just a matter of cheaper materials getting swapped out so someone could pocket the extra cash?" Eric suggested.

"What do you mean?" Leila asked. It was strange, this secret investigation they were running. He'd helped her make an excuse for the armor shipments that weren't going out this week—claiming delays on the military's side. Her employees had seemed to buy it.

Instead of making her feel like they were in on something together, her time with Eric was just making her uncomfortable. She needed to repeat what she'd said earlier, that her feelings weren't the same as when they were younger. But she didn't want to dive into that discussion when there were so many more important things to figure out right now. The future of her company—not to mention justice for the soldiers who'd been killed—depended on her rooting out the traitor.

Pushing her worries about hurting Eric's feelings to the back of her mind, Leila tried to focus on what he'd said. What if it wasn't just a matter of cheaper materials being used for someone to pocket the extra money? "What do you mean?"

"What if *both* sets of armor were made?"

Leila shook her head, still not understanding.

"Leila, what if it's kind of like the guns?" Eric asked. "What if someone sent cheap armor to the military, but sold the good ones at a huge markup to criminals? I know convicted felons can buy body armor. But if these sales are as big as Davis seems to think they are, maybe the same criminals who are buying up boxes and boxes of illegal weapons are also buying armor now? Maybe they're willing to pay more money and keep it on the down-low to keep from attracting any attention from law enforcement."

The idea made a chill run through Leila strong enough to make her reach for the blazer she'd set aside an hour ago when she and Eric had started digging through purchase receipts, looking for anything unusual. Davis hadn't told her what kind of criminals were buying the illegal Petrov Armor pistols. But criminals who needed boxes of them *and* wanted armor to go with it? That sounded like a massacre in the making. She had to stop it.

She couldn't change the past. But she could help find the person responsible, prevent any more illegal sales. And hopefully when they found the traitor, that person would give up their sales list, help the FBI bring those people to justice, too.

"Even taking into account the cost of buying cheaper armor, it's a lot more profit," Eric continued, probably not realizing he didn't need to convince her that his theory made sense. "And I know you think Davis is crazy…" He paused and scowled a little. "Believe me, I don't like agreeing with the guy. But the person who's got the right security level at the company *and* the easiest access to the armor?"

"Theresa," Leila stated. She didn't even like the woman, not really. So, why couldn't she quite bring herself to believe that Theresa would betray Petrov Armor?

"It has to be her," Eric insisted, obviously reading

her reluctance to believe Theresa was the culprit. "It just makes sense."

He stared at her, eyebrows raised until she nodded slowly. Maybe he was right. Maybe he and Davis were both right.

"We don't need Davis here anymore," Eric said, sounding relieved that she'd agreed with his suggestion Theresa was involved. "Tell him what you suspect and stop letting him muck around in the company's private information. Send him on his way and let him deal with the investigation from the outside, where he belongs."

"Eric, I can't—"

"You need a break from all of this. It's been too much, with your father's death and now this. I know you care about the company, Leila. I know you feel like it's your father's legacy. But you're wrong."

She shook her head.

He smiled at her, this time a sadder, more serious smile. "Don't you get it, Leila? *You're* his real legacy. If everything you've told me is true, this company is finished. You need to cut your losses and let it go. Come with me. Let's start over. A new business, a fresh start together. It doesn't even need to be in Tennessee. Let's get away, take a break and go somewhere." He stared at her with those dark blue eyes she'd fallen for so long ago. "Maybe overseas, lie on a beach for a while. Then we can figure it all out."

She shook her head. No matter how much she wished she could pretend none of this had happened—not the faulty armor or the gun sales or her father's murder—she couldn't leave. Couldn't just run away and hope someone else fixed the threat inside Petrov Armor.

It was *her* business to run now. *Her* responsibility to find out the truth. She owed it to the soldiers who'd been killed, to the employees who'd done nothing wrong and to her father.

She saw the disappointment on Eric's face even before she spoke. "I have to see this through to the end. No matter what happens."

YESTERDAY, AT THE end of the day, Leila had slipped out of the office without Davis spotting her. She'd left him a text message telling him she'd gone home to rest and that she'd see him tomorrow. This morning, she'd been shut in her office nonstop. Davis was tired of waiting for her to emerge, tired of waiting for her to explain why she was avoiding him.

He strode to the door of her office, had his hand on the door handle when he heard Eric's voice from inside the office. Davis froze, withdrew his hand slowly as he realized how often he'd stopped by Leila's office to talk to her in private over the past few days and found her and Eric "talking business."

Initially, he'd been unconcerned. Eric was her head of sales. But last week, she'd answered his questions quickly and efficiently, rarely spent more than an hour or two in meetings with Eric. The last few days, it seemed as though Eric and Leila were constantly meeting.

A bad feeling settled in his stomach. Could she have confided in Eric about the investigation?

Like they had been all week, the blinds on the inside of Leila's window into the main part of the office were down. But there was a gap on one side where a few slats had stuck together. Davis glanced behind him to make sure other employees weren't paying him attention as he put his eye to it.

Inside the office, Leila was sitting at the chair behind her desk as usual. But instead of being at the chair on the other side, Eric had pulled his seat around next to Leila.

Eric was frowning, pointing at something on the computer while Leila looked serious and determined. As though they were investigating this case by themselves, the head of the company and one of his main suspects.

Davis stood straighter and backed away, and someone's hand clamped on his shoulder, preventing a collision. He felt himself heat with embarrassment at being caught spying as he turned and found Joel standing there.

Joel held out his hand. "Davis, right?"

When he nodded and shook hands, Joel said, "Why don't we go down the street and grab a drink, have a chat?" Not giving him a chance to say no, Joel added, "Come on," and headed for the door.

Giving Leila's closed office door one last look, Davis followed him to a pub a few blocks away. It had been hard to get to Joel to talk to him, so he wasn't about to let this opportunity go to waste. The man didn't keep regular hours, and hadn't returned Davis's few phone calls, on the pretense of doing business for Leila.

Joel was silent most of the walk, keeping up a good pace. It wasn't until they were seated in a booth and they'd both ordered club sodas that Joel finally spoke. "You're more than just an assistant, aren't you, Davis?"

Davis felt a flash of panic and surprise, then Joel continued. "I can tell you're ambitious. Assistant is a starting point for you."

He nodded at Davis's club soda as it arrived. "I respect a man who doesn't drink while he's on the job. Some people think it's social, but it can make you lose focus." He paused meaningfully, then added, "Women can make you lose focus, too."

Davis nodded, hanging his head a little. Trying to appear embarrassed wasn't a stretch. For an undercover agent, he hadn't done a very good job of hiding his interest in Leila.

At least Joel didn't suspect he was FBI. Leila's uncle reaching out to him like this was a perfect way to get information. Davis just needed to steer the conversation in the right direction.

"It's great working for Leila," he started, "but yeah, I took this job as a chance to see the inner workings of a big company. My degree is in business management," he added, sticking to the cover résumé TCD had made him. "I am wondering, though…" He trailed off, hoping Joel would prompt him.

"What? Spit it out. I'll give you one rule of business right now—you'll never get what you want if you're not willing to ask for it. Then you've got to be willing to follow through."

Davis nodded, wondering how much of her can-do attitude Leila got from her uncle, rather than her father. "I was actually wondering about Theresa. It seems like she's been here a lot longer than Leila. I was kind of surprised—"

"That Leila was made CEO?" Joel finished for him. "I know people see it as nepotism, and let's be honest, I'm a little biased. There was a period where I basically raised that girl. But if you underestimate what Leila is capable of, that's a mistake. She might have come into the role a little young, but she belongs there."

Davis felt pride swell in his chest at the words, even though the feeling was ridiculous. He had no reason to feel anything but impartial interest. But no matter how much Leila was pushing him away right now, he was never going to feel impartial toward her. Never.

The thought gave him pause, but he pushed it to the back of his mind. Something to pick apart later, when he wasn't undercover. When he didn't have a dead friend who deserved his full attention on finding out who had caused her death.

"Theresa's great," Joel continued. "She's driven and ridiculously intelligent when it comes to innovation. She can be too intense sometimes, but she's reliable. She's a workaholic, too, but believe me, that's because she loves the research, loves the process of creating a new product. Theresa has no interest in being CEO. Eric, on the other hand…"

Davis had been staring pensively into his club soda, and he couldn't stop his head from popping up at Joel's statement. Theresa was still the stronger suspect, but Eric's time stamp had shown unusual activity too. Davis wasn't sure how to approach him, especially if Leila might have confided in him.

"Look, I like Eric. I've known him since he was a kid. Even back then, he was always hanging around wherever Leila was." Joel fiddled with his glass, still mostly full. "So I'll just say this—Leila has a blind spot when it comes to Eric."

"How so?" Davis asked, wondering why Joel had reached out to him. Was it just to give him career advice? Or was this really about Eric? Did Joel suspect Eric of something and need a sounding board?

Joel sighed, sounding conflicted as he spoke. "Eric loved my brother like a father. His own old man was never around. Which is better than what Neal and I had, but that's a whole other story. Anyway, when Eric graduated from high school, my brother saw something in him. Knew he'd be a hard worker, could succeed with the right mentorship. Talked Eric into going to school at night and working here during the day."

Davis nodded, having heard as much from Leila.

"The thing is, Eric *wasn't* my brother's kid. Leila was. So, when it came time to suggest a name to the board for CEO…" Joel shrugged, took a long sip of his club soda.

"Eric's jealous that Leila took over?"

"Resentful, is more the way I see it." Joel set his glass down, looking troubled. "He still loves Leila, that I know. But I'm not sure that love is pure. It's too tied up in him wanting all the things he thinks should be his. That's not just Neal's daughter. It's also her job. I think he'd do almost anything to get it—or if he can't do that, to take it away from Leila."

# Chapter Seventeen

Most days of the week, there were lots of employees in the office well into the evening. Leila's father had hired a dedicated group, people who cared about what they did. But on Fridays, many of them took off an hour early, got a jump-start on their weekend. A fair trade for the extra work they'd put in during the week, so both her father and Leila encouraged it.

Tonight, Leila wished she had a different policy. It was only six o'clock, but because it was Friday, the place was eerily empty. Normally she didn't mind being in the office alone. She should have been happy to have some time alone to think.

Right now, though, she wanted the background noise. She wanted the reminder that she wasn't all alone in the world, that she still had people she loved and who loved her, that she still had a company to run, to keep her going. When she was alone, it was too easy to fixate on what she'd lost. Her mother, so long ago. Her father, so recently. And soon, probably her father's company, too.

It was too easy to focus on Davis. Too easy to think about how much she already missed him, after a week of barely talking. Definitely too easy to worry about what else he might have uncovered in her company that he wasn't telling her.

By this point, he'd figured out that she was keeping something from him. But he hadn't pulled the plug on his undercover operation, so he didn't realize she'd told anyone about who he really was.

Guilt nagged her, an itch to come clean with him that she couldn't give in to. Half the reason she'd blurted the truth to Eric had been to stop him from kissing her. Right now, she wanted to talk to her uncle about what was going on. But even though Davis had betrayed her, she didn't want to do the same to him. She'd broken her promise by telling Eric, but Davis's words had rung in her head about the secrecy of the investigation. So, she'd made Eric promise repeatedly not to tell anyone else. And as bad as she wanted her uncle's insight right now, she'd resisted confiding in him.

She wondered if Davis had decided to do it himself. He and her uncle had disappeared in the afternoon. They'd returned after an hour, both looking serious. Her uncle had given Davis a pointed nod as they'd headed to their separate work spaces. It was a nod Leila recognized, one that said the men were on a shared mission.

It was a little surprising that Davis would spill FBI secrets voluntarily, but her uncle was persuasive. And he was insightful. If there was anyone who knew the ins and outs of the company as well as she did—or maybe even better—it was Uncle Joel.

Before Eric had taken off, Davis had popped his head into her office. He'd told her he was heading home in a subdued tone, given no hint that he still believed the lie she'd told him earlier in the week.

The desire to call him right back, demand that he come clean with her so they could figure out not just what was happening at Petrov Armor, but also what was happening between them, had almost been too strong to resist. But she had resisted, and now Davis was gone. A little voice in the back of her mind told her it was unlikely he'd be back on Monday morning. She wondered if a group of FBI agents holding up badges and making a scene would arrive instead.

Leila swore, rubbed the back of her neck and stood up. The darkness beyond her office was depressing, almost spooky, especially knowing that the person who'd attacked her had followed her from her office. But he was in jail, Leila reminded herself. After enough time had gone by without another incident, the police believed she was safe, so she no longer had cops following her. Davis seemed less convinced—or maybe he was just overprotective—but she needed to focus on things she could control.

Besides, what better time was there to get a jump on Davis's investigation? The question was, where could she look that she hadn't already checked?

The security access logs. It was one of the few things Davis had reviewed without her. She and Eric had talked about Theresa's easy access to the armor materials, and they'd looked through supply orders. Since Davis had already found Theresa's access card used at strange hours, Eric had suggested they not waste their time rechecking.

Still, Davis wasn't telling her everything. So maybe he'd found more than a single late-night access. Maybe he'd found a pattern. And as much as she didn't want to believe Theresa was involved, Eric was right. She was the most logical choice.

Besides being the one most familiar with the armor material, she was the one who'd have the easiest time swapping it out. Of all the employees who'd been here a long time and had sufficient security clearance to be able to pull this off, she was one of the few who hadn't been brought in by her father. Uncle Joel had found Theresa. When her father returned to work, he and Theresa seemed to have a mutual admiration, but maybe Leila had misread it.

She sank back into the chair behind her desk and pulled up the security card logs, scrolling back to the time when the defective armor had been shipped out. A single late-night access by Theresa, just as Davis had said.

Frowning, she leaned back in her chair and sighed. Then, she slid forward again and went back a few weeks. Before the shipment had been sent out, around the time the armor would have been made. Three late-night access logs that week. Her heart pounded faster, the excitement of finding something mixed with the anger of Theresa's betrayal.

Her breath stalled in her throat as she read the name on the log. Not Theresa, but Eric.

"No," Leila said out loud, leaning closer to the screen as if the proximity would suddenly change the name in front of her in black and white. "No way."

"No way what?" a familiar voice came from the doorway to her office.

Her heart seemed to freeze, then take off at an intensity that was almost painful as she lifted her gaze to find Eric leaning against the door frame, scowling.

DAVIS TOSSED HIS button-down on the floor and kicked out of his slacks, trading them for the jeans and T-shirt he preferred. He probably wouldn't be wearing the office attire again anytime soon. He doubted he'd go back to Petrov Armor on Monday morning. When he'd said goodbye to Leila in her office, it had felt final.

He was closing in on a suspect. As much as he'd hoped it would be Theresa, because it would be least devastating to Leila, it looked like Eric Ross was the traitor. After talking to Joel, he'd come back to the office and dug through the security records a little closer, going back much further than he had before. What he'd found was a pattern of unusual access. It wasn't a slam dunk, but it was enough.

The most logical next step was to send in a team with warrants in hand, and he expected that would happen before Monday morning. Joel had just thought he was helping Davis with a little career advice, then venting a bit about a guy he didn't think was good enough for his niece. But he'd given Davis the final pieces he'd needed to send his team in the right direction.

Joel had solidified the motivation for why the man who'd thought of Neal Petrov like a father would try to steal from him, then kill him. Jealousy and revenge. It was the thing Melinda, ever the profiler, would want to know when they asked for warrants. Why would Eric Ross do it? Well, he finally knew.

No way had Eric worked with someone else, least of all the man who'd forced him to break up with Leila. Eric had been in it alone.

It was time to get out. Davis still wasn't positive what had happened to make Leila suddenly stop trusting him, but as he'd thought back on the timing, he'd realized she'd started avoiding him after his phone call with Kane at his house. They'd mostly talked about the BECA side of the investigation, but Davis's progress at Petrov Armor had come up briefly. Still, once he'd remembered the few words he'd spoken about it, he'd known. That had to be what had changed. He'd been whispering, but Leila must have somehow overheard him say the people she cared about most were suspects in his investigation.

She hadn't denied him access, probably still believed the truth would come out and exonerate them. It physically hurt him that he was going to shatter that belief. But they couldn't go on like this. Especially not with Eric probably getting suspicious that Leila suspected something, which might explain why he'd suddenly sought her out at every opportunity. If she hadn't already, eventually, she'd let Davis's identity slip and Eric would start to cover his tracks. If that happened, he might do a good enough job that the FBI couldn't prove it, or he'd run off on a convenient "vacation" to a country without extradition.

The whole drive home, Davis had reached for his phone over and over, wanting to call Leila, wanting to explain that he'd never intended to hurt her, that he'd never intended to fall for her. But he couldn't tip her off that he was finished at Petrov Armor.

If she didn't hate him already, she was going to hate him soon.

Davis took a deep breath, trying to calm the urge to hit something, because he didn't have time to go to the gym and work out his aggression on a punching bag. He grabbed the attaché case he'd tossed on the floor and took it to his desk, dumping out the contents. Notes on relevant information about Eric. He needed to put it all together and present it to Pembrook so they could make the strongest case for the warrants. He wanted to serve them as soon as they could, get this over with, then move on with his life.

He was going to have to do it without Leila. Davis rubbed his temples, where a headache had suddenly formed. How had she gotten to him so quickly, so completely?

*Focus*, he reminded himself. He couldn't control what happened after those warrants were served. Couldn't control whether or not bringing down the person who'd swapped out the faulty armor dragged down the entire company with him. Couldn't control whether Leila's career and the legacy she'd tried so hard to preserve for her father crashed down around her.

All he could do was his job. He'd sworn an oath as an FBI agent to uphold the law. And he'd made a personal promise that he was going to find the person responsible for Jessica's death.

Gritting his teeth, Davis lined up his notes on Eric with the time line of possible illegal arms sales Kane and Melinda had put together. When his phone rang, he scowled at it, debating not answering. But it was a local number. Maybe Leila, calling from her office?

"Davis," he answered curtly, still in FBI mode. And trying to put as much of a barrier as possible between himself and Leila. Because if she asked him straight out, he wasn't sure he could lie to her and not hate himself.

But the voice that came over the line wasn't Leila. "Davis, it's Joel. Look, I'm sorry to call you after hours like this, but I've found something."

"What is it?" After Joel had shared that he thought Eric was out for Leila's job, Davis had acted like he was hesitant to say anything, but finally blurted that he'd felt something odd was going on at the company. He'd said he suspected it was preparation for a hostile takeover of Leila's CEO position, that maybe Eric had cut some corners in ways that would come back to her. Joel had promised to look into it.

When the end of the day had come and Joel had just headed out without a word, Davis figured the man had either been humoring him or hadn't found anything. But the intensity in Joel's voice now said otherwise.

"After we talked, I took a look at our purchase records. And you're right. Little things seem off, especially with recent armor purchases. All the odd purchases were logged in by Eric. There's nothing obvious enough to draw attention, but looking at it all together, it's not quite right."

"Not right, how?"

"Well, I know you thought Eric could be cutting corners and trying to make it seem like Leila's fault, but these purchases all seem just a bit too high. Like he was paying for more materials than he actually received."

Or he'd received plenty of materials, but he'd only

brought some of it into the office and kept the rest of it for illegal sales. "What if he wasn't paying for more than he got?"

"If we got all this material, I'm sure Theresa would have noticed. She's the one receiving it."

"What if she wasn't?"

"What do you mean?"

"Would Eric know how to build the armor? Theoretically?" Davis pressed. Could he have swapped out the faulty material himself?

"Sure," Joel replied simply. "He's been here a long time. He's seen Theresa and her team do it. But why would he want to build it himself? Anyway…"

"Something's not right," Davis stated, summing up. His pulse quickened at the thought of new, potentially more conclusive evidence to take to his boss. If he could get Joel to willingly hand it over, even better.

"Yeah," Joel agreed. "Normally I wouldn't talk about this at all with a brand-new employee, but I didn't even suspect anything until you brought it up. I'm going to have to tell Leila at some point, but she's been through so much lately. I don't want to bother her with this if there's some other explanation."

"I think that's a good idea," Davis agreed. For the investigation, he needed Leila to stay ignorant of this new development. But knowing that didn't stop guilt from flooding him. It didn't matter that they hadn't even known each other for two weeks. He owed her more than lies.

"I'm glad you agree," Joel said. "Even though I don't necessarily want to see my niece get back together with her ex, the truth is, Eric isn't the only one who still has feelings there. Leila never totally got over him, either. He broke up with her so out of the blue, but it wasn't his decision. I don't want to see my niece hurt, so if I'm wrong about this, I'd rather you help me figure it out before I break the news to Leila."

"What do you mean that breaking up with Leila wasn't Eric's decision?" Davis asked, a bad feeling forming.

"I'm sure my brother meant well, but asking Eric to break up with Leila all those years ago might have fueled some of this. I'm sure Eric figured one day Neal would change his mind, then hand over the company to him and offer his blessing on dating his daughter again, too. But it didn't happen that way."

"And his resentment has been building up ever since," Davis stated.

"Exactly. I think the other part of what's behind Eric's need to be CEO is to prove his worth to Leila. Doesn't make a whole lot of sense, since it would be at her expense, but it's a power thing." Joel sighed heavily. "At least, that's my suspicion. The fact is, I need an outside view. I've known Eric for so long, it's hard for me to be objective. Because there's something else I found."

"What is it?" Davis pressed when Joel took a breath.

"Something at our remote testing grounds. It could be connected to Eric too, but—"

"*Remote* testing grounds?" Davis knew about the second testing area in their office, a soundproofed area where the guns used to get tested. But Leila had never mentioned a remote facility. He resisted the urge to swear, held his silence while he waited for Joel to explain.

"Yeah, it's the other place we used to test the guns," Joel continued easily, probably not sensing Davis's anxiety.

But why would he? Joel thought he was uncovering a simple plot by Eric to undermine his niece, take over her position as CEO. He had no idea he was helping to unroot a long-running criminal enterprise.

"When Leila shut down the gun side of the business, we

didn't really need it anymore. We already had two testing areas inside the office, and those were much more convenient. So, this one was shut down. Or at least, it was supposed to be."

If it wasn't, it was the perfect place to test excess guns before selling them to criminals, instead of destroying them like Leila's plan dictated. It was probably also the perfect place to swap out the materials on armor, sell the good ones to criminals at a marked-up price and send the cheaper versions for contracts that had already been sold to the military. Make some cash and destroy the reputation of the woman he was trying to unseat at the same time.

Davis glanced down, realizing he'd fisted his hand so hard that he'd actually stopped blood flow to his fingertips. He forcibly loosened his fingers as he asked Joel, "Where is this place?"

"I'll text you the directions," Joel said. "Is it too much to ask you to meet me there tonight? I want to show you in person what I found before I tell Leila, get your thoughts on what the hell is going on here."

"Sure, I can do that," Davis said, fighting to keep his voice even and offhand.

Inside, he was screaming. This was it. He could feel it. This was the missing piece of the puzzle that would help him finally solve who was responsible for Jessica's death.

"Great," Joel said. "I just texted you the address. When can you meet me there?"

Davis glanced at the address. The remote testing facility *was* remote, at least in the sense that it was in a deserted area on the edge of Knoxville. The perfect place for Eric to conduct meetings with criminals, too.

"I can leave right now," Davis said.

"Great, I'll see you there."

Davis hung up, glanced at his phone to see if he had

any other messages. None, not a peep from Leila. Then, he grabbed his leather jacket and headed for his car. Right now, the rest of the TCD team was prepping for their own big arrest. They knew he was feeling close to finding answers at Petrov Armor. He'd contacted them after he checked out the initial lead from Leila's uncle, giving them the name of his suspect. But if this revealed what he thought it was going to, there'd be no delay in getting the warrants.

He'd be ready to make an arrest tonight.

# Chapter Eighteen

"No way, what?" Eric repeated, striding into her office as if it was his.

Leila's fingers felt clumsy as she moved the mouse to exit the supply order information she'd been reviewing, the logs that listed Eric's name next to orders connected to the faulty armor. Her heart pounded way too fast as she finally got it closed, just before Eric rounded her desk to stare at her now-blank screen.

Eric's suspicious gaze traveled from the computer to her face, assessing with seventeen years of experience reading her. She scrambled to come up with an answer he'd believe, even as her mind struggled to accept that Eric could have been the person betraying the company for so many years. That he could have killed her father, and tried to have her killed.

She stood abruptly, her thighs bumping the chair awkwardly and sending it sliding backward into the wall. Her legs tensed, ready to run, and her hands fisted with the desire to take a swing at him so strong she was actually shaking. *Eric had killed her father.*

Seventeen years of memories flashed before her eyes as Eric put his hand on her arm, leaning close with wide, innocent eyes.

"Are you okay?"

Images of Eric at fifteen years old, lanky and shy, asking to sit next to her and not taking no for an answer. A few months later, meeting her father and seeming to bond with him almost immediately, their connection as strong as his feelings for her, just different. Supposedly, the father he'd never had. And all the years since, in the office, laughing with her father, celebrating new deals with him, breaking down and weeping at his funeral.

Were all those memories lies?

Had everything he'd done since been a lie? Pretending to help her with the investigation in order to keep her close, see what she knew? Pretending to have romantic feelings for her again, suggesting they go to some foreign country together, so she'd help him get away before the FBI closed in?

Leila pulled free without answering. She wanted to run, but she was breathing so fast it felt like she was going to hyperventilate. Eric had been a track star in high school. Was there really any chance she could outrun him?

Would he kill her himself? Make it look like another mugging gone wrong?

Her hands fisted again, her breathing evening out, becoming more measured, deeper, as anger replaced her panic and disbelief. If he'd killed her father, she wasn't running away, hoping to save herself. She was fighting. She was making sure there was no way it would look like anything but a deliberate murder if he killed her. If fury mattered as much as brute strength, she'd take him with her, the man she'd once loved so deeply.

That fact made his betrayal so much worse.

"Leila," Eric whispered. "What's happening right now?"

His tone was worried, but there was an undercurrent of something else, something she couldn't quite identify.

"Hey, Leila, I was wondering—oh!"

Leila spun toward the sound of Theresa's voice and found the head of R and D in the doorway of her office.

Theresa was looking back and forth between her and Eric with surprise and concern. She was also backing away, as if to give them privacy. "Sorry about that. I can come back la—"

"Theresa!" Leila's voice came out too high-pitched and she tried to breathe deeply, calm herself down. Even though it made her want to cringe, she clutched Eric's arm and gave him her best "follow my lead" look.

His forehead creased and his lips turned up, telling her he either didn't understand what she was doing or didn't believe it.

*Pretend you still think it's Theresa*, Leila told herself, as the way out came to her. *Pretend you'd been freaking out because you found something to suggest Theresa was the traitor.*

Could she pull it off? Avert Eric's suspicion long enough to tell Davis, to get him to check out Eric? Maybe even avert his suspicion long enough to save her life? Because if Eric was willing to kill her father over this, he was probably willing to do the same to her.

"It's come to my attention that you didn't ever want me to be CEO," Leila said, making her tone aggressive and taking a step toward Theresa. She mentally apologized to the woman, who'd never been particularly friendly with her, but as far as Leila knew, had never publicly questioned her leadership.

Theresa shook her head, but she seemed more baffled at the sudden outburst than denying the accusation.

"Worse than that, Theresa, I'm seeing signs that you've—"

"Is this about the security card discrepancies?" Theresa cut her off. She sighed heavily, meant to be heard. "Your assistant already grilled me about this. Didn't he tell you?" She frowned, glancing from Leila to Eric.

Leila followed her gaze. Eric wasn't looking at Theresa, but at her. There was still suspicion in his gaze, but it seemed more like confusion than malice.

"Look, you're right," Theresa blurted as Leila continued to stare at Eric, uncertainty hitting.

Had she misinterpreted the records? Could there be some other explanation? Hope filled her. Eric's friendship when they were kids had altered the trajectory of her life. And she knew Eric's assertion that her father was the dad he'd never had wasn't one-sided. Her father had loved Eric like a son. She desperately didn't want all of that to be tainted.

"I don't think you should have been made CEO," Theresa continued, as Leila only half listened. "But I've never said that publicly. Within the company, I always supported you. I did my best to protect you. I felt like I owed it to your dad. And your uncle, even though I shouldn't really owe him anything." She let out a nervous-sounding laugh that was unusual enough from always confident Theresa to get Leila's full attention.

"Why not?" Leila asked.

"Why not what?" Theresa squinted at her, her expression saying she wasn't sure if Leila had totally lost it or if she legitimately needed to defend herself and her loyalty.

"Why wouldn't you owe Uncle Joel anything?" He'd been the one to hire her after all, not Leila's dad.

"Well, I mean, he should feel pretty good about what he's gotten from me." She flushed a little, shrugged.

"You and Uncle Joel..."

"Yeah, for the last couple of months again," Theresa admitted, her gaze darting from Leila to Eric as her cheeks turned an even deeper red. "It's foolish, I know. We've been on-again, off-again for years. It's casual. Your uncle will never do serious."

"How casual?" Leila asked as a new, terrible possibility nudged at her. Davis had told his team that Theresa, Eric and Joel were his top suspects. If Uncle Joel had been dating Theresa, he could have easily swiped her card. Maybe even borrowed her car.

She tried to shrug off the idea. She loved her uncle. He loved her. He'd half raised her. And he loved her dad. The two brothers had grown up with abuse so bad that Leila had never met her grandparents. Uncle Joel and her dad had been incredibly close, until her dad had met her mom. Even afterward, they'd stuck together. Uncle Joel had taken over her dad's company at a time when it would have folded otherwise.

He'd saved her father's livelihood, ensured they still had the money to send Leila to the best schools. But that act had also given Uncle Joel a level of access to everything that he never would have had otherwise. It had given him contacts and opportunities. And he was often out of the office, something she'd never questioned because of all the years he'd put in holding the company together. What if he'd spent that time using the company for his own gain, the way he did women?

*No way*, Leila told herself, ashamed for even thinking it.

"…a charmer," Theresa was saying and Leila tried to focus, realizing the woman was talking about her relationship with Leila's uncle.

"It wouldn't have lasted anyway," Theresa said, still flushed a deep red. "I know you and your uncle are close, but there's a reason he's got a reputation with women as a love 'em and leave 'em kind of guy. He's…" She shook her head. "Never mind. Jeez. I don't know why I'm telling you this. And I don't know why there's suddenly all this scrutiny on my access card, but whatever you suspect me of, I didn't—"

"He's *what*?" Leila pressed, ignoring the rest of it.

Theresa shrugged, then said softly, "I don't know if he's really capable of loving anyone."

Theresa apologized, tried to backtrack, but Leila was only half paying attention. Words her father had spoken years ago, with embarrassment and a hint of shame popped into her mind. "He's just unreliable, honey. He's always in things for himself." It had been so long ago, before her mother had died, one of many times her uncle had promised to show up for something, but never appeared.

But he'd changed. Hadn't he? She couldn't possibly have misjudged him so thoroughly.

Leila clutched her stomach, which churned as she realized that if Uncle Joel had taken Theresa's access card to swap out the armor, if he'd been the one betraying the company for cash all these years, then it was so much worse than even thinking Eric had done it. It would mean Uncle Joel had killed his own brother.

"Leila."

Eric's tone, full of dark realization, snapped her out of her spiraling thoughts.

"I'm so sorry," he said, gripping her arm. "I know I promised I wouldn't, but…"

He looked from her to Theresa as Leila snapped, "What? What is it?"

"I told your uncle that Davis is FBI."

BECA WAS GOING DOWN.

Not all of the members, because the loosely connected organization had members across the country. But enough that Kane felt really good about today's arrest plan.

Except for one thing. No matter what argument he threw at her, Melinda refused to be shut out of the arrest.

Even now, she was babbling on in profiler mode, acting like she had any right to fish around in his mind.

He'd thought that when they'd last argued, when she'd revealed—intentionally or not—that she'd had some deep loss of her own, she'd back off. That she'd let him take the lead and she'd fade into the background, focus on the paperwork and the profiling. Let him dive into the danger. The way it should be, each of them focusing on their strengths.

But if nothing else, Melinda was persistent and stubborn. Even if she didn't want to work with him at all.

The idea stung. It was ironic, given how hard he'd tried to make her feel that way. Now that she did, he half wished he could take it back.

But not right now. Not with a dangerous large-scale arrest happening on a group known for its propensity for violence and a stockpile of ready weapons. The FBI had gotten a tip that a group was meeting that night. The arrest warrants had come in and the plan was to make a big arrest, grab a bunch of them before word could get out and anyone could run—or arm themselves and prepare for a standoff.

He didn't want Melinda anywhere near it.

"This is still about Pembrook's daughter," Melinda insisted, and Kane couldn't believe her audacity.

He ground his back teeth together, trying to hold in the anger that always rushed forward when anyone dared to bring up that incident.

"You're scared I'm going to get hurt like she did." Melinda kept pushing.

"Not *hurt*," Kane snapped. "*Dead*. She's dead."

"And I'm not her," Melinda stated, making him want to slap his hand over her mouth to shut her up.

Or maybe slam his lips against hers. Different method, same end result. She'd finally have to shut up.

"Let's go." Laura's voice preceded her. When their team-mate finally appeared at the doorway, her expression as buttoned-up as the rest of her, she gave them a searching glance. Then she added, "Whatever you two are arguing about this time, maybe save it for after the big arrest."

Then she was gone and Melinda was staring back at him, with eyebrows raised.

"Fine," Kane said on a heavy exhale. If Melinda wanted to rush into danger, instead of staying in the office and doing her profiler work, so be it.

He strode past her, following the rest of the team out to the SUVs. On the way, he grabbed a submachine gun and slung it over his gear. Then, he climbed in.

This was going to be a dangerous batch of arrests, the kind the FBI would often hand off to one of their SWAT teams. But Pembrook had felt confident her team could handle it, and no one was about to suggest otherwise. In deference to the level of threat, every agent crammed into the SUV wore more gear than typical. They all had body armor—not from Petrov Armor, thank goodness—and even helmets.

The submachine guns weren't standard issue, either. They were usually reserved for tactical teams. But tonight, that was the agents of TCD.

Kane glanced at Melinda as she hopped on board. The SUV had been converted, so the backseats had two rows facing each other. She sat across from him, looking even smaller than usual weighed down with all the extra gear. She stared straight at him, her face an expressionless mask. But there was something in her gaze that looked like nerves.

His gut clenched. She didn't have the same level of ex-perience on these kinds of arrests as the rest of the team.

Sure, she'd been a regular special agent once. Then she'd traded in the field for an office where she could analyze the mind-set of serial killers, terrorists and zealots. She didn't belong here.

But that wasn't his call.

He tried to hold in his anxiety, but it only got worse as the SUV started up, heading toward the site of the raid. With so much undercover work, he rarely felt anxious. But when he did, it always seemed to be a sign that something was going to go terribly wrong.

The last time he'd felt this much anxiety was the day Pembrook's daughter had died.

# Chapter Nineteen

Uncle Joel *knew*.

Eric had told him days ago that Davis was an undercover FBI agent. He'd never said a word to her. Never chastised her for giving the FBI such unrestricted access to the company. Instead, he'd gotten chummy with Davis, spent more than an hour out of the office with him in the afternoon.

What had happened during that time? If Davis still suspected Uncle Joel, why hadn't he said anything to her? If Uncle Joel was really involved, what was his end goal with chumming around with Davis?

More than anything right now, she needed to know Davis's whereabouts. He'd left that evening with barely a word to her. Deep down, she'd known he wasn't coming back.

She'd called him three times in the last ten minutes, and each call had gone to voice mail. Maybe he was busy and she was overreacting. She didn't believe he was the kind of guy who'd ignore her out of spite, not after the closeness they'd shared.

Then again, could she really trust her own judgment? She glanced from Eric to Theresa and back again. In the space of a few days, she'd suspected them both of being the traitor. Maybe one of those suspicions was right and thinking it was Uncle Joel was way off base.

But the way her stomach was churning with fear, horror and betrayal right now, she couldn't risk that she was wrong yet again. She needed to find Davis.

If Uncle Joel had really murdered his own brother, what was one undercover FBI agent?

"I need your help." Leila's voice came out a frightened squeak.

"What do you need?" Eric asked as Theresa repeated for the third time since Eric had announced it, "Davis is FBI? Your assistant?"

"Yes, Davis is FBI," Leila responded, turning to fully face Theresa, studying her expression. By now, she'd had a good ten minutes to disguise whatever she was feeling. If Theresa was the traitor, she was cool under pressure.

"So, *that's* why he was asking about my access card," Theresa said, sounding horrified. "I should have known you were lying about the armor. It was ours, wasn't it?"

"Yes."

Theresa sank into the chair on the other side of Leila's desk. She shook her head, sounding lost. "I'm going to be ruined. This might be your company, but I'm in charge of development. How did this get past me? We have so many checks in place."

"Whoever did it knows every one of them and how to get around them," Leila replied, thinking it less and less likely that the traitor was in the room with her.

"And you honestly think it was your uncle?" Eric asked, the pain in his eyes mirroring her own feelings.

He'd never been close to her uncle, so Leila knew that pain was for her. She was grateful for it, knew it reflected how deeply he cared for her. But right now, with Davis potentially in trouble, Leila knew for sure the words she'd spoken to Eric earlier were true. Their time was over. She'd fallen in love with Davis.

As Eric stared at her, the expression in his eyes shifted. He'd known her too long.

She shook her head, wishing he hadn't realized it like this, wishing she could say something to stop the pain she was causing him.

Before she could say anything, Eric said softly, "It's okay, Leila. What do you need?"

"We have to find Davis," Leila said. "I know this is probably crazy, but I'm worried that he's in trouble. If my uncle really is behind this—"

"You think *Joel* made the faulty armor?" Theresa asked, her face going deathly pale. *"Why?"*

"Money," Leila answered simply. Part of her still couldn't believe her uncle would ever betray his own family to such a degree. Another part of her, the part that remembered how her uncle had been before he stepped up when her mom died, said it was possible.

A sob ripped its way up her throat and Leila swallowed it, her eyes tearing with the effort. Now wasn't the time to grieve all she was about to lose if she was right. She needed to focus on making sure Davis didn't get tricked like her father.

"Theresa, I need you to go to my uncle's house," Leila said, her voice strong and clear now that she was thinking only about next steps and not emotions. "See if he's there. If he is, make up whatever excuse you need, but text me right away." She turned to face Eric. "I need you to go to Davis's house and see if he's home. If not, I need you to call the FBI."

"What about you?" Eric asked.

"I'm going to the remote testing facility." They'd closed it down a year ago. Long-term, the plan had been to convert it into another armor testing location, but they didn't need it right now. The ones inside the main office were enough. It made no sense for her uncle to be at the remote location.

But he'd loved to go to there. She'd find him there randomly when she'd stop by to do checks, back when they still sold weapons. He'd be shooting one of their pistols or even just hanging around. In response to her surprise, he'd always joke, "We make guns, Leila. We should at least get a little shooting in."

"Maybe we should all stick together," Eric argued. "Check each place out in order and—"

"No," Leila cut him off. "Look, I'm probably overreacting here, but I need to be sure. And I need to know *now*. Can you do this?"

Theresa stood, her face still paler than usual, but with two deep red spots high on her cheeks. "Yes." Then she reached across the desk and squeezed Leila's hand. "Be careful. I know you love your uncle, but he's got a dark side. If you find him, don't let him realize what you suspect."

Theresa headed out of the office, and Eric gripped Leila's arms, turning her to face him. "Leila, this seems risky. I still think—"

She pulled free. "Eric, I don't care what Theresa says. My uncle loves me. He'd never hurt me. You're the one who needs to be careful. If my uncle is with Davis, just leave and call the FBI, okay?"

He nodded, his lips pursed in an expression she recognized. He didn't like it, but he knew he wasn't talking her out of this.

Then he was gone. Leila stayed in her office, trying to text Davis. She stared at the screen for another thirty seconds, hoping a response would pop up. When it didn't, she took off at a run.

The remote testing facility wasn't that far from the office by car, but while the area around their main building had continued to be built up year after year, the spot where they'd put this facility had stayed mostly deserted. *The perfect place to murder someone.*

The unbidden thought made Leila shiver and she punched on the gas, taking the back roads way too fast. As she pulled into the lot, her heart seemed to slam down toward her stomach.

Two cars were there—her uncle's and Davis's.

There had to be some innocent explanation. Maybe her uncle had offered to give Davis a tour of the place. She'd never mentioned it to him, so Davis had probably jumped at the chance. It hadn't even occurred to her, since they hadn't used it in almost a year. Frustration nipped at her because it was the perfect location to put together inferior armor.

*Uncle Joel would never kill Davis. He'd never kill her father.*

No matter how many times she repeated those things to herself, the fear remained.

Climbing out of her car, Leila glanced around. The place really was in the middle of nowhere, with woods on one side and a huge, overgrown field on the other. The fence around the lot was still intact, but the guard gate had been up when she'd arrived, some kind of malfunction. She had no idea how long it had been that way. It had been months since she'd made a personal check of this place.

Locking her car, Leila took her phone out of her purse as she ran for the door. With shaking hands, she pulled up the internet, looking for the number of the local FBI. But when she dialed, she got a recording with a list of options and hung up, not willing to wait.

Whatever her uncle was planning to do to Davis, whatever he might have done to her father, he'd never hurt her. If there was one thing she believed without question, it was that. As long as she could get there in time, she could stop him from hurting Davis.

She slid her access card into the reader and yanked open the door, stepping inside.

The lights were on, but the front area with its handful of desks and storage cabinets was empty. Beyond the entry was the testing area. Leila couldn't hear a thing, but if her uncle and Davis were back there, she wouldn't. Since they'd been used for shooting, they were all soundproofed.

Leila used her security card again to enter the shooting area, and her heart gave a painful thump. The testing space at the very back had a green light glowing over the door that meant it was in use.

With every step toward the active lane, Leila's breath became faster, more uneven. When she pulled open the heavy steel door, in front of her was the thing she'd feared most.

Davis was kneeling in the middle of the shooting lane, blood on his head and swaying. Her uncle stood at the front of the lane, a Petrov pistol centered on Davis like a target.

BECA HAD KNOWN they were coming.

One minute, the SUV was driving down the narrow lane toward the mansion where one of the wealthiest BECA members lived, toward a meeting supposedly in progress. Each member of the TCD team had been clutching their submachine guns, gazes steady, jaws tight. Kane's gaze had been on Melinda, cool and slightly angry, as she'd stared back at him.

Then, the world around him exploded in light and sound and the SUV tipped sideways, slamming to the ground on the side away from him.

Kane's head bounced off JC's. The agent had gotten stuck in the middle of their row. Pain filled his head and something dripped in his eye, and then the team around him was scrambling, most of them responding on instinct and training. Across from him, Melinda looked dazed, one hand to her head, blinking rapidly. JC, with his military background, was the first to move, despite the conk to the head.

"Move, move, move," JC ordered. "We're target practice here."

BECA must have had some kind of camera or alert system at the beginning of the long, winding entry to the mansion. They were the kind of group that was always armed, always prepared for a fight. They'd had the place booby-trapped. And Kane knew the BECA members would get here fast, to finish them off. He could already hear them coming, the growl of a large engine speeding toward them, then the screech of brakes.

He scrambled to both brace himself against the seat in front of him and the door and release his seat belt. It took longer than he would have liked. Then there was a face at the window, one that managed to be both snarling and smiling as he lifted his gun.

Forgetting the seat belt, Kane went for his pistol instead. He'd always been a quick draw, but as he saw his face reflected back at him superimposed on the guy intent on killing him, he wasn't sure he was fast enough. Even as he fired three shots and the window exploded, showering glass all over him and the teammates below him, Kane didn't know if he'd hit his mark until the guy dropped out of sight.

He waited for the pain of a bullet to his own body to register, but he only felt the needle-sting of what seemed like hundreds of tiny shards of glass. Not the searing intensity of a bullet. Then more shots boomed, way too many, and Kane cringed, knowing the SUV wasn't armored. A scream from inside the car emphasized the thought, and Kane's stomach clenched even as his mind cleared.

This was it. There was no good way out of this vehicle.

He'd always known he would die on the job. He'd accepted that years ago, in some ways longed for it, because it was no less than he deserved.

But he didn't want to go like this. Not surrounded by more teammates.

His gaze shifted to Melinda, still tethered to her seat, an easy target if someone else managed to clamber up to the side windows—now directly above them. He moved his gaze past her, to the front windshield, now on ground level. Past the two teammates in front, who were either hit or out cold, to the man bending down there, a furious intensity on his face as he lifted his weapon.

Kane shifted, aiming and firing at the same time as JC. Apparently Laura in the driver's seat wasn't as unconscious as she'd seemed, because her gun hand rose at the same time. The guy dropped in a shower of bullets. The front windshield shattered, too, and as shots started coming through the floorboards—now facing toward the zealots—JC yelled, "Ballistic shields!"

Then, someone was handing him a shield and Kane propped it between him and the bottom—now side—of the car, protecting him and the agents below him. Across from him, Melinda was being handed a shield, too. But she urged Evan Duran, in the seat next to her, to trade places.

Awkwardly he swapped with her. Melinda almost fell, but managed to slip between the agents, down to the other side of the SUV, pressed to the ground. But the vehicle wasn't entirely flat, Kane realized. The SUV had landed on something—maybe a boulder—putting the vehicle at a weird tilt. The front of the vehicle was actually slanted downward, too. And as Melinda shoved at the passenger door, it opened a crack.

"Time for BECA to get a surprise," Melinda muttered.

Kane grabbed for her, realizing what she was going to

do. Melinda was tiny—five foot four and no more than 115 pounds. She could fit through that crack. But no one else would be able to follow.

Kane's fingers closed around Melinda's shirt, gripped hard. But his angle was awkward, and the SUV was crowded, especially as Laura yanked the other agent who'd been sitting up front—Ana Sofia—into the back. More shields were pressed around them and JC lifted his arm over Kane's, firing through the space in the middle. A BECA member screamed outside the front of the vehicle.

Then, it was too late. The fabric slipped out of his grasp and Melinda was gone.

Out of the SUV, alone, facing an unknown number of armed BECA members.

# Chapter Twenty

This was a very bad idea.

Melinda had been a regular special agent once, working a Civil Rights squad. With her background in psychology, her supervisor had figured she was a perfect fit for the myriad of human trafficking cases that came their way. That work had been dangerous at times, but it had been the people she'd run into—both victims and perpetrators—who'd made her go into profiling.

She'd been there so long, she'd started to forget what it was like in the field. Profiling sometimes sent her into the thick of a case, but often it left her buried in paperwork. Too many of her days had been spent fixated on the tiny details of a case file that gave her a behavioral analysis and helped her track down the criminal.

When she'd come to TCD, she'd needed a refresher in fieldwork. Right now, as the only agent not hunkered down in the SUV, it didn't feel like even close to enough.

She had no backup out here. Not unless one of the other agents could get clear long enough to rush through the shot-to-pieces windshield. And that was a death wish only one agent was likely to try.

Thinking of Kane made Melinda move faster. She sucked in her breath and turned her head sideways, shoving herself the rest of the way through the SUV's open door.

The helmet barely cleared, but she felt Kane's fingers peel away. Her shirt tore, but she kept going, worming her way toward the rear of the vehicle and praying the whole thing didn't crash down on top of her.

Her submachine gun wouldn't have been an easy fit through the door, so she'd left it in the SUV. Right now, she longed for the comforting feel of the big gun. Sucking in dirt and dust, Melinda angled her pistol awkwardly, praying no one saw her before she was ready. Body armor and a helmet wouldn't be enough if they saw her while she was still trying to squeeze out of here.

When she'd realized the SUV wasn't flat on the ground, that the back door would open just enough, she'd known what she had to do. Yes, the agents inside had covered themselves well with strong ballistic shields. But eventually, the BECA members would either get lucky or simply force their way inside. With no option of retreat, her teammates would be in serious trouble. Especially if the BECA members had other weapons, like grenades—which wouldn't surprise her.

The thought put a heavy weight on her chest, like the SUV really had sunk down on her. She was the agent least prepared for this. But failure meant they would probably all die here today.

She'd get one chance. One chance to take out as many of them as possible, provide a distraction that would give her team time to rush through the front windshield. If she did this right, together, they could eliminate the threat.

Boots came into view and Melinda froze, afraid to even breathe. Then, another pair joined them, and another.

She was trapped. No way to slip out from underneath the vehicle, dart behind the cover of trees like she'd planned. If she fired from here, they'd know exactly where she was, be able to hit her while she had limited visibility and few ways out.

"Climb up," one of them whispered. "You two hit them from the side, and we'll hit them from the back. Tell Don to stand near the front and pick off anyone who tries to escape that way."

Melinda's gut clenched, her breathing came faster, and her vision and hearing narrowed. Tunnel vision. Knowing it was happening—that her fear was overriding her senses—didn't make it easier to fix.

BECA had a good plan. The agents inside were still firing periodically, but only out the front windshield. A distraction, hoping to give her a chance. Not knowing what she'd planned to do, since she hadn't told them, since she hadn't fully known when she'd slipped out that door.

She was a pretty good shot. But there were at least four BECA members near the side and back of the vehicle, at least one up front. Even if she could hit the four closest to her, she had an angle only on their feet and calves. Enough to bring them to the ground, sure, but to take them out of the fight entirely? Unlikely.

All that mattered was taking them down long enough for the other agents to get out the front, not getting shot herself before she could yell a warning about Don's position.

If she was going to die today, she prayed she'd be able to do it giving the rest of her team a fighting chance.

Not daring to move her hand up to touch the ring dangling under her T-shirt, she focused on the feel of it. The simple gold band she'd picked out for her late husband. It always gave her strength. Thinking of it made her breathing even out, her senses sharpen.

Just as one of the BECA members started to clamber up the side of the SUV to get a shot through the window, Melinda lined up her first shot. Then, she said one more prayer, fired two shots in rapid succession. Someone—maybe two someones—dropped to the ground, screaming in pain, but moving around. Probably aiming their own weapons, a new target in sight now that they were lying in the dirt.

Melinda didn't waste time. She screamed a warning to her team as she pivoted toward the side of the SUV, toward the guy dropping off the vehicle, making it bounce up and down, too close to her. Then more shots joined her own and Melinda kept firing, wondering if the adrenaline was preventing her from feeling the bullets that had to be hitting her by now.

The two guys on the side of the SUV both dropped, and Melinda hit them again, not waiting to see if they were dead before she swiveled once more toward the two she'd hit first. The two who had to be recovered enough to shoot her fatally by now.

But as she turned, a new pair of boots slammed down to the ground and someone else fired, taking out those BECA members. One of them had his gun up, pointed directly at her head, and Melinda squeezed her eyes shut, expecting it to fire anyway. But instead of a bullet, she felt a hand on her leg.

She jerked, opened her eyes. And there was Kane, kneeling down, pulling her out from under the SUV.

"Nice job," Evan told her as he ran around from the front of the vehicle, Laura close at his heels. Both of them still swept the area with their weapons even though the shots had ceased.

Kane yanked her to her feet, took the pistol from hands she realized were shaking and holstered it for her. "You did good," he said, his voice deeper than usual.

Then he was pulling her against his chest, and she could have sworn his hand stroked the back of her hair before he let her go, started talking logistics.

Ana Sofia was hurt. Not shot, but knocked cold when the SUV crashed. Evan had taken a bullet to the arm, *Just a nick*, he'd said. Laura had a nasty bruise on her forehead and blood on the side of her face. But they were all alive, their suspects all dead. Not even remotely the plan, but better than the alternative.

Melinda sank to the ground, her heart rate—so calm in those important moments—now off and running again. She closed her eyes, tried to will away the nausea, as she let her teammates handle the logistics. Dead suspects still needed guns moved away from them, hands cuffed. It was procedure. Calls had to be made, to deal with the bodies, to report back to Pembrook.

Through her haze, Melinda felt Laura's hand on her arm, her calm, understanding words. "It happens to all of us. Just breathe through it. You'll be okay."

Then, from farther away, JC's voice, obviously on a phone call. "What do you mean we don't know where Davis is?"

She tried to focus, to contribute in some meaningful way. She was FBI, for crying out loud. She could handle this.

But the buzzing in her ears just got louder, the uneven cadence of her breathing got worse. Then, somehow, it was Pembrook forcing her head up, staring back at her. Her voice that finally snapped Melinda out of it.

"It's over, Melinda. We're getting help from the Knoxville field office to manage the scene. We'll need statements, but right now, we need your profiling brain. We need to figure out where Davis might have gone."

Melinda frowned, took a deep breath. "Last I heard, he'd left the Petrov Armor office. He'd gone home."

"We're going to send an agent there now. Davis's phone is off, so we can't track it, but Hendrick is doing his magic back at the office. In the meantime, maybe Davis went back to Petrov Armor headquarters or—"

"He said he was finished there." The brief text she'd gotten earlier from Davis said he strongly suspected Eric Ross, flat out announced his undercover time was over. She'd texted back, asking for more detail, but hadn't gotten a response. "Did you ask Kane?"

"Kane said he had nothing more to offer on this," Pembrook replied, and something about the way she was scowling made Melinda glance around.

JC was still on scene and Rowan was here now, too, looking a little queasy. But the rest of the agents had cleared out. Probably some of them had gone to get medically checked out, some had gone to the office to either fill out statements about tonight or help with the search for Davis. And yet...

"Where's Kane?"

Pembrook shook her head, her face scrunching up apologetically. "He's gone."

Dread made her press a hand against her chest. "Gone?"

"Back undercover."

*"What?"*

"It came up days ago, new movement on a major drug smuggling operation where Kane had a deep cover a few months back. We'd pulled him, but his cover was intact. It's not great timing, but—"

"He's really gone? Just like that?" After everything that had happened tonight? After all their hard work to bring down the members of BECA? And not even a goodbye?

Pembrook stood, dusted off the knees of her pants. "You're the profiler, Melinda. You should understand." As she turned away, she added, "Get moving. I need you."

Grimacing at the stiffness in her arms and legs and back, Melinda stood. Her mind whirled as she followed her boss.

Kane was gone.

She'd thought that the way she'd proven herself tonight, the way the entire team had banded together to survive, would have shown him that being part of a team could be a good thing. That being part of a partnership could be a good thing. Instead, it had just reinforced his desire to run.

Pain sliced through her chest, not at all connected to her sore limbs being forced to move again after she'd held them so stiffly while under the SUV and during her panic attack afterward. But she ignored it and hurried after Pembrook.

She couldn't worry about Kane now, couldn't think about losing him as a partner. Couldn't think about how much she wanted to keep working with him. How much she wanted to keep seeing him, talking to him, arguing with him.

Right now, she needed to focus on Davis. Right now, she needed to help *find* Davis.

JOEL PETROV HAD ambushed him.

The realization hurt more than whatever Joel had used to knock him out when Davis had arrived at the remote testing facility.

He'd come here full of excitement about a new lead on Eric Ross, but as he slowly sat up and discovered himself in the middle of a firing lane, Davis knew. Joel had planted all the records leading to Eric, the security card access times and the supply orders.

"When did you know?" Davis asked. His words didn't sound quite right, his tongue heavy in his mouth. He pushed himself up to a kneeling position, got ready to try to stand.

"Don't," Joel warned.

Davis looked up and his vision blurred, but when he blinked a few times, the two versions of Joel merged into one. And that Joel was holding a pistol, aiming it straight at Davis. Close enough not to miss, far enough that there was no way Davis could rush him.

Subtly, Davis used one hand to pat his pocket, searching for his phone. The other pressed against the back of his head, felt the sticky evidence of blood.

He wasn't sure how long he'd been out, but it was long enough for Joel to have dragged him into this firing lane. Between the heavy throbbing in his head and the blood now smearing his hand, he knew he had a concussion.

It wasn't the first time. He'd been too close to an IED on a ranger mission once, been knocked nearly twenty feet from the explosion. But back then, he'd had a team to drag him out of the line of fire, get him on a medevac helicopter. Now, he was alone, and he had no one to blame but himself and his desperation to close this case.

He'd told his team he suspected Eric. He hadn't told them he was meeting Leila's uncle.

"Looking for this?" Joel asked, holding up Davis's FBI phone and then setting it on the counter near the front of the shooting lane. "I've known you were FBI for days." An ironic smile lifted one side of his lips. "Eric told me. After I knocked you out, I turned the phone off."

His team couldn't track him. Davis swayed a little on his knees, felt nausea rise up his throat. How hard had Joel hit him?

"Sorry," the man said, seemingly reading his mind. "Couldn't take any chances you'd wake up before I was ready."

"And now what?" Davis croaked, his voice sounding as off as his head felt. "You shoot me? You honestly believe this won't come back to you? This isn't exactly a good site for a botched mugging."

Joel's lips twisted into an angry snarl. "You think I don't have a plan for you? You think this is going to be hard for me? After what I had to do to my own brother? I had no choice then. Neal figured it out. Believe me, if there'd been another way—"

"He wasn't in on it?"

"Neal? Not follow the rules when it came to his company, his baby?" Joel snorted, a nasty, jealous sound. "No way."

"It was you all along," Davis stated. "Did you step in after Leila's mother died to help your brother out, or did you just see an opportunity right from the start?"

He heard the anger in his own voice, knew it was for Leila. She'd been right about her father. He wished she hadn't been so wrong about her uncle.

"I took over the company for Neal," Joel bit out. "He needed me. It was the two of us again—mostly—like it had always been growing up. Back then, he tried to look out for me. Our parents were no picnic, you know. This was finally my chance to repay him."

As Davis remembered how Leila had mentioned the abuse her father and uncle had suffered from their parents, Joel continued. "We'd been so close once. But as we got older, we grew apart. Then he got married, something both of us swore we'd never do. I tried to be happy for him, but I never quite knew how. When they had Leila, Neal wanted me back in their lives and so I came." The bitterness turned wistful. "But when his wife died, I knew it could be the two of us against the world again."

Melinda would be fascinated by the psychology here. Davis's mind was drifting, probably the concussion. He shook his head, trying to focus on what mattered, but only managed to make it pound harder, putting zigzagging lines over his vision.

Focusing made his head hurt worse, made him feel like he might pass out again. But if he did, he wouldn't be able to talk Joel out of shooting him, and he'd never wake up again. So he pressed on. "Leila is just collateral in your quest for money? Isn't the millions you've already made illegally off that company enough? You needed to kill soldiers, destroy your niece, too?"

The anger turned to fury, enough that Davis imagined he could rush Joel, take him down. But it was wishful thinking. The man was too far away, and even when he wasn't moving—or didn't think he was moving—Davis felt like he was swaying back and forth.

"That armor wasn't supposed to kill anyone."

"Yeah, you sound all broken up over it," Davis snapped, unable to help himself as an image of Jessica—proud in her army uniform, showing him a picture of her three kids—filled his mind.

"Look, those parts were cheaper, sure, but they were going to be sold to someone. How was I supposed to know they'd fail so badly? You think I wanted that kind of scrutiny?"

Davis gritted his teeth, trying to hold in a nasty response. Eighteen soldiers and seven locals had died in Afghanistan, and Joel Petrov was still thinking about himself.

"As for Leila, she never should have found out anything was wrong," Joel said. "When her dad convinced the board to put her in the CEO role, I thought it was perfect. She was too young for the job, too trusting of the people she loves." He frowned, deep grooves forming between his eyebrows, then he shook his head and muttered, "She never should have stopped the gun production," as if what had happened was Leila's fault.

"You can't go back now," Davis said. "She let me into the company. She knows I'm FBI. If something happens to me—"

"She'll blame Eric, the way I intended," Joel said, finishing for him. He glanced at his watch. "And now, I'm sorry, but I'm finished talking." He centered the pistol more carefully, steadying it.

"This won't work," Davis insisted, putting a hand to his temple, the knock to his head or the blood loss making him way too woozy, making his brain feel like it was several steps behind.

"I'm sorry," Joel repeated, and Davis closed his eyes, knowing he was out of options.

Bullets traveled faster than sound, so Davis didn't expect to hear anything, but a noise made his eyes pop open.

"Uncle Joel, stop!"

Leila stood behind Joel, out of breath and looking horrified.

Joel shifted sideways, so she wasn't directly behind him, then took a few steps forward, toward Davis. But he turned his pistol on Leila.

"You shouldn't be here," he said, a note of finality in his voice.

"No!" Davis yelled, trying to lurch to his feet. He stumbled and fell back to his knees, his hands scraping against the hard floor, but Joel's gun whipped back in his direction.

"Uncle Joel," Leila said, her voice full of fear and disbelief. "Please don't do this."

"I'm sorry, Leila," Joel said, and he actually sounded it as he centered his gun on Davis once again.

"I love him," Leila burst out.

The gun wavered and Davis shook his head, as if there was water in his ears he needed to shake out in order to hear properly.

She loved him? Was she saying it just to stop her uncle from killing him? Or did she actually mean it?

Either way, his heart started pounding double-time, telling Davis two truths: he loved her, too, and he was probably going to die without ever getting the chance to tell her.

## Chapter Twenty-One

The man she loved was about to die. And the man who'd helped raise her was going to kill him.

Leila took a deep breath, took a step closer. She kept her gaze centered on her uncle, not daring to look at Davis right now. She was too afraid of what she'd see. Not just because of the declaration of love she'd blurted, but also because he looked badly hurt. Blood saturated one side of his head, dripping down his neck and onto his T-shirt. He'd been swaying on his knees when she walked in, had almost face-planted when he tried to stand. Even if she could convince her uncle not to kill him—not to kill them both—he might not make it.

"You killed my father," she whispered, pain in her voice. "How could you do that? He was your only brother, your only real family besides me."

Her uncle's jaw quivered, but his gun hand didn't waver. "I didn't want to do it, Leila."

"Your greed was really worth more than my father's life?" Leila burst out, almost a yell.

"It wasn't about greed," her uncle Joel replied, his tone almost apologetic. Almost, but not quite.

"What was it about, then?" Leila demanded, still not daring to look at Davis. Maybe if she could slowly move closer to her uncle, get him to lower his gun—or try to take it from him—maybe she could save them both.

"Power," he said simply.

"Power? Is that supposed to be any better?"

"No." His gun lowered slightly, his attention on her instead of Davis.

From the corner of her eye, she saw Davis inch slowly forward on his knees. His chest heaved as he took in deep breaths, obviously in danger of passing out.

"I don't expect you to understand," her uncle said. "Your dad wanted to spare you the details of what happened to us as kids, but—"

"I know it was bad," Leila said softly. Her dad hadn't shared much of it, but he'd told her enough. Their childhood had been horrific. They'd only been able to rely on each other. Once when she was supposed to have been upstairs in bed, she'd heard her dad confiding to her mom that he was afraid Uncle Joel had locked up his emotions so tight that he'd never be able to feel anything.

But that couldn't really be true. He'd moved in with them for several years. He'd been there every morning, making her breakfast, walking her to the bus even when she insisted she was old enough to go by herself. Him telling her sternly that she didn't understand what dangers could be out there, how he'd never let her be hurt the way he'd been hurt.

He loved her. She knew he did.

That certainty bolstered her courage, made her take a big step closer. "Uncle Joel," she whispered, "I love you, too. Please, you can't do this."

"I can't go to jail," he whispered back. "Power. Control over my own life. It's all I ever wanted growing up. I know it sounds crazy, but no amount of money, no safety net, ever feels like enough. I know you don't approve, but I worked hard for this. I'm not letting him destroy it."

"You destroyed it," Leila snapped just as Uncle Joel started to focus on Davis again.

Davis, who was still inching forward, but so slowly he'd never get anywhere near close enough to rush her uncle. It would be a fatal mistake for him to try. He was way too disoriented from whatever her uncle had hit him over the head with.

"You destroyed my father's company," she continued, anger rushing back in. "You killed my father. You betrayed all of us. *How could you?*"

He shook his head, backed slightly away from her, his face shuttering, and Leila knew she was losing him.

"You love me," she insisted, stepping toward him again, even as she slid one hand inside her purse. "I know you do."

"Maybe I'm not truly capable of loving anyone," he said softly, sadly, as he aimed his gun at her again.

But it shook badly and he quickly re-aimed it at Davis. No matter what he said, she was pretty certain he wouldn't kill her. But she couldn't say the same about Davis.

"Yes, you are," she said, her fingers closing around the small pistol she'd carried since being attacked. Her own threat to counterbalance his, a last resort, since she wasn't sure she'd ever be able to actually fire on him. The man who'd help make her who she was, who'd taught her to be strong, made her feel like she mattered when her whole world had been crashing down. "You love me. You protected me. You always did."

As she said the words, her certainty grew. The fury she felt was still mixed with confusion, disbelief so strong that she knew it hadn't fully set in that he'd killed her father. It sounded so unreal, even in her own mind. The love she had for him, the man who'd put his whole life on hold for *years* to make sure she was okay? Even knowing what he'd done, she couldn't just erase it all.

Yes, he'd stumbled onto an opportunity to make money illegally in her father's company at the same time. But that hadn't been his original goal. If it had been the only thing that really mattered to him, he could have bailed on her at any time. He'd had enough control of the company at the time that a takeover would have been easy. Back then, he would have signed over his company without a word of protest. In his darkest moments, he'd tried to sell it to his brother, wanting to be rid of it. Uncle Joel had never accepted; he's just kept it going for his brother.

He'd never once, in all those years, let her down. As much as he'd betrayed her now, deep down she knew that her life could have taken a very different path without him. Children's Services had been on the verge of taking her away, placing her in foster care. She would have been alone in the world. Knowing how lost she'd been back then, there was no doubt it would have destroyed her.

In so many ways, she had her uncle Joel to thank for how she'd grown up. She'd never be able to forgive him for killing her father, destroying her company. Even now, hatred was blooming in her chest as she stared at him. But she couldn't completely turn her back on him, leave him alone in the world either.

"I still love you, Uncle Joel," she told him. She choked on the words, which felt like a betrayal to her father. But she reached a hand out to him, held it palm up, silently begging him to set the gun there. To be the man who'd raised her. To choose her over himself, to go to jail rather than kill another person she loved.

Because she did love Davis. She wasn't quite sure when it had happened, or how it had happened so quickly. She might doubt his intentions, doubt if what he felt for her was real, but she had no doubts about her feelings.

"Please," she begged her uncle, stretching her hand even farther.

His chin quivered, his gaze drifting to the weapon, then to her hand. If he noticed that Davis was a few feet closer than he'd been before, he didn't show it. Or maybe it didn't matter, since he still wasn't close enough.

"Please," she begged again, knowing he was wavering, knowing *him*.

His throat moved as he swallowed hard, and then his gaze went back to the weapon, his head giving a little shake, and she knew he'd made his choice.

She had a choice right now, too. The man who'd helped raise her, who'd without question saved her life when she was a child, the uncle she loved despite everything. Or the man she'd fallen for, the man who'd planned to leave in the end, but she loved anyway.

Leila let out a wail that sounded almost inhuman as she lifted the hand still hidden inside her purse, and fired her weapon.

And a man she loved fell to the floor.

# *Epilogue*

Leila had killed her uncle.

One week ago, there'd been a single instant to make a choice—Uncle Joel or Davis. It had been half instinct when she'd fired that shot. But her aim had been true. Center mass, the way her dad had trained her so many years ago. A kill shot.

She'd never thought she'd need to use it on someone she loved. Never thought she'd do it to protect someone else she loved.

Davis had spent two days in the hospital. One of his teammates had updated her a few hours after she'd shot her uncle, telling her Davis had a pretty severe concussion. She'd been numb by then, having given her statement more than once to local police and then Davis's team, who'd rushed in a few moments after she called 911.

The woman who'd told her about his condition, a profiler with kind eyes, had called her a few days ago to let her know Davis had been released from the hospital, cleared to go back to work. Apparently he was already working on a new case.

She hadn't spoken to him since the paramedics had loaded him into that ambulance, clinging to consciousness through sheer will. In that moment she'd squeezed his hand, pressed a brief kiss to his lips despite all the FBI agents watching. Then she'd walked away.

Leila had killed her uncle for him. In that instant her entire life had changed.

Leaning back in the chair in her father's office, Leila glanced around at the familiar room, somehow made foreign without her dad in it. She hadn't officially moved into his office—and she didn't plan to—but being here made her feel closer to him. She hadn't been able to go into her uncle's office yet. She wasn't sure when that would happen, if it ever would. Every memory she had of him now was tainted by the knowledge that he'd killed her father, by the look in his eyes when she'd known he was willing to kill Davis, too. Yet, a part of her still loved him, the man who'd claimed he wasn't sure if he even knew *how* to love. But he'd loved her. She still believed that.

Pressing a hand to her chest—where her grief seemed to have taken up permanent lodging—Leila stood and walked around the office. It wasn't large, but with framed copies of some of her father's earliest deals, it reflected how hard he'd worked to build this company.

Petrov Armor might not survive. Once news broke about the armor, about her uncle, she'd received letters of resignation from more than a third of her employees. The rest had stayed, but each day they eyed her with uncertainty, looks that said she'd betrayed their trust by keeping the truth from them when news of the faulty armor first surfaced.

The military—their biggest client—had canceled all of their orders. Petrov Armor had taken a hit so big that Leila knew she might have to let go some of the employees who'd stayed loyal, stuck around to fight with her. But she'd made her decision and for now, the board was willing to let her try. She was going to rebuild, prove to everyone that she could go back to the company her father had once envisioned, that he'd worked so hard to build. A place where the mission was to help *save* lives.

Peering through the open doorway, Leila saw lights on in Eric's office. She knew Theresa was still here, too, hard at work creating plans for more transparency, more security in their build process. People who would stick by her, stick by the company. People who cared about her, too.

But they weren't her family. That was all gone now, no one left except her father's abusive parents, who she'd never contact, and her mother's family in Pakistan who she'd never met, except over a few brief video chats.

They weren't Davis. Davis, who'd somehow wormed his way into her heart while he was digging through her company's darkest secrets.

He hadn't called. Maybe he'd been too concussed to hear her declaration of love. Maybe it wouldn't have mattered even if he'd known how she felt.

Because he was an FBI agent. And she was just the CEO of a company he'd been investigating. His job was finished here. He was gone.

Even if he wasn't, could she be with someone who— intentionally or not—had put her in a position where she'd had to kill the only real family she had left?

A shiver racked her body, a sob lodging in her chest. But she blinked back the tears, forced the sob down. She'd already cried for her uncle. Knowing what he'd done, what he'd been willing to do, she refused to give him any more of her tears.

She couldn't cry for Davis, either. Couldn't cry for what might have been. Not yet, because that would mean admitting she'd truly lost him, too. And she wasn't sure she was ready to admit that yet.

"Leila."

The soft voice speaking her name made her jerk. Realizing her eyes had gone unfocused, she blinked and there was Davis. She blinked again, certain she'd imagined him, but he was still in front of her. Real.

Beyond him, in the dim lights of the space outside the office, Eric gave her a sad smile and a nod. Then, he slipped back into his office and she refocused on the man in front of her.

"What are you doing here?" she whispered.

"I couldn't stay away," he whispered back, stepping closer.

There was still a big Band-Aid on the side of his head. Underneath, she knew there were a dozen stitches. But his eyes looked clear, his gaze steady as he took one more step toward her, then reached out and took both her hands in his.

It was something Eric had done in her office not so long ago. But Eric's touch hadn't made her heart race, or made hope burst through the pain in her chest.

She gazed up at him, trying to read his intention in his eyes. And yet—did it matter? Had anything really changed in the past week? They'd lied to each other. And she'd killed one of the people closest to her in the world. For him. Could she ever get beyond that?

As he brought her hands up to his lips, closed his eyes almost reverently as he kissed her there softly, she knew: she desperately wanted to.

"I'm so sorry about your uncle," he said when he lowered her hands from his lips.

The pain he felt on her behalf was in the crinkling around his eyes, in the downturn of his lips, the way he gazed at her. But there was something else there, too, and even though it didn't seem possible, Leila's heart beat even faster.

"I never expected it to end like that, Leila. I never expected…" He gave a shaky—could it be nervous?—smile. "I never expected to fall in love with you."

The words that followed were a jumble she couldn't quite piece together, about being sorry he'd taken so long to come here, about wanting to start fresh. But all she could hear was the thundering of her own heartbeat in her ears, those most important words repeating over and over in her mind. *I never expected to fall in love with you.*

"What are you saying?" she finally interrupted him, unable to process too much about the past, needing to know more about the future.

Davis stepped even closer, as far inside her personal space as he could get without physically pulling her into his arms. "I'm saying I can't let go, Leila. Maybe it's what makes the most sense, given everything that's happened, but I can't do it. I love you. I want to give this thing between us a real shot. No more lies, no more half-truths. The same side." He turned one of her hands in his, stroking her palm enough to send shivers of awareness over her skin. "I think we've always been on the same side, even if it didn't always feel that way."

She nodded back at him. They'd always been searching for the same thing: the truth. And they'd found it, even if it wasn't what she'd wanted, wasn't the way she'd wanted.

"A new start," she said, feeling more certain as the words burst from her mouth without thought.

He smiled, tentative but genuine. He shifted his grip on her hand until it was more of a handshake. "Agreed," he said, an echo of the promise they'd made to each other weeks ago, when he'd first gone undercover in her company.

Then, he pulled her closer still, until she was pressed against him. She rose up on her tiptoes, the first smile she'd felt in a week shifting from a small, hopeful thing into a full-blown grin. "I love you, too, Davis."

"I know," he answered. "And I promise you this—whatever comes next, we're in it together."

Then, he sealed that promise with a kiss.

* * * * *

# MILLS & BOON MODERN IS
# HAVING A MAKEOVER!

The same great stories you love,
a stylish new look!

Look out for our brand new look
# COMING JUNE 2024

MILLS & BOON

**afterglow BOOKS**

From showing up to glowing up, Afterglow Books
features authentic and relatable stories,
characters you can't help but fall in love
with and plenty of spice!

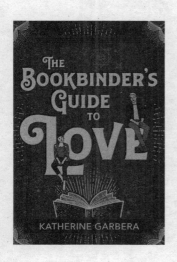

## OUT NOW

To discover more visit:
**Afterglowbooks.co.uk**

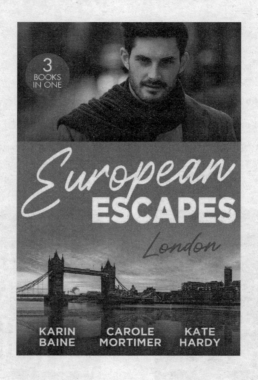

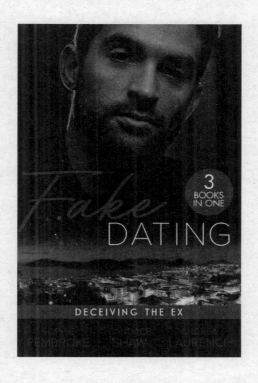

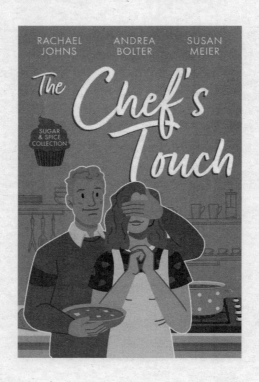

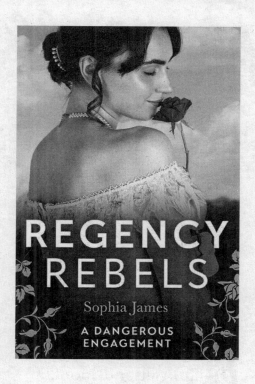

LET'S TALK

# Romance

For exclusive extracts, competitions
and special offers, find us online:

**f** MillsandBoon

**X** @MillsandBoon

**◉** @MillsandBoonUK

**♪** @MillsandBoonUK

Get in touch on 01413 063 232

# MILLS & BOON

## THE HEART OF ROMANCE

---

## A ROMANCE FOR EVERY READER

---

### MODERN

Prepare to be swept off your feet by sophisticated, sexy and seductive heroes, in some of the world's most glamourous and romantic locations, where power and passion collide.

### HISTORICAL

Escape with historical heroes from time gone by. Whether your passion is for wicked Regency Rakes, muscled Vikings or rugged Highlanders, awaken the romance of the past.

### MEDICAL

Set your pulse racing with dedicated, delectable doctors in the high-pressure world of medicine, where emotions run high and passion, comfort and love are the best medicine.

### *True Love*

Celebrate true love with tender stories of heartfelt romance, from the rush of falling in love to the joy a new baby can bring, and a focus on the emotional heart of a relationship.

### HEROES

The excitement of a gripping thriller, with intense romance at its heart. Resourceful, true-to-life women and strong, fearless men face danger and desire - a killer combination!

###

From showing up to glowing up, these characters are on the path to leading their best lives and finding romance along the way – with plenty of sizzling spice!

To see which titles are coming soon, please visit

## millsandboon.co.uk/nextmonth